WHO AM I SUPPOSE TO LOVE

By

W PARKS BRIGHAM

I would like to dedicate this book to my family and
friends for the love, support, and constant
encouragement. Thanks guys!

Who Am I Suppose To Love

Copyright © 2013 W Parks Brigham

All rights reserved.

ISBN: 9780984806836

IS

ACKNOWLEDGMENTS

Special thanks to family and friends for their constant encouragement, support, and love. I would like to personally thank those who took time to listen to the unfolding of Ruby Jewel and Caleb's story. I couldn't have done it without you.

Special thanks to the many book clubs for their support, encouragement, suggestions, and most of all their valuable constructive criticisms.

I would also like to thank my editing team for their hard work and input. Thanks a million guys

CHAPTER 1

"Ruby Jewel we need you to come home. Your mother is not doing so well."

"What do you mean Daddy? Have you taken her to see Dr. Alford?"

"Baby she's just not herself. She cries at the drop of a hat, irritable, don't want to do anything, and gets angry if you say something about the way she's behaving. She won't go to the doctor and I'm at my wits end. You know you're the only one she'll listen to. I know Junior is here, but he's no help. He runs in and out and can't see what's going on. The only thing on his mind is baseball. Tori have noticed some changes but she's bogged down with the kids and her teaching job. Babygirl I know you have your business, but."

"Daddy don't say another word. It's a little after seven, let me tie up some loose ends here and I'll be home by noon. Don't worry yourself, and in the meantime call Dr. Charlotte to make an appointment. I'll get her to go."

Ruby Jewel was the eldest of Robbi Jean and Henry Ray's five children. They were what you call stair steppers. She was thirty six and the others trailed behind. It's really ironic but true, she was the only one that could handle her mother. They have butted heads since she was a teenager. She was a daddy's girl and everybody knew it. Growing up with Robbi Jean had not been easy if you were overweight

1

and didn't have a desire to be an educator. All of her siblings were in the field of education, from kindergarten teacher to a college professor. She was proud of her younger siblings but an educator she was not.

Ruby was widely known as Attorney RJ McHarding and was one of the best in her profession and has allowed no one to stand in her way. Graduating with honors from two universities and working extremely hard she's established a top notch legal firm. She specializes in assisting small businesses in a wide range of issues from copyright and trademark to tax and employment law. Using technology supremely, well she has an extensive and successful database network service for attorneys who specialize in various fields. Looking at her agenda, most of her business was to be carried out in the office via telephone and computer today. She did have two new clients scheduled for this morning, and wanted to visit with Kellie Larson the owner of Kincaid Larson Transportation Service, (KLTS) mainly so she could see the triplets. However they did have a legal problem she handled, afterwards she would be free.

RJ went back to her bedroom to pack. The sooner she put her things in her small bag she would be ready to start her day, and leave for her parents' home. She approached her roomy walk in closet to get a few pieces. Although it was unintentional, she often found herself packing to please her mother, but time was not on her side for this trip. Besides, whatever she chooses she would stand out anyway. Ruby Jewel was something to behold with her five eleven height (without shoes), large firm frame, smooth dark complexion, and thick long curly black hair. She had a love for fashion with her own unique flair which was bold.

Pondering over which selections would not cause a

negative reaction from her mother should not be an issue for Attorney RJ McHarding, but it did. She was like any other daughter who wanted their mother's approval. However, there wasn't any pleasing Robbi Jean. She wanted complete control. Her mother lost that privilege when she defied her eighteen years ago and made the career choice of her dreams. She broke the chain and was no longer under her rule. In doing so, Ruby Jewel had to accept she may not get a pat on the back or praise from her. Over the years she's formed a thick skin for her constructive criticisms (as she calls them) and anyone else's' for that matter and proceeded to live a successful single life. Naturally she was the only McHarding unattached by choice and does not dwell on that either. She pulled out a few pieces from her closet that would accommodate the weather and laid them on her bed. Her traveling designer's bag in the hall closet was already partially packed with the essentials for emergency trips. All she needed to do was add her street clothing and accessories and she would be on her way._____

"Good morning Baby, what time is your appointment?" Jalen leaned over and kissed his sexy wife as she mumbled nine o'clock. He couldn't help being pleased this fine morning, today they were making contact. The wheels had been set in motion to finally get his revenge on his old adversary Ruby Jewel McHarding, caressing his baby. He recalled that warm autumn day when he saw her leaving her office, and couldn't believe his luck. Although he spent only eight months and twenty-four days behind bars, his livelihood had been changed because of her. He had lost everything! Yes he was able to keep a nice little stash hidden away, which helped him save face until the perfect job came along. The setback had been devastating and she was the reason. In the beginning he wasn't good for anything

but meaningless hard labor jobs before meeting up with one of the dudes he did time with. He was the one responsible for turning him on to Gregory Larson and the rest is history. It was still hard for him to forget that he brought shame to his mother who had worked hard to help him through school. She deserved better and so did his baby who loves him unconditionally. He kissed her eyelids as they fluttered open and then her sweet lips. "Come on girl it's time we get up."

Cathena did her cat stretch and held on to her Boo. Finally she had true love, Jalen Dalton. He was everything a woman wanted, a BMWJ. They met at her congregation during one of their singles' group activities and were a perfect match in every way. Their life had been great; all they needed now was to start their family. For some reason Jalen was not ready to become a father and she couldn't understand why. They had a nice home that he fixed up himself with a mother-in-law's suite in the back, money in the bank, and a good job. Her part time job as the church secretary and his mother's retirement were their extra income. Since he came in contact with Gregory Larson his life had changed for the better. He first started out as a hotshot driver and then was asked to be the transportation operator for Wiley Collins Senior Citizen Facility and Clinic. With the center developing more services they needed more drivers, which provided him with a stable and secure job plus a new title as their transportation manager. Overall he has been a hard worker and a good provider in every way in spite of his past troubles. Even his mother was now after them to start a family; she was ready to become a grandmother. They both just wished he would let go of the past and be thankful for what they have, each other._____

RJ pulled into the parking lot of KLTS where she shares

4

a suite with Lana Harvey CPA. When a unit became available they jumped at the chance to lease a space in the Kincaid business park which became the launching of McHarding and Harvey. The location was ideal for the two professionals along with the size of the suite. Since they were self-employed and needed minimum space everything worked out perfect. As you walk into their unit there's a small lobby section for their clients and a workplace for their shared office manager/receptionist and office clerk. The rest of the unit was basic with maintenance and security provided within their contract.

RJ secured her silver metallic STS Cadillac and went inside. Angela, her longtime friend and office manager had sent a text, her nine o'clock appointment was already present which was good to know. She could get started and be able to leave by eleven. Her associate Destiny, had prepared portfolios with guidelines and informative materials needed to give a thorough explanation of procedures and strategies, as how to get started in business.

"Good morning RJ."

"Angela," acknowledging with a nod, "Give me five minutes and then bring Ms. Gurley." She could forget about her morning tea and breakfast wrap. She did not have time but she will make up for it later. Dolly's Kitchen was calling her name and she would pay her a visit once she takes care of her mom.

A knock, "RJ, I would like for you to meet Ms Cathena Gurley."

"Good morning Ms Gurley and welcome. Please have a seat. Can we get you something to drink, we also have pastries."

She cut her off. "No thank you, I had a healthy breakfast before I left home. I would like a bottle of water."

"RJ, would you like something?"

"Yes, Angela I'll take my usual, plus two cake donuts." Angela stepped out of the office and closed the door with a big smile because she knew her friend and boss well. Trying to intimidate Ruby Jewel McHarding about her multiple plus sizes (depending on the designer and style) was a waste of time. She's a proud and assertive role model for all, especially for plus size women.

Okay Ms Gurley, I caught that hint but you're talking to the wrong gal. "Let's get down to business shall we," she suggested and presented her a packet, including a pen engraved with the company's name and began. Two and a half hours later her business plan had been meticulously explained. Her client realized starting a tutorial program for the church was not going to be a breeze. The goal was to help prepare students for the standardized tests, which were scheduled in late spring and hopefully continue in the summer and during the following school year. After the presentation, she requested refreshments. RJ didn't help the situation any when she pointed out they only had a few weeks before spring and applying for government grants was time consuming. Regardless of Ms Gurley being a snob, she remained professional and provided her with alternatives while they applied for funding. Destiny met with her next to assist in starting the paperwork. Looking at her watch, RJ knew in about another thirty minutes Ms Gurley would want lunch which wasn't a bad idea she thought, approaching the door to get their next client. She too had arrived early and was waiting in the small dining area having refreshments._____

Cathena Gurley Dalton couldn't wait to get in her car. She let out a deep breath and started the ignition. She had no idea it was going to be so in depth. Thanks to Jalen she had all the necessary information needed. He had coaxed her well, in spite of Attorney McHarding being very thorough and sharp. She had to give her credit she definitely knew her profession. Most likely graduated with honors humph, probably didn't have anything else to do but study and eat junk. Other than being smart and having good business sense, she didn't see anything spectacular about Ruby Jewel with that real lame name, something left over from the old days. She called Jalen at work.

"Hey, cupcake how did it go?"

"Hi handsome everything is done. You were right about her, she's pretty heavy in more ways than one," smirked Cathena.

"I know what you mean and you did a good job cupcake, now all we have to do is lay low and let Ms Know-it-all take us there." Cathena didn't understand how starting the new program at the church would help him get back at RJ McHarding. She just didn't get it, motives and all. And what does he mean about taking them there? This was a program for the church that she and his mother were going to spear head. And why did she have to use her maiden name instead of her married name? Besides, Bro. Lockhart trusted her. Again she just hoped and prayed that he would focus more on their future and leave the past behind._____

RJ had completed her consultation session with client

7

number two who wanted to start a secretarial and bookkeeping business in her home. After providing her with the necessary business proposal she too was referred to Destiny. Before closing down she gave Angela instructions concerning scheduling office appointments for the next couple of days, just in case her parents needed her to stay. She was to consult with Destiny first because she knew the ones she was comfortable with handling alone. She said her goodbyes to the staff and went next door to give Kellie the news before leaving for Hempstead. Her father had called and said he had a 2:30 appointment which was perfect. Her mother had also agreed to go since she was informed she would accompany them.

"RJ don't you look pretty," said Clyde opening the door for her. He was such a sweetie she thought and thanked him for the compliment. She knew Cherri was another happily married KLTS female. First it was Kellie, next Ann, and then Cherri, all tied the knot within three years. Whenever she sees them she can't help thinking If only she could be so lucky. But how could she when she's avoided every man that's shown an interest in having a meaningful relationship with her. Although she dates, no one was calling her number, and up until now she never really cared. She closed her eyes and shook her head, where was all this coming from anyway. For the last ten years she had been busy building a successful business. Like she and Kellie often said, marriage did not go with their outfits, just business. Humph, Mrs. Larson was wearing marriage very well now and so were Ann and Cherri.

Ruby Jewel knew she had lost her chance at real happiness, when she walked away from her true love and soul mate fifteen years ago. He was the main reason why she had failed in finding someone special. But of course it was all her fault why they weren't together. She had allowed herself to be bullied because of a narrow minded old woman. This was the twenty-first century to have such old ancient ideas. Intelligent people didn't think that way anymore. She had been a frightened blind fool and made it possible for some other lucky woman to have him. She should have been truthful when he asked her *Why?* I guess you could say that's been the drive and motivation she's feed off of to become the no nonsense attorney. She was known for being shrewd and ruthless when it came to defending or providing services for her clients. Cherri was at the front desk and told her to go right in. She was about to ask when Cherri gave her the answer.

"Yes, the babies are here." RJ had fallen in love with all three little sweethearts who would be three in August and were practically potty trained. She often came over to visit whenever she could. Although she would never admit it, being with the triplets and her siblings' children often made her think about trying out motherhood. *Lord, she really was trippin.* She could hear the chatter and singing as she approached the door. Knocking before entering she joined in with their favorite song, *the insy weensy spider.*_____

Ruby Jewel took the exit to her parents' home. As usual she spent more time with the triplets than she had planned. They were so adorable and very active today. Kellie had them dressed so cute in blue and yellow playsuits. Of course Kyla was the cutest in her ruffled bottom stretched pants and headband around her curly top. It's always a pleasure to spend time with the Larsons and their clan. She pulled into her parents' driveway and blew the horn to let them know she had arrived. There was just enough time for her to run for personal business and then they would be on their way.

"She's here," shouted her father. He was out the door to give his big girl a big hug. He loved all of his children but she was the apple of his eye; dependable, considerate, loving, and had a heart of gold. If the truth be told she was the prettiest of his three daughters and certainly the smartest out of the five. Yeah, he was a wee bias because she was a carbon copy of his mother and grandmother, down to color, size, and hair. She had the White Cloud makeup all the way. Ruby was more like them than their other two daughters.

"Hi Daddy, is Momma ready?" His hug was more of a squeeze. She could tell he was relieved, it was all over his face everything would be alright now that she was there. Her mother walked into the living room, there was a sadness about her that caused RJ to have concerns. "Hi Momma, how are you feeling?" She gave her a hug and kissed her forehead although she was a bit distant.

"I'm good baby, just a little tired. I told your daddy not to bother you. I probably just need some vitamins for energy, and then I'll be back to my old self."

"Momma I wanted to come. Now let me go to the powder room so I can freshen up and we can be on our way." Ruby took off her black jacket and pulled at her cap sleeves to her fuchsia jungle print dress and disappeared.

Robbi Jean watched her beautiful first born walk away with much admiration and love in her heart. She was everything a mother would want in a daughter. She graduated with highest honors from high school and both colleges, a successful lawyer and business woman with numerous awards. She was very proud of her although she's never uttered the words. Why would a mother do that to her child? Why would she do that to her own flesh and blood? She knew how important it was for children to have their parents' approval and acceptance. She's taught hundreds in her career and was aware of the ingredients for a child to be strong, healthy, and happy: emotionally, physically, mentally, and spiritually. But something has always held her back when it came to Ruby Jewel. She's never had problems providing support and encouragement for her other four children. But they have always looked to her for that special touch and needed that extra push. But not her, she was born with confidence, spunk, determination, and brilliance. Ever since she was a little tot she was independent and always had it in her mind she could do it herself. She's excelled and accomplished whatever she's set her mind to do. Even being overweight was really not an issue for her. She had a certain air about herself that often said you can look at me if you want, just don't get too close. With her cool and touch me not exterior, she still had it all together and knew it regardless of what someone thought. And she's demanded nothing but respect from her and anybody else that's crossed her path.

CHAPTER 2

Caleb Gerald VanLee the 3rd had finally completed all of his packing and the movers were on their way out. His housekeeper had supervised the entire operation and personally labeled every box so it would be easier to set up his new home. According to her his place would be ready when he arrived. Recommendations from his new co-worker, he was able to lease a two bedroom townhouse on the outskirts of Hempstead that put him close to the center and hospital.

Caleb was joining his mentor Dr. Charlotte Alford and team in Hempstead, Texas at the Jordan Memorial Clinic that's also affiliated with the Memorial Hospital System. It was awesome and one of a kind. He was very impressed when he visited the clinic last year and was honored when they offered him the position as the clinic's neurologist and one of the medical consultants for the hospital annex in Cypress. More so, he was happy to relocate back to Texas, and had been walking around on a cloud since he made the decision to do so. Of course, his Grandmother Mildred didn't understand why he had to move to a back in the woods place when he had such a wonderful position at General. He knew all the talk in the world would not make her understand. Thank God for his parents, Uncle Daniel, and Aunt Carrie who truly understood his two-fold mission in life.

They always said he was so much like his biological

mother and father; not caring what their parents had planned for their future, they did what made them happy. They chose community service careers and helped establish a free clinic for the less fortunate instead of being prominent doctors at General. Caleb Gerald VanLee the 3rd was adopted by his mom and dad's best friends, Vera and Lawrence Nicholson when he was barely a year old and they are the only parents he's known. His birth parents were killed in an automobile accident. Although both sets of grandparents wanted custody, his parents had made legal provisions in case of their death as to who would raise their only child. He always felt blessed growing up. His adoptive parents gave him a strong foundation and instilled in him the necessities of life. They worked hard at him having a relationship with his biological family. He was able to spend quality time with both birth family as well as his adoptive parents' families. He had some wonderful summers and holidays in Bellville, Texas. Although his parents had some challenging times they managed and provided him with a nurturing happy productive childhood. He had the better of two worlds for sure growing up in Denver, Colorado. His grandparents insisted on him having nothing but the best, but his mom and dad managed to keep them under control and well grounded. He did not grow up being a spoiled; rich kid just privileged.

Nevertheless, he was now looking forward to moving back to the southwest and start a new life and have complete happiness. He had some fond memories while living there during his college days and with his extended family. Both of his adoptive parents' families were in Texas, in and around the Bellville and Hempstead area. His parents had been so happy when he chose to attend their alma mater, Prairie View A&M University. And his dad was ecstatic when he announced he wanted to pledge his fraternity, man was that a trip. Those were some difficult days but he made it through and proved himself worthy to wear his frat brand on his heart and the colors purple and gold. Of course his biological grandparents were appalled. But he made it clear if they wanted to continue being a part of his life they had to accept him for who he was and not pressure him into being who they thought he should be. It all worked out well with him receiving the best education to carry out his dreams. Besides, he's done alright. His parents had done an excellent job and he was proud to be their son....

Touching his diamond earlobe he thought about the conversation he had with his uncle who had encouraged him to take the move and more so in finding and claiming his true love. He was the only one other than Aunt Carrie who knew he still carried a torch, once he was able to admit to himself he still loved her. At one time he had been angry and hostile, and stayed that way which seemed like eternity. But it was his Uncle Daniel who was understanding and played a big part in him finally accepting his true feelings. Although she broke his heart into a million little pieces and dismissed him; he was ready to give it to her again and again, until he makes her accept they were meant to be one. Because he felt deep down in his heart she was his true love and soul mate, the decision to relocate to her hometown was easy. Yes, he was excited about his new job and was looking forward to finally specializing in the area he had studied considerably for; but she was his main driving force.

It was obvious to his entire family there was a change about him. The sparkle was back in his eyes according to his aunt; he was no longer just existing. They were right and he was going to make it happen too; a new career and be with the love of his life. He didn't care if it has been fifteen years and it was going to be a challenge. He has never walked away from one except that time, but he was now determined to make it happen._____

They had a very successful doctor's visit at the Jordan Memorial Clinic. Dr. Charlotte gave Robbi Jean a thorough examination and ordered a series of tests and blood work over the next couple of days at the senior citizen's clinic. Dr. Charlotte Alford and three other doctors who specialize in geriatrics medicine had the aspiration to establish the clinic five years ago. They provide excellent services for their seasoned citizens in the Hempstead proximity regardless of their income. Ruby Jewel had been their consultant and provided them with an excellent grant writer who was instrumental in them achieving their goals. Now the seniors have their medical check-ups and tests done right in the area instead of traveling to Cypress. The clinic has been extremely successful and was bringing in two prominent doctors from Denver and Chicago, a neurologist that specializes in geriatrics and a cardiogeriatrics. Ruby Jewel had to contain herself as her heart did flip flops when Dr. Charlotte revealed the name of one of the new doctors. She was glad her parents were not in the room with them. It was hard enough fighting back the excitement and longing she felt in Dr. Alford's presence. She knew trying to fool her parents concerning her true feelings for him would have been impossible. Her heart screamed OMG; he was coming back. Never in a million years did she think he would come to a little town like Hempstead to practice medicine. She heard of his success in Denver, working with his grandfather who was also a distinguished neurosurgeon. However, she didn't know any real personal information about him, whether

15

or not he was married nor had a family. His life had been his own and private after he left PVU to attend the finest medical school money could provide. Dr. Alford did not volunteer any personal info and she dare not ask.

Again, Ruby Jewel knew she had been a fool to walk out of his life. Because of him she had not been able to get close to any other man. Her insecurities resurfaced which made it difficult for her to have a meaningful relationship period. She found herself always second guessing their motives and her worth. Her motto was simple; she was too big a cat to be played by the kittens that's approached her. But it was him who tried everything in his power to break that barrier and did, he just wasn't aware of his accomplishment. That wall had been built since high school and was stronger than ever, thinking it was impossible for someone to really want her. Humph, all behind trying to get a date for her senior prom, which was a catastrophe. She made it hard for herself with her *don't you dare try to talk to me* attitude and really didn't care about her senior prom.

It was her mother who was embarrassed, she being the only one not going to the prom out of her friends' children. Therefore, she set it upon herself to get her a date. The boy she thought was the ideal date was a terrible choice with his demands. Ruby Jewel didn't care if he was one of her good friends' sons; she was not going to yield to his ultimatum. That was the day she decided to please herself instead of her mother. She was not going to let her mother make any more decisions for her unless it was what she wanted. Of course Robbie Jean didn't hesitate to tell her she was going to find herself alone if she didn't watch her attitude. She had been harsh in voicing her opinion about her breaking the date and made it clear he agreed as a favor for her. In so many words Ruby should have been glad he even considered and if she didn't watch it, she would find herself alone with her disposition.

Her mother had no idea why and made the decision to just let it be. Besides, Elliot DuWayne Parker was nothing but a spoiled egotistical bully. He was no match for her which he found out that very day and became the joke of their senior class after she finished putting him in his place. To keep down the drama she never said a word to her parents. Furthermore she always felt her mother would have found a way to put all the blame on her. So as bold as she pleased, she went to the prom alone and had a wonderful time with the other dateless seniors. Of course her mother was totally out done and furious, and tried to find reasons to put some of the blame on her father. She always said he was responsible for her mind-set because of all the foolishness he filled her head with. She was perfect the way she was and when her time comes she will find the right man. Her father was right about that, she did find him, her soul mate, and best friend but she walked away.

RJ cleared her head because it was no use in hashing over past history. What was done was done, but she could never forget the hurt and pain he showed when she broke it off that day. She gave some flimsy excuse about love and marriage was not what she wanted at the moment. He stood there looking distraught and told her he didn't believe a word she said. She was then challenged to say what she knew he had to hear from her lips, and she did. *I really don't love you the way you want me to*. As the lie escaped from her lips, she wanted to take it back, especially with the devastating hurt shown in his face. She too was heartbroken, but for his sake she had to live with her decision. After they graduated from PVU they went their separate ways with their paths never to cross again....

"There you are, we were looking for you," said her father. She was sitting on the bench in front of the clinic. "Your mother and I just finished registering at the senior citizen center." She could hear the excitement in his voice. He had been trying to get her to attend the center for some time, but she always made excuses. Dr. Charlotte suggested it would be great if they signed up and participated in the center's programs, and be around people their age instead of sitting at home missing out on some fantastic fun.

"That's terrific Daddy and a wonderful decision. You and Momma will have a great time, they have lots of activities including field trips. According to Dr. Charlotte they have interesting outings every month. They even have weekend trips."

"I don't think I want to go on any trips," said her mother. "Maybe we can do the ones for a day. I don't want to spend the night with strangers."

"Robbi, sweetheart these people are our neighbors and friends."

"I still don't want to spend the night away from home." Ruby Jewel suggested they go to Ms Dolly's for dinner, her treat and they could talk more about it then. She didn't want to push the issue for fear her mother may back out going period....

"Ruby Jewel, are you going to eat all of that?"

"Yes Mother, I'm going to try hard and all that I don't eat I'm taking home to eat later." She knew the day could not end with her not saying something about her weight.

"All right then, you won't be able to wear that dress next time you put it on. It's already clingy." She didn't see a need in explaining the cling was because of the fabric. In actuality her dress was simple, flattering, and comfortable like all her wardrobe in general.

"Well Mother dear, I'll just have to spend a little more time on the treadmill, because I am very fond of this dress." Well she's back to her old self thought RJ, continuing her meal. Henry gave his wife a disapproving look that said enough. But she knew it as well. When her daughter refers to her as mother dear, RJ has surfaced. Constructive criticism is accepted with no problem, its sarcasm that's not tolerated under any circumstances. She had a way of letting you know just that without showing any disrespect.

They practically finished their meal in silence except when her mother did her usual bragging on her siblings. She sung praises for her sister and brother who were expecting little bundles of joy sometime during the summer; Kami was having another girl and Aaron's wife was expecting their first son. She knew first hand and had been asked not to say anything. RJ never understood her logic; there was no competition between her siblings. They have a close relationship and are very supportive for one another.

Before she could get to her office all four siblings had called to thank her for stopping with her business to go home. Tori was in tears because she felt bad about not being able to take more responsibility with their parents since she lived close by. Junior was his typical self, totally in the dark about everything. She didn't know how his wife puts up with him. Thank God they had boys which help him

19

to be a decent father with sports being his life. Of course it was understood about Kami and Aaron who lived in other cities with demanding jobs and families....

Ruby Jewel had unpacked her bag and settled in the bedroom she uses when she visits her parents. Her father was proud of their home which he had rebuilt after he married. It was the house he grew up in and came back to after he did several years in the army with a wife and two small children and a third on the way. In spite of the conflicts she had with her mother she's had some heartwarming memories growing up in Hempstead. Besides, her father was always there to smooth things over....

All her correspondence had been completed and Destiny had rescheduled two clients for the beginning of next week and the rest of her business would be done via internet, she loved technology. She closed down her laptop and snuggled up on her comfortable chaise lounge to rest her eyes for a few minutes.

Her father knocked softly on the door. "Ruby Jewel, are you still working baby."

"No Daddy, you can come in."

He stood in the doorway and asked, "How about we share that chocolate cake we got from Ms. Dolly's with some ice cream." He was singing her song she thought jumping up. That's where she inherited her sweet tooth from, him.

CHAPTER 3

"Dr. VanLee, telephone, it's your mom."

"Thanks, hi Momma. How are you and Dad this fine day?"

"We're doing as well as can be expected son. Are you all boxed up?"

"Yes Mama, I'm all packed and plan to leave in the morning, I'll be over before I get on the road." He could tell she was sniffling on the other end. It was understandable she did not want him to move so far away. He was their only child and her baby as she often says. What she didn't know was he had practically talked his father into relocating back to Texas once he retires from his second job which was actually next month. He always felt when his father retired at fifty-five that was it, but he insisted he needed something else to do and accepted another part-time position at the same company. Lawrence Nicholson was almost sixty-five years old and this was it. If things go the way he planned his parents would be joining him soon. After talking to his father for a little while, he decided to pay them a visit tonight instead of on his way out. He knew his mother was going to cry but again that was expected....

Caleb's visit with his parents was great. When he got there surprisingly enough his mother was in good spirits and had a delicious dinner waiting. One of his favorites...chicken

21

spaghetti with green and yellow squash, green salad, garlic bread, lemonade, and banana pudding for desert had been prepared just for his taste buds. She even packed up the leftovers for his breakfast. His stomach didn't know what time of day it was according to his father, and he was his father's son._____

Ruby Jewel had been up for a couple of hours and had a busy productive morning. She had a conference call with her siblings about their mother's doctor visit. Afterwards she took her bath and managed to take care of some of her business. She answered several emails and accepted contracts for two new clients. Angela had also emailed the news of her being the recipient of two awards; Houston's Steps to Success Award and Sister's Black Angels Award. The award ceremonies would take place late summer. She would also be featured in one of the local magazines. That's what she's talking about as she drew in a deep breath. The smell of success and the wonderful aroma of her father's breakfast filled her nostrils. He was fixing her favorites; hot biscuits, sausage, bacon, and eggs. She was sure he had grits for them, which they could have.

She joined her parents for breakfast on the screened in back porch. Her father knew she loved having breakfast there. The backyard was private with shade trees, beautiful flowerbeds, a vegetable garden and fruit trees, thanks to her parents who love to play in dirt. The sweet-smelling mixtures filled the air with wonderful fragrances. They enjoyed their breakfast with pleasant conversation. She shared the news about her awards and the article that would appear in one of the local magazines regarding her accomplishments. Naturally her father expressed how proud he was; her mother shocked her when she conveyed the same sentiments. She even put forth an effort to show interest and asked her to tell them about the awards. Not one time did she make any comments about the portion of food on her plate. Of course Henry Jr. had been by to visit before he left for work which with his news of Heather expecting. They were going to the doctor this morning to confirm it, that's why he wasn't at work. He had actually taken off to accompany his wife.

Ruby Jewel looked at her watch and announced it was time to get ready so they would be on time for her appointment. Her mother looked at her father and wanted to protest but decided against it when Henry Ray got up to clear the patio table. Instead she looked at her daughter and asked if she was wearing what she had on. Lord she wished she would give it a rest, you would think. She's been dressing herself for ages. Now what was wrong with her outfit? It was a nice warm day for the beginning of March and she was dressed casually for the pre-spring weather. This year they really didn't have much of a winter. The moderate warm days started in the middle of February, warm during the day and cool at night. Her ankle length multi print tiered skirt with appliqué flowers was cute. Certainly she wasn't complaining about the brown one piece top that had the appearance of a shrug and camisole. Her colorful jewelry and causal brown flats were ideal. She decided not to take her mother's question as a criticism and simply said yes.

"What about your hair?"

"Momma there's nothing to do with spiral curls except let them hang and add a scarf or headband for more color. I'm sure we can agree I have enough colors with the browns, oranges, and turquoises in my skirt." If she only knew how hard it was to get this look she would let it go, thought Ruby fingering her hair. She wished she could be like Kellie and wear her hair natural but it was just too thick especially when she had the urge to run a comb through it, too much drama and pain. RJ knew her mom preferred her to have it hanging and flowing down her back like her sisters. But that was not her style. If she was going to wear a relaxer her hair style must reflect her personality.

"Ruby Jewel I think you look pretty and Robbi sweetheart you need to get your purse so we can go." She thanked her father and helped him remove the remaining dishes._____

Once again their visit to the clinic was a success. Her mother was very cooperative and had a pleasing temperament. Their next appointment would be Friday afternoon for consultation concerning her test results. That was fine for Ruby Jewel; she would meet with clients and be back in time. Instead of going home her parents decided to go to the center and visit for a while. She chose to sit in the park which was across the way. It was such a splendid day with total relaxing surroundings. The light winds caused the branches to sway back and forth providing a cozy atmosphere while spreading sweet scent of outdoors. Quacking swimming ducks in the park's small pond, chirping insects, and singing birds orchestrated a soothing melody. Sitting in one of the swings under a shade tree, she watched baby squirrels at play. Swinging back and forth with her hair blowing, RJ couldn't remember the last time she actually went to the park just to relax and enjoy the scenery. All she needed now was a picnic lunch. That was a thought smiling and enjoying the cool breezes. Maybe when they come back for the results they'll do just that and take in nature's wonder.

The signs and sounds of an early spring everywhere would certainly guarantee a peaceful and pleasurable outing._____

Caleb was exhausted as he parked his metallic gold Range Rover in the parking lot of one of the inns along the interstate. Although he was about four hours from Houston, Texas; he couldn't go another mile. When he completed his visits with his entire family, it was after twelve. He couldn't believe his Grandmother Van Lee, and then on the other hand he could. She actually gave him a telephone number to get in touch with someone who was working at the hospital. Her goal was to see him married and give her great grandchildren. It was simple, she wanted an heir and he was her only hope. He was thankful his biological mother had two siblings which provided Grandmother Stratton with six grandchildren. He would hate to be pressured from both sides. Of course his mom had been hinting around that it was time for him to settle down, but it wasn't a song like Grandmother VanLee and she was not trying to pick out his future wife. He couldn't make her understand it was not necessary; his heart already belonged to someone else.

Caleb stood at the front desk to get a room for the night and was too tired to go out, room service would have to do. His plans were simple; take a hot shower, eat, and lay his weary body down. He was not expected at the clinic until the beginning of next week, but he had decided to pay the clinic a visit Friday Before starting his new job, he had planned to have a little fun and couldn't wait to hook up with his frat brothers in Houston. Over the years they had been busy building families plus careers while he spent his years alone specializing in his field. Caleb knew they had stories to tell and he couldn't wait to hear them.

CHAPTER 4

Ruby Jewel was back in H-town and in the office. Of course her father hated to see her leave but she promised she would spend the weekend when she returns which made him happy. She really didn't know what in the world she was thinking to make a promise, but it was done. Attorney RJ McHarding could handle a weekend with her mother, she'll get her sister to bring over the children.

"RJ, Ms. Janet Cook is here."

"Thanks Angela, I'll come out front and get her." This was the last client for the day. Because she had to rearrange her schedule to be with her parents for the test results she had several potential clients come in today. For anyone else this day would have been hectic, but for her it was a high and not because of the dollars she earned. Enabling her clients to fulfill their business aspirations was incredibly rewarding, especially since she too had taken that giant step in chancing and embarking on her own business venture. Of course her mother was not happy with her leaving the state controller's office, but she had to follow her heart and at least try. Needless to say she had done well and had an impressive clientele plus a lucrative business.

RJ walked to the front to greet her last client. Ms Cook's appointment would not take long. She was looking at expanding her restaurant and was in the process of purchasing the property next door to give her more sitting room and parking. She wanted her to look over the contract before she signed. As Ms Janet put it when she called, it wasn't that she didn't trust her realtor because she did, she just felt better with her lawyer taking a *look see*. "Hey Ms Janet, it's good to see ya. Come on let's go to my office." She had a shopping bag and RJ knew exactly what was in it, dinner!

Well, that was it for the office visits. RJ had completed a few other pressing matters before calling it quits at the workplace, but not for the day. On her way home she was to stop by Wiley Collins Senior Citizen's facility. Nathan Collins had called and needed her to take care of an urgent problem._____

Caleb cruised into the Houston city limits on the 45 interstate along with the evening traffic. He was spending the night at the Grandeur Inn and meeting Alton Ray Russell, Tyler Hamilton, and Nathan Collins around six. He hadn't seen his frat brothers since the last convention he attended which was six years ago. He was anxious to see *Silky Silk, Wolf,* and *Mudpuppy* and was looking forward to their visit. When he called Nathan to tell him he was moving to Texas and would be passing through Houston he insisted they meet for an early dinner. In the past they had gotten together at the conventions whenever he was able to attend. Even though he never attended their homecomings or reunions at the university, he still managed to keep in touch with Silk. He didn't know why he hadn't stayed in touch with his own line brothers; it was only four of them. When they tried to contact him back in the day he ignored their calls. Eventually the calls stopped and he truly lost contact with them altogether.

It was a shame because they had a strong bond back then and were the brothers he never had. They even spent time with his families in Bellville and Denver. He hadn't seen any of them since he left PVU. Who was he fooling? He knew the real reason why. He was angry and embarrassed, walking around the yard like he was Mr. Omega himself with the finest sistah on his arm with much attitude, and then the unexpected happened and everyone knew she had shattered his heart. He left PVU a broken man and couldn't take being around people that was a constant reminder of what he once had. Maybe if she had given him a reason; but she didn't and it wasn't any need in pondering over the past. He was dealing with the future now.

Nonetheless, with him moving to Hempstead he would be closer to her. Caleb's smile revealed it all, his assertiveness and determination where she was concerned. She may as well get ready to deal with him because he was there to stay. Dr. VanLee was also planning on locating his line brothers. Caleb checked at the front desk and was already registered in one of the VIP suites; compliments from his frat brothers.

"Frosty...Frosty!"

"Mudpuppy, Wolf!" The three friends did their frat grip along with hugs and taking turns lifting him completely off the floor. It was a happy reunion; the only person missing was Silk. They decided to take their little get-together to his suite. Wolf ordered room service and the friends strolled down memory lane sharing old stories and pictures of their families bringing him up to date with their present lives. No one mentioned HER, so he thought he would wait awhile, besides Silk was not present and he knew he would know something about her. She was the lawyer for his business as well as the hotel.

"Hey guys, where's Silky Silk?" he asked finally sipping on his drink. With food in his mouth Mudpuppy told him he was meeting with his lawyer. Caleb put his drink down and gazed at his frat brothers._____

"Nathan, I'll get on this right away and make some calls. But I do want you to discuss some of the other alternatives I suggested with your partners and get back with me." Because of the economy, the center has lost some fundings which has affected their programs for some of their residents. He was especially concerned about those whose rent was subsidized along with some of the other services. Besides the clinic, the Wiley Collins Residential Center was developed to provide homes and services for all senior citizens, especially those with low incomes. They needed RJ to work her magic and find some additional funding which was one of her specialties. Nathan and his partners maintained a sense of optimism that the economy would eventually make a recovery and gain strength. Their main concern was the possibility of having to waiver some of their services which they did not want to be an option. What they needed was cushion monies to continue their different programs at the present time. She had already come up with some lucrative ideas which he needed to talk over with the others. He was very confident that she would handle the situation ASAP, and she started off with her own personal donation of twenty-five thousand.

"Thanks RJ for initially getting the ball rolling and I will talk to my partners. Now there's something else I wanted to talk to you about."

"Oh."

"Guess who's moving back to Texas and setting up residence at the new..."

"Caleb," she answered interrupting him before he could say another word. Nathan looked at her for any indication that she was still carrying the torch for him as well. He remembers clearly how much in love they were and everyone thinking they were the ideal couple on the yard. When you saw one, you saw the other hand in hand. Caleb Gerald VanLee 3rd had been one proud dude back then. He had pulled one of the finest and smartest sisters on the yard. There were a lot of brothers jealous because she wanted him instead of a real brother. It was understood she was his woman and no one stepped to her. That went on right until graduation, then *bam* they were no longer a couple. They went their separate ways and never looked back. It was just a few years ago they ran into each other at one of the fraternity conventions. Since then they have kept in touch and looked forward to meeting up every two years. Nathan was glad to hear that his frat brother and friend was planning to relocate to Texas and was arranging a little get together at the Grandeur Inn with the others. He looked at his watch and knew the group was chilling right about now.

"So you know he's moving back."

"Yes, Dr. Alford told me he was joining their staff. And no I do not plan on seeing him." Why was she lying to Nathan? He was the one that has stayed in her heart all these years and now he's constantly on her mind since she's learned he's moving to Texas. The way she behaved, she's certain he's never given her another thought. It wasn't like she was hard to find. He did know where her parents lived.

"Ruby Jewel, you know we go way back. Are you being

fair to yourself and Frosty?"

She hadn't heard that name since she left PVU, his line name. She thought it was so cute and fit him perfectly. The surprised smile on her face said it all whether she wanted to admit it or not. "Nathan, please don't push the issue. That was so long ago and he's probably never given me another thought once he left PVU. For all we know he's probably married and has a family. I was just a."

"Don't even try it RJ. You broke that man's heart. Do you know as close as he and his line brothers were they have yet to hear from him? He has alienated himself from all of us, until me and my boys just happened to run into him at one of the conventions. We made a promise then to stay in touch and no, he's not married nor have a family."

"Nathan please," she turned from him to hide her emotions. She was sad on one hand, because she too remembers that time and pleased on the other that he was not married. It was pointless to say she could never forget the hurt and pain she caused the only man she's ever loved and still loves. The expression on his face when he asked her, *"who am I supposed to love Ruby?"* has yet to escape her and still tears at her heart every time she recalls that regretful moment. For him to even think she did not want him because of who he was, still pains her after fifteen years. And what really hurts is she didn't put forth any effort to make him think differently. Nathan got up from his desk to stand next to her. Turning her around to face him he saw her vulnerable state which was so unlike her. He has seen her in action. She was one tough sistah, but he knew love was capable of making the strongest weak and defenseless. He was speaking from experience.

31

"Hey I tell you what, when I see him tonight I'll real causal like, see where his head's at, and get back to you."

"Nathan don't, just let it be," she sniffed. "I'm not ready to face him yet. I need some time. Besides, I'm just getting use to the fact that he's moving to Hempstead and working with Dr. Charlotte at the clinic. I'm bound to run into him sooner or later and I'm praying for later."

"Okay Babygirl, I'll let it be for now. But if my brother is still carrying the torch I'm going to be back at cha for sho au'ight?" She shook her head indicating yes and wiped her tears. "Come on I'll walk you to your car." Nathan watched her drive off and started for the door when he heard a horn blowing, it was the brothers._____

Jalen watched her leave the facility wiping tears as he snapped more pictures. What in the world could she be upset about? She had the whole world at her feet. Mr. Collins was holding her pretty close and the Mrs. was nowhere around. I thought she and the Mrs. were good friends. Mmmm, I wonder? Maybe this little information will be useful. Maybe that's the angle he should take instead of involving the new church program and his family in exposing her as the backstabbing snake she is!_____

Ruby Jewel was an emotional wreck when she left Wiley Collins Facility. It was God's doing for her to leave when she did. They drove up as she was driving off. She couldn't help but get a quick glimpse when she past their vehicle. The mere sight of him caused her to feel every accelerated heart beat while dancing butterflies performed in her stomach. Her breathing had become more of a chore than a necessity. He was the only man that caused her body to react in such a manner. She couldn't believe after all these years he still had that kind of effect on her. Since she heard he was coming to Texas and practice medicine, she's had sleepless nights and during the day her thoughts were consumed with him. When Nathan told her he was not married she had to literally take hold of herself because she could feel her heart taking wings to escape. She was filled with excitement and anxiousness, but at the same time she couldn't deny her feelings of hopelessness and despair. How could she expect him to still be interested in her after the way she treated him. The night he gave her the most wonderful experience ever, she repaid him by pushing him away. She knew what the gossip on the yard was, but it was far from the truth. There has never been another man for her._____

Ruby Jewel made it home, went through her rituals and decided to call it an early night. She was completely drained and knew she still had another busy morning before leaving Friday. Whether or not she gets any sleep was another issue altogether.

Cell phone. "Hey Tori what's up baby sis?"

"Ruby Jewel, Daddy said you were spending the whole weekend." Hesitating, "I need a big favor if that's true."

"Yes, Tori I'm planning on staying until Sunday and you know I'm good for babysitting." Tori and her husband had a fourteen year old and two small school age children.

"No, Ruby I don't need a babysitter this time. But I do need your help." She could sense whatever she wanted to ask was difficult.

Tori couldn't imagine why she was having a hard time asking her big sister for help. She knew there was no limit to what she would do for her or her family and Lincoln has always held a special place in her heart. It was her big sister who stood up for him when her parents thought he was not good enough for their baby girl, which was far from the truth. Lincoln has worked hard since he was big enough to push a lawnmower. He was a good provider then and was doing a fantastic job now. But with the economy like it is; the plant where Lincoln was employed, had decided to cut employees' hours instead of passing out pink slips a few months ago. Although they were happy he still had a job, the cutting of his hours had caused them to get behind on some of their bills. They had already returned one of their vehicles and now stood a chance of losing their home if they didn't get some help in a hurry. Although they had filled out the required forms to be considered for the new mortgage assistance program, by the time their paper work is assessed they would be too far in debt. They didn't want to go to her parents who were retired and on a fixed income and their other siblings were not able to help; everyone's money was tight.

"Tori what do you need? You know you can ask me for anything."

"Ruby do you think you could give us a loan, we?" Ruby Jewel cut her sister off immediately. She knew Lincoln and Tori were very independent and had done well. Things must be pretty bad for them to ask for money.

"Tori, of course I can, now how much?" Although she expected that response she could not fight back the tears that had threaten to fall since she dialed her number. Ruby sensed she was now upset and waited patiently for her to pull herself together. "Tori sweetie, come on. How much do you need?"

"Ruby Jewel," it was her brother-in-law, "I don't think we're in the position to get any assistance from the government. We have a mess on our hands and it's going to cost a good penny to set us straight and.

"Lincoln tell me, what is the problem and let me decide how we should handle the matter." When her brother-in-law finished telling her their troubles she was fit to be tied.

Lincoln had inherited property that has been kept in the family for three generations, twenty acres of rich grazing land that had been passed down to him by his great grandfather before he died. They had a beautiful hundred year old farmhouse that had been restored and modernized which sits on an acre. So far he had been able to make the payment for the taxes and his bank loan. Their bank note has now fallen behind along with other bills. If that wasn't enough, today he received his termination notice and had to tell his wife he no longer have a job. The severance package he received was not nearly enough to set them straight, but it was a help. Ruby Jewel assured them their troubles were over and she would meet them bright and early in the morning at the bank. She knew Elliot Parker had been after their property for years. Well, not as long as she had a dime would he ever own any and that was a promise. She called Angela to let her know she wouldn't be in at all tomorrow._____

Dr. VanLee had a wonderful visit with his brothers and promised to return to H-town soon. He was given a grand tour of the facility which was very impressive. He was sorry to hear about them facing financial difficulties and blessed him with a generous check along with Tyler and Alton Ray which would help them to continue all of their services, plus some until the economy improves. Their contributions caused Nathan to become overwhelmed and emotional, but that's what brothers do for a worthy cause.

Caleb was disappointed to hear he had just missed Ruby Jewel, but he had been given hope. According to Nathan he was sure she still loved him and was encouraged to pursue her whether she wanted him to or not. That news caused his heart to dance. He vowed then to bring Ruby Jewel to her senses. Once and for all she was going to accept they had an undenying love and he was not going to stop until she was his.

Driving into the city limits he noticed the changes from Houston to Hempstead. Wooded areas were now freeways, businesses and beautiful suburbs. While on the way he couldn't resist visiting his old alma mater. The campus had grown considerably. Caleb could visualize the parking lot filled to capacity at the tailgate parties during homecoming and couldn't wait to participate and see the rest of the brothers this year. *Turn left on Chambers.* Modern technology, thought Caleb as he followed the directions given by his GPS. He could be at his new home in ten minutes, but he needed to make a stop first. He really didn't have to be in a hurry, or worry about unpacking and setting up his townhouse. That chore had been taken care of and was completed thanks to his well-organized housekeeper.

Chapter 5

"Good morning Baby Girl. Are you on your way home?"

"Hi Daddy, yes I'm in the city limits right now." She was actually in the bank's parking lot which was practically empty and parked right beside her sister's SUV. "I have a little business to take care of, but I'll be at the house as soon as we finish. How's Momma?"

"She's doing fine. Her mood and attitude has been pretty good since the last time you were home. She's even been working in her flower beds and we've gone to the center every day."

"That's good Daddy. Now…"

"Wait Ruby Jewel before you hang up. I just want to thank you for helping out Tori and Lincoln. He has worked so hard and deserves better. You're such a blessing to this family, you know that don't you?"

"I'm just glad I can be there for them Daddy, but we'll talk later they're waiting on me now."

"Bye Sweetheart."

"Bye Daddy." She was glad her sister told them their problem, which keeps her from having to withhold information. That was pressure she didn't have to encounter. Her adrenaline was already running pretty high due to the little business she was about to handle. What she was about to do was delightful pressure and she came prepared. Stylishly dressed in a vibrant sleeveless red knit dress with a double layered empire waist band, gold accessories, red crisscross shoes and matching bag in hand, she was ready for action. Her curly locks were drawn up in a cascade of curls with a red and cream zebra print scarf, just like the cardigan she was wearing. Robbi Jean may not approve of her choice for today, but she felt alive and ready to kick some tail...Elliot Parker's for sure. With dark shades to shield her eyes from the bright sunlight, she stepped from her Cadillac and walked toward the front door of the city bank.

"Good morning Ruby Jewel don't you look fine this lovely morning." She thanked the kindly older gentleman who was a harmless flirt and sweetheart as she entered the building. Tori and Lincoln were on the far end of the bank waving to her. With the grace of a swan but the demeanor and face of a shrewd competent business woman, she sashayed to their location and embraced them both. Before she could take her seat Mr. Parker walked over.

"Hello Ruby Jewel, I can see life is still being good to you. If you will allow me to say so, you look absolutely gorgeous."

"I think you're already said so, but thank you for the compliment." He had that sneaky grin on his face, but today she was going to wipe it completely off.

"Now what can I do for you fine folks?" Lincoln asked him how much it would take to bring them current on their loan along with all the penalties. RJ talked over her plans with them last night, but if that didn't work she had an ace in the hole that they were not aware of. She met with her banker before leaving for Hempstead to get a cashier's check of an estimated balance of their loan plus a little cushion money.

Elliot pulled up their information. "I'm afraid you're now in foreclosure and…"

RJ interrupted him and requested the remaining balance of their loan and the deeds to their property. Her sister and brother-in-law were about to protest when she held her hand up silencing them both.

He looked at her with a smirk expression, "RJ there are other alternatives we can…"

"Again Elliot we would like the payoff balance of their loan and the deeds to their property. That's the alternative we will take, thank you." Her persona and attitude was obvious, she didn't need him to tell her what she already knew. He asked for a few minutes and left them alone. By this time Tori was wiping tears and leaned on her husband. Lincoln kissed her forehead and whispered thank you to his sister-in-law as he struggled to retain his own tears. They didn't have to ask, because they knew exactly what Ruby Jewel McHarding was getting ready to do. Elliot Parker came back with the payoff banknote but not the deeds and had that look that not even she could pull this off in one sitting. He gave her the print outs, and with that lawyer's instinct she looked over the paper work while pulling out an envelope from her designer's bag. Giving him the envelope, "I think this will cover the payoff and put a little extra into their account since Lincoln was terminated yesterday. You two need to sign and, wait a minute I don't see anywhere to sign or the deeds." Her eyes pierced him with a deadly glare.

Giving her the envelope back, "I…I…I'll…excuse me for a minute, I'll be right back." Elliot rushed from his desk.

I know you will, thought RJ as she handed the envelope to Lincoln. "Now handle your business brother-in-law and when you two finish meet me over at Ms. Dolly's for breakfast, I have a business proposition to talk over with you." She strolled out of the bank the same way she strolled in this time wearing a well pleased smile of satisfaction. Humph, she deserved some of Ms Dolly's grand slam country style breakfast after the way she had Elliot Parker stuttering like a small child. Next she'll wash it all down with a cool glass of lemon-apricot tea and then buy a dozen homemade teacakes for later. She was feeling real good and decided to walk instead of driving since it was right around the corner from the bank.

A few minutes later Elliot came back with all the necessary documents for the Sims loan payoff. He was truly upset with Ruby Jewel. He had already notified the client who was interested in purchasing their property. He was going to get a decent price and stood to make a nice commission. Leave it to her to run to their rescue…

Ruby didn't get far before stopping at one of the little shops that featured antiques. She loved window shopping in downtown Hempstead. During her browsing she's found some charming and unique vintage jewelry, plus a lace tablecloth with matching napkins. One of her most precious pieces and her pride and joy was an exquisite crystal serving set and vase that's sitting on her table this very moment. It was a special gift from Caleb. He said it was their first pieces for when they set up house after they were. She couldn't bring herself to say the word nor did she want to even think of that day. Besides she had the crystal set that was a constant reminder of how it could have been....

Caleb couldn't believe his luck when he spotted her leaving the bank. His insides were smiling as he watched her pass by. She was more beautiful than he remembered, as he fingered his diamond stud. Her silky looking dark skin was actually glowing against a vivid shade of red, one of his favorite colors to see her in. Her curly hair pulled back into a ponytail danced from side to side with each movement of her head. Naturally he preferred her silky tresses flowing around her face and down her back. The mere sight of her caused his body to go completely haywire, especially when he noticed she was still wearing their twin diamond stud around her ankle. That and the red dress that hugged her curves caused him to travel down memory lane to their one and only time making passionate candid love. She had been so shy and self-conscious mainly about her body size at first. But once he assured her it was her luscious curves that attracted him from the very beginning, eased her mind and allowed him to pleasure her to the best of his ability. He did have a little help; one of their favorite songs, *Let's Chill* was how it all started. A night he relives more times than he would like to admit. It was a good thing he was sitting behind the desk with Ms Daphne Lambert facing him as he recalled that evening. She had honored him with her precious body which was a sure indication that what they had was real, he was her first. He loved her so much and thought she loved him as well. Then she mangled his heart when she ended their relationship a week later. He had gotten his mother's engagement ring from his grandmother and had made plans to propose to her that very weekend. He wanted her by his side for the rest of his life and still do. It was a new day and time, and he was not going to let her walk away from him without putting up a fight.

Now if he could get Ms Lambert to finish this business transaction that should have been done thirty minutes ago. Somehow she managed to prolong the completion of him opening a simple account and was using every minute to flirt during the process. He hated to be rude it was not his nature, but he was fed up with women coming on to him. Caleb did not have a conceited bone in his body, regardless of his assets and women considering him a great catch. His heart belonged to only one woman and she just passed the window. The only way he was going to catch her was to hurry Ms Lambert along and let her know he was not interested period....

Cell phone. "Hi Nathan, what's up?" She took a seat on one of the sidewalk benches that was in front of the shop.

"RJ you're not going to believe what I have to tell you! I have some fantastic news!" He was practically shouting.

"What is it Nathan, tell me!"

"Our troubles are over at the center!"

"Are you serious, you didn't win the lottery?"

"Might as well have won the lottery the way money is coming in. Gregory Larson called this morning and pledged a hefty sum from him and Kellie, plus KLTS. Neblett Enterprise, J&E Associates, Delana, and Ms Janet all called to say they would be sending their donations. Here's the clincher, the brothers came over right after you left and wrote some hefty checks themselves. Can you believe that Ruby

Jewel? Of course it was Caleb's check that brought me to my knees. I tell you I'm still in shock. I offered him partnership in the center, that's how serious his check was. But you know Frosty; he turned it down and said he was glad to be of service. RJ you started it and I'm so happy and grateful at the same time to report we now have over two million dollars. Can you believe that? I'm telling you it's awesome RJ and I can't thank you enough. Now have you seen my brother yet, he should be there."

"No, Nathan not yet and please don't start with me."

"I'm not, but I do want you to know he did ask about you and made it clear of his intentions, so get ready baby girl, you know how a brother can be persistent. His very words were *he was not letting you walk away from him this time.*" Before she could respond a voice from the past captured her soul, her very essence. The deep sensuous vocal cords belonged to only HIM.

"Hi Ruby." Disconnecting her call she stood to stare into the most gorgeous baby blue eyes ever. Lord she was not ready to face HIM yet, but as fate would have it, she had to acknowledge his presence or look foolish. And looking foolish was not a part of Attorney Ruby Jewel McHarding's makeup.

"Hi Caleb," six three, perfectly suntanned, drop dead specimen of a man! Long powerful legs were clad in faded worn jeans. A starched ironed white long sleeve shirt opened at the neck with the cuffs turned back was stretched across his broad well-developed chest. With great pleasure, she continued examining every adorable inch of him. His golden chestnut curly hair was no longer in a ponytail that she loved and thought was so sexy. He now had a stylish haircut layered and tousled in the top and tapered on the sides. A light shadowy beard blended right into side burns and his mustache, which conveyed sex appeal and sophistication. Ruby looked at his right earlobe and noticed he was still wearing their twin diamond stud. He even had a little fuzz under his bottom lip that called out for caressing. Handsome and fine was an understatement for Caleb VanLee 3rd as his lips turned up into a fetching contagious grin showing two deep dimples. She couldn't contain her own smile while trying to control her rapid heartbeat.

He reached for her and she did not resist. Pulling her into his arms he whispered, "Girl, it's been so long and you're more beautiful than ever." He pressed her tightly against his powerful body that was a heavier than before. He felt absolutely divine, she thought returning his hug which initiated a sensuous intense growl to escape his lips and her heated insides to sizzle. They both inhaled each other's intriguing and intoxicating scents of melded spices with sweet sensuous fruits and florals, while they continued lingering in each other's arms with spectators passing by smiling.

Cell phone his. Still holding on to her he reached in his pocket to answer his cell. "Caleb Gerald VanLee 3rd! How dare you not come and see us while you were so close. Your grandparents, uncles, and aunts waited all evening for you anticipating your visit. We got word from your mother that you were on your way to Hempstead. I just don't believe you!" This call had to be taken sitting down. It was his father's baby sister and she was in rare form. He sat down on the same wooden bench and pulled her by his side, putting his arm around her making sure she stayed while he talked to his aunt.

"Auntie I'm sorry, please forgive me. It was late when I got to Houston and I decided to just spend the night and I got a late start this morning." He could tell she was making up a cry, as she sniffed while he explained. She was tough and crying was not a part of her character at all, unless her feelings were hurt. "Auntie don't cry, I was planning to come for a visit as soon as I finished getting settled. I didn't want to be pushed for time and run in for a few minutes and then leave. Really and truly I had planned to come to Sunday worship and spend the whole day. You know we're nowhere from each other now and I promise you'll get to see a lot of me."

"You're just saying that because you know I'm upset with you."

"No I'm not. Come on now, tell me you forgive me and say you'll have all of my favorites Sunday."

"Ok, I'll tell everyone you'll be here Sunday and yes, I'll have all your favorites."

"That's my little rosebud."

"Alright flattery will get you nowhere." He could hear the smile in her voice and knew he was back in her good grace.

"Dr. VanLee! Dr. VanLee! We need you! Please hurry!"

"Auntie I need to go someone's calling me. There must be an emergency. I'll see you soon, love you and give my love to the family."

He and Ruby headed in the direction where the voice was coming from hand in hand. It was the security guard meeting them. Caleb unlocked his truck and called out for him to get his medical bag. He met them at the bank entrance and they followed him inside to the back office where one of their female customers was lying on a loveseat. The older gentleman informed him they had called the ambulance but it would take them a few minutes. Caleb asked if anyone was with her and of course she was alone. He asked for her purse and told Ruby to check inside for any kind of information that would be helpful. He then ordered everyone out and began examining her. Ruby found medical cards and a list of her medicines and gave it to Caleb.

"Smart lady," he said as he glanced at the meds while checking her vital signs. She moaned softly as her eyes opened which was a good sign. Each time he called her name she looked at him. She tried to sit up but he asked her to t lie still for a few minutes. After looking at her meds he decided to check her glucose and sure enough it was extremely low. Becoming aware of what was going on she pointed to her purse that Ruby was holding. He asked her to look inside for a peppermint. Not only did she have the mints she also had orange juice which was much better. He reached in his bag for a straw and raised her up just a bit so she could slowly sip a little juice at a time. Gradually her color returned. Caleb asked her the number one question, had she taken her medicine for the day and when was the last time she had eaten? The blank expression on her face and her eyes clouding up with tears made the answer obviously clear. She had neglected to do both. Just as he was about to let her sit up the paramedics and her daughter entered the room.

"Mother, you forgot to take your medicine again." It was more of a statement than a question.

"Ms..." Caleb wanted her to stop with her accusing tone, her mother was already upset and surely she could see that.

"And just..." The look on her face and the voice in her head screamed wow! Slinging her hair from out of her eyes she smiled up at Caleb.

"Dr. VanLee and you are?

"I'm sorry Dr. VanLee, her daughter." After the introductions he informed her of her mother's condition and said he wanted her to go to the clinic to have her doctor examine her. She was about to protest but he assured her it was for precautionary measures to make sure it was only her low sugar count and the absence of her meds and food that caused her to faint. He would feel better and appreciate it if she would do that for him. His dimpled contagious smile pulled one from her.

"Can my daughter take me instead of riding in the ambulance?"

"If that will make you happy." Her face lit up with relief. Ruby gave her daughter her purse while Caleb helped her up. She thanked Caleb for helping and he gave her a tender pat on the shoulder expressing he was glad he was available. Together he and Ruby walked her out of the bank to her daughter's car. After making sure she was buckled in he told her daughter she should get her a sandwich before going to the clinic. Holding hands again they watched them drive off.

Caleb looked around and noticed Tori. "Is this who I think it is, little Tori Nicole all grown up into a beautiful young woman." Dropping Ruby's hand he grabbed her up with feet dangling and gave her a big hug.

"Yes it's me, married with three children," pointing to her husband and introduced them. Caleb put her down and shook Lincoln's hand and told him it was a pleasure to meet the man in his little Tori's life. "We were going to Ms Dolly's for breakfast why don't you join us." He looked at Ruby and said he would love to. Lingering and dragging out the word love. It was obvious she was still the love of his life to everyone including Ruby Jewel....

The two couples enjoyed their late breakfast. Ms Dolly was so happy to see Caleb she took a seat and insisted their meal was on the house. Ruby was also pleased she joined them; it kept the conversation light and ongoing. She was also relieved the subject of them and whether or not they were now a couple entered the conversation. Obviously she had to admit she was intrigued with Caleb's revelations concerning his passion working with senior citizens. She was fascinated with his ideas and hung onto every word, as his deep baritone voiced lulled her to no end. Ms Dolly was delighted to learn that he had moved to Hempstead and was joining the medical staff at the clinic. She was really proud that one of her children as she often referred to them; would be a part of the clinic that was named after her grandfather.

Ruby glanced at her watch and wondered where in the world the time had vanished to. Her mother's appointment was at 1:15 and it was already after twelve. She needed to make a move now and so did Tori and her husband because the children have early dismissal on Fridays. Standing on her feet, "We hate to leave good company," she spoke for her sister too. "But we must leave, our mother has a doctor's appointment and the kids get out of school at 12:30 today. Ms Dolly once again the food was scrumptious, and as always we truly enjoyed your company. Can I please get my standard doggy bag?"

Ms Dolly ordered them to stay put and she would be

right back. Before going into the kitchen she stood at the door and observed the young couple. She always thought Ruby Jewel had met her match with Caleb and was heartbroken when they went their separate ways. Well things are already looking up for the both of them she thought, as she watched the couple not being able to take their eyes off one another. They made a beautiful couple, ebony and ivory.

Caleb also stood beside her with his cell phone out. "Ruby, please give me your number before you leave. I would love to call you later. With all the excitement we haven't had time to talk." He thought he would play it safe and not rush her by telling her he wanted to call her. Nevertheless, he was sure she got the message with the way he used the word love.

There he goes again with that word love and that enticing smile she thought, as she granted his request. He embraced her and planted a sweet kiss on her cheek. Lord she was thankful she was pushed for time as her insides shuddered. She was definitely going to have to get a hold of her emotions. Ms Dolly came back with a treat for her and the children.

"'I'll be right back Ms. Dolly for a takeout, I'm going to walk Ruby to her car."

Cell phone. His apologetic look said he needed to take the call. She told him to go ahead and that she looks forward to talking to him later. Ruby couldn't believe she uttered those words as soon as they left her lips, but it was the truth. She didn't need to think she was fooling anyone concerning her true feelings for him. It was written all over her face. What's more, she had noticed the sneak peeks she was getting from her sister and brother-in-law._____

Ruby managed to get her parents to the clinic just a few minutes before her appointment. Her mother's tests were all good including her MRI which showed no signs of what she had suspected. Her cholesterol and blood pressure were a little up and she did have a low performing thyroid which explained her mood swings and irritableness. Dr. Charlotte assured them the prescribed medication would get everything under control. Instead of prescribing medication for the other concerns, she wanted them both to start a special diet along with exercising which would help lower her pressure and cholesterol. She also noted she was in better spirits since her last visit and was pleased to know she was attending the center and taking her vitamins that were recommended. They were all relieved that her health was fine except for a couple of small issues that could be taken care of relatively easy.

They did not stop at Ms Dolly's this time for a meal. Her father had informed her he had cooked one of her favorites, a big pot of beans with sausage, hamburger meat, cornbread, and raspberry lemonade, and frosted chocolate brownies. He was singing her song, thought Ruby. She knew her brother and sister, with their families would also come for dinner.

CHAPTER 6

The McHardings had their early dinner and gathered on the back porch for dessert, which was their routine with family meals. Her mother was busy fussing over her grandchildren who wanted ice cream cones. Ruby Jewel was engaged in her favorite pastime when she's home, rocking in her wooden antique rocker. It was a form of soothing relaxation which she needed after leaving Caleb. She was thankful for all the interruptions and was relieved she had not been alone with him. Then she had to do something foolish and give him her number which he would have gotten anyway. Besides he did know where her parents lived. For once she was lost for words and did not know what in the world she was going to say to him. *I'm sorry for the way I acted fifteen years ago. I'm still madly in love with you. Every time I hear the songs Let's Chill and A Piece of My Love, I relive that night. Okay Ruby, get a hold of yourself. Don't forget your persona confident bold and assertive. You're….*

"Guess who I saw today and invited him over for dinner tonight. He was going to be a surprise but I guess he couldn't make it," announced Junior. That snapped Ruby right out of her private thoughts and reminiscing further into the past. All eyes were on him as they waited to hear who, but Tori stole his thunder and made the announcement for him.

"Dr. Caleb Gerald VanLee 3rd and we had the pleasure of having a late breakfast with him. He's moved to Hempstead to head the new Neurology Department at the senior citizen's clinic, specializing in Dementia and Alzheimer. And he is some handsome, tall fine and sexy than ever, huh Ruby?" Her mother and father looked at her with questionable faces. Not one time had she uttered one word about him moving here nor did she say she even saw him today.

"Well, Ruby," said her mother. Needless to say she just sat there and agreed with what was said.

"Yes Momma, Tori is right." And she left it at that.

Cell phone, It was him. "Hi Caleb, I understand you were invited for dinner." All eyes were on her. She knew leaving the room was not a good idea as everyone anticipated his answer.

"Ruby that's what I wanted to tell you and your family. I laid down for a short nap and I'm just waking up. I know dinner is over at the McHarding's house, but did Junior leave me some chili beans." Good ole Junior, thought Caleb. He had given him a chance to spend time with her and then he sleeps the evening away.

"Yes Caleb, there's plenty of daddy's dinner. Right now we're having dessert on the back porch and no, it's not too late for you to come over for your share." A smile spread across his face, she still remembers him that well. He said he'd be there in ten minutes. She disconnected and told the family Mrs. McHarding got up immediately to fix his dinner and asked for her help which was unusual.

"Ruby what are you going to do this time?"

"What do you mean Momma?" Her mother gave her that look that said don't even try it. Regardless of them butting heads she knew her daughter too well. She noticed how quiet and distant she was during dinner. Her body was there but her mind was somewhere else, now it was crystal clear as what was going on with her. She recognized fifteen years ago there was something very special between the two of them besides friendship. Why things went sour she didn't have a clue, but was sure her daughter was the reason for them going their separate ways.

"Baby, I don't know what really happened between the two of you although I do have my suspicions. I just don't want you to make the same mistake again. Caleb is a wonderful man and he loved you so much. You deserve someone like him." Ruby looked at her mother in amazement. Robbi Jean looked at her beautiful daughter and embraced her tightly.

"Momma, I don't know what to do. Surely he can't feel the same way after the way I treated him. I was thoughtless, self-centered and…" She couldn't go on, for fear of breaking down right there in her mother's arms.

"Shhhhhh. The mere fact he's coming over lets you know all of that is in the past and he still has feelings for you. Just take it one day at a time and don't push him away this time. Let him know how much you care for him too." Her mother paused for a second. "You still do don't you?"

Ruby Jewel looked at her mother with tears in her eyes and whispered, "Yes."

"Okay then wipe those tears, take a couple of deep

breaths, and pull yourself together. I need to see that confident, assertive, and beautiful daughter of mine with all her charm work her magic. I want to see that woman right now." Although she wanted to bawl like a toddler she held it in. Her mother has not said such encouraging words to her since she decided to make her own decisions. Not once had she ever said she was beautiful, pretty yes, but never beautiful. Robbi Jean watched her daughter's expressions and knew what was going through her mind. It was their first positive mother and daughter talk in such a long time. She gave her an extra squeeze and kissed her on the cheek. There was a knock on the front door. Her mother smoothed back her curls and told her to go handle her business. Ruby looked down at her casual dress, a red printed tunic over a pair of black leggings and slides.

"You look fine, now go on and stop fretting." Ruby did as she was told. Taking another deep breath, she walked toward the front door. Looking back she mouthed, "Thank you Mommy." Robbi Jean had to now fight back her own tears. Her baby hadn't called her mommy since she was a little fellow._____

Ruby Jewel stretched and kicked her covers off as she thought about the wonderful evening she had with Caleb and her family. Her mother had been a life saver and made sure they were never alone for any length of time which kept her from being under any kind of pressure. He had every one hanging on to his every word including her. While listening to him she became more at ease and lost all apprehensiveness about their past relationship. His sense of humor and storytelling was even better. They also played a new board game Junior introduced to them called Scrabble Flash. She couldn't remember the last time she had so much fun playing a simple game.

After playing a few rounds Caleb became fascinated and thought *Scrabble Flash* would be perfect for some of the senior citizens at the recreation center. He explained how simple activities dealing with words and numbers were beneficial for intellectual stimulation. These kinds of activities were effective as one preventive method that may inhibit the symptoms and slow the progression of Dementia. He went on to give some vital information that was very interesting concerning AD and Dementia. She watched how his eyes lit up as he continued talking about facts concerning risk factors and preventive methods. He was a wealth of knowledge and she knew he was an excellent and caring doctor. She witnessed firsthand his bedside manners with Mrs. Dayton and could tell he had a genuine love for his work. The clinic was getting an extraordinary doctor as far as she was concerned.

They ended the evening with everyone sitting on the front porch and steps enjoying ice cream cones and then called it a night. Before leaving he told her he had a wonderful evening with her family, but would like to spend some time with just her. They made a date for dinner and a movie Saturday night. Even though it was after twelve she was too excited to sleep. She kept thinking about their date. You would think it was their first and she was sixteen instead of thirty-six. They were only going to the movies. Humph, she hadn't been to the movies with a man since heck was a pup. In all honesty the only time she's gone to the movies was during girl's night out with her entourage, and that was whenever they could fit it into their demanding lives. Lately with everyone busy with families, boyfriends, and she with her business, they hadn't had a girl's night out in a while.

Cell phone. She couldn't believe it, it was Caleb. "Hi Ruby, I didn't wake you did I?"

"No, I was still awake. What's up?"

"You don't' want to know."

She giggled to herself, "You dirty ole Q-dog." He growled and then barked like a big dog. They both burst into laughter. She hadn't heard that in years.

"Ruby, I'm just not sleepy, plus I needed to hear your voice. I had a long relaxing nap earlier remember."

"Oh yes that's right and you want me to do what about that?"

"Sneak out the house and let's sit on the back porch and enjoy the moonlight."

"Are you serious?"

"Of course I am I'll be there in ten minutes."

"Caleb! Caleb," a dial tone.

Sure enough ten minutes or so later he was throwing a pebble at her bedroom window. She had just enough time to put the girls in a bra. Her lavender pajamas were nothing fancy and could be mistaken for a lounging outfit since they were trimmed in a girly lace. When she purchased the set she thought they were cute for sleeping, not for entertaining a man. But it was too late to change, they would have to do. Looking out the window Caleb stood grinning up at her, shirtless in a pair of purple and gold jogging pants and an opened matching jacket with his frat symbol on the front. She pointed to the porch and closed the curtains. Tiptoeing past her parents' room she went to the back door, deactivated the alarm system and went out to meet him.

Caleb was sitting on the bottom step of the porch. When he heard the door open he pounced on her and had her in his arms before she could think about resisting; of course she wasn't going to.

"Did I tell you how pretty you looked today," he whispered. She nodded her head as she inhaled his male scent, a fresh shower mixed with a mysterious fragrance of woods and spices. She couldn't resist nipping him gently on the neck. "Au'right don't start something you're not going to finish." She smiled up at him and kissed both cute dimples.

"Come on, let's sit on the swing and study the moon and the stars. You can give me a lesson on the kind of moon we have tonight." Caleb smiled at his ebony princess as they walked over to the swing. She knew next to medicine he was fascinated with the science of astronomy and always said their stars were in sync and they were meant to be together.

"Before we get into the science of the stars and the moon I need to ask you a question. I know from the past you were never good at expressing your feelings. I've always assumed how you felt about me by your actions. But I've never heard you actually say in words how you felt." *Lord please don't let him ask me why I broke up with him begged Ruby Jewel.* Caleb could feel her uneasiness and knew she probably thought he was going to bring up the past or force her to explain her feelings. He had made up his mind before he relocated to leave all that behind him and look toward the future. "Ruby can I assume there's still something strong between us since you're still wearing our twin diamond studs."

She tried her best to steady her emotions and not reveal how bad off she really was where he was concerned. But at the same time she felt he needed to know the love she had for him has never left her heart and was deeper and stronger than ever. Ruby looked up into the clearest blue eyes and admitted, "Yes Caleb there's still something very much between us."

"What do you suppose we do about us?"

"What about we take *us* slow for now which will give *us* time to reconnect." Caleb held her to his chest as he thanked her because he knew that had been difficult for her. He also let her know he thought taking *"us"* slow was a great idea, but he did want her to understand he had never stopped loving her. She acknowledge as she cuddled in his arms pressing her breasts against his hard chest. With his insides filling up with joy he was convinced more so than ever that he had his first and only love back. He just needed to be patient with her for the time being. Caleb vowed he would take their relationship slow, but he secretly promised he would romance her to no end. He then started his lecture with her snuggling even closer in his arms hanging on to his every word. She watched his eyes sparkle and dimples dance as he held class which went on for over an hour then he started to yawn.

"Okay Dr. VanLee you're getting sleepy. Although I'm enjoying the lecture, you need to leave so you can get home safely."

"Are you trying to get rid of me?"

"Definitely not," she said. "I just don't want anything to happen to you."

"You still care that much Ruby?" He had to hear her say something if it was nothing but yes. He thought he could wait but his heart just wouldn't let him.

She looked into his gorgeous blue eyes and confessed, "Yes Caleb, I still care very much." His heart went out to her because after all these years, he was seeing the same heartbreaking troubled expression she had when she broke up with him. He wanted to ask what was holding her back but decided to let it be for now. Caleb reached for her hand and placed it on the symbol of his fraternity branded on his chest. She knew very well what that implied. *He would love her until the day he dies*. He then held her hand to his lips to caress each fingertip with gentle kisses.

Caleb stood and pulled her into his arms once again. "I give you my word to take *"us"* slow because you asked. But I'm putting you on notice; I'm not going to play fair Attorney Ruby Jewel McHarding. And I want you to also know I'm going to do everything humanly possible to make you my wife before this year is up. I promise you that!" He knew he caught her off guard with his revelation and then went on to shock her more. He covered her mouth with his and kissed her with the burning passion that he's held since they laid eyes on each other. She hadn't been kissed like that in fifteen years, breathless and swept away by a sizzling shuddering wave. While gasping he placed soft butterfly kisses at the corner of her mouth. He leaned her against the banister to support the both of them as he kissed the tip of her nose. He needed to leave because he made a promise. "Good night and sweet dreams."

Ruby watched him leave out of the back gate with tears in her eyes and then slipped back into the house. Why couldn't she be honest with him tonight and say how she truly felt? Why wouldn't the words come out? She was going to have to do something about her insecurities. All she could think of was the life she has been living. The almighty Attorney Ruby Jewel McHarding who has everything under control and can handle any situation and resolve most problems; needed to come to grip before she loses the man that means everything to her again. She had some issues to resolve and she would with the help of the man up above and her mother. Ruby smiled because that was certainly a switch. That's love for you....

"Was that somebody coming in the house," asked Henry Ray.

"Yes, Ruby and Caleb have been out on the porch for the last couple of hours."

"Are you serious?"

"Shhhhhh, before she hears you." Robbie Jean waited to hear the bedroom door close before she said another word. "Oh Henry, I've been so unfair to her and have made life so difficult with all my criticizing. Regardless of her success, I've made her feel insecure and she doubts whether she has what it takes to have a healthy relationship."

"Did she say that, Sweetheart?"

"No, but a mother knows these things Henry. I've done that poor child an injustice and I just pray the Lord allows me time to make it up to her. It's all my fault Henry. I'm the blame for my baby feeling inadequate when it comes to men," Robbie Jean began shedding tears. Henry Ray didn't know the last time he had seen her cry. He consoled her with tender caresses and assured her things were going to be alright. She could only pray that the burden that she's inflicted on her daughter would be taken away and she would certainly do her part to help.

CHAPTER 7

"Momma, do I look all right?" Ruby Jewel couldn't believe she was actually asking her mother for her approval, but she was.

"You look wonderful Baby." They both stood gazing into the full length mirror on the closet door. The flattering seasonless hot pink, olive green, and black colorblock dress was fashionable and accentuated her curves. Matching bracelets, dangling earrings in the three colors, and olive green T-strap shoes completed her look. They both turned their attention to her hair. Robbi Jean wanted to make sure she didn't offend her daughter in any way. But she thought with the round neckline and adjustable back tie, her hair would look real nice in an upsweep. Ruby must have read her mind. She twisted and pinned her locks up toward the front which provided a crown of cluster curls.

"Perfect," said her mother. "Wait; let's pull a few curls for bangs and your sides." She turned Ruby around so she could see what she had done and they both agreed with a smile.

"Well I guess I'm ready, all I need now is a wrap in case it gets too cool in the movies."

"Oh no Baby, don't take a wrap. Let him be your wrap."

"MOMMY!"

"Oh I think I hear the doorbell. Add a little more color to your lips before you come out." Robbie Jean turned to leave her daughter's room but not without giving her a sassy wink. Ruby shook her head and smiled. She was seeing a side of her mother that she had never seen and liked it very much. She added color to her lips grabbed her olive green clutch and went out to meet her date.

She could hear him and her father talking. She made her entrance and he stood to greet her with a tender kiss on the cheek. He was so handsome she thought in his dark denim jeans and tailored long sleeve black collarless shirt. He also wore a vest that pulled together his look. He always could wear a pair of jeans, Ruby thought as she smiled her approval.

"You look beautiful Ruby, you ready?"

"Yes, and thank you for the compliment," she said. You look pretty jazzy yourself."

"You're welcome and thank you."

"You two are going to be late if you don't stop with the manners," said Robbi Jean. Everyone chuckled and the young couple said goodnight and left holding hands...

Caleb had decided that they would drive on the outskirts of town to Cypress, a dinner theater that was recommended. The setting was for a mature crowd. You could have a nice meal and watch a movie all at the same time. The atmosphere was cozy with beautiful garden plants and plush comfy seating. The big comfortable round couches were a bonus in her book. She hated having to squeeze into anything especially a chair. Caleb escorted her to one of the half-moon shaped tables which were easily accessible for getting in and out. Naturally they received some quick glances, but she was use to people checking her out. But this time she was sure it had something to do with him. She was on the arms of a fine specimen of a man that just happened to be white. And it was no doubt she was special to him the way he held her close to his side when they took their seats. Menus were on the table to place their order. They decided to share a platter to keep from having a lot of dishes on the table. Caleb had the waitress to add extra and winked, saying he was hungry. The waitress set place settings for two and told them she would be back shortly with their food. Caleb whispered shortly under his breath and Ruby shook her head, he hadn't changed in that department either. They engaged in light conversation and watched previews of upcoming features while waiting for the arrival of their food. The evening had taken off to a wonderful start. Ruby felt at ease and was truly looking forward to the meal and movie.

"Dr. VanLee, what a surprise to see you here!" Caleb couldn't believe it, Daphne Lambert.

"Good evening Ms Lambert. It's a surprise to see you too. I was told this was the closest theater where you can watch a movie and have a nice dinner all at the same time. Excuse my manners, I would like to introduce..."

"There's no need, me and Ruby Jewel go way back, hey girlfriend."

No she didn't, thought Ruby. "Hey Daphne, how's your family?"

"They're fine. Mom and Dad are in Europe for a month. You know Danni lives there now and she and her husband are expecting their first baby."

"That's wonderful." Both of the Lamberts girls were spoiled brats since their family owned the bank.

"Are you Dr. VanLee's lawyer," she asked as she flipped her hair out of her face. Ruby never understood women combing their hair to the front and then flipping it back over and over.

"No, she's my date for the evening. As a matter of fact I'm trying to rekindle a little something, if you know what I mean." Daphne Lambert's big smile turned into a silly grin. "Oh Baby here's our food." She was standing in the way of the waitress, who politely asked to excuse her so she could set their dinner on the table, that's when she turned red.

"Daphne if you're alone you're more than welcome to join us. As you can see there's plenty."

"Oh no I have a date also." She pointed to a nerdy looking dude on the other side of the room who was watching her. "I just saw Dr. VanLee and thought I would come over and say hello."

"That was nice of you and I guess I'll see you next time I come into the bank. Enjoy the movie. Baby I'm hungry, let's say grace." Talking about being dismissed, he reached for Ruby's hand to bless their meal. Ruby dare not say a word. She knew from the past he was very protective of her and her feelings. She has seen him become very indignant, especially when someone invades their privacy unless it's a frat brother but he didn't waste any time putting them in check too...

The meal was great and so was the movie. He had chosen an action packed remake of an old western that had both black and white cowboys who were small cattle ranchers and merged together to protect their land from a big cattle baron. It was filled with lots of action and romance which made it a really great flick. That was a DVD she would like to add to her collection.

On the way home they talked about the movie and their favorite parts. She couldn't believe the romantic part where the cowboy won the heart of his true love. That was her favorite part too but she dared not say. She did tell him he had done a fantastic job with dinner and the movie selection, and she truly enjoyed the evening. Ruby admitted she couldn't say when the last time she had such a wonderful time. Of course she realized she had given too much information. But it was the truth and she was going to stop holding back with him. At least she was going to put forth every effort.

Caleb was delighted she had a terrific time. He was glad he had pleased her and this was just the beginning. He really loved it when she had to snuggle up to him because it was a bit cool in the theater. He wanted to spend every waking moment with her, but knew that was not possible because of their careers unless he was coming home to her. Caleb made a promise to himself that they were going to spend as much time together that their busy schedules would allow. He didn't care if it was nothing but a quiet evening parked in his car. They spent the remainder of the ride in silence listening to a quiet storm CD, both minds and hearts racing with thoughts of love and romance. It had been so long for the both of them but longer for her. Ruby Jewel had not allowed anyone to touch her since their special night. He knew her silence indicated she was traveling back to that night, because he too had done so many times. Right now he's so tempted to take her to his place instead of her parents. He must have patience and restraint. He had promised!

He pulled up in front of her house. He looked over at his ebony princess whose eyes were closed and leaned over to kiss her lips. She moaned sweetly.

"Ruby we're here". She looked up into his handsome face and smiled. "Before I walk you to the door can I see you tomorrow before you leave for home?" He knew her parents were planning a visit with her mother's oldest sister who lives in one of the new suburbs right past the college with her daughter and family.

"Caleb I usually drive my car to Aunt Rita's and afterwards I head home since I'm not far from the freeway. This Monday is pretty busy, I had my office manager to reschedule appointments for Momma's test results."

"Ruby can't we meet somewhere in between. You know I'll be at Aunt Ruth's visiting with both families. Can't we at least try to arrange something?"

She could hear the pleading in his voice and it was true she wanted to see him just as bad before leaving. "How about we meet at the local drive-in country store that's off the freeway between Bellville and Prairie View, you can't miss it."

"That's a deal. Now I just need to know what time I'll be able to slip away."

"You have my number; give me a call if you can't. After

all, your family hasn't seen you in what."

"It has been at least four years," interrupting her. "I didn't get to come with my parents the last few times. So I do owe them a good visit. If I can't get away at a decent time, is it asking too much for you to stay one more night?"

She was so tempted to say yes, but knew she needed to get back to the office. Business was good and she needed to stay focused as much as possible; clients and staff were depending on her. But she did want to spend more time with him. Ruby knew in order to make this relationship promising and work she would have to be flexible and organize her time. And she was ready to take the necessary steps to build a future with HIM. Future, now that was a switch. She recalled his very words, *"He was planning on making her his wife before the year was over."* She would have to be a working partner in his quest which meant developing a schedule that would include Caleb VanLee. Another switch, she thought smiling. Ruby Jewel was actually anticipating building a relationship and becoming his wife by the end of the year.

"Let's just see how things work out and what time permits." He agreed and walked her to the front door where they said their good nights with a sweet embrace and kiss._____

Caleb pulled into the parking lot of the church where his parents were raised. He could see people standing in the foyer greeting one another and figured Sunday school was over. Which meant he was right on time to visit before the morning services begins. The Nicholsons' and Beasleys' were two of the oldest families who still attended West Victory and were instrumental in building the church which was the first Church of Christ in the area. It was a nice size congregation that serviced the local and neighboring areas. His father often said West Victory was responsible for introducing him to the woman of his dreams. Everyone knew Vera Denise Beasley and Lawrence Gene Nicholson were made for each other and Caleb had to agree. They were extremely happy and still very much in love after forty-eight years of marriage. And he knew without a doubt he would have the same happiness with Ruby.

He reached over and got his suit coat. Regardless of the Texas weather being warm to him, he knew West Victory was an old fashion country church where everyone dressed. Of course his grandmothers and aunts never stopped wearing their hats and gloves which has set the dress code for the other women. He was pretty clean himself in his brown suit, vanilla cream silk t-shirt, brown designer shoes and his gold jewelry. Nothing too flashy, just enough to represent and fit in with his family. As he approached the front door he saw his cousins who had been his partners in crime when he spent his summers in the country. Roy and Douglas recognized him and made their way. The cousins hugged and gave the frat grip. They were also members of the same fraternity. That was the Nicholson's and Beasley's way. The men were Qs and the women were Deltas or *non-pha-non*.

"Frosty you look mighty sharp my man. All buff and grown up, where's the ponytail little bro?" asked Douglas with a hearty laugh. The male cousins were known for teasing him about his ponytail. His response was always the same, the women liked it and they did. The model for the butter commercial could have taken lessons from him in seducing women with his long hair.

"What can I say cuz, I had to cut it off to go with my new image." He hunched his shoulders and flashed his dimpled smile. Before he could say another word he was grabbed from behind in a big bear hug and lifted completely off the floor. He knew it was Tiny. "Tiny! Tiny! What's going on my main man?"

"You got it little bro. Man it's been ages since we've seen you last. I heard Mama gave you one good chewing out."

"Yes she did." Arnold Jr. knew his mother was a piece of work and was nothing nice. She still comes in everyday to the family business he now operates, to give him a hard time.

"Caleb! Caleb!" shouted the twins Kaili and Kailey. They both jumped in his arms. It had been some years since he had seen them. They were the closest to sisters he's had. The twins were both married with their own children, three each. As a matter of fact, all of his cousins on both sides were married with children and doing fine. Since they lived in nearby suburbs two to three miles from Bellville, they still attended West Victory Church. Every weekend was pretty much a family gathering. They have dinner and fellowship on the grounds then a three o'clock service afterwards and call it a Sunday evening. That's how they've spent their Sundays as long as he could remember. He thought it was a great idea because it kept both the church family and the physical family close. Not to mention the wonderful meals prepared. While the men left for brothers' meeting they have before worship, he walked in the sanctuary where his grandparents and aunts were sitting.

"There's our vanilla grandbaby," said both grandmothers

as he gave each one a big hug and kiss. That was his pet name for the older women in the family. Color was not an issue in this family and his grandparents made sure he was not treated differently because of his skin color. He never knew there was a difference until one summer during his visit, Uncle Arnold's nephews from Chicago came down. They had the rest of the cousins calling him whitey during a baseball game. Caleb struck out PJ who became angry; the next thing you know he and his brother BF started calling him names. They got into a fight and the rest was history. Aunt Ruth whipped tails that summer and made it clear there would be no name calling and fighting in this family. She talked to him at length concerning the incident and his true ethnicity and because he had black parents he would run into those kinds of situations. She could control what goes on in her home but she had no control of what takes place on the outside. He needed to get a thick skin to be strong and ignore ignorance. That was the summer he truly grew up even though he was just a child. He became aware of the real differences of the two worlds he was involved in. Whenever they get together with those two, Tiny always bring it up and they have a big laugh about it still.

He hugged and kissed his aunts and the other saints that he had come to know and love. Of course his Auntie popped him upside the head and then gave him a big kiss. She always had her nephews taking side steps to keep from being hit. The men came out of the meeting room and service was about to begin. He shook hands and got hugs from his grandfathers and uncles as they took their seats on the front row. He was about to take a seat beside his grandmothers when his Uncle Junior grabbed his arm and told him to sit up front with them. As he took a seat beside his Great Uncle Pete and grandfathers, he knew he may as well be prepared and reached for a songbook.

Uncle Arnold took the pulpit and started the worship service, with opening remarks, prayer request, and then congregational prayer.

"Brothers and sisters we have a special treat today. I know you've seen my nephew from Denver this glorious morning. He's making Hempstead his home now and will be joining the Memorial Hospital staff and the West Victory family. Let's put him on the spot and insist that he leads us in songs." The church said amen and applauded until he was up in the pulpit himself.

He could hear his grandmothers and great uncle still saying amen and his Aunt Lucille "Sing for aunty." Caleb did just that as he started off with one of their old one hundred favorites *Victory in Jesus* and ended with *I Love My Savior Too*. Needless to say he had to sing the last song over. He was embraced and thanked by his grandfather and great uncle for singing their song. They had a wonderful uplifting worship service and the spirit was high as his grandparents often said. Afterwards they enjoyed a great fellowship meal. He was able to get away at a reasonable time and was meeting Ruby at the country drive-in.

CHAPTER 8

RJ was late coming into the office for the first time in years. Even though she had about twenty minutes before her first client she was still late according to her norm. She said good morning and at the same time ignored the stares she received from her staff and partner. She asked for her usual breakfast and switched right past them. Although she was dressed for business she was exhausted from her weekend which brought a smile to her lips.

RJ McHarding had a fantastic three days. In addition to seeing Caleb again and rekindling their relationship, she and her mother had actually bridged a gap that had been between them for some time. When she got home from her date she found her still baking and icing cakes for Sunday. While they completed the task together, she told her about her date which had been their first. For once her mother showed genuine concern for her happiness and what she wanted. But she had not been ready for what Robbie Jean had to say next. She recalled their little talk word for word and it will always stay with her.

Ruby I know you're lonely, but you don't have to be. Let go of your insecurities and allow your prince charming to sweep you off your feet. Baby he can't love you if you won't allow him. He can't give you what you need and deserve if you don't let him. Don't tie his hands. You need love like everyone else. I want you to have that happiness that your father and I have had all these years and I do believe Caleb is the one. But you have to give in Baby and stop holding back. I'm begging you to let go of the past and start new with the man that's perfect for you and I'll say it again, Baby he is THE ONE. I can truly say that now with much admiration and convection in my heart. I watched how the two of you stole glances at one another when you thought no one was paying you any attention. I saw the love Ruby, and if you're holding on to the past because of the things I've said, please let it go for the both of our sakes. I'm so sorry my precious Jewel for making you uncomfortable about who you are, because Baby you're a beautiful vibrant woman with an unlimited amount of qualities to offer. I had no right to make you think you were not worthy. Any man of merit should be proud that you would even give him the time of day and I mean that from the bottom of my heart. For the record I've always been proud of you and I want you to always remember that. You are very precious to me. Please forgive Momma for not being supportive and there for you when you needed me. I love you so much.

That revelation put her in her mother's arms. When her father came into the kitchen, he found them crying and holding one another. He pretended to want a glass of water, but did ask was everything alright? Her mother assured him they were fine just having some mother and daughter time. She knew her father was relieved and happy, because for once he did not have to be a mediator between the two to keep peace. As a matter of fact she knew he had a strong feeling he would never have to be a referee ever again between the loves of his life and it was about time.

The family visit with Robbi Jean's oldest sister was real nice.   They had a special treat when her three sons and families were present.   Her aunt was thrilled to have her baby sister and all her family over at the same time for a visit. Everything had been set up on the back patio for an old fashion Sunday picnic instead of the usual Sunday dinner since it was a nice warm day.

The highlight of the evening was she was able to leave at a decent time to meet Caleb at the corner drive-in before going home. They sipped on strawberry banana smoothies and ate homemade pound cake while he brought her up to date with his family. He shared pictures he took during the fellowship dinner of his family.   His grandparents really looked well. Both sets are in their early eighties and didn't look a day over sixty-five. He was hugged up with every woman at the church young and old. He teased her about being jealous and she had to confess she was a tiny bit. But he assured her she had nothing to worry about because his heart and soul belonged to her if she wanted them. She couldn't believe she actually told him she did, maybe her mother's little talk had truly been a wakeup call and the key factor in her finally taking hold of her senses. She was now content and felt fortunate that they were given a second chance at having a new beginning. After a while conversation was not necessary, simply being together had pleased them both. They were satisfied just holding hands and listening to music which made their evening so incredibly special....

Angela knocked on her door and entered before she could say come in. "Well I can tell we had an enjoyable weekend, because we do look kind of tired. And where is your jewelry? Here's your breakfast sandwich and tea." RJ touched her ears; at least she had on her diamond studs which she wears twenty-four seven. She couldn't remember the last time she forgot to put on jewelry. She did have a backup, and "that don't miss a thing Angela" was already in her closet. She opened the top drawer that held some of her personals for situations like this. She even had two extra changes of clothing and a nice pair of black shoes if needed. Angela gave her the emergency jewelry box, just some good costume, nothing of real value. While picking out accessories she was informed of the four appointments she had back to back until four. That meant she would be with clients or at least in the office until six.

"Will this do?" RJ held a multi-strand necklace up against her teal princess line sleeveless sheath dress which had a round neckline. Angel nodded yes and she took out the matching earrings and bracelet.

"I think you'll look more presentable if you scoop that wild mane to the side instead of a plain ponytail hanging in the back," said Angela and gave her a mirror and some hair pins. "Girlfriend, you must tell me about your visit with your parents. It must have been a whammy of a weekend; the evidence is crystal clear. Plus there's something different about you that I cannot put my finger on."

"Thanks Angela and when you get back to the front desk ask Carla to come in before my first appointment." Humph, she was right about that as she scooped her hair up and over to the side. Mmmm, that did look much better and she now had more of a relaxed appearance than that wild get-up. And the jewelry was perfect lying on the wide lapel of her matching jacket.

"RJ you need to come out front for a minute," requested

Angela and turned off the speaker before she could ask why. Now she was not in the mood for Angela's games today. She just left her office, what in the world did she want now. RJ got up from her chair and made her way down the short hall. As she came close to the front she could see a large arrangement of assorted flowers. They were simply gorgeous. Angela gave her the card with a smirky grin. She turned it over to and saw his name at the bottom. She had everyone's attention as she read it.

Something beautiful for a beautiful lady. Hope these brighten your day like the mere thought of you brightens mine. Looking forward to the weekend.

Love Caleb

"My, my, Missy. You've been holding out on us," said Lana who had joined the group.

"Later girls, I must get ready for my first client." RJ took her floral arrangement to her office with her heart singing. She removed the green plant that sits on the small accent table she had by the window and replaced it with her flowers. The fresh blooms filled the room with spring colors and a lovely aroma._____

The day was finally over with her seeing the last client. It went by relatively fast considering how she started out. Everyone that entered her office admired her flowers and said how beautiful they were. She avoided her co-workers as much as she could and tried to have a working lunch but they wouldn't hear of it. They met in the small dining area including Kellie and Ann from next door. She told them about her weekend and Caleb while they ate a light lunch of grilled chicken, vegetable dish and tea. They were so happy for her and couldn't wait to meet Dr. Caleb VanLee 3rd. When she showed them his picture on her cell they gave out cat whistles and shouts of "you go girl." Kellie had the biggest grin ever when she recognized it was him. Angela was shocked, not only was he white he was a Q, and they both graduated from PVU. Ruby smiled as she recalled Angela's other remark Dr. Caleb VanLee had to be hellavue to have pledged a black fraternity and win the heart of Attorney Ruby Jewel McHarding. When she was about to deny he didn't have her heart, the lunch bunch said in unison, *"Don't even go there!"* Kellie gave her that look to remind her she knew her story. They had some of the same hang ups. But she got over hers and RJ was more than confident that she would too.

After they were all satisfied with her detailed account of Caleb and her weekend, she was able to return to her office and complete her work day. It was late now and she was the last one to leave the building. Even the cleaning crew was just about through with her office being last. All business transactions had been completed along with attorney referrals.

Cell phone, CALEB. "Hi Sweetheart, are you on your way home yet?"

"No, I'm still at the office. Caleb the flowers were absolutely wonderful. I received so many compliments. I had to tell my co-workers about you and my weekend. I'm just going on. How was your day?"

"Fine, I just miss you so."

"Is that right?" Ruby Jewel couldn't contain her smile

and giddy emotions she felt inside.

"Yes, Ruby I don't know how long I'm going to be able to live like this, missing you like this."

"Oh Caleb, I miss you just as much. The flowers were a constant reminder of you and our time we spent together."

"I'm glad. How long will it be before you get home?" He was tired and wanted to take care of his personal needs and then stretch out with her in his arms for the night. He spent his entire day at the clinic and never made it to Cypress Memorial. They rescheduled the visit for tomorrow, he did get a lot done. After spending a couple of hours with human resource and setting up his office, he spent the remaining of his day making his clinical debut visiting and meeting the entire staff. His day had been filled with lots of activity and more was promised. He didn't intend to come to Houston but he found himself heading straight to the freeway instead of going home.

"It should take me about fifteen to twenty minutes depending on the freeway traffic; I'm practically right down the street."

"Hurry Baby, I'm waiting on you."

She couldn't believe her ears. "Caleb are you here in the city?" she asked excitedly.

"Yes Sweetheart, I'm sitting on your front porch speaking to the neighbors and enjoying the scenery. Bro. Bruce walked over, introduced himself and asked if I needed anything. According to him your next door neighbor, was threatening to call the police. He talked her out of it and said he would investigate. They all thought you would be home by now. I told them I was a very good friend from out of town and was trying to surprise you with a visit. Oh, and one of the other neighbors from down the street also walked over after she got her mail. "

"Caleb I'll be there shortly." Ruby got tickled because she knew Ms. Johnnie was having a stroke with a white man sitting on her porch.

"Okay Sweetheart, hurry but be careful." Caleb leaned against a decorative dark green pillow on the antique bronze bench admiring her set up. She had her very own garden right in her doorway which made a comfortable relaxing spot.

CHAPTER 9

Ruby Jewel said her goodnights and left the building. She didn't waste any time getting out of the parking lot. Traffic was a little slow but she was taking the second exit and would be home in a matter of minutes. She still couldn't believe he was actually waiting for her. Was he spending the night? Would that be safe? It was no use pondering over that foolishness, she was just glad he was here. She exited 288 and drove down the feeder until she got to the boulevard that would take her into her subdivision. His Range Rover was in view as she turned on her street.

Cell phone. "Ruby."

"Hi Momma, is everything okay?"

"Yes Sweetie, I'm calling to let you know Caleb is on his way to Houston. He called to get your address. It seems he's going to spend the day at Cypress Memorial tomorrow and decided to come into the city to see you."

"Momma don't worry he already called and he's at the house waiting on me now."

"Wow, he didn't waste any time did he? Now Ruby don't forget what we talked about. He can't love you if you won't let him, remember that. "

"I will Momma. I'm getting another call, tell Daddy I said hello and I love you." Clicking over, "Nathan, what's up?"

"RJ, I hate to call you after hours but we're having a problem with one of our vendors and we need some legal advice about our obligations concerning their contract. If possible we want to get out of it. Can I come by and we take a look at it?"

"Sure Nathan, let me check my schedule and I'll have Angela get back with you." She pulled up beside his vehicle and gathered her belongings as she continued her conversation with Nathan.

"That sounds like a plan, now how's?"

"Fine, he's waiting for me to get out of the car as we speak."

"Wow my brother is still smooth as silk, *Ruffff*. Tell him to holler at me."

"I will goodbye Nathan."

"Bye Baby."

He opened her car door and she walked into his waiting arms and gave him a peck on the cheek. "Hi baby, how was your day," he asked as he held her close?

"Busy, but very productive, I picked up three new clients. Before I forget Nathan said give him a call. Come on let's go inside." RJ waved to some of her neighbors who were outside while getting her mail. Caleb threw his medical saddlebag over his shoulders and grabbed his clothes bag. She opened her mahogany front door and screen to her modest home.

"Welcome Dr. VanLee, you can set your keys there." She pointed to the tray on a wood accent table with a distressed gray finish. Her entryway was a continuation of outside, a welcoming enchanting indoor retreat. A garden gate wall art with the same distressed finish hung above the table with a richly patterned stained glass lamp and a crystal vase with running ivies. "You can give me your bags and I'll put them in the guest room."

He had a strange look on his face when she said guest room. Had he planned to sleep with her? She was not ready for that, not yet. Besides, she's waited this long she may as well wait until she was officially a *Mrs*. Call her old fashion or whatever, that's how she felt. If it had not been for them drinking a whole bottle of champagne that night, things wouldn't have gotten out of hand. It was an act of mercy from the man above that she didn't' get pregnant. So her strategy was to ignore his expression and deal with it later. Right now she wanted to get him to his room and see what she could pull together for a meal. Thank God her mother and aunt had packed her a nice care package. It won't last for the week as it was intended, since she's having overnight guest. Ruby smiled to herself, it had been ages since she's entertained anyone in her home and she's never had a male guest overnight except for family. She usually met her friends at the office or a designated place.

With his bags still in his hand, "Ruby the only way I'm going to be comfortable is to take a hot shower and put on sweats."

"Come on, I think I can make that happen." He followed her down a short hallway to one of the bedrooms which had its own personal powder room and shared a tub and shower with another. She opened the closet door for him to hang his bags. "Now you take care of your business and I'll see what I can do about getting you something to eat."

She looked in his tired handsome face and asked, "You are hungry huh?"

"Enough to eat a bear," was his response with a dimpled smile.

"How about some grilled chicken, tilapia, salad, baked potato slices, and homemade dinner rolls?"

"No dessert?" She told him he had a choice of bread pudding or carrot cake, or have both.

"That sounds like a winner." Before she could leave the room he reached for her and gave her a gentle kiss on her lips. "See you in a few," he whispered. Ruby stopped by her bedroom to take off her jacket and put up her briefcase.

Caleb unzipped his bag got a change of clothes and laid them on an embroidered silhouette comforter. The soft vivid colors peach, green, and chocolate certainly would provide a sensual nighttime sanctuary for most people, but not him with them being under the same roof. Looking around the room he made note of her simple furnishings of modern pieces mixed with antiques. Instead of having a head board for the queen size bed, various sizes of decorative pillows against a bronze tone laced ridge wall screen. Very ingenious he thought as he sat on the oversized chocolate ottoman to take off his shoes and socks. The plush cream colored rug felt good to his tired bare feet. He was glad she had another on the side of the bed. He loved the look of hard wood floors but appreciated the feel of lush carpet.

Caleb walked into the bathroom and wasn't a bit surprised

of the color scheme at all. She had the same warm shades were used against white stressed furniture, antique looking fixtures and a marble counter top with scented candles and running ivies. He walked to the tub and shower area, a little bit of heaven he thought and turned on the water. A built in bench and shower head with different jets to provide a body with a relaxing spa shower...

Ruby's kitchen was small but ideally designed to meet her needs with all the necessary appliances in smoke and stainless steel. She removed an attractive plant basket off of her oak wood table top with black rod iron legs to set up for their meal. An attractive petite size four-shelf rack with similar designs was used to hold condiments for the salad, bread, and desserts. Place settings for two were placed on the table along with a pitcher of raspberry-banana punch. She thought it was best to wait before adding the hot entrees since he was not present and to make a quick change.

On the way to her room she did not hear the water which meant he had completed his shower and would probably be ready to eat in a few minutes. She hurriedly changed into a sleeveless abstract crinkled waist dress, a pair of dangling earrings and silver slides. As she stepped from her master suite into the hallway she could hear the television. Knowing him he had found an old western or Star Trek. Ruby stood in the doorway of the family room and sure enough he had made himself comfortable on her deep platinum sectional sofa. He had his legs stretched out the ottoman with his head resting on a jacquard design pillow of platinum, peach and green. She was surprised he didn't sit in her oversized wing back recliner. Ruby was sure he didn't know it was a recliner since it resembles a classical antique upholstered in the same jacquard print as her pillows. He didn't know what he was missing. She's spent a many nights in that chair reading and fell asleep.

"Hey you, I thought you were hungry." She walked over to where he was sitting and extended her hand. He accepted and flashed his come on smile as he stood. "Bring the remote control in case you want to change the channel." She walked to the oven to get the rest of warm containers while he took a seat.

"Ruby your home is very nice and inviting. Hummm, the dinner smells delicious too. "

"Thank you Caleb." She took a seat across from him. "Say grace so we can eat." He blessed the food and thanked God for bringing them back together. Smacking his lips and rubbing his hands together he served her first. She commented on him still being a clown regardless of all his titles.

"I'm being my natural self," he growled and barked.

"Alright this is a small house and Ms Johnnie's dog will hear you. We're close with our yards connected in the back, we do have private patios."

"It's not that small but if your yards are connected, that's close." He helped himself to a nice portion of everything. While enjoying his meal he looked around to observe his surroundings. "I can say this much for you, it looks like you've utilized all your space and have everything you need without having that crowded feeling. I love the way the bedrooms have their own personal powder room and share a tub and shower. That was smart, did you think of that?"

"Nope, I can't take the credit for the architectural designs.

The previous owner built these two houses for himself and his parents, but his job transferred him out of the country before they could move in. Since he was not going to be in the country for a while he moved them into Wiley Collins Residential Center and I was able to buy the entire property for a very good price. The house next door is not quite as large as this one and it's built with handicap provisions, but just as nice. There was a connecting screened-in walkway that I closed off so I could rent the property out and secure our privacy. I use mine as an exercise room."

"You made a good investment and I really like your colors. It's truly a reflection of your personality, bold and vibrant. The furniture in your family room is very comfortable. I didn't know if I wanted to sit in the big recliner or stretch out on the sofa. Are you responsible for the décor?"

"I'm afraid not, my interior designer's team gets all the credit for choosing and blending the different colors as you said, to reflect me; together we picked the decorative items. I'll give you a tour of the front of the house when we finish eating."

"Looking forward to it, are all the bedrooms on the same side?"

"Yes they are."

"How many do you have?"

"Three." He looked at her with that same expression and once again she chose to ignore and continued giving him the make-up of her compact but roomy home.

After their meal and dessert, together they cleaned her kitchen and then took a grand tour. The powder room located in the entrance was in plum and cream blended and with the front of the house. The living room had a medium gray sofa with plum, teal, and gray throw pillows with a sculptured arrangement of walnut wood trimmed mirrors resembling pebbles in a stream that shimmers in the sunshine. There were two stackable zebra walnut wood end tables with a woven basket holding a mixture of green plants in a corner. A circled padded arm chair of dark plum woven fabric was placed in front of them at a slight angle. In another corner stood a metro mix display shelf with five tiers that held pictures and decorative ornaments. Ottomans used for storage and additional seating were placed on opposite sides of the sofa. Although the furniture was arranged for conversation, a television was mounted in a built-in niche. Separating the dining and living area was a sofa table with twin crystal lanterns. Dark walnut furniture was in the dining area with a beautiful light fixture hanging down over the table for added elegance. On the table was the crystal set he bought fifteen years ago. He couldn't believe she was still holding on to it after all this time. She looked at him with a smile silently letting him know he's been with her the entire time they were apart. Caleb was pleased as he observed her art pieces that were placed in the niches. He noticed more pieces throughout her living areas which enhanced her home with sophistication and class.

"Well Dr. VanLee, that's the end of the tour of my humble abode. Oh I forgot to show you the back yard." She opened the customized shades and turned on the light so he could see.

"You have a nice size yard and your flowers are beautiful, plus the plants inside. Who takes care of your flowers?" He couldn't see her playing in dirt.

"Believe it or not Ms. Johnnie takes care of the plants and for exchange I pay for lawn services for both yards."

"Sounds like a good deal to me." He stood by the back door staring at her with his arms folded across his broad chest. So sexy she thought with his bare arms and flexing muscles. She wanted to caress every inch of him. He didn't know she checked out his back side while he looked out her window. It was evident he spent time in somebody's gym. He was physically fit, but he always was one who believed in eating healthy and exercising. He was still profiling looking at her with that expression.

"What?"

"You haven't showed me the other bedrooms," he said with a grin.

"Okay. I thought I would do that last when it's time to go to bed. Why don't we take a stroll to settle our dinner?"

"I don't feel like going out. I was really planning on calling it an early night. I need to be at the hospital at nine in the morning."

"You cannot go to bed after the way you just finished eating Caleb. Come on we're taking that stroll."

"Why can't we use the exercise room?"

"Come on," she sang, "you need some fresh air." She pulled him all the way to the front door. They began their walk down the street holding hands. Most of her neighbors had already taken their evening strolls, and were sitting in their front yard which was routine. She was behind schedule because she got in late. She stopped and introduced him to those neighbors who were still outside. It was such a lovely clear night; a slight breeze made it even more enjoyable.

"I'm going to need another shower when we get back," he grunted.

"Oh stop being a killjoy and enjoy the evening."

"I'm being a killjoy. You've got to be kidding watch this GRRR...RUFF RUFF...GRRR...RUF RUFF." Ruby couldn't believe him; all the neighborhood dogs started barking. She stopped his nonsense with a quick kiss. GRRR...RU...she kissed him again. They both laughed and continued their stroll with the noise of the neighboring pets barking their heads off. They made it down the end of the block and turned around to head back to the house. After a few minutes the barking ceased and she threatened him with sleeping on the patio with Ms Johnnie's dog if he starts that foolishness again.

As soon as they walked up her drive his cell rang. They both took a seat on the front porch. "Hello Grandmother, I'm doing great. Yes, I'm to meet with the department tomorrow." Ruby decided to give him some privacy. She mouthed she was going inside to take her shower and left the doors opened. He couldn't believe the nerve of his grandmother. Already she's trying to fix him up with her friend's granddaughter that lives in the Cypress area and works at the hospital as an OBGYN. He thought he had made it perfectly clear before he left home he did not need or want her help in that department. Caleb hates to hurt her feelings but she's going to have to stop. That's why he didn't hesitate to make it known he cares very deeply for someone and it was serious. She wasn't too happy hearing it was someone from his college days at PVU, but he didn't care. He had never let her dictate to him and was not about to start now. Caleb walked inside the house and made his way back into the family room with a smile, he knew someone who would be glad to hear the news of him rekindling his relationship with her. "Hi Mama."

Ruby had completed her bath and put on one of her ethnic loungers since she had company. She could hear him still on the cell this time he was talking to his mother. Since he was busy she thought she would go over her schedule for the week. He was back in the family room sitting in the recliner. She sat on the sofa with her feet reclined and pulled out her iPod tablet to check her agenda for tomorrow and was glad she did. She had a morning appointment at the beauty salon which was close to Wiley Collins center. That would give her an opportunity to stop by and take a look at the contract Nathan called her about.

"Okay Mama. Tell Daddy I said goodnight and I'll see you two soon. Love you. Well I've taken care of family. What are you doing?"

"I'm going over my schedule for tomorrow."

"How does it look?"

"So far it looks like I'm going to have an easy day after all, which I could surely use, especially after today."

"Do you think you can schedule me in for lunch at the hospital?"

Ruby looked at him as her mother's word surfaced mentally. "Can I call you once I get into the office?"

"Sure, I guess I need to turn in, my appointment is at nine. Even on the beltway it will take me at least forty-five minutes to an hour. How long are you going to be up?"

She looked at the time on the flat screen and couldn't believe it was already ten thirty. "Not long," closing her briefcase, "but let me get you settled. Do you need anything from the kitchen?"

"Ruby must I sleep by myself?"

She got up from her seat and grabbed his hand. "Come on now, you're a big boy. Let me get you a bottle of water." He stood there grinning at her like a little fellow watching her turn everything off and setting the alarm. She led him to his room when he announced he wanted to take another quick shower. Ruby sat his water on the table, kissed him goodnight and went into her room. She took her hair down and put on a pair of yellow print capri pajama bottoms and a solid yellow t-shirt with a printed front. Ruby said her prayers and asked for extra strength while temptation named Caleb Gerald VanLee 3rd was in her home. She removed her throw pillows that matched her fringed bottom stone blue chenille bedspread, pulled back the bed covers, and crawled in for the night. Before she could turn off her bed lamp there was a knock on her door. Ooooooo...he was really being a baby. "Yes Caleb!"

He opened her door, "Ruby you didn't show me your room yet." He looked around with a smile and wasn't a bit surprised that her room would reflect an old charm country retreat. The bed lamp glowed against the vanilla cream walls and different shades of the blues and greens she used.

"Caleb get in this bed and promise me you'll behave yourself."

"Now Ruby I can't promise you that," he said with a sly grin.

"Okay, go back to your room!"

"Au'ight I promise."

"I thought so, and I mean I don't want to hear a peep out of you, do you hear me mister."

"Yes ma'am." He climbed in close beside her and draped his arm around her waist drawing her even closer breathing in her soft fresh fragrance. Man she felt wonderful in his arms. "Thank you Baby." He kissed her on the cheek and closed his eyes and slowly drifted off into a pleasant sleep. Ruby really couldn't believe how peaceful and relaxed she felt being in his arms. You would think them together this way was the norm. Mmmmmm, she could get use to this in a hurry she thought as she inhaled his masculine scent drifting off into a sound sleep too.

CHAPTER 10

Caleb's cell alarm went off, it was time for him to rise and start his day. Due to his early morning meeting at the hospital he needed to get up now because of the traveling distance; if he wanted to be on time. Although he had a restful night he hated to leave her bed. He kept his promise to be on his best behavior, only because he was asleep the entire night with her snuggled in his arms. Trying hard not to wake her he slowly eased out of bed. Standing on the side he watched his ebony princess stretch and turn over to face him. With her tousled hair in her face she had an exotic beauty about her that unnerved him to no end. She was simply breathtaking as she stretched again. He knew she was awake now and leaned over to kiss her forehead.

"Good morning beautiful, I was trying not to wake you but I see I was not successful."

She smiled up at him, "Good morning yourself, and I don't know about that being beautiful with my hair all over my head." She attempted to push it out of her face and he leaned down to assist. Their eyes locked as she took a deep breathe, anticipating his next move. Her mind screamed you're not ready. "Caleb."

"I know you're not ready."

Goodness was he a mind reader or something. After all this time he still knew her oh too well. Lord she has missed so much all these years. Thank God she's getting a second chance, that's why she should be honest and tell him what she's never said to anyone else. Humph, there has been no one else to tell. "Caleb, I have not been with anyone since that night. I made a vow I would wait until I'm married before having sex again. So I've practiced celibacy for fifteen years." She blew out a deep relieved breath, "Now I've said it." That wasn't so hard she thought as she felt Ruby Jewel's spunk ascend. She reached over to the little crystal dish on her night stand for a breath sheet. He burst into laughter when she offered him one and took one for herself. That was his Ruby Jewel, a realist with no shame.

"Now that our breaths are fresh what do you suggest," he said with a sly smile. She pulled him down on top of her and kissed his forehead then his nose while he nestled between her bosoms. She caressed the side of his face.

"Caleb why did you cut your ponytail and cover your dimples with facial hair," asked Ruby?

He nuzzled her neck with his lips and then covered her mouth with his as they shared a passionate kiss. Rubbing noses he said, "It's a long story and I'll be glad to tell you over lunch."

"Okay, I'll wait till then. We both should make a move so I can make that lunch date."

"Sounds like a great idea but not before I do this." He raised her t-shirt up and kissed her naked breasts. She gasped and he covered her mouth once more in a lingering kiss and left her smiling…

He was dressed and ready to leave. He peeped inside her room but she was in the bathroom. He could see clearly the layout of her master suite now. Two medium sized windows provided lots of natural light. Sheer curtains of sage and stone blue with matching hanging scarves were hung at each window. Her queen bed with wood posts were connected to decorative rod iron and placed in front of one of the windows. A light walnut antique chest was located in the far corner. Three tier accent tables of the same color were used as night stands. A chaise upholstered in a soft chenille fabric of dark sage with accent pillows sat by the other window with a glazed ceramic garden stool with crackled finish beside it. Her home was quaint and smartly done by talented decorators.

"Ruby it's time for me to leave." He had already put his clothes bag and saddlebag by the front door. She came out of the bathroom in a short blue satin robe and matching slides. He reached for her and kissed her again. She walked him to the front door and disarmed the security system. "Baby, will I see you later," he asked?

"Yes, I'm going to do my very best."_____

RJ made it to the beauty salon right on time. As a matter of fact she and Bronwyn drove up together. Today she had to get a relaxer and then a roller set. Kellie, Nisey, and Cynthia were also scheduled and came in while she was still under the dryer. That's where she spends most of her time under the hair dryer due to the length and coarseness of her hair. But she didn't really mind because it gave her a chance to relax and hang out with her girls. Bronwyn had already made it known a little birdie came in yesterday evening, giving her the scoop of an old beau that has come back into her life. She wanted to know if a new romance was in bloom. When Ruby gave her the rest of the story she was grinning harder than her. She was like everyone else, thrilled that their girl was courting and wished her well.

Bronwyn checked one of her curls in the back to make sure she was completely dry. "Okay girlfriend, I think you're done. Come get in the chair."

"Well Ms RJ, I understand you're dating again and someone from the past," said Cynthia. Ruby Jewel loved Cynthia but sometimes she's a pain in the butt.

"You've heard right. How's your romance going?"

"Oh girl, Kellie hasn't told you the news," she waved her finger with a gorgeous diamond solitaire.

"Congratulations! When's the big day?"

"Mid-June, you'll be getting an invitation. Now, when are we going to meet your ivory prince?"

Well she knows he's not black, thought RJ. "Soon I promise you." Bronwyn finished taking the rollers out and her hair was just perfect as always. Tight spiral curls hung right at her shoulders. She used a gold headband to keep the curls from falling in her face. Bronwyn also gave her a complete facial then applied her make-up. The House of Beauty was a fantastic place and provides excellent service in taking care of all your needs. She paid her bill and left a hefty tip to show her appreciation. Now if she wasn't pushed for time she would go right next door to Delana's Boutique. If she was going to meet Caleb for lunch she needed to make a move because she did have one more stop....

RJ stopped at the front desk of Wiley Collins facility to sign in. She could feel someone watching her. Turning around she stared in the face of her ex-coworker Jalen Dalton. She hadn't seen him since they left the attorney general office back in the day. They both left about the same time. She decided to go into business for herself and he went to jail. He was an excellent computer analysis with special talents in developing and organizing non-profit programs, he was the man. She always felt he was set up by the real culprit in his department. She knew it was some dirty dealings and had nothing to do with him. He was the fall guy for that complete mess. She was glad to see he was doing well.

"Hello Jalen," she extended her hand. He was hesitant along with his dry hello, but he obliged her with a weak hand shake and abruptly walked off. She stared at his departing back and shook her head.

Mr. Collins is ready to see you now Attorney McHarding." She thanked the receptionist and went straight to Nathan's office.

Jalen couldn't believe the nerve of Ruby Jewel McHarding. She actually acted like she was glad to see him. Who was she fooling? All she was trying to do was throw her success in his face. Now she'll probably run and tell Mr. Collins he was rude to her. Instead of him getting even with her, she was getting ready to make some more trouble for him. All his plans had backed fired. The plans for the tutorial program had actually begun with some cramming sessions for seniors in math for their exit exams. His wife had solicited his help which caused him to have a change of heart and not use the tutorial program in getting back at her.

As a matter of fact up until now he had not given her much thought since she hadn't been at the center. He even had the nerve to recommend her to his old cell mate who was having some problems with his rental property. They had an appointment to see her. With his job and working with the children he hadn't had the time to think about RJ McHarding. Their minister had also kept him busy developing software for their other non-profit organizations. Being around him had depleted the thirst he had for revenge. He had even come to the conclusion he did not want to cause any problems for Mr. and Mrs. Collins which prompted him to discard the pictures. They had been good to him. But now that he's set eyes on her face to face he was determined to cause her some pain like she did him. He just needed to find another way and not involve his church or his employers that he respects and appreciates....

"Nathan, they have breached their contract by not providing the services they promised to render. In doing so that gives you the right to cancel and terminate any other ties you have with them. I'll have a letter drawn up canceling your contract and send to them before the day is out."

"Thanks RJ; I knew you could handle it. Now what's the scoop? "

"Hey RJ, I missed you the last time you were here. Girl friend don't you look gorgeous. Mmmmmm, Nathan told me Caleb was back in Texas." Jazper couldn't believe the no nonsense RJ McHarding was actually blushing. "Stand up sistah girl and let me see that dress." RJ stood with the both of them staring at her. She did look good. The classic blue crossover crepe dress was a flattering fit with its elbow length butterfly sleeves and wide elastic waist. Delana would be proud of her, instead the dress's tie belt, she used a gold scarf with specks of blues and green for color. Her layered beaded gold necklace set enhanced her outfit. She even dressed up her blue comforts with a gold button clamp. Her look was professional but with a splash of glamour.

"Okay now that we've had the fashion show, what about Frosty?" Nathan had wrapped his arms around his wife as they both waited for her to fill them in. They were such a handsome loving couple.

"He's fine Nathan as a matter of fact I'm meeting him for lunch at the hospital. So I don't have time to visit today, but I will be in touch." She was just about to walk out when she thought about Jalen. "Nathan, I saw Jalen Dalton. Just what does he do here?"

"He's our transportation manager."

"Well I'm here to tell you he's not utilizing his talent." She told him about his background and how he would benefit them in other areas. They were surprised to hear all of his credentials. He was recommended highly by Gregory Larson even though he had some trouble with the law and had served some time. Nathan was also like Gregory when it comes to giving ex-offenders a second chance. RJ strongly suggested they needed to reconsider his position and put him where they all can benefit. They both agreed and walked her to the front door. On their way Nathan saw Jalen and asked him to come to his office after he returns from lunch.

He knew what that was about thanks to Ms McHarding.

CHAPTER 11

Caleb's morning had started off on a good note after leaving Ruby. Although he missed her terribly he did have their lunch date to look forward too. The breakfast meeting was a success; he met with the hospital board. He couldn't believe one of his grandparents' long time good friends, who is now retired and on the board. According to Dr. Alford, Dr. Nason was also involved in developing their senior citizen clinic. On a whole, they had a nice visit and he even called his grandparents so they could speak to one another for a few minutes. Dr. Nason introduced him to his granddaughter who was a resident in the OB/GYN department, and just happens to be the woman his grandmother had in mind. Caleb knew his grandmother encouraged him to do so, he heard pieces of their conversation. He then met the staff in the geriatrics unit and visited with some of the patients in the sunroom. His last stop was the ground floor which housed the basics, but he was particularly interested in the emergency area, radiology and especially the lab facility where his cousin worked.

Cypress Memorial Hospital and the Professional Building were very impressive. He had come to the conclusion he was going to enjoy being affiliated with the hospital district. It was almost lunch time and he still had not heard from Ruby. Some of the doctors including Dr. Lauren Nason had asked him to join them for lunch in the cafeteria which they highly recommended. Just as they were leaving the medical records department he heard a familiar voice from behind. It couldn't be, he thought, as he turned to face the person the voice belonged to.

"Q-Note!" A tall handsome brother with a wide grin turned and looked his way. He couldn't believe his eyes.

"Frosty, is that really you." He walked quickly to his line brother. Both reached for one another, embraced and did their frat grip. "Man I can't believe my eyes, it's really you." The doctors he was with watched the two men who obviously were old friends and had not seen each other for some long time.

"Yes Q-Note its old Frosty here in the flesh," exclaimed Caleb. They hugged and held on to each other still in disbelief that they were finally together after fifteen years. "Brother it's so good to see you. You're looking great too. How's Ms Joyce?"

"Man Mama is doing fine. She's retired and living with me and my family. And how's your blended families?" Q-Note let out a big hearty laugh. The brothers always joked with him once they met his entire family.

Before Caleb answered he noticed the doctors were still standing around waiting. "Say man, we were on our way to lunch, can you join us and then we can talk and make plans to meet later and really catch up."

"Hold up, let me tell my staff where I'll be." Q-Note went inside the office they just left. Caleb smiled. So he was the Mr. Travis everyone referred to and responsible for a well-organized medical records department, Roderick Charles Travis Jr.

Q-Note joined the group. "So Mr. Travis you're the big hunch-cho in charge of medical records."

"That's me Dr. VanLee." They both hit their chest and broke into laughter. "Say man you're going to have another surprise in a minute." Caleb looked at his smiling frat brother. "Forget it, my lips are sealed." Q-Note had his co-worker to call the surprise; frat brother number three who he knew was in town and at the hospital. He and his mother were visiting his grandmother who was recuperating from surgery. As they entered the cafeteria on the side of the door stood the surprise, Spikey. Caleb looked at Q-Note then at the man standing against the window, Wesley Lloyd Tillman III. All he could do was shake his head in amazement. They walked into each other's arms and didn't care how it looked. Stepping back they did their frat grip and all three brothers hit their chest and let out a dog howl. This time all three embraced. They were sure they made a spectacle of themselves, but it was worth the embarrassment. It had been fifteen long years for these three who were inseparable once upon a time were.

Dr. Charles Nason and the other doctors were a bit surprised as they watched the trio and knew they may as well get their lunch. Before Dr. Charles was able to get in line, he received a text to return to his office. He whispered to his granddaughter he had to leave. Instead of joining the others she continued to study her new prospect. Humph, Dr. VanLee was prestige, single, fine, and rich. Although money was not a prerequisite it would be nice to have someone who was in the same circle.

"Gentlemen let's join the others," Lauren said.

Caleb looked at his two brothers. "Are you two down

with this company?"

"Yeah, Frosty we can handle it, we can get together later," said Spikey with **Q** cosigning. "I'm going to be in town till the end of the week. **Q** and I had planned on getting together anyway before I leave."

"Okay let's hang with the aristocrat for a spell." He looked at his watch and assumed she was not going to make it. He had not noticed his brothers were also looking at their timepieces; diamond Omega watches that had been a gift to them from him when they all graduated from PVU.

Dr. Nason had two tables pulled together so they all could eat comfortably together. Since she had her eye on him she needed to accept his friends for now. Today's special was mama's meatloaf with several choice sides. Caleb and his brothers chose garlic mashed potatoes, steamed cabbage, cornbread, banana pudding and lemonade, the others had grilled chicken and salad. He insisted on treating and paid for lunch. The men wearing suit coats took them off so they could be comfortable. Frosty and Q-Note had the attention of the doctors because their brands were now visible. Both had on sleeveless silk T-shirts. Caleb asked the group to have a word of prayer with him. He and his brothers held hands as he thanked God for their meal and bringing together old friends.

Everyone enjoyed their meal while the trio was questioned about their friendship and the significance of their brands. Next they wanted to know Spikey's profession. He told them he was in partnership with his father and uncle who were both dentists in Tyler, Texas. He specialized in reconstruction, implants, and oral surgery. Q-Note and Frosty shared a quiet smirk, he told them. Spikey had a wife and three boys. Q-Note had a wife and four children two of each. The three knew they would have to get together at another time so they could really reminisce.

Cell phone, it's her. "Hey, where are you?"

"I'm in the hospital cafeteria." He couldn't believe she was there.

"Gentlemen I have a surprise for you now." Caleb stood and watched for her to walk through the cafeteria doors. Lord he couldn't believe his eyes his ebony princess was absolutely breathtaking. He along with his brothers eyeballed her from head to toe; her flowing bouncy hair, the slight jiggle of breasts, the sway of her hips, and long shapely legs.

"Dang man is that Ruby Jewel," exclaimed Q-Note.

"Yes it is." Caleb was by her side and kissed her in front of an audience. Holding her close enough for her to feel the beat of his heart, he whispered. "Girl you oughta to be shame of yourself. Are you trying to give me a heart attack?"

She honored him with her sexy smile and told him, "Certainly not, but you are in the right place." She looked over to the table where he was sitting and couldn't believe her eyes. "Q-Note! Spikey! Where did you two come from?" Both men were now at her side and took turns squeezing her tightly kissing both cheeks.

"Girl if you don't look like a million dollars," said Spikey. All Q-Note could do was grunt.

"Enough of that," growled Caleb. "Baby, let me introduce you to some of the doctors that work here at the hospital." Calling each one by name, "I would like for everyone to meet

Attorney RJ McHarding." They all said their pleasantries. "Baby what would you like?" Ruby Jewel looked at everyone's plate and decided she would have the same meal he was having. "I'll be right back," and kissed her lips.

"Man get me a carry out," requested Q-Note as he watched him disappear. "I couldn't wait for him to leave," he said with Spikey acknowledging the same sentiment. "Does this mean you two are a couple again?" She looked at their old friends and told them yes. "Ruby please *don't* break our brother's heart again." She assured them she had no intentions of ever doing that again.

A couple, humph not if she could help it. And he let her break his heart that was hard to believe. "So, Attorney McHarding what kind of law do you practice? Criminal?"

Ruby was expecting some sort of sarcastic remark from old girl. She saw the way she was drooling over Caleb. She might as well forget it because he belonged to her. "No, Dr. Nason. I represent small businesses with various issues and concerns. I also have a database network service for attorney referrals. So if someone does need a criminal attorney I can refer them to some of the best." *Cell phone,* "Please excuse me, this is my office calling." RJ got up from her seat and walked over to the window for privacy.

"Ummm....Ummm," said the brothers with the doctors also showing appreciation. Caleb watched them with a smile. He couldn't blame them. She was something to behold.

"Man I want ya'll to stop slobbering over my woman."

"Frosty are you sure you can handle all of that?"

"Every ounce, besides man, I thought you had a family."

"You know I'm just kidding little brother."

"I got your little brother," said Caleb stomping his foot, and he had to leave it at that since they were in mixed company. Spikey and Q-Note burst into laughs they knew exactly where he was coming from, that old myth did not apply to him.

Lauren Nason couldn't believe how all the men were taking turns eyeing her big butt and cleavage. She thought inquiring about the type of lawyer she was would indicate she was just another wanna be. But she had to give it to her she was one smart lady. While everyone was glued to her chest she pulled her up and quickly scanned her website which was impressive, but she could care less. She had her eyes set on him and sistah girl as they say is going to have a fight on her hands. She guarantees it!

Ruby walked back over to the table.

"Is everything alright?" asked Caleb.

"Yes, just my office touching base with me." He held her chair and took his seat beside her.

"Dr. VanLee, it was a pleasure meeting you and your friends. I'm looking forward to working with you and Mr. Travis I'll see you around," said one of the doctors. The other two men also got up and offered the same sentiments.

Dr. Nason had made up her mind to sit for a few more minutes, she wanted to invite him to her grandparents' home for dinner tonight, but it was evident that was not going to be a good idea this time. So much for that, however there was her grandfather's...Text...She was needed in delivery.

"Caleb, my grandmother asked me to extend an invitation to you for my grandfather's seventy-fifth birthday celebration the last Saturday of this month. We're having an old fashion barbecue with all the usual fixings plus a square dance. Family and friends, board members, department heads, and the clinic staff will be present along with city dignitaries."

He looked at Ruby and said, "We'll have to check our schedule." She pulled out a business card from her pocket and told him to give her a call.

"Frosty, I'm going to have to get back to work also. Here's my card, let me know when we can get together, especially before our man leaves." Caleb got up and hugged his friend and told him he would do just that. "Ruby Jewel it was wonderful to see you again baby, and I know with you on my brother's arm, I'll get to see plenty of you. Later people."

Caleb, Ruby, and Wesley continued with their meal and had some interesting conversation. Ruby had him to tell why he had cut his ponytail and was wearing the shadowy light beard. It was all due to image since he had specialized in geriatrics. He wanted to be taken serious, and not be looked at as his grandmother said a hippie; or somebody wild and did not know what they were doing. Of course he had ignored her advice and tried to practice anyway. On his first day he went in to examine a ninety year old lady at his grandfather's clinic, she became frightened and hysterical which caused her blood pressure to elevate considerably. He went on to say it was not worth all the drama. Besides all the women say I look good. Ruby gave him a playful slap on the arm and continued eating her dessert while he and Wesley shared family pictures. Wesley had a beautiful family, an attractive wife who was their business manager and three fine little boys.

"Now Ms RJ, what have you been doing for yourself besides getting more beautiful than ever?"

"You're too kind Wesley; I've spent the last fifteen years building a successful business. I share an office suite with an excellent CPA and have some very influential clients. As a matter of fact I represent some of your frat brothers." She looked at Caleb and asked him if he told them about Silk, Wolf and Mudpuppy?"

Wesley eyes lit up with excitement. "Man you mean to tell me you've seen those guys?"

"That's right and they are doing very well. What about Stay Ready? Do you know how to get in touch with him?"

"Yeah, man he went back to his little home town somewhere near here. Hold up I got it written down, because I told him I would be here this week, yeah here it is. It's called Hearne, Texas that's it. After he completed law school he went back home and took over his father's job as the sheriff. A few years later the people appointed him as their justice of the peace, now he's the Honorable Judge Ross of the county courts. We're supposed to get together before I leave."

Caleb would love to see his old friend. They had been the closest of the four. He was the first to accept him as a potential line brother. He didn't care about the color of his skin. When Ruby broke up with him it was Marcus Wayne Ross's shoulders he literally cried on. Then he had the nerve to throw their friendship away. He wouldn't blame him if he didn't want to see him.

"Man please let me know. I tell you what give me a date and time as soon as you can and we can pull something together."

"Sounds like a plan and I'll do just that. I guess I need to go check on my mother and grandmother."

"You mean Mrs. Tillman is here?"

"Yeah man."

"Let me get my satchel and then we'll be up to see her. You ready Baby?" She told him yes. He got his suit coat and they left the cafeteria. Where he needed to get his bag was on the way. He also wanted her to meet Dr. Charles Nason. Besides being one of the board members of the hospital and the clinic, he was also his grandparents' dearest and oldest friend.

They had a nice chat with the older gentleman who seemed fascinated with Ruby and then they went to visit with Wesley's mother and grandmother.   While Caleb was giving his thank yous and saying his goodbyes Ruby made a couple of calls, one to her parents to let them know she would be in Hempstead for a couple of hours, but they were out. She then called her office to let them know she would not be in today and would see them Wednesday afternoon. Of course Angela would not hang up until she admitted she was with him. Ruby could hear the hand slaps, everybody knew.

CHAPTER 12

Ruby and Caleb left the hospital around two. Instead of driving two cars he insisted she ride with him and they would come back later for hers. His plans were to stop by the clinic and wanted her with him. Although his official full day was not until tomorrow he wanted to show her his office among other things. He needed to be seen with the woman that has his heart to confirm he was not interested in any other woman except her. No more foolishness for him, he was ready to start a life with Ruby as his wife and the mother of his children. His friends had all accomplished what he's wanted for so long, a family and a career. Dr. Caleb VanLee 3rd had the career, now he was determined to get started ASAP with his other goals and that was a promise.

"You've been mighty quiet."

He reached for her hand and kissed it. "I was thinking about my boys. It was really great to see them today. But I have to admit for once in my life I'm jealous of my brothers. They have everything I've yearned for, they have it all." She knew exactly what he meant. If there's anyone to blame it would be her. She was the reason why he felt his life was incomplete and vowed to do something about that. They pulled into the clinic's parking lot and parked in the space that was designated for him. "Come on let me show you around." He went around to her side to assist, holding hands they walked inside the clinic._____

Jalen Dalton couldn't believe what just took place in Nathan Collin's office. He was offered a new job as their new program director. One of his duties was to develop and spear head activities for the Wiley Collins facility. Nathan had given him a list of the services he and his partners were providing and needed him to fine tune them. According to Ruby Jewel McHarding he was the best man for the job and she had recommended him highly. That's what threw him. He always thought she was responsible for him being charged with fraud and misappropriating funds. She actually told Mr. Collins she always felt he wasn't the guilty one, just the fall guy. It was hard to swallow that he owed her gratitude of thanks. Man, he needs to call Cathena and his mother who were probably at the church. Humph, he was going to go home and fix his favorite women a fantastic dinner to celebrate. Hummm, he was going to take care of some other desirable business and make both women happy. Jalen smiled to himself and was thankful he hadn't done anything stupid. His minister said the word was powerful if you let it dwell in you and allow it to destroy the trash from your heart of understanding. As of this very moment Jalen Dalton was turning over a new leaf._____

"Girl did you see that new doctor, he's fine as he wanna be for a white man."

"Baby please he's what you call God's gift to all women and I heard he was single."

"That's right but I heard Dr. Nason from Cypress Memorial was already trying to stake a claim along with a couple of other nurses that was over at Cypress."

"Girl get outa of here, where did you get that little bit of news?"

"Dr. Nason called Dr. Alford trying to get his private number. But you know Dr. No Nonsense was not budging at all. Baby, she let sistah girl have it. She didn't care if her grandfather was on the board or not. That was privileged information and she was respecting his privacy. My sister said when he visited their department the head nurses were falling all over themselves trying to get all up in his face."

"Girlfriend can you blame them. But they may as well forget about that dude and just enjoy the view. Did you see what he had on his arm?"

"No not what, who and face it, that sistah looks good and she ain't no chump. The way he was grinning at her said it all. You got to give the sistah her props, she got that all wrapped up."

"I guess you can say that, but girl why would he want somebody that big."

"All right friend, you letting that skinny girl mentality surface?"

"Girl I am not skinny."

"Okay then that size eight attitude for sure. Besides, the next time you see her you better take a good long look. That sistah is gorgeous, curvy, and represents. I have two cousins with wives about her size give or take five pounds or more. Baby they love them to death, treats them like queens and one of them don't even work. Girlfriend I'm telling you, we should be so lucky."

"I wonder..." One of the stall doors opened and out

stepped Ruby Jewel. Both ladies froze in silence. Ignoring the pair she walked over to the vanity washed and dried her hands. Next she took out hand cream and lipstick, added color to her lips and then rubbed cream on her hands. Looking out of the corner of her eye she could see the duo was still silently standing at attention with sorry and embarrassed written across their faces. It was no need for them to feel bad, because she was a big sistah and was proud of it. Pulling at the locks of curls and checking her dress to make sure she was straight, RJ walked over to the two with a big smile.

"You were right he is wrapped up and tied down with this sistah!"

"You go sistah," said one of the ladies. They all gave each other a high-five and RJ sashayed out of the ladies bathroom.

"OMG! OMG!"

Ruby Jewel thought she would take a seat in the waiting room with the patients until Caleb was ready to leave for the day. He had given her the grand tour of the clinic, his office, plus introduced her to the staff that was available. She couldn't believe he had an old college picture of them on his desk. He had his ponytail and she was wearing her old *Jill Scott* look that she's not even wearing anymore. After pleading with him, he gave her the picture, but made her promise to replace it very soon. She promised to get on it right away. Ruby looked at the clock on the wall. It was almost 4:30. The day hours for the clinic were eight until five and then they went into their after hour's service which was until midnight. Saturday appointments can also be scheduled as needed until noon. Caleb was really going to be happy here at Jordan Memorial.

"Hey, there you are. I've been waiting for you. Why didn't you come back to my office?" He grabbed her hand and took her back to where he would be working. Stopping at the nurse's station he introduced her to the two nurses she saw in the bathroom; Belinda and Lornetta. Ruby winked and told them she was glad to make their acquaintance and mouthed "again." His nurse and the physician assistant who would also work closely with him were now standing by to be introduced. Both ladies were attractive and trimmed. After meeting the rest of the staff they went back to his office. Instead of letting her sit down he pull her into his arms and kissed her senseless. She was still in his arms when they heard a knock on the door. He said, "Come in." It was his nurse.

"Oh excuse me Dr. VanLee." She turned an embarrassing red.

"That's okay Nurse Silsby, what can I do for you?"

"I...I just wanted to say if you don't need me for anything else I'll be at the nurse's station. I do have a few minutes before it's time to clock out."

"No, I think we've covered everything for now, you have a good evening."

"Thank you." She closed the door and Caleb kissed her again.

"You know you're not right." *Cell phone.*

"What," smiling at her, she just shook her head and answered her cell.

"Hi Momma, I called to let you know I was in the city with Caleb. Where are you and Daddy?" Caleb mouthed to tell them hello. "Caleb said hello."

"Tell him we said hello too Baby. Daddy and I are over at the center getting ready to play bingo." Ruby Jewel couldn't believe what she was hearing. "Why don't you two come over for a few games?"

"Okay Momma, we'll be there in a few minutes." She hung up and told him to come on so they could leave.

"Where are we going?" He grabbed his satchel, coat and followed her out of his office.

"On a double date with my parents," said Ruby. His strange expression caused her to add, "The center to play bingo." She has never played bingo, at least not to her recollection. This should be fun. Caleb was having the same exact thoughts, catching her hand squeezing it._____

"Charles I talked to Lauren this afternoon. She told me that Mildred's grandson had some big black woman vulgarly dressed all over him."

"Liny I did what you asked of me. I introduced them and made it possible for them to have lunch, but he was already expecting a lunch date. And she was not some big black woman as you say and certainly was not vulgarly dressed. She's a beautiful well educated and highly successful lawyer with her own business. He introduced her as his very special friend. And if you ask me he's a man deeply in love. As a matter of fact I had Lauren to invite them to my birthday celebration so you can meet her yourself."

"Charles how could you? Mildred and I were trying to

get him and Lauren together. He would make a wonderful husband for her."

"Well Sweetcakes, I don't think you two have a match. I'm telling you that young man is very much taken. What do the young folks say; she has his nose wide open. When's dinner, I'm starved," he asked as he walked over to his favorite chair.

"Oh Charles, that's all you think about is food. Maria said dinner would be ready in about twenty minutes."   Linda Nason was vexed with her husband.   They had already talked about introducing Lauren and Caleb. He knew darn well she and Mildred were planning on those two being a couple. Well she'll just have to have some help to make this work.   She went to her master suite to make a private telephone call. Charles smiled as he watched her leave the room. He loved his granddaughter very much but she was no competition for her as he recalls their meeting. Ruby Jewel McHarding was her grandmother all over again, bold and beautiful.   The two could pass for twins.   She had inherited her extraordinary features from her tall healthy statue down to her smooth silky dark complexion.   He thought his eyes were playing tricks on him when young Caleb introduced her; it was like he had stepped back into the past. How he missed seeing her during the planning of the clinic he didn't know.   He was aware of her name but never associated it with *The Mc Hardings'* of Hempstead, besides RJ McHarding was from Houston.   Lord he didn't think his brother would ever get over.

"Charles dinner is ready."

"Okay Sweetcakes."

CHAPTER 13

Caleb and Ruby along with the seniors had a wonderful time. The biggest joy was watching the senior citizens have fun. The center even stayed open passed their normal hours because of his generosity. When they walked into the large area he turned the evening into a festive occasion. First he paid for all the seniors to play bingo and then had the program director to order party trays and beverages for the entire group. She watched him move around the room spending time with each one as they enjoyed the refreshments. He even helped serve those who were on canes and walkers. He was truly in his element. She knew he had to be tired because of his full day, but he was like a kid turned loose in a candy store. He had a genuine love and concern and demonstrated it well. She noticed her parents also had an enjoyable evening regardless of them not winning had Caleb to donate their prize money to the event fund. They were sure after tonight the next bingo night would be full to the max. Because Dr. VanLee was a hit making sure everyone went home as a winner.

Ruby couldn't remember when she's had fun playing games and had to admit she was looking forward to next Tuesday herself. Something was happening to her. Her attitude was changing and for the better. There was more to life than work and making sure others were taken care of.

Not that she resented looking out for her siblings and parents, she was the eldest. But it was true she needed a new lifestyle besides just being a care giver. And it was time to stop thinking the life she had was sufficient. She had a wonderful man who's made it absolutely clear he loved and wanted only her. Ruby Jewel was going to have to make some adjustments as of right now so they could move forward in their new relationship.

Caleb looked over to where she was sitting and walked over to get her. He wanted her to meet one of the little ladies from his grandparents little home town. She was now living with her daughter in the city since the passing of her husband.

"Why Caleb she's beautiful."

"Thank you Mrs. Felton, I think she is too."

"Am I going to be attending a wedding soon?"

Caleb revealed his fetching smile and said he sure hopes so. Mrs. Felton didn't let him get off that easy. She took Ruby's hand and said she did not see a ring and he needs to get some fire under his bottom. Her daughter shook her head and said for them to please look over her mother because she does speak her mind. They assured her no harm was done and they all had a good laugh. Mrs. Felton and her daughter whispered to Ruby he was definitely a keeper, they knew his whole family well and he was raised right. She told them she had planned too. He went to get his satchel and her purse and said good night to the staff. Along with her parents they walked the two ladies to their car and wished them good night. Next they walked her parents to their car, she gave them a hug and told them good night.

When she embraced her mother she whispered she liked what she saw. Ruby mouthed thank you and watched them drive off…

"Okay, what's the plan?" Ruby looked at him with that sistah girl's expression. They were not going to go there. He had an early day tomorrow. He was due in the clinic at 8:00 am. He needed his rest and that was that.

"The plan is for you to take me to get my car and we go our separate way."

"Baby, I don't like that plan."

She stopped walking and asked, "What other options do we have?"

"I'm glad you asked. Now, I take you to get your car, stop by Wallyworld, you buy a change of clothes and whatever else you need; spend the night and then leave in the morning. My townhouse is right at the freeway and farther down you can catch the beltway. I'm not going to be able to get a goodnight sleep with you on the road."

"Caleb it's less than an hour's ride. You know that."

"But Baby I'm going to miss holding you in my sleep. Just one more night please."

"What am I going to do with you?"

"Say you'll marry me. You heard Mrs. Felton I'm a keeper."

"You actually heard that?" He had a big smile on his face when he confessed he could also read lips.

"Caleb!"

"And yeah I saw that wink and sistah girl look when you told those two nurses *again*." She was too thru and would have to remember he now can read lips. "I'm waiting."

"Yes Caleb, I'll marry you!"

He shouted, "Yes to the top of his voice," and lifted her up twirling them both around. People were walking by and he announced, "She said yes! Everybody! She wants to marry me." The passerbyers congratulated them both.

"Caleb put me down; you're making a scene and exposing more of me than I care to show." He did and they walked to his vehicle.

Two sisters from the senior's residential facility were walking to their cars when they heard the commotion. "Who was that?"

"That's the new doctor at the clinic and he must have just asked that sistah to marry him and she said yes." Both women slapped high five and got in their cars.

Caleb drove to Cypress Memorial so she could get her car. He wanted to press her with a date but thought he would give her a little time, like the end of the week.

"Now when do you want to get married?"

Dang she must have been reading his mind he thought and asked, "How about the last Saturday in March?"

"Caleb are you serious. That will give us only two weeks. What about your new job, a convenient and accommodating place for both families in this short time span? Me making some adjustments to my career, a wedding gown, but that won't be a problem? I think the first Saturday in April is too soon Sweetie."

"Ruby I can't wait any longer. I really wanted to say this weekend but I knew that would be stressful and rushing it since we want our families there. In all honesty I only have to worry about my grandparents in Denver. I know my parent's family and your family won't be a problem since they all live close by. I think we can pull it off with the help of your family and your girls. Baby, please give it some thought. Let's not say anything to our families yet and sleep on it tonight and then we can set a definite date tomorrow." They were already at the hospital. Like he said it was actually down the street. He turned the motor off and looked at her. "Ruby don't leave me, I need you so much," he pleaded. He pulled her in his arms and told her how much he loved and wanted her desperately. She weakened terribly with her love for him and ached just as much. They kissed with so much emotion you would think this was it. After she caught her breath she told him to follow her to Wallyworld so she could pick up a few things. With the biggest smile ever he was out of the car in a flash opening her door. She called her parents to let them know she was staying over and left it at that....

"Welcome to my world Attorney McHarding. Make yourself comfortable while I take your things upstairs." He placed her bags in the second master suite so she could have privacy in the morning. Her eyes followed him up the winding mahogany staircase covered in a mocha runner. She noticed an open loft area that was probably used as an office and private den knowing him. Downstairs she observed his world as he put it. Simplicity, organization, and rich vibrant colors of wine, mocha, and cream were displayed throughout a carpeted opened spacious room. It provided basic living areas for an individual or small family. Located in his foyer in front of a stained glass window was a beautiful planter box which held a green plant with white flowers that resembles flags. Beside it was a small accent table of mahogany wood and graphite colored touch floor lamp. The seating area had a contemporary dark plush wine sofa with two handcrafted sculptures of steel curved strips hanging above it. Twin mocha wingback chairs with nail head trims faced the fireplace. Tucked away were three ottomans upholstered in textured fabrics of his colors for extra seating. She looked around for a television and noticed a space saving cabinet in a black finish. Ruby was sure he was using it as an entertainment center.

The dining area was simple but grand. It was set up for four with a round mahogany table, mocha cushioned chairs, a space saving matching buffet and three antique pictures. A beautiful cactus plant graced the center of the table looking like a living work of art and a magnificent replica of an old world hanging chandelier. She peeped into his stainless steel kitchen with streaked black granite countertops which were clutter free. The small breakfast nook was located in front of a bay window. She decided to take a seat at his round Bristol table. Hand painted watercolor design ceramic dinnerware for two graced his table. In the center was a wine water picture used as a vase with silk flowers. He found her gazing out of the bay window.

"Would you like to go out and sit for a spell and watch the stars, it's still a bit early."

Why not, she wasn't sleepy yet, "Okay." She could see patio furniture and a beautiful landscaped yard.

"Would you like something to drink?"

"Water will be fine." He opened the fridge and took out a large chilled bottled water and two glasses from the cabinet. She waited for him to open the patio door and they went out. It was a beautiful clear night with the sounds of life moving about. He poured water into their glasses; they sipped and enjoyed the view. After a few minutes she broke the silence and told him what a charming place he had. He thanked her and they settled back into a comfortable silence.

Caleb made the next move and got up from his seat and knelt in front of her. "Ruby I want to make it official." He reached in his pocket and pulled out a worn velvet bag and then took out the most exquisite diamond solitaire engagement ring ever. She gasped and covered her mouth, she was totally surprised. It had to be at least five carats, with tears Ruby gazed into his eyes. "This was my biological mother's ring that my mother has kept for me all these years. It was stated in her will for her only beloved son to have her jewelry to give to the woman he plans to spend his life with. Now once again will you do *me* the honors of being my wife and wear my mother's ring?"

"Yes Caleb, I'll be your wife and wear your mother's ring." He slid the ring on her finger. It was a perfect fit. She looked at him in surprise. He explained to her he had it sized fifteen years ago and nothing else needed to be said.

"Simply beautiful," said Caleb and kissed her hand. Beautiful was putting it mildly thought Ruby. It was the most extraordinary twenty-four carat white gold ring ever, a pear shaped solitaire with large baguette diamonds on each side.

"Oh Caleb, I love you so much. And I've always loved you and only you." He stood and pulled her into his arms and led her back inside. He keyed in the alarm.

"Let me show you where you're going to sleep and yes I'm going to be on my best behavior." He looked down at her loveliness and said, "Until after I've had my shower." She wanted to tell him she didn't ask him to and would be disappointed if he didn't display the same conduct he did last night, but thought she would keep it to herself. Together they walked up the staircase.

He opened the door to the room she would use for the night. It resembled a show place from a magazine. Her bags were placed on an old fashioned rod iron bed in a bronze and copper finish, covered with a reversible teal and chocolate print comforter set. Throw pillows in the same pattern were placed at the head of the bed. A thick cushioned chocolate colored metal bench with curved detailed arms and legs was sat at the end of the bed. Contemporary abstract wall sculpture of multi-hued cooper concentric hoops hung above the bed. Teal curtains and valance covered the large window. A slender chest stood on the opposite wall with small crystal sculptures. Two accent tables were placed on each side with miniature ginger jar lamps.

He walked over to the closet and showed her where she could hang her things. "You have your own bathroom right through that door. I'm going to make a few calls and let you get settled. He kissed her gently and told her he would be back to tuck her in. She smiled and he disappeared behind the door. She hung up the clothing she bought. A pair of navy cuffed crop pants, matching satin strap cami, and a smock blouse in a teal print that she could wear with her navy shoes without the shoe jewelry. She also purchased her essentials and a pair of gold hoops. She was set for the night and sat on the bed to gaze at her engagement ring.

She should look like a million bucks with a diamond this size when she walks in the office tomorrow. Ruby smiled, a Wallyworld outfit will have to do...

All was done and she closed the door to the chocolate and teal bathroom. She had pampered herself with a relaxing shower in one of the body gels she purchased. A sparkling fragrant cocktail of orange blossoms and fruity peach perfumed her body. The combination of the moisturizing lotion and plain old petroleum jelly left her skin soft and silky smooth. She put on a lace blue satin gown that stopped above her knees and slipped her feet in a pair of satin blue slippers. She placed the pillows on the bench and pulled the comforter back. With her briefcase she stretched out in the bed and pulled out her tablet to check her emails. She had to make three referrals and accept two appointments for next week that was set up by Angela. She ignored her additional questions about him. It was no use trying to do anything else tonight, concentrating was becoming a problem. She wanted to talk to her mother and share the news. But they agreed to wait until tomorrow. Staring at her ring she decided to call it a night and slid under the covers.

Caleb had given her plenty time to get situated. He had taken his shower, talked to his parents and had done everything in his power to keep from blurting out the news of Ruby accepting his proposal of marriage. His thoughts were to give the news and all the details at one time. He knocked on her door and waited for her to tell him to enter, no answer. He opened it, she was asleep. Caleb was disappointed she didn't wait for him to tuck her in. He walked over to his sleeping beauty and tenderly nudged her sweet lips as he eased down beside her.

She stirred and winked an eye. "What took you so long?" She did wait.

He took her in his arms and caressed her face with his. She could feel the smooth silky texture of his soft facial hairs touching her cheek, chin, and nose. She weaved her fingers through his tousled damp hair that was freshly shampooed. He gazed into her caring eyes that bared passion and desire for him. His sentiments were the same as he captured her trembling lips. Her body language displayed uneasiness. "Don't be nervous Baby," he whispered softly. "Just let me love you like there's no tomorrow." His tongue penetrated her sweet lips, searching for hers. Capturing her moist luscious organ he tasted the sweet flavor of the minted candy she had before she retired for the evening. Peach flavored just like the blended scent of her smooth chocolate skin. Their tongues circled and danced a seductive tempo as she caressed his suntan corded shoulders down to his strapping back squeezing him tightly. His hands traveled all over her perfumed body touching and feeling while easing her gown to expose her ample soft curvaceous body. With each tender stroke on her nakedness she shivered while her breath rushed in and out. He felt her shudders as he massaged her large hips and thighs. Sensuous moans escaped her lips while he fondled her plump rose petal and peach fragrant breasts; her eyes fluttered shut. His tongue circled and massaged one nipple while his hand kneaded the other. Unconsciously she arched her body into his as he continued his magic. She pulled his face closer to nuzzle and scorch his skin with hot kisses. Slowly moving up and down her body with magical strokes leaving no skin untouched, she writhed and whimpered. She called out to him as he gently pushed her legs apart and caressed her inner thighs, pausing at her velvet top that guarded her secret jewels. Every tender stroke gave a breathtaking hint of mindless ecstasy that was rising by each intense second. With cries of passion she shuddered and clutched his shoulders rapidly losing herself as incredible pleasures took her to a glorious place. He held her tightly as she became captive by a rush of sensations so powerful; it caused her to come completely apart in his arms. Keeping her under his spell he captured her mouth with her struggling for more oxygen. Showing her no mercy he traced kisses down her hot steamy body stopping again to tease her taut nipples. She clenched her stomach as he traveled down to her adorable little navel. He had to hold her down with his body because hers had taken a mind of its own. She felt the evidence of his desire as he continued his assault stopping only to whisper words of love and devotion. Caleb knew his ebony princess was now ready as he tenderly joined their bodies and made them one. Together they began their unified rhythm with trickles of ecstasy flooding through their souls. Tidal waves of pure passion took them over the edge as she screamed his name shattering into tiny pieces holding on to him for dear life. He buried his face in her bosoms muffling his shouts while surrendering to the longest release of his life. Swelling with pride, he knew his seed had been planted as he gathered her in his arms.

CHAPTER 14

Ruby Jewel parents agreed to meet at the country truck stop that's on the way to Houston which was known for serving delicious meals and pastries. Beforehand she sent a text to her siblings announcing her engagement and wedding. She wanted to tell her parents face to face. Caleb wanted so much to be with her but his first patient was at 8:45. He left practically running because they did get a late start due to circumstances beyond their control, a full night of unadulterated passion. She was the one who had to lock up his place and set the security system. He gave her his key on a diamond and gold butterfly keychain which also belonged to his mother, and told her she now held the key to his home and heart. Another special gift she thought, that would be treasured for the rest of her life. He made her promise if anything ever happens between them for her not to return them, because she was his first and last choice and the only woman worthy enough to have his mother's jewelry. They then agreed the third Saturday in April, which would give them at least five good weeks to make all the arrangements and his Denver family enough time to make plans and reservations. He was leaving everything up to her but insisted on paying for everything. She told him they would split the cost down the middle and he agreed. At least they didn't have to worry about rings; they were using his parents'.

Ruby Jewel pulled into the crowded parking lot looking around to see if she could spot her parents' car. They were parked close to the back which made them easily visible. She pulled up beside them and got out to get in the back seat. Naturally her daddy bought breakfast, something simple that could be eaten in the car because she was pushed for time. Her father gave her one of the breakfast sandwiches and juice. Before she could ask he handed her a little bag with her blueberry muffin. He knew his first born very well.

"Okay Ruby, what's this all about," asked her mother.

"Oh, just that Caleb and I are engaged to be married and our date is the third Saturday in April." Ruby held her hand over the seat to show them her ring. "Isn't it beautiful and it was his mother's."

"Ruby Jewel beautiful is putting it lightly. It's absolutely gorgeous and very expensive. Congratulations Baby."

"I know Momma." Her father was quiet and that wasn't like him. "Daddy, you are happy for me aren't you?"

"Yes Baby you know I'm happy for you, it's just that April is around the corner. Don't you think that's a bit soon?"

"Daddy he wanted to get married at the end of this month. I talked him into waiting until Easter weekend since the family would all be here."

"What about his grandparents in Denver?"

"What about them? All they have to do is come, we're paying for everything."

Henry Ray was not going to bring up the past or dampen

his daughter's moment. He could see her happiness and knew she had never stopped loving Caleb VanLee and the same thing for him. "Baby I'm happy for you and I can pay for my daughter's wedding. I paid for the other two."

"Daddy I want to help since we'll be pushed for time and remember; I'm over thirty. To accommodate his blended family we're going to have everything at the Grandeur Inn Hotel in one of their large banquet halls. Caleb has already called and reserved the room. His frat brothers own two thirds of the hotel and another one owns a large nursery in Bryan and has a florist shop right there in the hotel. We will also be close to the airport and other hotels if additional rooms are needed. The event planner will handle all the arrangements after we decide what we want. Caleb is leaving all the details to us. He's confident that we can pull it off since money is not a problem." Ruby smiled when she said that because it was a true fact.

"Okay Baby, Daddy and I will be there for you and do whatever you need us to do."

"Thanks, I knew you would. I need to run because I must get to the office as early as I can. As you can see, I need to change into something a little more conservative." Ruby and her parents got out of the car and walked over to hers. She gave them both hugs and told them she loved them.

CHAPTER 15

RJ made record time to the office. She could hardly get inside the door with all the morning company. All eyes were plastered on her with all her girls present. She looked at Angela and shook her head. What was the use she thought, then displayed the biggest smile she's sure they've seen on her face in a long time. As they crowded in, she was embraced and congratulated by each one. During the well wishes Ruby caught sight of a huge bouquet of purple and lavender roses and hydrangeas tied with a large gold glittered ribbon and netting sitting on the counter in an elegant design crystal vase. The arrangement was absolutely breathtaking. She held her hands up to cover her mouth when Angela grabbed the one with her ring. Screams and *ahhhhs* filled the room.

"Now that's what you call a diamond, girlfriend and cost somebody *bank*," said Kellie. She told them it belonged to his biological mother. They started back with the *ahhhhs* and *ooohs*. Cynthia interrupted them to announce she had delivered the arrangement herself when she got the order to reserve limousine service for the third Saturday in April from the hotel event planner. The women covered their mouths when they heard the news about her date.

"The third Saturday in April, that's just about"....

"Five weeks and five days," announced Cynthia completing her cousin Nisey's count. "And we have work to do!"

"Girl isn't your hands full with your own wedding in June?"

"Baby everything is done. All I'm waiting on is to say I Do!"

"Girlfriend we got this," exclaimed Angela. "You just make sure the hotel does its part."

"Sistahs I hate to break up this wonderful celebration and leave good company but I must change before my client gets here."

"Humph, you haven't seen a celebration," said Lana.

"Okay, but we have to finish this conversation over lunch, Nisey and Cynthia we'll put you two on speaker phone." Everybody agreed that was the plan and allowed her to leave to change. Before she made it to her door she looked back at her girls and did something that was totally out of character for Attorney RJ McHarding. She ran back over to the group screaming, "I'm getting married ya'll! I'm getting married!" The cheers, screams, and hugs started all over again...

Angela had given her enough time to change and knocked on her door. She walked in with her bouquet of flowers and exchanged them with the older arrangement. It still had live blooms and greenery, so she put them on the front counter.

"Now Ms RJ, I'll have all websites ready for us to look at and we can print out what you're interested in and start your portfolio. I will also have a checklist printed so we can keep tabs on what we've done and still need to do. Oh, you have about twenty minutes before your clients arrive, hurry and don't forget makeup!"

Ruby slipped her feet into black and white spectator pumps and went back to the closet to get her spare makeup. When she looked down at herself she saw her black and white jacket blouse was buttoned wrong and put it all on Angela. She was just plain rushed fidgeting with one of her silver dangling earrings. She did not need a necklace because of the three rows of flouncy ruffles that cascaded down the front of her top. After adding a little make-up and her silver bracelets, that Attorney RJ McHarding flair was no doubt visible.

"Attorney McHarding, Allen and Cornelius Baines are here."

"Thank you Angela, I'll be right there." Ruby stepped in the hallway and walked toward the receptionist desk, two gentlemen stood. No wonder Angela buzzed instead of bringing them to her office, they were fine and some handsome.

"Gentlemen, I'm Attorney RJ McHarding." They shook hands. Ummm they smelled nice too she thought. "Can I offer you refreshments…coffee, tea, or juice and fresh pastries?" They both agreed to coffee and pastries. Angela quickly got to her feet to fix a tray for the brothers as they walked to her office. "Please, have seats gentlemen. Now, I understand you're having some problems with the housing association in your neighborhood." They both acknowledged and Allen gave her a folder with four certified letters. While she was examining the first letter Angela knocked on the door, with the refreshment tray and sat it down on a cart and excused herself. Ruby asked them to help themselves and then they could get down to business. Already she detected an inexperience lawyer had messed up royally and Dixon & Dixon Law Firm whom she was well familiar with would have to pay. Humph, this was not going to take long at all.

"Attorney McHarding I want to let you know before we get started that I am an ex-offender. I served ten years in the federal penal system and the core of our problem centers around ex-offenders." RJ made a mental note the youngest brother, Cornelius was the spokesman. Both brothers share ownership of a four unit duplex that was willed to them by an uncle who had never married nor had children. They were also ideally located, especially for someone starting over because of special circumstances. She listened attentively as he explained the delicate nature that was also involved. After he finished, she advised them several violations had been made against them including harassment and she would put a stop to all of it …ASAP holding the folder which contained the letters. RJ assured them their problem would be handled in strictest of confidence. She believed everyone deserved a second chance and should be able to live their lives accordingly. Excusing herself to make a telephone call to the law firm, they understood why she came highly recommended and with a hefty price tag.

"Attorney H. Dixon, please…"_____

Lunch was later than usual due to her second client who was having some problems with getting their government funding for one of their church programs for the homeless. She was able to give them some other alternatives for now that would help along with her donation. She needed the tax write off to help balance the business she was steadily picking up. She and Lana both were doing extremely well and were in the process of hiring additional help. Lana was now working a half day in the office and the remainder of the day teaching at the community college. Plus she and one of the assistant ministers were having an old fashion courtship. Ruby knew with her getting married and moving to Hempstead she could use another young attorney and trainee law clerk that could assist her and Destiny.

Ruby walked in the dining room with her iPod, everyone was waiting. Angela had her laptop and printer set up so they could print out immediately. Hot lunches had been catered by Ms. Janet…steamed vegetables; twice baked potatoes, individual meatloaves, and pound cake. Ruby knew what was expected of her, but she was ready to eat.

Cell phone, Caleb. "Hi Sweetie," she had everybody's undivided attention and thought she would take the call outside.

"Caleb the flowers were simply gorgeous as usual. You're spoiling me."

"That's my intentions to spoil you and my children rotten."

"Oh Caleb, have you had time to call your grandparents on both sides?"

"I called my Grandmother Audrey and she's going to tell that side. I had Mom and Dad to pass the news to their families and I dealt with Grandmother Mildred which was drama."

"You know she never did like me."

"Well she may as well learn to because you're part of me

Ruby. You're responsible for this smile I'm wearing inside and out. You're the one I want to spend the rest of my life with, so she needs to blend in with the rest of the family. Besides grandfather can handle her well, now did you get the hint with the flowers?"

"Oh, were you giving me a hint? What?"

"The colors," Caleb said. She knew that, just wanted to hear him admit he wanted a purple and gold wedding, most Q's do.

"Yes Sweetie I got the hint. As a matter of fact everyone is waiting on me now to look at pictures and make decisions on what we need. I'll probably have a folder with every little detail down to my underwear."

"Tell them not to spend much time on that because all I'm going to do is tear them off." Ruby covered her mouth in shock. He knew she was stunned at his boldness just like she was last night and he loved every bit of it because she was his prudish ebony princess. "Ruby I love you." Once again her heart melted a little more. "Before I hang up, I heard from Stay Ready; the Judge was able to clear his calendar and we're going to get together the weekend and Dr. Nason called. She wanted to know if we would be attending her grandfather's birthday celebration, are we?"

"Well you be sure to tell her hello, and yes we can attend the celebration since he's your grandparents dearest friend and on the board. You know she wants you, not me." He didn't hesitate to say she may as well understand they were a package deal.

"I better get back with the group before that Angela comes looking for me. Before I go, how was your morning?"

"Great. I've seen four new patients and tonight I'll do the afterhours shift so I'll call you back when I have another break." They expressed their sentiments and ended the call. Ruby walked back inside and ran into Angela.

"There you are we're waiting."

The working lunch was a success although she didn't get to complete hers for looking at this picture and that picture. She had Angela to add a little more and she would have her lunch for dinner. She had a complete portfolio of her wedding plans. Everybody was eager to help and was pleased with the job they had been assigned thanks to her efficient assistant. She was having a small wedding party which worked out perfect. She didn't have to choose between any of her girls. They were just happy she was getting married. Her two sisters and teenage niece would stand up with her as matrons and maid of honor. They would be responsible for choosing their own tea length dresses in light gold; her little nieces as flower girls would be in purple and lavender short dresses with gold ribbon sashes; and nephews as ring bearer and basket holder would wear black tux like the groomsmen.

Angela even tried to pick out some sample wedding gowns with the encouragement from her two sisters who had emailed pictures. Technology, but that's where she stopped them cold. She already had the type of gown she wanted in mind; ivory ornate lace, off the shoulders, sweetheart neckline, high-waist, full tea length skirt, jeweled headpiece, and accessories to enhance. Everyone smiled when she finished describing her dream dress because it sounded just like her. Now she needed to call Delana to let her know what she wanted and have her check her stock to see if she has anything like it or close to it available. Yes it's true, she had thought about what she wanted to get married in for years and always knew her colors would be purple, lavender, and light gold…his colors.   Now it was time to make it happen…

What a day thought Ruby as she pulled in her drive. She couldn't help remembering the last time she came home he was waiting on her, but not tonight he was in Hempstead. Although they had talked twice before she left the office she stilled missed him terribly.   Ruby Jewel McHarding had to admit for once in her life she was madly in love and now understands the behavior of her baby sister and good friend Kellie Kincaid when they rushed into marriage to their soul mates. A smile crossed her lips as she thought about how Tori and Lincoln waited a week. Her parents had pleaded with them to at least give them a few days and have a small ceremony at home. They agreed and gave them exactly one week to make preparations for what turned out to be a beautiful garden wedding in their parent's backyard fourteen years ago. Kellie's husband on the other hand surprised her with an elaborate wedding in their hometown, the big city of Edna in a day. She had been at a seminar and hated she missed that grand affair. But now she understood the urgency. Maybe they could move their date up to the first Saturday in April instead of the third, since money and a place was not a problem. The way Angela and her entourage pulled together all her wedding plans in one sitting she was confident, that group could pull it off.

Cell phone. Caleb. "Hi Sweetheart."

"Caleb I was just thinking about you and was getting ready to call."

"You miss me, huh?"

"You can't imagine how much."

"Girl you're turning my insides to jello."

"You're so silly," she teased. Caleb we've completed the plans for our wedding. I just need to find a dress which is not going be a problem. I was thinking what if we move our date to the first Saturday in April that's just two weeks earlier. What do you think about that?" She paused and waited for his response.

"You got it bad too, huh? You sure we can't have everything ready by next week?"

"I'm sure we can, but two weeks and a few days would make it easier for your Denver family. We'll just have to be patient and keep ourselves busy until then. I may not be able to attend the birthday celebration because I do have to help with the final arrangements.

"If it means us getting married two weeks earlier, I'll go alone. That will give me something to do and stay out of trouble. I think I'll put in some extra hours at the center and hang with the old folks."

"Both of those are great ideas, I don't have to worry about Dr. Nason and somebody under forty trying to steal my man. I'll also get in touch with Mrs. Felton and her daughter and have them keep an eye on you." They both enjoyed a good laugh.

"Ruby I'm looking forward to spending the rest of my life with you. And I promise we're going to have a wonderful life together."

"I know Caleb."

"Baby, I forgot about a honeymoon!"

"Sweetie our life together will be a honeymoon."

"There you go again girl, melting my heart

"Dr. VanLee we need help, this lady..." He could hear the commotion going on in the waiting room.

"Baby there's an emergency, I'm being called. I'll call you later. I love you."_____

Ruby had just finished talking to her parents and told them they were moving the date up to the first Saturday in April instead of the third. She wanted to know how they felt about that before she made any other calls. They made it clear they were behind her one hundred per cent. She sent a text to her siblings, Angela, and her entourage. She knew she would be getting calls in about...now.

"Hello Angela."

"Kellie and Cynthia are also on the phone. Hold up...Is that you Nisey?"

"Yes ma'am it's yours truly. Where's Lana?"

"On a date," said Angela. "I'm to fill her in later. Now girlfriend, you couldn't wait huh?"

"How do you know I'm the one instead of him?"

"Ruby Jewel I know you. He probably wanted to get married at the end of this month and it was your idea with this third Saturday in April stuff. Now are we sure because we need to see the printer Friday for sure and you need to see Delana in the morning. You don't have an office visit until after lunch tomorrow. Kellie can you meet her at

Delana's to help her choose a couple of selections until I can get there. I don't see me getting away until after 11:30. You know I have two bosses."

"Yes, Angela I can do that."

"Okay that's settled. Now Cynthia you need to make the changes with the hotel."

"Done."

"Oh, go ahead and order the flowers and let's use the exact ones the ivory prince sent her today. Flowers will not be a problem that's his frat brother's shop."

"Done."

"Now Ruby we need a count of corsages and boutonnières by the end of the week. Can you handle that?" Silence.

"We're here Angela."

"Hey Tori and Kami, Ruby Jewel we need you to say something."

"I didn't think you needed me," she said.

"Ah, we hurt her feelings. We need you Sweetie. You're the bride. Now can you get us a count of his family and Kami you do the McHarding clan. The cake, Ruby we also need to make a decision on the cake by the weekend. Tori and Kami we need you two to be available tomorrow around 12:00 so we can help her chose her dress, we'll send pictures. I think we've covered everything, any questions?"

"I'll speak for the group I think you have everything covered," said Kellie.

"Good now let's get in Ruby's real business. Sistah girl he must can…"

"Good night Angela and friends." Everybody laughed as they hung up. Ruby went into her kitchen and warmed up her lunch/dinner and sat in her favorite chair and watched an old sitcom._____

Tonight had been busy but good, no life threatening emergencies. No one was sent to Cypress Memorial. The little grandmother was the only highlight of their evening. There were a couple of minor problems, heartburn, a couple of sinus sufferers and two diabetics who were out of their medicine. They even kept two little old ladies who were absolute dolls while their family members ran a couple of errands in the area. They sat and watched old shows from back in the day. He was also able to solicit more seniors for the center. Caleb had a brainstorm for providing after hour day care at the center for families that needed services and planned to talk to Dr. Alford and Dr. Nason. According to the office clerk they have people to drop off their love ones at least two or three times a week especially on the days the center closes early.

He was able to call Ruby back to say good night before she turned in. She told him everything was in place and all she needed from him was a count for corsages and boutonnières plus three men that would stand up for him. That was a simple enough task. He told her his mother and aunt were on the flower detail and cousins would stand up with him.

CHAPTER 16

Ruby and Kellie met at Ms Janet's for breakfast and thought they would head over to Delana's around 10:30. They didn't see a need for them to be there as early as Ms Angela suggested. She had called Delana and told her what she wanted. Once she and Kellie settled down and ordered their breakfast she knew she was going to have to come clean with her. They went way back and she knew her far better than Ms Angela. She was in love the worst way and didn't want to be away from him period. Kellie understood from her own experience. Ruby told her she didn't know how she was going to endure being away from him regardless with her having a lot on her plate.

A receptionist was to start immediately since Angela will have to focus solely as their office manager. Interviews must be conducted for potential employees with the changes being made. She had made the decision to move to Hempstead and come into the office a couple of days a week once she gets married. When she told Caleb he was touched that she would consider his career over hers. Ruby Jewel was ready to be a wife and mother. She's had a career for fifteen years. Kellie looked at her friend with the biggest smile ever when she revealed her plans. Her girl was certainly in love and she truly understood.

"Okay Ms Ruby Jewel I'm like Angela, are you sure you can wait, what three weeks?"

"I don't have a choice and it's not quite three weeks."

"Well come on let's get over to Delana's before Angela beats us there. You know we have a schedule to keep."

"Girl please, I write Angela's check. But come on anyway, it's time for us to move around." They giggled like teenage girls, left a tip, and made their way to Delana's Boutique. Pulling into the parking lot they recognized her car and looked at each other. They couldn't believe she actually beat them. The duo walked in the boutique with Ruby carrying her shoe box, Angela met them at the door looking at her watch. They decided it was best not to say a word and followed her to the private dressing area Delana had already set up with her selections.

"Momma, Tori, I can't believe you're actually here." Her eyes teared as she embraced them. Talking about surprises, her daddy came in with Delana. She walked right into his arms with tears streaming down her face. The new entourage dabbed at their eyes as they worked hard at holding back tears.

"Okay ladies this is a joyous occasion. Let's get this show on the road." Delana clapped her hands and told everyone to leave the room but Ruby. She unzipped the first dress and helped her in it. She told her it was not quite what she requested but as far as she was concerned this was the dress. It had most of the features and definitely fits her personality, lace completely embellished with tiny crystals and pearls. The satin pleated off the shoulders waist dress was almost a perfect fit with its flowing lace skirt. Delana had to pull it in a bit under the arms which caused it to flow beautifully with the lace scallop hem stopping at the top of her ankles. When she put on her three inch white pearl sandals it was the perfect length. Delana was determined this was the one and already picked out the head piece and jewelry for a complete presentation. She swirled Ruby's hair up with her curly tresses coming to the front. She then put the headpiece in place which had large curly flowers coming to the front and detailed with the same ornaments as the dress. The detachable tulle mini blusher covered her face. To add the finishing touches large crystal teardrop earrings hung from her ears, a teardrop necklace fell right where the pleated neckline met, and three strand matching bracelets for her wrist.

"One word, said Delana. "Gorgeous! Absolutely gorgeous! Now you look in the mirror." Ruby did as she was told and couldn't believe the image facing her, she was right it was beautiful. The back was as stunning as the front with an inside pleat of flowing ornate lace. She felt like Caleb's ebony princess for sure and knew he would be pleased. Now if everyone agrees, this is the dress, and Delana's work was done.

Ruby Jewel walked out to the front and the entourage was speechless with gapping mouths. She turned so they could see the back. Her father was the first one to finally speak, "Baby you look absolutely beautiful. It's perfect. I don't see a reason for us to look at anything else. Maybe your mother..." Mrs. McHarding said she couldn't have said it any better as she wiped her tears and looked back at the others for their opinion. But they were still wiping tears also. At last Angela said she agreed with Mr. McHarding, with the others nodding their heads for a yes. Ruby turned and faced

Delana and told her she could put her name on this dress. Her father reached Delana his bank card and held his hand up for his daughter not to say a word.

"Can I say thank you Daddy and Momma?"

"Yes you can, and you're welcome." She embraced her parents and then started to the dressing room.

"Wait let me take a picture for Kami," exclaimed Tori. She modeled her dress once again and then left to change. Angela checked off wedding dress on her today's list and announced the remaining task that needed Ruby's attention. She volunteered her parents and sisters to help make the final decisions on the menu and cake as long as the cake was decorated in purple, gold, and white. It didn't matter about the design since they had narrowed it down to two choices she liked. Because Delana chose the perfect dress, they could use the extra time left to choose the invitations so they could get them to the printer tomorrow. They had to give it to Angela she had everything under control. Cynthia and Kellie had their checklist and they too were just about completed. She was pleased how everything was working out so well. Humph with these girls by her side along with her family they probably could have pulled off an end of the month wedding without any problems.

CHAPTER 17

The remainder of the week had been productive and busy for the staff at McHarding and Harvey. Ruby had asked to meet with everyone in the dining room at the end of the day before they left for the weekend. She wanted to make them aware of the decisions she's made once she's married. Destiny and Lana were already aware and had given her a couple of people who they felt would fit in with their little family.

Angela texted, *Boss Lady we're waiting on you*. Ruby Jewel shook her head. She didn't know how she does it, talking about being efficient. She was worth every dime of her salary and the raise she was going to receive. Because of her they had accomplished all of their wedding assignments plus their workload for the entire week. The only thing left to do for the upcoming nuptials were the invitations and the keepsakes for the guests. She wanted to touch base with her *Boo* before she ordered them. *Boo*, that brought a smile to her lips, she had a *Boo*. She packed up her things and walked down to the dining room to meet with her coworkers._____

The VanLee's had an early Saturday morning flight and would arrive at 6:45 am Texas time. Linda Nason was having their driver pick them up from Hobby and drive to their ranch which was located on the outskirts of Hempstead.

The old friends were looking forward to their visit plus surprising Caleb. They started out trying to surprise him but he overheard their conversation the other night when she and Mildred were scheming. She had to cover it up and tell him Caleb Sr. was coming for his birthday party.

Of course Mildred had a time convincing her husband not to call their grandson. He did not like surprises himself nor did he like imposing on others. Regardless of him being their grandson, he still respected his privacy as a man. But Linda insisted they would make Charles so happy with their presence and it had been some time since their last visit. But he knew his wife well and suspected she was up to something that involved his grandson and his future bride. Nevertheless, Caleb could handle his Grandmother without a doubt._____

Dr. VanLee had seen his last patient for the day. He, his cousins, and frat brothers were all getting together this evening. Wesley's grandmother had been released from the hospital and was doing fine. He was leaving on an early morning flight tomorrow for Tyler Texas. Tonight was the last chance for all of them to hang out. *Stay Ready* and his cousins had freed up their calendars for the rest of the day and insisted on seeing the future Mrs. Caleb VanLee 3rd plus their old frat brothers in Houston. Caleb couldn't argue with that and miss a chance of seeing her. He contacted Nathan and he made it all happen. He purposely didn't call Ruby because he wanted to surprise her. They were to meet up at Cypress Memorial parking lot. Roy was shocked to find out he and *Q-Note* worked at the hospital all these years and had never run into each other. But it was possible with their different shifts; **Q** in the day and Roy at night.

Caleb pulled in the hospital parking lot and called Tiny.

"Where are ya'll man?"

"Frosty, we're parked in the back up front in the visitors' section in the Sheriff's black Escalade."

"I see you cuz." He pulled beside him. Silk recognized the metallic gold Escalade and had the driver to follow it and block them in once they parked. They had no idea Nathan would be there waiting on them in a luxury stretch limo to take them into the city in grand style. The limo door opened and three brothers got out; Silk, Wolf, and Mudpuppy. Tiny, Roy, and Douglas jumped out of the SUV, because they recognized Silky Silk right off the top.

"Put me down Tiny Bear," shouted Silk while the other brothers embraced.

"Don't do that cuz, keep him in the air," said Douglas (Bare-None) with Roy (Q-Chips) co-signing. "Let's get our licks back first."

"You're on your own with these country boys," teased Wolf and Mudpuppy.

"Hold up cousins I smell vittles." Tiny Bear put Silk down and turned to face Frosty.

"Where man, because I'm hungry as a Tiny Bear." The brothers burst into laughter. Food was always there weakness and Silky Silk had a huge spread for his brothers.

Cell phone. "Frosty, man where are ya'll Judge Ross is about to drive me crazy."

"Q-Note come around to the visitor's parking lot and you'll see a stretched limo, that's us."

"What he say **Q**?"

"Now doc don't you start acting like the Judge here."

"Man it's been fifteen years since I've seen these brothers, I can't help it," exclaimed the Judge. "Is that them," shouted Stay Ready. He saw seven men, six black and one white. He would have jumped out of the vehicle if it had been possible. These new vehicles are a pain in the butt sometimes. Q-Note stopped his SUV and the doors automatically unlocked.

"Frosty! Frosty! Man it's been too long." The long lost brothers grabbed one another in the biggest hug. "Frosty, I've missed you so much man. How could you do that to us?" Stay Ready was trying not to become emotional because they were the closest out of the four. The others had no idea how he had blessed him financially. He and Yolanda got married their senior year, and Frosty made it possible for their lives to be stress free with them expecting their first child. He was able to work part time, finish school, and attend law school all because of Caleb Gerald VanLee. He had tried many times to contact him, but he refused to even acknowledge him or his line brothers in any way. The one and only time he did talk to him, was to simply let him know to make him proud and forget Frosty ever existed. How could he when his oldest son and baby girl are named after him; Caleb Gerald and Callie Gabrielle. Frosty held his brother and told him the love has always been there and he had made him proud.

"Come on brothers' share the love," shouted Tiny Bear. It was a wonderful sight to see old friends reunite and seal their bond once again. Silk looked at his watch and announced they needed to make a move because the traffic was going to be a mess once they get close to the future Mrs. VanLee. Spikey got his suitcase out of Q-Note's SUV while everyone secured their vehicles and loaded up in the limo. Nathan gave the driver directions that led them straight to the business park with less traffic. In the meantime, they enjoyed a wonderful fulfilling spread. Tiny Bear wanted to know where was the *Kool-Aid*. Nathan hadn't disappointed him. He had two homemade gallon jugs just for his Tiny Bear. The guys ate, told stories and passed around brag books of their families. Poor Caleb didn't have anything to brag on yet, but he soon would. He was thankful she decided to move their date up. He couldn't wait to enjoy the real happiness of life. When he saw Caleb and Callie his eyes clouded up. Silk patted his leg and told him it wouldn't be long…

Nathan and Caleb spotted her car right out front when they pulled into the parking lot. Good she was still there he thought with a big dimpled smile. The limo stopped and the men piled out.

"Nathan, what's happening man," said Gregory who was coming down the sidewalk with three little people hanging onto each leg and one around his neck.

"I'm doing good man, but you look pretty busy." Nathan burst into a hearty laugh because he definitely could relate. "Man, I like for you to meet my frat brothers who came down to hang out for the evening." Gregory looked at Caleb and then back to Nathan. "He knew exactly where he was coming from. Yeah G-Man, he's earned the right, meet Dr. Caleb Gerald VanLee better known as Frosty." Nathan continued with his introductions and told him they were there to surprise Ruby.

"Let me unlock the door, the staff is in a meeting and have the front doors locked, for security reasons."

The men said thanks and followed him in. Gregory put the triplets down and they ran straight to the dining room where the juice was kept. You could hear the pattering of little tennis shoes.

"See what you got to look forward to," said Silk as they followed the little people but hung back a bit.

"What in the world…"

"Juice…juice…juice…"

"Who's with you babies?"

"We are, **Q**-dogs in the house!"

Ruby couldn't believe her eyes. Ten of God's finest walked in the dining room behind Gregory hitting the wall and stomping their feet as they stepped across the threshold, a frat thing. Caleb was the last to enter. Their faces lit up like children opening presents when their eyes met. He reached for her and was pulled back by Tiny Bear.

"Little cuz you're last. Ruby Jewel you look absolutely delicious," Tiny lifted her off the floor and gave her a big kiss on her cheek. It was a good thing she had on a long skirt. She went from arm to arm. She couldn't believe they were all there.

"Marcus, (alias Stay Ready) it's been too long." She hugged him the longest.

"Ruby Jewel you're a sight for sore eyes. You're more beautiful than ever." All the men agreed.

"Is it my turn yet?"

"Go ahead little brother," said Q-Note.

"I told you before I got yo..." Naturally he didn't finish the phrase. "Come here girl." He opened his arms for her to walk into them. He didn't care who was watching because they did have an audience. He kissed her lips, and then captured her mouth with an urgency parting her lips, sweeping and tasting her sweetness. He kissed her until she was deliciously breathless.

"Let her catch her breath man," exclaimed Silk! They stopped and he rubbed his face against her cheek while holding her close. Angela coughed to get her girl's attention.

"Oh excuse me, where are my manners. Let me introduce everyone, ladies PVU's finest."

"You can say that again," said Destiny with amen coming from the others.

"Okay, they're all married except this one. Ladies this is my fiancé, Caleb Gerald VanLee 3rd better known as Frosty. She continued until everyone was introduced.

Caleb and Ruby then tried slipping out of the room and ran into Nisey and Cynthia.

"My, my, where are you two love birds going," asked Nisey?

"Exactly," added Cynthia. She knew she may as well let it go and introduced them expressing they were his Soros.

"Soros, it's a pleasure meeting you both. Can we bribe my sisters to allow us to slip off for a few minutes?" They were seduced and conned with his mesmerizing deep baritone voice and potent smile. Both stepped aside to let them pass but not before he kissed them on the cheek and whispered, "Thanks for helping a brother out." Ruby rushed him into her office. "Lock the door," he ordered and then pinned her against it pressing his hardness against her soft thickness, devouring her mouth while absorbing her warmth. His body ached terribly for hers with their heartbeats pounding the same tune. He held her hands over her head with one of his while kissing the bend of her neck and then each earlobe. Soft groans escaped her lips as he unbuttoned her pleated paisley blouse and placed hot kisses on her fragrant soft plump mounds. She gasped as she felt his warm breath against her velvety flesh. He nudged the center of her bosom as he cupped and gently molded one of her breasts with the palm of his hand. She whimpered softly and called his name. A taut nipple showed its appreciation as he moved to the other, but not before capturing her mouth with a searing kiss that left them mindless. He stopped abruptly, he was being summoned. Sucking air through his teeth he vowed to fix that Tiny.

They willed their bothered bodies to return to normal as they tried pulling themselves together. He walked over to a chair and she straddled his lap. She held his face between her hands and kissed his lips as he caressed her bottom.

"Let's not start that again," she pleaded. "We should go back into the dining room and join the others. But first I need to find out how do you want the invitations to read so I can tell the printer tomorrow?"

"What do you mean?"

"Do you want your grandparents' name on the

invitation?"

"Ruby I have four sets of grandparents and a wonderful set of parents that raised me. I wouldn't dream of taking that honor from them nor will I insult my black family. Are you considering putting your grandparents' name on the invitation?"

"No Caleb, you know my grandparents are deceased."

"There's your answer Baby. Mine does not have to have any special treatments; they are who they are grandparents. Worry your pretty little head about something else." A knock on the door said their special time was over. Ruby smoothed down her flared burgundy skirt and attempted to button her blouse, when he lightly pushed her hand aside. "I'll fix it back like i found it." He then put her gold heart pendant back in its place. He kissed the inside of her wrist that held the matching bracelet. She sucked in her breath. "Oh you like that."

Ruby took hold of his hand, "come on mister," and pulled him to his feet. She unlocked her door and together they joined the group.

"It's about time. What in the world were you two doing," asked Tiny Bear?

"None of your business, where's everybody?" He told them the group was satisfied with spending the evening just hanging out here and had made themselves comfortable next door. Silk and Mudpuppy wives are now here and the Houston brothers ordered dinner.

"You two need to come join the party or do I need to call Gran and let her know what you were doing." Caleb hit at his cousin who was trying to make it to the door. The loving couple walked over with Tiny Bear to join the others.

Angela met them, "There they are. I figured you didn't need your purse for anything so I locked it up in your trunk. Here are your keys."

"Thank you Angela and we can go ahead and order the invitations the way we wrote them. That's what Caleb and I were talking about."

"Girlfriend please, it's all over his face what you two have been doing. Here," she gave her a napkin and told her to take care of her *Boo* and told Caleb it was nice meeting him. She winked at her and said she would see her in the morning and walked off. Caleb burst into a hearty laugh and told Ruby he liked her.

When they entered the dining room Gregory was busy adjusting the screen. Ruby questioned Kellie as to what he was doing. She shook her head and told her he was setting up his toys, a laptop and his new iPhone for the brothers to call their families and introduce them. He was just about ready when the triplets started clapping their hands and chanting, "Grandmommy...Granddaddy." So the first thing he had to do was let them talk to their grandparents and then he would be able to do the same for the others.

Ms Janet had catered a delicious meal that was enjoyed by all. It was nice meeting the brothers' wives and families, especially Q-Chips family. His three year old wanted to know if he was coming home tonight so he could sleep with his mother and wouldn't let him talk to his wife. They all had a big laugh. Plans were also made to attend the wedding of course with everyone giving Alton the okay to reserve rooms for their families.

"I hate to be bearer of sad news guys, but it's time for us to head back to Cypress." Nathan thanked the Larsons for their wonderful hospitality with the brothers expressing the same sentiments and how much they appreciated their kindness. Thank yous, hugs and kisses went around the room as the guys began making their way outside to the limo. Caleb and Nathan were the last ones to get in.

He hated to leave Ruby because he didn't know the next time they would see each other, hopefully sometime before the weekend was over. He knew he would have to be understanding since she would be his wife in two weeks. He held her close and kissed her good bye. Nathan walked over after putting his family in their SUV. He patted Caleb on the shoulder and gave them both a squeeze and got in the limo.

"I'll call you when I get home Baby I love you," he kissed her one more time and got in the limo with his brothers. She watched them drive off. Ruby thanked Gregory and Kellie who were putting the little people in the vehicle and hurriedly got into her own car. She did not want them to see her tears.

Ruby hated to tell him she probably wouldn't be home until Thursday of next week. She had a full schedule this weekend; a church function for the senior citizens and ladies bible class Sunday that she had to facilitate. She also had three interviews which were scheduled for Monday for additional staff. Ruby had to admit the bare facts, if she wanted a smooth transition into his world she would have to be around to help make the necessary preparations at McHarding and Harvey. She and Lana along with the staff have worked too hard building up their business for her to put it in jeopardy because of the new life she's encountering. There were people with families depending on her. Besides, they only had two more weekends and the next one would be theirs. She and Caleb would just have to manage being away from each other for just a little while.

Before she could get out of the parking lot her cell rang, it was Tori and Angela calling three way and talked her home. For once she was happy to listen to those two which helped her to stay focused and not burst into tears like she wanted to. Turning onto her street, Ruby thanked her sister again for making this day perfect. Angela had also filled her in about Caleb and the guys surprising her with their visit. Today had been emotional, but good.

"Okay girls I made it home. Thanks!"

CHAPTER 18

Linda Nason and her granddaughter were sitting out on the screened-in patio enjoying the evening sipping tea. It was such a peaceful night.

"Grandmother it's all over the clinic that he's moved the date up to the first Saturday in April. There was hope if it had remained the same, but we're looking at two weeks. What in the world is Mrs. VanLee going to do in that short of time?"

"Darling I don't know, but Mildred said for us not to worry and leave everything up to her. You did contact Sarah Williston at the newspaper?"

"Leave what up to whom," asked Charles Nason as he joined his wife and granddaughter. Both ladies became silent; they knew he did not like underhanded deeds and confusion. He would eat them alive if he knew what they were trying to do. She poured her husband a cup of tea and offered him a sweet roll to avoid answering his question. For some reason he was impressed with Attorney RJ McHarding and she couldn't understand why? Linda Nason had actually pulled up her website to see for herself and didn't see anything special about this woman. Yes, she was a dark beauty but so what, she came to the conclusion you can't believe everything you see on internet anyway. "Liny, you didn't answer my question."

"What was that Dear?" Okay, he was well familiar with that game, and knew he would find out sooner or later. But he wanted to know what they were up to now. He didn't want any foolishness tonight because he was too excited with the news of his early birthday present. One of his dearest and oldest friends was coming in tomorrow and stay the entire week for his celebration. He was looking forward to seeing Caleb Sr. It had been a couple of years since he and his fine wife were here last.

"I asked, leave what up to whom?"

"Oh Dear, the event planner told us not to worry about the musicians." Very good Grandmother thought Lauren announcing she was turning in for the night. She had decided to stay over in her room she's had at her grandparents' ranch since she was a little girl. She kissed them both and went inside. Grandmother was on her own now, but she's had him wrapped around her little finger as long as she could remember._____

The limo pulled into the hospital parking lot, all the brothers agreed the evening had been fantastic and couldn't wait to do it again. It was set they would all return for the wedding and was looking forward to it. They even told Alton to be sure to put them in the same hotel and on the same floor if possible with a hospitality suite. Judge Ross suggested they should do something like this periodically and include their families. Everybody was receptive to his suggestion, promising never to be out of touch with each other ever again. They hugged, said their goodbyes, and got in their vehicles to leave. Caleb offered Q-Note a ride around to where he left his truck. Before leaving he told his cousins to say hello to the family and he might see them Sunday, but he didn't know for sure. The way he was feeling right now, he may take a drive to Houston to see his baby. Yeah, he was missing her terribly already.

"There's my truck right there Frosty." He pulled beside it. The brothers hugged once again and Q-Note got out. Caleb waved and blew his horn and before he could move…Bammm! Someone hit his side bumper. He looked in his rear view mirror and spotted a red sports car kissing his right bumper. All three got out about the same time. The guys walked to the side back to examine the damage. He knew his truck would not be hurt but he couldn't say the same for the little toy car. She had a smashed up side front, he didn't have a scratch.

"Didn't you see me," she yelled.

He did not feel like entertaining any drama tonight. He just had a wonderful evening and was missing his baby right now. "Miss if I'm not mistaken you hit me. I was parked and I do have a witness."

"Dr. Nason!"

"Mr. Travis…Dr. VanLee, oh I'm so sorry for my behavior and I didn't mean to run into the back of you. I don't know how this could have happened." She knew damn well how she did it; she did just what he said, hit him. When she recognized him she couldn't let the opportunity pass without making contact even if it did mean hurting her baby. She probably did about five thousand dollars' worth of damage, oh well.

"Alright Dr. Nason."

"Please call me Lauren. Our vehicles are connected now." The guys looked at each other and then at the car.

She was right about being connected; her front end was slightly under his bumper.

"Lauren if you will get back in your car and when we lift this side put your car in reverse and back up." Both men felt foul play but it was nothing for them to do but handle the situation.   She nodded a yes and did as she was told. Bulging biceps, triceps, and back muscles surfaced as the two men easily lifted the back side of his vehicle.   Both agreed she was going to need a wrecker so she would not damage her car any more than it was.

"Lauren, I think its best we call a wrecker service instead of you trying to drive your car anywhere," said Roderick.

"I agree," added Caleb. She pulled out her cell and called her 24 hour car service. "Man why don't you go on home, I'll wait with Lauren since I don't have anyone waiting on me tonight." He said that with much longing and sadness.

"Okay my brother, but remember it won't be long before you have your baby by your side for the rest of your life." They embraced and said goodnight. She took in everything that was said and knew her work was cut out for her. Her grandfather was right, he was deeply in love with Ms McHarding; it was in his voice.

"How long will it be before your service arrives?"

"It usually takes them about thirty minutes,"

"Why don't we sit in my truck while we wait?"

"I hate to put you out Caleb since it's late."

"That's okay; I can spare thirty minutes or so. Anyway why are you out this time of night, late delivery?" She shook her head yes and walked over to his SUV. He held opened the door and then went around to the driver's side. Her lips turned up into a satisfied smile as she watched him walk around to the other side. He turned his ride on to run the air conditioner. This Texas humid weather was getting the best of him especially with this unwanted company robbing him of his time he usually spends with Ruby. Thirty minutes was all she was getting and then he was going to have to excuse himself and call her before she goes to bed.

"So Dr. VanLee, tell me how did you manage to go to a black university?" He looked at her and knew she really wanted to know why he was engaged to a black woman.

"I decided to follow in my family footsteps and attend their alma mater. We are a Prairie View A&M University alumni family." Her strange look told him to make it simple and clear and he told her the entire story of his family background.

"Where did you meet Attorney McHarding?"

He turned to look at her before he answered, she could see the twinkle in his eyes and his enticing dimpled smile as his thoughts channeled in on her. It was his first smile since their encounter. "We met at PVU our freshman year," before he could continue talking about the love of his life flashing red lights shone in his rearview mirror. "Lauren I think your service is here." Thank God she thought, as he got out of the car to open her door. She certainly did not want to hear him sing praises about her. The drivers put her car on the flat bed and then gave her a set of keys to a baby Mercedes. She had some kind of car service and was glad he did not have to take her home, because he had a gut feeling Dr. Lauren Nason caused this whole little scene, just couldn't prove it.

"You're all set Dr. Nason," said one of the drivers. "Do you want us to follow you home?"

"No, that won't be necessary and thank you for bringing me my car." Nobody told them to go by her grandparents' home and get her another car. She had it planned for him to take her home. Oh well, they did get to spend some time together and they would spend more during the weekend.

They both said goodnight and he got in his SUV and waited for her to drive off in the same direction he was going. Surely they didn't live in the same housing complex. They took the same exit and she pulled right up to his security gate of the Shadow Creek Townhouses. Yes, they lived in the same complex, but she took a left and he took a right, what a relief. Lauren Nason waited a few minutes to make sure he was home and inside before she turned around to see which townhouse he lived in. She couldn't believe her luck; they lived in the same complex. Lauren spotted his metallic gold SUV and had the biggest smile on her face as she drove off._____

Caleb looked at his watch and called her anyway so he could hear her voice before he called it a night. "Hi Baby."

"Hi yourself."

"I know it's late I just needed to hear your voice and say I love you before I closed my eyes." He was right, it was late and she had fallen asleep dreaming of him. But she was glad he called so she could hear his voice too.

"Caleb I know it's late but can you sing me a song before we hang up." The biggest smile spread across his face, he hadn't done that since their college days. He serenaded her and her roommate many nights.

"What would you like to hear?"

"Surprise me." And he did just that with the first song he had ever sang to her...a *Teddy Pendergrass* ballad...*And If I Had.* She smiled as she recalled the first time he sang that song which caused tears to flow from her eyes. The lyrics compelled her to tell him that he did have somebody who truly cared and loved him back. That was the very night she declared her love for him and promised to always be there. When he finished singing, she repeated she loved and needed him, wishing they were together so she could show just him how much. They ended their night with settling for the words from their hearts and drifted off to sleep.

CHAPTER 19

Dr. VanLee was in good spirits this fine beautiful morning. He decided last night he would drive to Houston after work and spend the rest of the weekend with Ruby. Yes sireee, thought Caleb as he packed his clothes and other personals. If he had not signed up to work at the clinic this Saturday he never would have left her. It was evident that being apart was only causing sadness between them which was not necessary. Hempstead was just down the street and the beltway was a great help, besides he would be traveling away from the real heavy traffic going and coming. Caleb didn't care since it would only be two weeks._____

Lauren had just hung up with her Grandmother. She couldn't wait to tell her about last night and had called at the crack of dawn. Her Grandmother laughed and called her a little conniving devil. They both agreed it got the job done and she even found out they lived in the same complex. Lauren squealed with that wonderful discovery. She was also able to show her appreciation from last night by sending him an edible fruit basket. With him being raised as a gentleman, she was sure he would give her a thank you call. Lauren Nason had to admit he was going to be quite a challenge since he thought he was in love with her. She has never backed away from a challenge before and with the help of her grandmother and his, she would be the winner.

Grandmother's idea about soliciting the help of her good friend was fantastic and would be perfect in causing a rift between the two lovebirds. What more could you ask for than someone whose family owns the local paper and promised to have pictures taken that would cause suspicion and maybe some mistrust. All they needed to do was provide the scenes and she would have her people take care of the rest._____

Caleb walked through the front doors of the clinic singing which was not the norm for the doctors. They always used the back entrance, but he enjoyed seeing and speaking to the patients. It makes his job that much more inspiring and rewarding. Besides he felt real good and was looking forward to surprising his baby tonight.

"Hi Nephew." Caleb looked around and who did he see but his Aunt Ruth pushing his Great Aunt and his grandmother following behind them.

"Is that my Grandbaby," she asked.

"Aunties, Gram, what a surprise." He walked over and gave each one a big hug and kiss. Aunt Lucille told him his great aunt had an 8:00 appointment. Ever since the clinic opened, Aunt Bea has had her doctor's visits the first thing on a Saturday morning. If they expected her to come on an empty stomach and do blood work, it was best they make sure her appointment was early. He asked them how were they doing? They said fine as they walked over to the desk to make her next appointment. He said good morning told the ladies to take care of his family. Before leaving Gram asked was there anything special he wanted for Sunday dinner. He told her chicken and dumplings and peach cobbler would hit the spot. She smiled because she had already received that request from Tiny and knew they had gotten together. Although his grandmother was in her early eighties she was still active and could make you hurt yourself with her cooking. She had no intentions of disappointing her grandbabies although they were grown adults with children of their own. It was a funny thing they got a kick out of being referred to as her grandbabies especially the adult men.

"See you Sunday Grandbaby." The biggest smile spread across his face, you would think he was a small child. He walked back and gave his Gram another kiss and hug.

"Okay Gram," and disappeared behind the doors. The front staff sat quietly as they observed the genuine love shone between them. They dare not say the obvious and went on with their duties. The three Nicholson Matriarchs shared their private thoughts and took care of their business. They knew everyone was wondering how in the world they were family, the explanation would have to come from him._____

"Mildred Charles, it's so good to see you. How was your flight?" Linda Nason accompanied their driver to pick up the VanLees from the airport. She had instructed her driver to take them to the hospital to meet Charles. They were going to have breakfast with him in the cafeteria. Linda Nason was use to the finest of restaurants and country club cuisines, but nothing beats the scrumptious food served at the hospital cafeteria. It really should change its name to something real fancy because it was that good. She was certainly not going to tell Mildred where they were dinning. They enjoyed the scenic route while passing the time with small talk. She couldn't go into details regarding the recent developments of their little project, but assured her they were making progress._____

Ruby Jewel walked inside the cafeteria / dining room looking like a million bucks and feeling like she was on top of the world. Why wouldn't she, she was marrying the love of her life in two weeks. Ruby had a smile deep inside of her as she recalled last night. He serenaded her with two love songs. His deep baritone voice was still soothing and hypnotizing. He had truly put a spell over her, because she had a good night's sleep and was ready for the day. Humph, she was the first one to arrive at the church except for their security and Bro. Bobby over the kitchen. Yes ma'am she was in good spirits. She even felt like she could endure their little separation for now, but came to the conclusion she didn't have to.

Bro. Bobby had made the coffee and was in the process of preparing a nutritional brunch. Kellie and Nisey had come by earlier and dressed the tables appropriately for the occasion. Her job along with Cynthia and Angela were to facilitate and make the necessary arrangements to make sure it was a success. Cynthia was the commentator and she and Angela were responsible for making sure the presenters' needs were met along with providing the seniors with pertinent information. Ruby knew she was early, but she wanted to start on time so they could leave on time. She had the screen and laptop in place for the presenters and was now waiting on Angela to bring their box of handouts so they could prepare a folder for each senior.

Angela Lacey couldn't believe her eyes; Ruby was already there as she held the door for the brother bringing in the boxes. She just knew she would be late because that Dr. Caleb VanLee was some kind of catch, not only was he a brilliant doctor, a fine and handsome specimen of a man. He was rich and very much in love with him some Ruby Jewel. She didn't see him leaving her last night, not by a long shot. Another lucky sistah, thought Angela as she went inside the church. She could smell the perking coffee brewing and was ready for her fix.

"Are my eyes deceiving me or is this Ruby Jewel McHarding already setting up for the seminar. I thought for sure you would still be at home with Dr. VanLee."

Ruby smiled at her friend. "He left last night with everyone else. Wow, you look real nice and very springy this morning.

"Thanks boss lady and you're mighty sharp yourself. Girlfriend is that new?"

"Only my blouse, you know I can't resist ruffles and cap sleeves. The jewel black tank and purple and black tweed skirt you've seen before. The skirt has a jacket I just switched up for a more casual look.

"Well you truly pulled together an attractive outfit mixing the old with the new. Your mesh jewelry…"

"I know completes the look." The friends laughed and began unpacking the box to make their folders.

"Sistah girl those were some of the finest men I've seen in a long time. I mean every one of them. And all happily married, huh?"

"Yes ma'am happily married with children, except Caleb and he belongs to me"

"Please, everybody could see that even if they were blind. You hit the jackpot my friend and you deserve it."

Ruby looked at her friend of many years and knew where her mind had wondered off to. Lately Ruby had noticed her far away expressions quite a bit lately, and she was well aware of their meanings. Once upon a time she had the love of her life and was living the sistah girl's dream. But he allowed outside forces to get in the way of their happiness and marriage and ended up behind bars. It was obvious she still loved him, but she's made it clear talking about him was off limits. Pretending she didn't care and was over him was ridiculous. Six years and she still could not bring herself to divorce him.

"Angela when's the last time you heard from him?" Although she hesitated a bit, it wasn't any need of her denying anything because Ruby Jewel knew her too well.

"He wrote me a letter two days ago and said he would be up for parole in two months. They moved him somewhere close and he wanted to know if I would come and visit him."

"Why didn't you say something before now? What are you going to do?"

"Ruby, I don't know what to do, he said he never stopped loving me and pleaded with me to give him another chance.

"Wow, you really have something to think about."

"I tell you what, after the seminar we'll spend the rest of the day doing what we like best to clear our heads. Afterwards we can come up with a solution." She rewarded her with a smile that said thanks friend.

CHAPTER 20

The Nasons and VanLees had a delicious meal. Mildred VanLee was utterly shocked when Linda Nason announced at the last minute where they were having breakfast, not the country club but the hospital cafeteria. She actually had to go through a line like she was in some fast food restaurant. It didn't seem to bother the others the least, but she was appalled. She suppressed her vanity and accepted the predicament she was in for the time being. But couldn't believe Caleb Sr. and Charles when they went back through the line for extra pastries to take home, even Linda requested a homemade cinnamon roll. She had to agree whether she wanted to or not, the food was tasty and the décor was unexpected for a hospital lunch room with the atmosphere being relatively pleasant. Overall their breakfast date was enjoyable, and she was now ready to see her grandson.

The driver pulled right up to the clinic's front door and parked. Dr. Nason told him to stay put and not to worry about opening the doors; he would take care of that. He didn't want to block the entrance any longer than they had to because they would be there for a while and it was business hours. The VanLees were going to have a grand tour of both facilities. The front desk receptionist recognized Dr. Nason and his wife and alerted the skeleton crew that he was there.

Although the staff was always about the business of the clinic and performed their duties well, it didn't hurt to be aware VIPs were on the premises. The older black gentleman, who was the day security, met them and welcomed all to the clinic. Dr. Nason has always been a down to earth guy thought Andy. They shake hands every time they see each other, after all Hempstead was a small town. His wife on the other hand was a snob and he knew her friend wasn't much better.

Dr. Nason stepped in the doorway speaking as always. "Hello Andy, how's life treating you?"

"Pretty good Dr. Nason, good morning Mrs. Nason and company." He tipped his hat.

"Andy, I would like for you to meet Dr. and Mrs. VanLee Sr." The smile on his face said he recognized the last name. He knew the story behind Dr. VanLee's family background but he kept it to himself.

"It's a pleasure." He shook the older gentleman's hand and tipped his hat once again.

"It's a pleasure meeting you Andy. Is my grandson doing a good job here?"

"Yes sir, he's a fine doctor and the staff and patients have fallen in love with him. He's making his family very proud. As a matter of fact his Grandmother Nicholson and aunties were here early this morning. Ms. Bea had her annual check-up. I know he'll be..."

"Please don't say anything to him it's a surprise," interrupted his grandmother with a scolding uppity tone. He knew he had ruffled her feathers real good when he mentioned his black family. He knew all about Mrs. Mildred VanLee. Andy pretended to zip his lips and told them to have a nice visit and walked off to assist a patient being transported by ambulance service.

Dr. Nason walked around the facility greeting and introducing the VanLees. He was very pleased to show off his pride and joy. Then they walked to the area where his doctors and medical team carried out their excellent care. Mrs. VanLee was anxious and wanted to see her grandson and his office. Dr. Nason inquired at the nurse's station whether or not he was available to have visitors. They were told he was not at the clinic at the moment. He was on an emergency home visit. While the nurse was explaining his whereabouts Dr. Alford stepped out of an examining room.

"Drs., Mrs. Nason, and Mrs. VanLee what a pleasant surprise; Caleb didn't say you were in the city." She hugged the men and then the women. Mildred VanLee hasn't changed one bit with her snooty ways, she thought.

"He does not know, we were trying to surprise him," said Dr. VanLee.

"Good, he just called a few minutes ago and said everything was under control and he would be in shortly. We're so happy to have him join our staff he's offering a service that's so well needed. He's such a wonderful and nurturing doctor and. You should be very proud of him. "

"We are proud of him. I just don't understand."

"Grandmother! Grandfather! I can't believe it. When did you get here?" He hugged and kissed his grandmother and then hugged his grandfather. "I still can't believe you're actually here. Come on let me take you to my office. Oh, wait

175

a minute let me introduce you to my nurse and PA." After the introductions he turned to his grandparents and told them he was glad they were here, but what was the occasion.

"Caleb darling, we decided to come for Charles's birthday celebration and stay until the wedding." It never dawned on him that they would come for Dr. Nason's celebration.

"Well that's great. That means you'll be here two whole weeks."

"That's right," said his grandmother excitedly. All he could do was smile, because he knew something was up.

"Dr. VanLee we hate to leave good company but I want to take your grandparents to the center. I know it's almost twelve, so we'll leave and let you wrap up your day."

"Grandfather before you go, where's your luggage so I can put it in my SUV."

"Son that won't be necessary, we're staying with the Nason's for a few days. Then we will spend the remainder of our visit with you." He was convinced for sure his grandmother and Mrs. Nason were up to something that involved Lauren Nason.

"Okay Grandfather I'll see you after I get off." Dang, he had his own bag packed and in his vehicle. He had made plans to spend the evening with Ruby. His grandfather noticed his strange expression and asked was there a problem? Caleb shook his head and said nothing, because he knew his grandmother would have a *"hissy fit"* as Gram would say, if he tried leaving. He knew Ruby was busy making the final arrangements for their wedding and had some church work to do. He would just have to suffer and be alone for a couple of more days, but he was going to get one thing straight with his grandmother once and for all about his personal life. Butt out!_____

"Baby you won't believe who's here in Hempstead at this very moment." No hello or I love you and he didn't give her a chance to give an answer before he blurted out his grandparents from Denver. Ruby couldn't believe it herself, the VanLees were here and staying until the wedding, he told her the only good thing is that they are staying with the Nasons."

"Well that's good Caleb, isn't it?"

"Baby are you for real? You know how my grandmother is. She hasn't changed at all and I don't feel up to her drama with Linda Nason as her accomplice making these two weeks difficult.

"Oh Sweetie it can't be that bad."

"Take my word, it's that bad. You know she has a granddaughter and grandmother has already set us up as dinner dates tonight at the old mansion supper club. Ruby Jewel McHarding I'm telling you I'm not having it."

"Calm down Sweetie." She knew when he said her whole name he was vexed.

"I don't want to calm down. You know I love my grandparents, but Ruby I smell trouble. Aunt Bea, Aunt Lucille and Gram were also here this morning. Dang that means I won't get any of the chicken and dumplings Gram is fixing for Sunday. Uh uhn, no ma'am, that knucklehead Tiny is going to pack everything he can't eat."

"Caleb if you don't stop. Call your grandmother and ask her to take some out for you and put it in the freezer and you can have it later."

"You can't freeze chicken and dumplings Baby!"

Ruby saw she was not getting anywhere with him. He was upset and in rare form. "Caleb, didn't you say they were staying until the wedding?"

"Yes Baby."

"Well, why can't you go to your Gram's tomorrow and come back after you hang out with your cousins? You do have two whole weeks to be with them. Invite them to worship with you."

"You know what, that's a great idea. Thanks for thinking for me Baby. That's why I love and need you by my side." He felt better, but was still a bit agitated about the whole situation, them showing up and surprising him.

"I love you too Caleb and wish I was there so I could hold you and kiss away those ugly frowns," she said softly. She had him down pack and knew he had a sourpuss appearance for sure. Those were the words he needed to hear as he gradually calmed down with a smile slowly spreading across his handsome face. "Feel better now?"

"A little."

"Caleb VanLee, what am I going to do with you?"

"Repeat what you said."

"Caleb I love you and wish you were here or me there with you. Be patient Sweetie, we'll be together soon. Now stop your whining and get your mind set to have dinner with your grandparents and be polite to your boss's granddaughter. *I'm sending you a kiss...you can put it where you want it...boy I understand what you're going through so I want you to have this kiss...Remember, I love you and I love you... I'll text you during dinner.*" They both burst into laughter after she completed her borrowed tunes.

"Girl, I love you and can't wait to get my kiss and hold you in my arms."

"I know Sweetie me too, love you." He felt better and was ready to handle whatever.

Angela watched her faraway look when she disconnected. She had traveled back to a dark unpleasant time. "He has the *I miss yous* bad, uh? And I must add you're crazy."

"I am not and yes he does...plus he's a mess, but that's my *Boo* and I love him. Come on let's get the ice cream to eat with our cake so we can help you reach a decision about your *Boo*." Ruby was well aware of how overpowering his grandparents could be and especially his grandmother when she's trying to have her way, but not this time. They weren't twenty-one and right out of college still in the process of furthering their education to obtain the career goals they aspired. Neither does he have anything to lose because he now has accomplished a rewarding and successful career in addition to having full control of his inheritance.

CHAPTER 21

Mrs. VanLee tried her best to get him to ride in the limo with them to dinner, but he flatly refused. Caleb was meeting them at the mansion for a late supper. He tried hard to get out of it but as usual his grandmother put a guilt trip on him. She even tried with the help of Mrs. Nason to have him pick up Lauren. God was on his side, one of her patients went into labor.

Caleb pulled up to the front of the establishment and gave his keys to the attendant. He hated supper clubs that insisted on a man wearing a coat and tie. That's why he and Ruby loved the Golden Regal Mansion; you only had to be practical in your dress. They allowed you to be comfortable while enjoying a great meal. Tonight he was dressed for the occasion because he did like to please his grandmother to a certain degree. He was wearing his basic black suit and shoes, with a dark plum silk t-shirt. Entering the door, he was greeted by a beautiful honey complexioned hostess dressed in a black cocktail dress.

"Welcome sir to the Golden Regal Mansion. Are you alone?"

"Thank you and no, I'm with Dr. Nason's party."

"Very good sir, please follow me." Caleb followed the cute little hostess to an empty table. He wondered why they were not there yet and if they didn't arrive soon he was going to start without them. The food was delicious and he was looking forward to having a fine meal. "Sir would you like something from the bar while you wait for your party?"

"Yes, I'll have a lemon-berry twister and I would like to see a menu now." The waitress looked at him a bit puzzled but granted his request. He pulled his coat off and hung it on the stand beside their table. His cell vibrated, it was his grandmother.

Caleb couldn't believe the nerve of his grandmother and her friend. They'll be a little late because they were picking up Lauren and hurriedly said she was only down the street. He knew where it was and what they were up to since they both lived in Shadow Creek. If they think he's going to wait on them to eat they were foolishly wrong. He got the waitress attention and told her he was ready to start with the first course of his meal.

The neighbors who lived next door to Ruby's parents walked in with his grandparents and the Nasons. He greeted them and made introductions. They congratulated him on his upcoming marriage and said they were looking forward to the wedding. They said their good evenings and followed their hostess. Before he could help his grandmother with her seat she started.

"Caleb are you sure you are not rushing into this marriage while you're still settling into your job?"

"Grandmother we have been through this before and I don't intend to wait another day passed the two weeks I had to grudgingly give Ruby." He returned to his chair which was now between her and Lauren, making him feel like a sandwich. "Grandmother I love her and need her by my side. For years you have harassed me to marry and have children, well that's exactly what I'm doing."

"*But Grandson.*" He shushed her and leaned over to kiss her rosy cheek and told her to be happy for him because he was bursting with joy and couldn't wait to start his new life with her.

"Well Son, I'm thrilled for the both of you. I can see happiness all over your face and I've noticed your new peaceful state and we both wish you the best." Dr. Caleb gently patted his wife's hand.

"Thanks Grandfather, now ladies, I must say you three look beautiful tonight in your conservative black." All three thanked him for the compliment. They did look nice including Lauren. She was attractive, he thought but didn't compare to his Ruby. "Can we eat because I'm hungry enough to eat a..." He looked at his grandmother and decided not to finish what he was going to say, wrong group...

Dinner was wonderful and he had to give it to his grandmother she was very civil and on her best behavior. Mrs. Nason and Lauren became solemn when she started showing an interest in his wedding and asked questions. Of course he really couldn't answer some of the questions; he only knew the basic information colors, place, and time. He told her Ruby had made plans to come home Tuesday so they could have lunch and go over the particulars. She seemed interested and a bit excited but he couldn't let his guard down yet. They spent the remainder of the evening talking about their week and the activities that would take place for the birthday celebration. During so, he received his text with some excellent news; Ruby would be able to attend the birthday bash after all. Dr. Nason and his grandfather seemed to be thrilled with his announcement, but disappointment quickly clouded the faces of the females and he definitely understood why. He would not be available for Lauren Nason to hang on his arm like she was doing tonight. She's touched and caressed him throughout the night including rubbing against his leg.

"Dr. Nason, can I get a picture of your family and guests?"

"Of course," answered Mrs. Nason.

"Move in a little closer please," requested the photographer, which really wasn't necessary. But it did give Lauren an excuse to practically be in his lap with her cheek plastered to his face, and her breast against his chest. "Thanks, I'll see you around."

"Good people I'm ready to call it a night." He was full and ready to hit the sack. His grandmother protested saying they haven't had their coffee and dessert."

"Grandmother, I couldn't eat or drink another thing. My dessert will have to be a carry out." The waitress appeared as if he had summoned her with his homemade chocolate cake. He knew that didn't set too well with her but she's used to him carrying out a doggy bag. "I have to drive to Bellville in the morning for worship and then I want to spend a little time with Uncle Pete. Aunt Ruth said he complained of having a pain in his chest and I want to examine him since they can't get him to come in to the clinic."

"You mean to tell me that old man is still living."

"Yes Grandmother," said Caleb annoyingly.

"I didn't mean it like that Caleb, it's just that he should be a hundred years old at least."

"He's ninety-eight and still going strong and I want to make sure he stays that way for a long time."

"But I thought we would go to service together with the Nasons."

"Since you'll be here for two weeks we'll go next Sunday." He got his suit coat and kissed her goodnight and hugged his grandfather who was now standing. "I'll see everyone tomorrow evening if it's the Lord's will. Goodnight." He left without giving them a chance to say another word including give Lauren a ride home. As he was leaving the table a group of ladies passed by greeting him with flirtatious remarks and big grins, two were Soros. He acknowledged them with a smile and hugs; spoke to the other three and continued on his way._____

"You're on your way to Hempstead, what happened to ladies bible class?"

"Girl it was canceled so some of the sisters could accompany their husbands to Barret Station's homecoming. A recorded message was sent out Friday, but with everything going on I hadn't checked my messages and neither did you. Mr. Green also left a message and said the invitations would be ready Monday evening. We can go ahead with our party after work for Tuesday, be sure to order something everyone would like for dinner and charge it to my personal account."

"I'll pick up the invitations since it's on my way." Ruby smiled at her friend as she cleared her cell.

Cell phone. "Momma I was just about to call to let you know that I was on my way home, hold on, I got another call, I'm sorry that was Caleb there's been a change of plans."

"Ruby, I called you about this Sunday's paper."

"What about this morning's paper?"

"There's a picture with Caleb and some white woman by the name of **Lauren Nason**!" They said her name together. "I know Momma; he called this morning to tell me before I got there. You don't have to worry, Caleb VanLee belongs to me."

"Alright then, you still need to watch your back. Mildred VanLee and that Linda Nason had approving smiles plastered on their lily white faces."

"Momma!"

"Ruby I'm sorry I don't care for either one with their uppity airs. How long will it be before you get here?"

"As soon as I get Caleb, we'll be on our way. All the arrangements for the wedding have been completed. The invitations will be ready Monday, my girls and I will address and mail them out no later than Wednesday. What's for dinner?"

"Your father had a taste for chicken and dumplings."

"You're kidding, so does Caleb. That's what his Gram fixed for their Sunday family dinner at his request, but he didn't get a chance to eat any due to the emergency."

"Well I can't say mine is as good as his grandmother's, but my family seems to enjoy them."

"Momma please, your chicken and dumplings are delicious and daddy's peach cobbler is to die for."

"Oh he wants peach cobbler too?"

"No, I do."

"Okay Baby, I'll tell your daddy and we'll see you soon." They said their goodbyes while she took her exit, recalling his instructions.

"Hi, I'm Ruby McHarding and would like to see Dr. VanLee." Six pairs of amazed eyes stared her up and down. He told them his fiancée would be arriving shortly. She wanted to look down at her top to see if she was exposing any more flesh than usual but decided not to.

"Ms McHarding, Dr. VanLee asked me to give you his personal belongings." She thanked the receptionist and found an empty seat. His cell rung, it was his grandfather.

"Hi Dr. VanLee this is Ruby, how are you?"

"Ruby, I'm doing great, I'm really looking forward to seeing you though. Caleb said you were coming for a short visit. Where are you two?"

"We're at Memorial; he rode in the ambulance with…"

"Is his Uncle Pete alright?"

"Oh yes sir, he's fine. He brought in the neighbor and he's now with the family. Evidently he left his SUV at his uncle's and asked me to swing by the hospital to pick him up. As soon as we leave my parents' we'll be over."

"Great Ruby and be sure to tell your family I said hello."

"I will sir and tell Mrs. VanLee I said the same."

"Ruby."

"Yes Dr. VanLee?"

"Thanks for loving and making my grandson so happy. I already see the change in him. He's at peace now and loves you so much. I'm so sorry we interfered before and I hope you will find it in your heart to forgive us."

"Dr. VanLee please don't even think about that. That's the past. I'm just so thankful we're getting a second chance. And thank you sir for," he interrupted her with a request.

"I think it's time you to start calling me Grandfather, Granddaughter." Mildred walked into the room.

"Okay Grandfather, see you soon."

"Caleb was that our grandson?"

Caleb Sr. got up from his seat, "No dear, our soon to be granddaughter." He kissed her cheek and asked if lunch was ready. She knew that subject was closed after their conversation last night. When he saw the pictures in the local newspaper he was not pleased at and expressed clearly when they had their long talk. She was strongly warned about interfering or causing any kind of trouble in any way. He took her by the hand and they went downstairs to join the Nasons._____

Caleb walked through the doors and spotted her. Ruby smiled when she looked up and saw him walking toward her. Sexy he was in his dark gray slacks and pearl gray collarless dress shirt. He had his sleeves rolled up and the first two buttons were undone.

"Hi Baby." He kissed her lips and reached for his medical saddlebag to put over his shoulder. He caught her hand and they walked out the door.

"How's your patient?"

"He's well as could be expected. He suffered a stroke and has a few complications along with some paralysis. He'll have to stay for a little while and have some rehabilitation, but he'll be good as new. Baby I'm hungry; I haven't had anything but a breakfast sandwich and juice."

"I am too so let's hurry and get to my parents'." She reached him the keys.

"Sounds like a plan." He opened and closed her door and went around to the driver's side. Her family's home was about twenty-five minutes away. He was glad when she called and said she was on her way home and could visit with his grandparents to go over the details for their wedding. Needless to say he was still upset with his grandmother and the Nason women, and hadn't planned to set eyes on them at all today. He had made up his mind to settle for a carryout from the hospital cafeteria and go to the townhouse and wait for his cousins to bring him his SUV. Caleb couldn't get over the nerve of the photographer and columnist insinuating he was *an eligible bachelor and well worth staking a claim. But Dr. Lauren Nason seems to have him in her clutch. Are they the latest promising couple? We'll just have to wait and see won't we.* When Caleb saw the morning paper he was furious and fit to be tied. He first called his grandfather who assured him he had taken care of his grandmother and warned her there would be some serious consequences if she causes any more trouble. Then he called Ruby to let her know so she would not be surprised when she sees it. He knew someone would make sure she gets a copy.

"You're mighty quiet. Are you worried about Mr. Craig?"

"No Baby, he's really going to be fine. Since I was there, I was able to give him some medicine to reverse the stroke which kept him from enduring anymore damages. I was thinking of that picture in the newspaper."

"Caleb, now you know that woman wants you and..."

"Well she *sho can't lickey split hav* me."

"Alright Uncle Pete."

"I did sound just like him, huh?" He had that appreciative grin on his face. He loved him some Uncle Pete and could mark him to the *T*. Whenever he and his cousins got together they always had him to imitate their favorite uncle. "Finally," he announced pulling in her parents drive. He noticed two other vehicles and knew her siblings were also there. "Come on Baby before your greedy brother eats up everything." She laughed because he was right about Junior. But her mother assured her it would be plenty.

CHAPTER 22

They had a wonderful visit with her family and a delicious dinner and were now on their way to the Nason's ranch. Junior and Caleb made a pig of themselves and certainly inflated her mother's ego in her cooking abilities. She now ranked with the best of them according to Caleb. Every pot and serving bowl had been scraped and licked clean thanks to those two who volunteered to wash the dishes. Her family was very impressed with how good he was in cleaning. They were well entertained by him with his stories of growing up with Vera and Ruth Nicholson as teachers. They both made it clear he was going to have survival skills regardless of him being a golden child as they put it. He said he had endured hard labor whenever he visited his Aunt Ruth and appreciates to this day her sternness....

They drove through the Nason's gate and followed the winding drive to the ranch which was truly something to see. It was a beautiful two story ranch home right out of a picture book for a western movie surrounded by lush landscaped gardens, massive shade trees, and a huge wrap around gallery with outdoor furniture and ceiling fans. There were also horse stables, corals, a huge barn, and green pastures for miles. It was truly a magnificent showplace.

"This is something, huh?"

"If you have to have this much space, I prefer Lincoln's farmhouse any day. Come on so we can get this over with." Oh, he was already getting himself worked up as he parked and came over to open her door. She handed him her satchel and pulled him close to her. He caught her around her waist.

She reached and caressed his face, "Promise me you'll be on your best behavior."

"I will if..." She silenced him with a gentle kiss. That wasn't enough, he thought as he reclaimed her lips with an intense thirst for more. Catching their breaths, he said, "I promise." She tried to wipe her lipstick from his lips with him kissing her fingertips. Their shared smiles said later, as he took her hand and walked to the front door and rang the doorbell.

The door was opened by a middle aged woman who welcomed them to the Nason's home and then escorted them to the family room where everyone was lounging. His grandfather and Dr. Nason met them at the entrance.

"Caleb and Ruby welcome to our home," said Dr. Nason, shaking his hand and giving her a hug. "I must say you two make a stunning couple and Ruby you look very lovely." They were well coordinated in their yellow and gray. Her belted floral sheath fit perfectly stopping above her knees showing curves and legs. You'd thought they had called each other and said what they were wearing. They even had on gray shoes; of course she had on her faithful crisscross comforts with pearl flower buttons to dress them up.

"I agree," said Dr. Caleb. "Come here and give your

future grandfather a hug and a kiss." There was truly something special about her, he thought. Not only was she going to be a wife in a few days, he had a strong feeling motherhood was next; at least he secretly suspected as much and could only hope.

She thanked both older gentlemen as she embraced her future grandfather. They all walked over to where the women were sitting. Caleb hugged and kissed his grandmother and Mrs. Nason. He spoke to Lauren.

"Ruby let me introduce you to the woman that still has my heart all tied up after fifty-five years of marriage, Linda Nason and you know my granddaughter Lauren." Mrs. Nason told her husband to stop with his foolishness as she blushed like a teenager. Ruby kissed his grandmother on the cheek and spoke to the Nason women. Mrs. Nason offered them some refreshments. Ruby declined with a pleasant no thank you, but Caleb said he would love something. She couldn't believe he actually had room for more, after he and her brother made a pig of themselves at her parents'. Mrs. Nason asked Mrs. Perez to make sandwiches from the leftover roast beef and ham, and bring them with lemonade and cake. She knew her husband would also be ready for his Sunday evening snack.

"Well now, I understand congratulations are in order. You two are getting married." They both said thank you and he held out her hand to show off her ring and told them it was his mother's. Mrs. VanLee had to swallow her emotions. She was the one that helped their son design that ring. Both Calebs noticed her disapproval expression, but thought the best thing to do was ignore it. Caleb 3rd didn't hesitate to reveal his mother's wishes for him to give her jewelry to the woman he chooses to share his life with. He also told them he had an exquisite heirloom charm bracelet with an angel that was to be given at the birth of their first born. He looked at Ruby and held up two fingers with a dimpled grin. She smiled back and held up four fingers. He mouthed thank you Baby and kissed her hand. All eyes watched their affectionate love play.

His cell rang it was Tiny, who was bringing his ride with Doug. Since they were about ten minutes away from the ranch he asked Dr. Nason if they could drop his vehicle off to him, that way he wouldn't have to leave. He told him of course and directed them straight to the ranch. Mrs. Perez rolled in a cart with the refreshments.

"Baby, show Grandmother your wedding portfolio while I eat a bite." Humph, she knew it would be more than a bite, shaking her head. She pulled it out and asked Mrs. Nason and Lauren, if they would like to see also? She was not trying to be presumptuous, but she didn't want to leave them out. Most women loved looking at wedding pictures, at least she did. They said they would and she got up to sit between the senior women and Lauren sat on the table in front of them.

"Wait Lauren, don't sit on today's paper," said Mrs. Nason. She tried picking it up with one hand and dropped it on the floor intentionally. The page with the pictures was folded down and visible. The older men froze.

"Oh let me see Mrs. Nason, Caleb told me about them." Ruby took the paper and admired the pictures and read the caption. "I must say Lauren you look gorgeous. I love your dress." She also told the grandmothers how ravishing they were with their handsome men by their sides. "Is that why they have big smiles and look at my *Boo*, he's definitely a

GQ man, handsome and debonair." She looked at him and winked, "Sweetie, you are going to have to put the word out that you are spoken for now," as she wiggled her ring finger.

"I will Baby," he mumbled between chews. She gave the paper to Lauren to do whatever and opened up her binder. Ruby explained her perfectionist office manager was responsible for all the extra frills, title page and table of contents. She also had it sectioned off with dividers and captions and pictures to let you know what you were going to see.

"I would like to see your dress," said Mrs. Nason. She turned to that section and showed them what she was going to wear.

"You've already had your picture taken in your dress," asked Lauren in a raised voice.

"Not professionally, my sister took these with her cell and had them enlarged to put in my album."

"Is this really a wedding dress or just a formal?" Dr. Nason put his sandwich down to say something, because he knew his granddaughter but Caleb shook his head and whispered she can handle herself well.

"It's what I'm going to use as a wedding dress Lauren. It's elegant and very chic, don't you think." She didn't wait for her to respond. "Surely you didn't expect me to have a ball gown with layers of tulle with my size." Lauren had a smug look on her face because that was going to be her next smart remark. But she was not to be out done while her grandmother and Mrs. VanLee continued to examine every detail of her wedding ensemble.

"Well at least you chose a dress that does not show your true size, and it seems to be slenderizing."

"Thank you Lauren I think it flows perfectly myself, that was one of the features I loved about the dress."

"Ruby, your dress does not have a train, does your veil have one," complained his grandmother. "You probably wouldn't have been able to find a formal wedding dress in your size at this late date anyway. But the dress is beautiful," she hurried up and said because the men now had disapproving frowns. They had done nothing but criticized, but she was still holding her own.

Ruby told her she was right about finding something on that line at this late date. But her dream dress just happened to be tea length and actually made on this style except this was not quite her color choice but she fell in love with the other features. She never wanted a long drawn out train nor veil especially at her age. By that time his grandfather and Mr. Nason got up to see and came to the conclusion they were just being plain mean.

"Ruby, you're absolutely gorgeous. You're going to make a beautiful bride."

"Let me see and I'll be the judge," announced Caleb."

"You can't see her in her dress that's bad luck and you're going to need all the luck you can get."

"Mildred," exclaimed his grandfather, "that's enough!"

"Oh Caleb, I'm speaking of them only having a short time to plan everything."

"She's right Grandfather, we were pressed for time but

believe it or not we have everything under control. Even the invitations will be ready tomorrow and my girls and I are going to address and send them off this week although we've notified everyone by phone, text, and e-mail."

"Sounds like you two do have it all together," said Dr. Nason, "and I agree with Caleb, you're going to make a beautiful bride and Son, you're very lucky."

"Thank you sir, that's exactly how I feel." He walked over and kissed her in front of them, because she had truly been picked on. Mrs. Perez came in to announce he had company at the front door. Dr. Nason told her to bring them in.

Tiny and Doug entered speaking. Caleb introduced his first cousins to the Nasons after they gave his grandparents a hug. Ruby watch his grandmother blush when the two cousins told her she hadn't aged one day since the last time they saw her which had been at least ten years ago.

"Would you fellows like some refreshments, we were having a little something."

"Cuz you need to try one of these roast beef sandwiches, taste like Papa's beef."

"I'm sure it does since my stock is from his breed and I buy my feed only from your father." Dr. Nason recognized him from the paper when they did a write up about their family business being one of the oldest in the county.

"Why you're the Charles Nason, of the C&N Ranch."

"That's me."

"It's a pleasure to finally meet you sir. Our grandfather

talks about you all the time."

"Hey, if his grandsons are anything like their grandfather you fellows can shoot a mean game of pool and tries hard to rule the domino's table."

All three cousins slapped hands and said, "Try, we rule."

"Fellows let's go out to the man cave and have a little fun. Liny have Maria fix some more refreshments and I'll send Hosea in to get them."

"Baby."

"Sweetie go ahead, as soon as I finish showing the ladies the rest of our plans I'll be leaving, I don't want to get home too late."

"Are you sure?"

"Of course I am."

He walked over and pulled her up to his chest declaring his love. His cousins began making smacking noises. He looked over at them and asked for his package Gram sent.

"Dang," said Tiny, "it's in your ride." He was about to

Dr. Nason told them they could put his care package in the barn's refrigerator. He kissed her lips then both cheeks. She whispered he had an audience. Ignoring her remark he winked and held her closer. He could feel her heart beating and it wasn't because she was excited from his kiss. Caleb knew she was afraid of what he was going to do in front of everyone. And she did have something to get embarrassed about, because he did believe in caressing her backside or breasts whenever they shared a kissed. Easing her mind he reached in his pocket to get her keys. Giving them to her with another kiss, "I'll call you later tonight, drive carefully." The men gave Ruby a hug said goodbye to the other women and followed Dr. Nason.

Ruby sat back down and shared the rest of her portfolio pictures. She told Mrs. Nason the grandmothers were wearing street or tea length dresses in shades of gold. Then she asked Mrs. VanLee whether or not she had found something to her likening which was a mistake. She didn't hesitate to say she brought a dress she's had for some time that would do since the wedding was last minute. Ruby ignored her remarks and continued sharing her pictures of how the banquet hall and cocktail area were going to be decorated for the occasion. No one had any comments or anymore insults which was fine with her and best. It wasn't promised whether or not she would be diplomatic the next time. When she finished sharing to her surprise the ladies thanked her. She expressed it was her pleasure and pulled out her key ring. Mrs. VanLee went ballistic!

Her voice was elevated and high pitched. "He gave you his mother's diamond key ring too? I bought that key ring myself for Caleb Jr. to give to Bianca. I can't believe he would give it to you." She said *to you so nasty.* She wanted to tell her the sterling silver jewelry she was wearing belonged to her too, but she didn't.

Instead, Ruby stood and took a deep breath before responding. "Mrs. VanLee it was her wish for him to give her jewelry to the woman he loves and plans to spend the rest of his life with; that's me. I just don't understand, I've done everything you and Dr. VanLee asked me to do. I've spent fifteen years of my life without him, wishing all the time things had been different. We are back together and I thank

God for that. We feel blessed to get this second chance and I love your grandson more than life itself. I know you are aware of that. I'm not so gullible in knowing I'm not your choice and you have someone else in mind for him," looking furiously at Lauren. "It will never ever happen! And Lauren, I strongly advise you to back off because I assure you, you don't want to deal with me."

"How dare you, that sounds like a threat!" exclaimed Mrs. VanLee.

She was trembling inside, but her tone was sharp and powerful. "No ma'am, that's a certified promise," she said giving Lauren that sistah girl angry stare down.

"We will not tolerate such insolence from you."

"Mrs. VanLee you're the reason for my insolence as you put it. But let me say this again and make it clear, I am the woman your grandson chose," pointing to herself. "And I plan to spend the rest of my life as Mrs. Caleb VanLee 3rd making him happy and being the best wife for him. Now I don't know what you have against me, surely it's not because of my color or is it?" Mrs. VanLee glared at her and was about to say something when she saw Caleb walking in. He needed to get his saddlebag before she left for home.

"That's a perfectly good question Grandmother; I would also like to hear the answer." Ruby whirled around to look him dead in the face. She wondered how much did he hear, but didn't ask. Of course his grandmother immediately started making her the villain.

"Caleb, did you hear the way she…" he held his hand to silence her.

"Don't even try it Grandmother. And I want to know what do you have against her because if it has anything to do with…"

"Caleb please, you know better than that. I am not a racist and I resent her even suggesting such. I have lots of black friends and you know I love Vera and Lawrence dearly they're family. She's trying to cause conflict between us." She wiped make believe tears to get his sympathy.

"Grandmother then what's the problem?"

"There is no problem I asked about her key chain and she jumped to all kinds of conclusions and insinuations."

"Grandmother listen to me carefully, I don't want you asking her about any of my mother's jewelry and anything else I give her of my mother's. All of my parents' possessions belong to me. Please make this the last time you question her, ask me because she's only accepting these gifts from me. And because they are my mother's, she understands how precious they are and she's just as precious. When you hurt her Grandmother you're hurting me also. If you love me, and I know you do, please refrain from doing so in the future. This is the woman I plan to spend the rest of my life with and be the mother of my children, your great-grandchildren." His voice cracked, as he caught her hand. They told everyone good evening, and walked to the front door without waiting for their responses. All three sat with ridiculous expressions on their faces all for different reasons.

CHAPTER 23

In general all was well and going according to schedule. The engaged couple was still engaged regardless Sunday mishap or his grandmother and her entourage's behaviors. As if that wasn't enough, just this past Monday Mrs. VanLee tried to set Caleb up as Lauren Nason's date for the spring fling dance at the senior citizen center, but the surprise was on them when she showed up. In spite of everything, they had a wonderful time socializing and entertaining the seniors. It was a sixties party with their music and dress. A karaoke machine had been purchased and the seniors had a great time participating. She and Caleb came as Peaches and Herb and did one of their love songs that brought the house down....

Ruby couldn't believe they were coming up on the last Friday in March and actually had eight days before their big day. It has been two weeks since the engagement and all the wedding preparations had been completed with invitations mailed, keepsakes were ready, flowers and cakes ordered and paid for, in addition to obtaining marriage licenses that she was still carrying around. All they were doing now was waiting to say the words *"I Do."* She even had two *Passion Lanier* suits for the day after her wedding that she took home. She was leaving it up to her mother to make the final decision, because she couldn't. Both selections were figure flattering and simply gorgeous, and she looked good in both! She had enough and was now becoming anxious along with her girls, which was unexpected.

She and Caleb kept themselves pretty busy between their jobs and their little rendezvous besides the time spent with his grandparents. Meeting whenever and where ever had kept them on the go…the center, dinner, a movie, and their favorite truck spot had worked out in their favor. They even managed to attend a concert in the park and jazz night at the mansion. On those occasions she spent the night at her parents. He protested and it was difficult for her too. But she assured him with time zooming by they could hold out till their wedding night.

Both were also involved in new projects. Caleb was in the process of submitting a proposal for additional clinical services and evening activities for the center. Since the spring fling was such a hit he thought they could offer more which would provide the seniors with daily social gatherings and a break for their caretakers a couple of hours in the evening. She personally prepared the necessary information needed and had contacted Jalen Dalton to develop the proposal. He was elated to take on the project and refused to give a fee which surprised her. He told her it was for old times' sake and he wanted to show his appreciation for her recommending him for the new position he now holds. She let him know under no uncertain terms he was the best and as far as she was concerned he was another innocent black man that had been the fall guy for corporate corruption._____

"Ruby, Mr. Baines is on line two."

"Thank you, Celia. Mr. Baines what can I do for you?"

She handled their problem practically the day they presented the situation. It just so happens she knew the law firm well that was trying to make a case against the brothers. When she contacted them she made it clear they didn't have a valid argument and legal actions would be taken against them in a lawsuit for several violations of the brothers' constitutional rights if they didn't take care of the matter ASAP. She knew she had ruffled homeboy's feathers but they knew better and was very much aware of her wrath. When she finished they were able to settle out of court with a nice little settlement for the brothers which had come as a surprise to them, but not her. They were expecting a long drawn out battle, but she didn't believe in such if she could prevent it. Humph, that's what she was known for and was good at it. This firm knew her capabilities well and did not want to tangle with her when they knew they did not have a defense of any kind.

Well that was nice of him, she thought as she hung the phone up; he had such a nice voice that grabs at you when you least expect. He called to thank her once again and informed her they had received their settlement and a letter of apology. He expressed how he and his brother were still surprised in the short time it took for them to agree to her demands. With four letters written in just two months on their stationery was enough ammunition for them to cut a check the day she called, but she kept that to herself. She expressed her appreciation for him calling and told him to do something nice for himself.

Angela walked in with her two purple roses that she's been receiving every day since she left Hempstead Sunday evening. Each rose was a reminder of how much she's missed and loved.

"You ready to leave yet?"

"Yes, as soon as I get my bag. Is everyone else gone for the weekend?" Angela told her all but their new clerk who was closing down the front office as she held the door open for her. They now had three new full time employees and a fourth was expected after she gets married. A college student would work with the data base network service along with her fulltime employer who she's still in training. Her mind had been made up concerning coming in the office two days a week; especially since she and her brother-in-law were going into business. She presented him her brainstorm of selecting a portion of his land and for a camping site for RV's and campers. He thought it was a fantastic idea since a creek ran through his land as well as a little cabin in excellent condition located on the property. It would be perfect for a caretaker. Her new employee, who's working under Destiny, had been given her first assignment. She was to develop a proposal for their camping site venture and present it to them. This was the same technique her mentor used to train her and knew it was an effective method. If she did this well Ruby knew she was capable of handling McHarding's business and client's.

This was the last Friday in the month and they were expecting a full weekend. Tonight was movie night at the center and Dr. Nason's birthday celebration was tomorrow. As Ruby and Angela walked to the front, they noticed Kellie was sitting in their van. They were also going home for the weekend. Kellie had told her Gregory's grandparents and aunts had requested a visit to take turns keeping the triplets for the entire weekend. Of course they were indecisive and thought that was a bit much. Ruby was the one who convinced them to at least give it a try, she and Gregory could use a break. Kellie had been quiet these last few days and when she questioned her if something was wrong she replied no, but yes was written all over her face.

"Hey girl, you're still here, where are my munchkins," asked Ruby?

"They're with their daddy. I left my bag and they went back to get it. Lately, I can't seem to get it together. I don't know what's wrong with me." She was tearing up and wiped her eyes.

"Sweetie don't, you're taking care of three babies and have done an excellent job where other mothers have only one at a time," said Ruby.

"That's what Gregory said." She was now crying. Ruby opened her door to console her.

"Come on Sweetie, it's going to be alright. You're just having mood swings and that's what women go through at certain times of the month." Gregory came out with his little army and rushed over to her side.

"Baby what's wrong?" The little people sensed something was wrong and started calling for their mommy. Ruby, Angela, and Ann each took a child and walked back inside to give him a few minutes to console her. "Sweetheart talk to me, what can I do?"

"Nothing, you've already done it," she sniffed.

"Baby tell me what have I done, so I can apologize. Better yet I'm sorry. I wouldn't do anything to hurt you. You know that don't you? You and the children are my life."

"Oh Sweetie, I know that. I'm just overwhelmed, that's

all."

"About what Baby?"

"I'm...I'm...pregnant," she cried. He held her close to his chest and rocked his baby with the biggest grin ever.

"Kellie, we're going to have another baby. What's wrong with that?"

"I thought you said you wanted to wait until the triplets where at least six and in school."

"Sweetheart, you know that was just talk, besides we can put them in private school this school year. I've already talked to Aunt Juanita and she thought that was a great idea. The program at the church would be perfect. I was going to talk to you about it on the way to Edna."

"So you're really okay with this."

"Kellie Larson I'm okay with anything you do."   She smiled and told him she was going to hold him to that as he kissed her breathless. Ruby came back out with Kyla and asked if everything was alright. They told her yes and the tot reached for her. Angela and Ann came out with the boys and they wanted to be in their mommy's arms too. Gregory let them fill her warmth and then told them it was time to go bye-bye. They knew the drill, the back seats.

"Baby tell them the news." She looked at her friends and announced she was expecting. Squeals of congratulations frightened the tots which started them to cry. The ladies calmed them down together with their favorite song...*the insy weensy spider*. Gregory finally had his family safely buckled up and went around and got in the van doing a dance. He knew the minute they started riding the triplets would be just fine; he had their favorite video, *Happy Feet*. After being entertained by Gregory's happy feet dance everyone said their goodbyes and went their separate ways._____

Ruby made it in time for movie night and refreshments. Tonight they were going to see a popular comedy and have refreshments. She spotted her parents with his grandparents, Dr. and Mrs. Nason along with a middle-aged couple who had to be Lauren's parents. She was a carbon copy of her mother. Ruby couldn't believe they were all sitting together as she walked over to speak. Dr. Nason made the introductions and she was right they were her parents. She embraced her parents and the VanLees and shook hands with the Nasons. Mildred VanLee harbored a quiet disapproval, but knew better than to display her true feelings openly. Her husband had given his last warning about her sour disposition when it came to Ruby. He demanded she put an end to her foolishness at once and have a civil tongue, period.

Henry Ray gave her his usual compliment. He has always made his babygirl feel special, particularly when he sensed she needed that extra little reassurance. He saw the taint expressions of the two older ladies when she entered the center and walked toward them. His Ruby Jewel portrayed grace, poise, style, and pure loveliness. He didn't know what their problems were, but they had truly picked the wrong daughter to ruffle feathers. Her mother could vouch for that. Before she could take a seat Mrs. Nason made a comment about her designer shoes which were exactly like the ones she had on the last time they saw each other just a different color. Mildred VanLee silently applauded her friend. Her daughter-in-law asked about the shoe ornaments she was wearing, they matched her jewelry and belt. Her father invited the men to follow him. He was sure it was something they could do to assist Caleb instead of listening to the women talk shoes. Besides, he wanted to know the relationship between Charles Nason and the Nason he heard about during his childhood.

The men left and Ruby began enlightening the women with her concept of *comfort*, and how we use it toward achieving our life goals, why not for your feet. When you find a good thing and it works, utilize it. She uses jewelry to give her shoes a unique look like the decorative set she has on. It was custom made and could be used with several pairs for coordinating and bringing together an outfit. The cute snap on brass buttons matched the buckle on her belt and jewelry that she was wearing. Leslie Nason thought her idea was brilliant and commended her for her talent; she was impressed and definitely had something to think about.

The men came back with paper goods and a large cooler filled with water and drinks. Ruby stood and straightened her jersey seamed espresso skirt and sand colored tailored shirt and walked over to help. She arranged the paper goods and was getting ready to open the packages of napkins when she heard someone calling her name. It was one of the little ladies who attended the center on a regular basis. Ms. Abigail walked over; caught her hand and announced loudly her *Boo* was in the kitchen. Everyone smiled because she was such a character and the cutest little ninety years old that actually blushes around her Caleb. She often says he reminds her of her late husband. Ruby gave her mother her purse and allowed Ms. Abigail to escort her straight to the kitchen.

"Dr. Caleb look who I have your pretty girlfriend." She

was so proud of her accomplishment. "You're going to kiss her, huh?"   Lauren was also there helping with the refreshments. They both gave polite hellos.

"Yes Ms. Abigail I am."

"Well we're waiting." Caleb walked over to where they both were standing and winked at Ruby and then kissed Ms. Abigail on the cheek first.

"Ms. Abigail are you trying to steal my *Boo*."   She covered her mouth as she giggled. He took her in his arms and gave her a lingering kiss. Ms. Abigail covered her eyes at first, and then peeped to watch. He told her he had been waiting for her to walk through that door ever since she called and said she was in the city limits. She asked if he needed any help and he told her she could roll out the cart that was already loaded with refreshments.   Ms. Abigail helped her set the food out and then took her seat with her friends. Caleb and Lauren came out with the extra trays He announced they could help themselves with refreshments and the movie would start shortly afterwards. Lauren had a ridiculous smug grin on her face like she had accomplished something major being by his side. Grandmother Mildred and Mrs. Nason had the same expression nodding a silent approval to each other as the show began....

The movie was hilarious and the entire group enjoyed it including the VanLees and the Nasons.   Afterwards, the seniors socialized and enjoyed the rest of the refreshments. As usual Caleb and Ruby had to tell their story of how they met and fell in love to Lauren's parents. When he finished Leslie Nason sighed and told them that was such a lovely story. He told Mrs. Nason he agreed, winking at Ruby. The evening had come to an end and the seniors were leaving along with the Nasons. Their house keeper had called to tell them his brother and family had arrived. He expressed how much he enjoyed himself and was like the others, looking forward to next time. Lauren told her father to drive her car; she would ride with the VanLees. She lied and said she had a headache and wanted to go straight home. Her father kissed her on the forehead and said they would see her later. Leslie Nason gave her spoiled daughter a strange look, but kept her thoughts to herself. She pecked her on the cheek and advised her to turn in early. But she silently vowed to have a talk with her daughter before she leaves.

Soon the center was in order and security was locking up. It was still early for the young at heart. Believe it or not, his grandmother was not ready to call it an evening and suggested they go somewhere and have coffee. That was unexpected! Caleb told her that was a splendid idea and he knew just the place winking at Ruby. He gave his grandfather the keys and told him to follow them. Taking Ruby's hand, he twirled her around in a two-step over to her car with a big satisfied smile; he knew he had beaten them both at their own game. She shook her head and laughed.

"You know you're being a rascal and your grandmother is going to have a fit."

"What? I'm grown and you sound like my grandfather."

"Okay grown but you are being a devil. You know darn well your grandmother and Lauren Nason are going to be upset." He burst out with a hearty laugh because she was right as they pulled out of the parking lot and headed straight to their favorite truck stop. It was still early and they wouldn't have a problem finding a table. His grandfather was following him with a hidden smile. He knew his grandson was a rascal and that was the only way to describe him.

They were at their favorite spot within minutes. He didn't waste any time opening the door for her and then rushed over to his grandparents and opened the ladies door with the biggest grin ever. She was right he was being a devil. He announced this was the spot and they were in luck because their favorite table was empty for now.

"Caleb how could you," exclaimed his grandmother with a look of disgust. He tried to play innocent and said they have the best coffee and homemade pastries in the county plus a relaxing atmosphere. She could actually let her hair down so to speak. She rolled her eyes as she allowed him to lead her to their table. Ruby and Dr. Caleb were already sitting down waiting with pleasant looks. The redwood picnic table did have comfortable cushioned seats and a nice plastic tablecloth. She had a hard time containing her smile as she watched the two ladies look at each other in total disbelief and repulse.

"Caleb can you believe this. I have never."

"It's a first time for everything Grandmother. Lauren would you like me to get you something for your headache?" Stunned she looked at him, because she called herself being discreet and whispered that to her parents. *Yeah, I read your lips.*

"Caleb I would like a cappuccino if they carry it. That will soothe my headache."

"You're in luck they do." He looked at his grandparents, his grandfather said surprise them. "I know what you want Baby. While I take care of the pastries and drinks, get our picnic basket out. Grandmother you'll be happy to know we have everything you need to make this a pleasant experience." His grandfather asked him if he needed any help with a smile on his face because now he was being downright mischievous. He told him he had it and disappeared inside the store front.

When he returned Ruby had everything ready with all proper essentials; plus something for Lauren's headache. Grandfather Caleb couldn't help teasing her as they prepared the table together. He told them they truly came equipped. Caleb had his hands full when he returned. He couldn't resist giving her a little smooch as she helped him empty the box that held their goodies. She mouthed rascal as the others inspected their hot drinks. Although this setup was fine for them, she knew his grandmother was not happy. She didn't care what Lauren Nason thought because she should have gone with her parents. Ruby was waiting for her to make one negative comment and she was going to put her in her place once and for all. She did have to put up with his grandmother but not her. The VanLees were surprised when they sipped their drink. It was exactly the same brand they drink at home. Caleb winked at his grandmother and told her to try one of the homemade pastries and she did.

For once they all had a civil and enjoyable time, good conversation and delicious treats. Grandmother Mildred even inquired about their upcoming wedding and told her she had found a very nice dress and hat in a beautiful light gold that was ideal for a daytime wedding. That had been another one of her complaints, but they had good reasons. Caleb wanted to give his family members who were not spending the night a chance to get home before it was real late. Ruby told her she was happy she was able to find something that truly suits her. She made it known she had been taken to one of the exclusive stores in Houston. Of course Caleb had already informed her. Lauren even shared the news of delivering her first set of triplets, boys which had been a surprise for her as well as the parents.

"Well it's getting late," announced his grandfather with a yawn. They all agreed and started the cleanup. They were flabbergasted when his grandmother pitched in gathering and throwing away the trash. Before leaving everyone wanted a refill and his grandfather requested extra pastries to take home. Ruby suggested he buy some for Lauren's parents to go with their morning coffee since she had been on her best behavior. Grandfather Caleb kissed his wife on the cheek as they walked holding hands to the car. Caleb walked Ruby to her car and held her in his arms for a few minutes before kissing her goodnight. He hated to let her leave him but they did have the rest of the weekend. He told her to call him when she's settled for the night and watched her drive off. He got in his SUV and was pleasantly surprised his grandfather was in the front seat instead of Lauren Nason. He smiled silently to himself and thought finally._____

Leslie saw the light on in her daughter's room and knocked on her door, they needed to talk. She came in barely speaking and went straight to her room. She gave her a chance to get a shower and was now ready to confront her in regards to her behavior.

"Come in."

"Lauren we need to talk," said her mother as she took a seat on her bed. She had a good conversation with her father-in-law who informed her about the trouble she and her grandmother have tried to create with Ruby and Caleb. He even showed her the pictures from the newspaper. She didn't want to believe it, but she knew her daughter well and the way she eyed him tonight was just pitiful. Once again she was setting herself up for a big disappointment. Father thought she would be the best person to get her straight because his son was blind when it came to his pumpkin and he was right.

"What is it mother, I've had a long day and I'm tired."

"Well Lauren you should have come with us and you would have been home at least an hour or so ago. I had a talk with your grandfather and I couldn't believe the things he said. Lauren it is totally preposterous for you to think Caleb VanLee is the man for you." Leslie Nason wished for once her daughter would set her sights on a man that did not belong to someone else. She was sure her mother-in-law had a lot to do with it. "Did you see the size of that diamond on her engagement ring? A man does not buy a ring that expensive if he's not serious and Lauren they are. He couldn't keep his eyes or hands off of her. Did you see that? It's evident he loves her very much."

"Mother please, I wish for once I could have your support and not be criticized."

"Lauren you have always had my support, but you would have to be blind not to see that man is deeply in love with Ruby McHarding."

"Ooooh, I'm sick and tired of hearing that name. Why would he want someone like her mother instead of me?"

"Someone like her, Lauren she's beautiful, smart, intelligent and successful. Why wouldn't he want her? You may as well accept the fact she's the women he chose before he even knew you existed." She began to cry. Her mother held her in her arms to comfort her. "Darling, I'm sorry for upsetting you, but you need to be realistic and accept the fact he is in love with someone else.

"Well Mother what am I supposed to do, answer me that!"

"Find you someone that's not already in love with another woman and in this case engaged. Baby you're making yourself unhappy and it's not necessary." Leslie held and rocked her grown daughter while she cried her heart out. She felt sorry for her but it was nothing she could do about it. This was not the first time she's done this with the help of her grandmother. The last man relocated with his intended and has been married for several years with children. Just like her grandfather said, she's had plenty opportunities to marry decent professional men with good jobs, but she's ignored or refused to give them the time of day. Well she should have, thought her mother as she finally quieted down. She gave her a tissue and told her to pull herself together. Lauren wiped her face and got in bed. Her mother kissed her forehead and told her to try and get some sleep. Humph, it was nothing else she could do but sleep after that good cry.

CHAPTER 24

"Dang, where in the world are we going to park," asked Ruby?

"Valet Baby valet." He stopped the car and was already at her door in seconds. "Come on let's speak and head to the food." She grabbed his hand and told him he better not run to the food for at least thirty minutes. "Is that etiquettes or something?" She shook her hand at him and repeated it again. He kissed her pouting lips and agreed thirty minutes was it, as they walked up the winding drive. The party was truly in high gear, the band was kicking it with Zydeco. He couldn't resist the temptation and did a couple of steps and twirled her around barely missing Dewey and Dr. Charlotte Alford.

"Frosty, welcome back brother, and Ruby it's good to see you again."

"It's so good to be back and to see you big brother Dewey. It's good to see you too Dr. Charlotte."

"Caleb you need to quit. We see each other every day remember we do work together." The couples laughed as the two frat brothers hugged. "Come on Ruby let's follow the music and join the party while they do their frat brother ritual." Both men were dressed in worn blue denim jeans, buttoned vest, and black hats. You would have thought a text had been sent out concerning what to wear. Her cowboy was wearing his jeans, the fit was perfect on his slightly bow legs with his vest showing off his well-developed upper body as well.

The men were right behind them as they walked around to the enormous back yard. Lights, lanterns, and insect streamers were hung along the walkway and around the entire area to provide a jovial bug free surrounding. A huge wooden floor had been laid for the band and dancing. Around the platform were large round tables and chairs set up for at least ten people covered with red checkered table cloths and matching napkins. Old fashion lanterns were placed in the middle of each table with picnic baskets of condiments and Eco friendly red eating utensils and napkins. Four buffet stations were available with a delightful spread. Standing in lines was not going to happen; everything was easily accessible including the men and women outdoor facilities. For added comfort large outdoor fans were located in various areas away from the guest which provided a welcomed breeze. Everyone was having a great time dressed in their western attire with good conversations and dancing. The few children who were present had their own area with water play and a small carnival.

Caleb's cell vibrated, it was his grandmother. "Hi Darling, I see you finally made it." He had dropped them off first and then picked Ruby up. He wanted to show her a piece of property he was thinking of purchasing for them if she was alright with it. The location was excellent not too far from her parents and the clinic. It was a fabulous old farmhouse with two cottages perched on five acres of land. One was connected by a wraparound porch to the main house. A newly constructed barn with stables and a coral was also on the property along with a small pond. It was everything he had dreamed of. He also had to break the news that his grandfather had talked about relocating to Texas since they were their only family. He wanted to spend his last days with them and his great-grands. But he wanted to make sure she was fine with the idea first. Ruby thought the farmhouse which had been restored with all the modern conveniences and practically move in ready was fantastic. The owners had even left some beautiful antiques. They were going to need very little furniture. And living close to his family was a wonderful idea, including his grandmother and gave him a thumbs up. He pulled over the SUV and embraced her while calling the realtor to get the ball rolling.

"Yes Grandmother, we're here. Where are you located?"

"We're in front on the left. Come sit with us at the head table with the Nasons." Lord that was all he needed.

"Grandmother I'm with Dr. Alford and her husband, Dewey. Is there enough room for four?" Dewey was shaking his head in protest. Hell, he was looking forward to enjoying himself. Dr. Nason knew how to have a party and he and his family were cool, but sitting with Mildred VanLee was not his idea of having a good time. He remembers her too well. Dewey mouthed he was on his own and they would get together and hang out at another time. He kissed Ruby on the cheek and grabbed his wife's hand and headed toward the mayor's table who was his partner in running the city. They were also frat brothers and good friends. Ruby tried pleading with them both, but Dr. Charlotte echoed her husband's sentiments and left grinning. Ruby and Caleb's expression was assurance that they had each other's back. He took her hand and walked over to a table full of strangers except his grandparents and Dr. and Mrs. Nason. He didn't see, yep there she was standing next to his grandfather.

"You ready Baby, he growled."

"As ready as I'm going to be and take that frown off your face." He stopped cold, faced her and ordered her to kiss it off. She pleaded with him to behave and be on his best behavior for her sake.

"Finally," exclaimed his grandfather as he walked over to meet them. They embraced and she kissed him on the cheek. "Ruby you're simply radiant. Son I can't say it enough, you're one lucky man."

"Thanks Grandfather, that's exactly how I feel." His look of love and admiration touched her very soul and caused her to reward him with a gentle smack on the lips, which produced a wide grin. With her in the middle the VanLee men escorted her over to the other guests who witnessed their display of affection. He walked over to his grandmother and brushed his lips against her cheek, then spoke to Lauren and Dr. and Mrs. Nason with her doing the same. Mildred VanLee could feel her husband and grandson watching her and decided to do the unmentionable. She embraced her future granddaughter which caught her completely off guard.

As her audience watched Dr. Nason told her how pretty she looked and voiced the same sentiments as his grandfather; adding she came from a good family because he knew her grandmother well. Ruby was surprised to hear that bit of information and would certainly have to find out how.

"Dr. Nason I have to agree with you and grandfather

she's truly something special." He brushed his lips against hers again.

"Stop you're all embarrassing me." She expected her Caleb to say sweet things he has always referred to her as his beautiful ebony princess and perhaps his grandfather. But she's noticed whenever she's in Dr. Nason's presence he gives her special looks as if she was someone else. It wasn't until he revealed he knew her grandmother, did she understand. She's seen pictures of her grandmother and great-grandmother and had to agree she had a very strong resemblance of both. She could have been either one of their daughters instead of the actual relationship they have.

"Granddaughter we're just calling it as we see it."

"Amen to that," said Caleb. Ruby gave all three men a peck and quickly changed the conversation and returned the compliments on their outfits. She told the ladies they looked very nice in their western attire. Ruby knew women of their caliber were fashion conscience and loved to hear how good they looked. That was one thing they all had in common which validated them in their little circle. Besides their expressions had said it all, enough was enough on how pretty she was. One thing about Ruby Jewel she was confident and knew she was attractive. Of course she had no choice being the daughter of Henry Ray McHarding.

The VanLees and Nasons really looked nice resembling movie stars from the old cowboy days. The couples were well coordinated and matching down to their cowboy boots and hats. The VanLees were in brown and beige with decorative brown fringe on their shirts and Mrs. VanLee's skirt. The Nasons were in blue jeans, with Mrs. Nason skirt beautifully embellished. Their red twin shirts were also decorated with the same colored sequins and beading. Their fancy boots and hats were black with jeweled red bands.

Lauren had on a more modern western dress, an ultrachic short red ruffled skirt with a white petticoat and a gingham puff sleeve blouse tied in the front that showed a little midriff. She accessorized it with gold and red western jewelry, a cute red cowboy hat and fancy boots. Her outfit really complemented her slender figure and the look she was going for, sleek and sexy. The ladies thanked Ruby and returned the same sentiments. She knew they were only being polite because her dress was simple and she could have felt out of place. But her outfit was casual and complemented Caleb's, a white washed blue denim skirt with raw fringed edges that encircled above and below her hips and hem. The matching pin tucked blouse had the same trimmings around the short sleeves and bottom. Worn navy cowboy boots and silver medallion jewelry set with western charms completed her look.

"I think we can say all our women folk look real nice, agree gentlemen," said Dr. Nason. The men acknowledged and Caleb pulled her to his side, the photographer was on hand snapping pictures.

"Baby can we get something to eat now," he asked. She looked at him with a smile because he did wait like he promised. It seems everyone had enjoyed a fabulous breakfast according to the evidence on the table. And Caleb was ready and she had to admit she was hungry too.

"Okay Sweetie."

"Here Caleb give me your medical bag, I'll put it inside the house."

He thanked Dr. Nason and they excused themselves and went toward the nearest food station. Caleb twirled her around a couple of times on the way to the upbeat country western tune. He had an appreciation for all kinds of music thanks to his Uncle Pete and Uncle Arnold._____

As Charles Nason approached the back veranda of his home he found his oldest brother sitting on the swing with a faraway look. He joined him for a few minutes. Collen had been told she was the splitting image of his beloved Ruby Jewel but he never believed the resemblance would be that strong. He was taken back over sixty years when he first laid eyes on his dark beauty.

"Charles, I can't get over how much she looks like her."

"I told you Collen she's her grandmother reincarnated."

"I mean to say. Is her father still here in Hempstead living in their family home?"

"Yes, he's still in the home you bought her, it's just been remodeled over the years to accommodate his growing family. As a matter of fact we were all at the center last night and we had a wonderful time." He could tell he wanted to ask if he said anything about her.

"Did he?"

"Not only did he bring up his mother, he asked about the relationship between us." He knew his brother well as he watched his various facial expressions.

"Lord you don't know how many times I wished he was my son, instead of that damn McHarding who didn't do anything but break her heart."

"That's all in the past Collen she made her decision when she married that jerk instead of you." Charles you know that's not fair the way things were back then in Texas. And our parents were not nice at all once they found out how we felt about each other."

"I know big brother. What's done is done. Let me put Caleb's grandson's medical bag up and we can go out and I'll introduce you. Where's Elizabeth?"

"She went inside to help the girls with the grands." Collen had a beautiful family and a wonderful wife who has been by his side for almost forty years. They had their own secluded self-haven in a little small town called Edmond, Oklahoma. He had married and started his family late in life and it was well worth the wait. Although he did not marry his first black beauty, his second was truly the love of his life. She has given him two fine sons and a beautiful daughter. Together they have nine grandchildren that's a handful and one on the way. This was the first time he had been home in years with his entire family and was glad they made the trip.

"You ready?"

"About as ready as I'm going to be," the two brothers walked over to the family table, but Ruby was not there.

"Caleb I would like for you to meet my big brother Collen Nason." He stood and shook the older gentleman's hand.

"Where's your fiancée?"

"She saw some of the staff from the clinic and went over to speak. So Mr. Nason are you a retired doctor like your brother?"

"Yes, I'm retired, but a college professor."

"Here she comes now." A vision of pure loveliness thought Collen. It was just plain unbelievable and the resemblance was remarkable. They had the same built and complexion. Her smile alone was like a breath of fresh air, just like his Ruby's. Caleb watched the two Nason brothers as they followed her every move. Turning back to her direction he too watched the sway of her ample hips, the slight movement of her luscious breasts, her ponytail swinging to and fro. Her sensual smile along was arousing as his heart beat quickening.

He extended his hand out. "Baby this is Dr. Nason's big brother, Dr. Collen Nason PhD. Dr. Nason this is…"

"I know Ruby Jewel McHarding." She was her grandmother's double. "Caleb may I congratulate your fiancée with a hug and a kiss?"

"Of course sir," it was clear they knew Ruby's grandmother well. The older Nason brother gave her a big hug and kissed her gently on the cheek. It was just like he expected, kissing his Ruby.

"Thanks for letting an old man revisit his past." His family was now by his side and he made introductions, his wife, daughter, sons and their spouses; a white son-in-law and two black daughters-in-law. He too had a well-blended family. For some reason neither Ruby nor Caleb were surprised that his wife was a beautiful black woman who was at least ten years his junior. Of course the older Nason brother was nice looking and had handsome sons. And wouldn't you believe it they were dressed like their frat brothers, talking about a coincidence.

"Dad she looks just like the woman from your childhood,"

exclaimed his namesake as he started that frat ritual with his brother following suit.

"This is her granddaughter."

"I don't know if I should be concerned Ms McHarding," teased his wife. Collen pulled her into his arms and kissed her lips.

"Daddy please," sighed their baby girl.

"Son-in-law can you handle your woman?"

"I believe I can Dad." Everyone laughed. Collen expressed to Ruby that he would love to spend some time with her and share his photo album with her before he leaves. She told him she would love to whenever he likes.

"Hey ya'll we're letting this good music go to waste," announced Collen Jr. "Let's step Deb." The Young Nason family went to the dance floor with everyone following, including their parents. Caleb was such a show off twirling her around keeping time with the steps. Of course his old school frat brothers joined in to show everyone how a Q-dog does it and started their ritual barking. Lord, Collen Jr. and his younger brother Colton joined in. After the stepping song the DJ played the *Atomic Dog* and the floor was cleared for them to stomp. It was ridiculous to see grown men carry on like they were still in college but they were having the time of their lives. Surely Dr. Nason didn't expect them to take over his party even if it was for one dance.

The ladies took their seats and watched. Ruby was glad it was not the long version as she explained to Lauren, her mother and grandmother what the stomping was all about. During the conversation Ruby noticed that Lauren and her mother could pass for twins. She found out last night her father was an engineer and they had lived abroad during Lauren's childhood. That's why she was fluent in several languages. Finally the song was done and the DJ played a song that enticed the other guest back to the dance floor.

"Ruby what are they doing now," asked Leslie Nason? She explained that when they hit their heart that symbolizes they will love Omega until they die and now they are inviting their women to join them.

"Watch," Ruby said. Dr. Charlotte and the mayor's wife were first and then the others started one by one keeping up with their husbands' steps. Once they were in their husband's arms they kissed the omega symbol over their heart.

"How in the world did they get that on their skin," asked Lauren with the other women looking on in amazement.

"They were branded cousin," answered Debra as she reached for her sister- in-law's hand who took Ruby's and they stepped over to their waiting men who let out a loud howl which started a chain reaction from the others all over again.

"Caleb has a brand," asked Lauren? Ruby held up three fingers and continued stepping.

Caleb closed his eyes when he felt the warmth of her lips against his naked skin; she caressed and kissed his symbol. He then put his finger under her chin and gazed into her sensuous dark eyes which were filled with love for only him and devoured her lips. They held each other and continued their dance. Lord he couldn't wait to make her his wife as he released her hair to let it blow in the breeze. He loved to see it hanging loosely down her back. He squeezed her tightly pressing her closer.

"Remember your grandparents are here watching, be nice," she said softly. He whispered against her wild curls only for her sake...

"Mother I'm telling you, do not mention that name to me again." Once more Lauren and her mother were having a disagreement.

"What name Pumpkin? How are my favorite girls?"

"Hi Daddy, when did you get up?" Charles 2nd kissed his wife and daughter.

"Now Pumpkin, what were you two talking about?"

"Mother brought up Heston Kamond again." Leslie shook her head and said she was going to get something to eat. She knew her spoiled rotten daughter was impossible and especially when she's scheming on some poor man. Well she can forget about Dr. Caleb VanLee. Speak of the devil.

"Hello Lauren, Mr. and Mrs. Nason." They all spoke. Lauren would you like to dance?"

"Of course she would, go ahead pumpkin. Come on Lee let's join them and then get something to eat." Lauren couldn't believe her father would even suggest she dance with this egotistical jerk. Heston Kamond was a big time rancher who thought he was God's gift to every woman because of his good looks and his family's wealth. He's been after her ever since she moved to Hempstead, she just wasn't interested.

CHAPTER 25

"Come on cowboy let's sit this one out." Ruby led him off the dance floor and to their seats. She needed to catch her breath and cool off for a spell; whether he admitted it or not the good doctor needed to as well.

"Caleb, why don't you and Ruby join us over here?" The Nason boys had found a frat brother and a new playmate and their wives and sister were also pretty cool.

"Ruby, we were on our way to the ladies room, want to join us."

"I don't mind if I do." She gave him a smack on the lips and accompanied her new friends.

"Sistah girl, where did you find that hunk? You know Lauren is about to die with envy," said Deb. "She's been shooting daggers at you whether you know it or not." Ruby fingered her ring as she told them she was very much aware of Lauren's looks and intentions. But they didn't have to worry she had that under control. The Nason women admired her engagement ring while she told them their love story.

"Ruby, that's so sweet, but we're serious about Lauren, you better watch her girl, she's something else and never stops. Trust, when you least expects she's weaved her venomous web. Tell her Corlette, how she tried to kept drama between you and your man before ya'll married. It's a good thing Yvette and I are married to her cousins."

"She's right Ruby, keep your eyes open."

"Sistahs, I do have that man safely tucked in my arms. He's mine and only the man up above can break us up and I pray that never happens for a long, long time." They did a high five and went into the fancy facility.

After completing their business, they started back to the table that was now empty. The men had disappeared.

"Where could they be," asked Yvette? They heard this big ruckus and walked over to a big crowd. Oh no, Uncle Charles didn't."

"Yes he did," said Corlette, "a mechanical bull."

"Son you don't know who my people are. I was born on a bull."

"Put your money where your mouth is old man, we each got fifty that says you can't last two minutes." Heston Kamond and his boys had no idea who they were really dealing with, as they flashed their money.

"Did he just call me old man?"

"I believe so frat, you need to shut this dude up. I'll collect their fifty."

"Naw frat that's chump change, they gon need a hundred, because I feel like riding." Caleb pulled his wallet out.

"Naw frat, we got this," and told him to put away his

wallet. They did their hand grip and the bet was on. Ruby and the other ladies ran over to the crowd just as he was about to get on the mechanical bull. She called his name. He turned around and she ran straight into his arms, she was trembling. "Hey, it's alright, now you know this is like play for me. I got this. Remember who my uncle is, Black Bulldog Pete."

"Who did he say," asked one of Heston's partners? He had heard that name all his life around the rodeo circuit. He was the best, but he was black.

The brothers didn't even let him finish, when they repeated it again. "You heard him; Black Bulldog Pete is his great-uncle." Heston grumbled he didn't care who his old gray uncle was and to put out or shut up.

"Caleb I'm afraid." She clung to him.

He gave her a big squeeze and looked at Heston and his partners he calls them and said, "Put the timer on three minutes and boys watch and learn *somthum*." The crowd let out a cheer as he mounted the bull secured himself like his uncle had taught him and told them to hit the switch. He rode it like an old pro with the crowd cheering him on. Poor Ruby was frightened to death with the way he was being jerked violently around on that contraption. His grandfather and the older Nason brothers had joined the crowd. She wiped the sweat that popped out on her forehead. His Grandfather put his arms around her and told her it was going to be fine. What seemed liked forever had only been three minutes when the timer finally went off and the mechanical bull stopped. Shouts of cheers and hats flying said he was a winner.

"Anybody think they can beat my man's time?" Collen held up the money, but there were no contenders. Caleb carefully got off because he knew he had taken a brutal ride and needed to sit down somewhere and just be still for a few minutes. He hadn't been on a mechanical bull in years, but he did represent. He reached for Ruby and told her he was alright, but she felt different. With his grandfather on one side and her on the other they walked slowly to the front porch as he gave high fives and hand grips. Even Heston and his boys did a cowboy bow with hats in hands acknowledging he was the man. Black Bulldog Pete would be proud....

The evening was winding down and the guests were leaving. Dr. Charles and his family had formed a receiving line thanking their many guests for sharing this wonderful celebration. Caleb and Ruby were also ready to call it an evening and made it known when he requested his medical bag. His new found frat brothers and their spouses pleaded with them to stay and join the family for the last event of the evening. A trail ride and hayride around the ranch with a weenie roast to follow. That's why the women had now changed into jeans but kept their same shirts except Ms Lauren. She was now wearing a pair of hip hugger jeans and a red midriff top underneath a jean vest. Again she had accomplished her goal, sleek and sexy as she stood with her family.

Caleb had been a bit quiet than usual for the remainder of the evening. They only danced a couple of times to ballads. He did a square dance with Lauren who made a pure spectacle of herself. They spent the rest of the party socializing with clinic staff and the Nason family. Ruby really wanted to decline, she felt he needed to go home and take a shower and go to bed early; but the announcement of the trail ride sparked excitement and was right down his alley. He loved horseback riding. She would have to sit this activity out because she was not dressed to ride a horse and would not get in the way of him completing the day with one of his favorite pastimes. The Nason family refused to hear of such and insisted she ride in the wagon with Corlette and the small children. She agreed and noticed out of the corner of her eye Lauren and her grandmother snotty looks said she was not welcome but they knew better than to voice it....

Lauren had been to the stable to make sure the livestock was ready for the trail riders and request a horse for Caleb. She didn't care what Hosea said and asked for Weeboy. The idea was for them to ride double once they get on the trail. She had it all planned, a moonlit stroll on her Chinadoll. She was fresh and ready to make her move since Ruby would be riding in the wagon with her cousins and aunt. This was her last chance to be with him without her. She would have him to herself, well almost to herself since he's hit it off with her male cousins.

The family walked to the stables with the children excitedly running to claim their ponies. The men assisted the small children and women and then mounted their horses. Caleb rode close to the wagon to give her his medical bag and another kiss. She caressed the soft hairs on his face and asked how about his headache. He said it was gone. But she felt he wasn't telling the whole truth and hoped the evening fresh air and ride would do him good. Her look let him know she didn't believe a word he said which prompted him to promise to take it easy and enjoy a slow pace trot.

The trail riders were blessed with a glorious natural light due to the golden sunset as they traveled down the path to the prepared sight. The Nason's youngsters were having the time of their lives galloping ahead and then turning around to get back with the group. Other than the bull riding event it had been a wonderful day, thought Ruby as she snuggled one of the sleepy tots to her breast. Corlette said that's why they have the RV already on the site. Ruby pulled another one to her side to let rest until they reached their destination. She met some new friends and enjoyed talking to Collen Nason who confessed her grandmother had been his first love. It seems her great-great-grandfather who was a full-blooded Cherokee Indian was a major part in building the Nason's horse ranch into one of the finest in the country during those days. He was a horse whisperer from way back and worked on this very ranch. He was married to a beautiful black woman and had two children, a son who died at a young age and a lovely daughter, her great grandmother Ruby Jewel White-Cloud....

"Whoa Weeboy, whoa now," said Caleb as he gently patted his horse who was becoming a bit spirited and started rearing up on his hind legs.

"Doc is everything alright," asked Collen Jr.

"Yeah, he's just a little high-spirited that's all."

"Okay now, I did promise your lady I would take care of you. She said you were a typical doctor, always putting yourself last. What kind of doctor is that?"

"I'm a neurologist, specializing in geriatrics."

"Get outa here doc," exclaimed one of the other Nason cousins."

"Man you so down to earth, I thought you were just a

typical educated dude with a good job. Not a walking medical book for brains, no offense my brother." Collen held up his hand.

"None taken bro and for the record my fiancée is an attorney, Attorney RJ McHarding."

"Wait a minute, I've heard that name before," said Deb. "Does she have a data base service for attorneys?"

"That's my baby," he said proudly.

"I'm in her Oklahoma database and have received several referrals; one is responsible for putting me in the loop." That explains everything, thought Deb. That why Lauren had set her sights on him. He and his grandfather were prominent neurologists from Denver, Colorado. She read about him in yesterday's paper, what a difference a pair of jeans and a cowboy hat makes. In the newspaper he was suave and sophisticated, now he's just a brother hanging out. She wouldn't fit into his world at all and he was definitely not a brother who would allow a woman to put him on a leash regardless of him being a **Q**.

"Yeah man, she's known for sending a brother to the cleaners," remarked Elvin.

"You just better treat my sister right mister."

"Hey, you know I love her dirty panties."

"It's draws white boy," shouted Colton with everybody laughing. Their brother-in-law was a jewel and good for their baby sister. He had a wonderful personality with a good sense of humor because they gave him a hard time whenever they could.

"I gotcha white boy."

"Brother-in-law, brother-in-law." Caleb smiled and knew he had found some real down to earth buds for real.

"Whatever, I need to go check on my baby and see how junior is treating her."

Elvin turned his horse to ride off when Caleb's horse started rearing up on his hind legs again. He tried the technique he had been taught by the best but it wasn't working. Collen was just about to suggest he might need to get off and tie him to the wagon when the horse started to buck. He steered him away from the other riders and children while trying to steady the black stallion. Nothing seemed to be working. The riders moved further away giving him room to continue trying to get Weeboy under control. The Nason men got off their horses to assist but it was too late. Caleb was thrown to the ground followed by screams and shouts. The horse continued bucking wildly as the men tried desperately to steer him away from their fallen friend who was not moving. The wagon stopped and all you could hear were yells and screams. Someone shouted a man was down and hurt.

Thank God it wasn't any of the children thought Ruby. "Corlette you stay with the kids while I take Caleb his bag." She stretched the two tikes she was holding on a blanket and climbed off the wagon. She ran to the crowd shouting his name and saying she had his medical bag, he was not visible. Someone took it from her and gave it to Dr. Charles. Through a small opening she could see him lifeless down on the ground with part of his face covered in blood. She screamed his name and begged him to get up. It seems she and his grandmother were taking turns until she broke down sobbing and had to be taken away. Someone put their arms around her and held on to her as she continued pleading with him to get up.

"Baby please get up." The person holding her whispered he couldn't hear her. She saw both doctors down on the ground with Lauren assisting them. Someone said they couldn't tell where the blood was coming from and to be careful. She could hear the sound of the ambulance nearby approaching the site. A voice shouted to give them room. As the Nasons moved aside she could see a helpless Caleb stretched out on the ground with a head bandage on his left side drenched in blood. The sight of it all caused her to moan his name over and over. Ruby was shaking and trembling like she was out in the cold as she watched the paramedics with the two doctors by his side. A helicopter was now looming over the area.

His grandfather came over to her. "Ruby we're going to life flight him to Memorial. I need you to be strong." his voice cracked.

"We'll bring her doc."

"*Oh God no ...Caleb...Caleb.*" Sobbing profoundly she was led to a vehicle. Everything had happened so fast in that short time. The wagon and horses were nowhere in sight or she just didn't see them for the blinding tears. She heard voices but she couldn't understand what was being said. Thank God for the person holding her because she needed their strength; she had been stripped and felt completely helpless...

They arrived at the hospital and rushed inside to the emergency area. She heard her name being called but did not recognize the voice.

"Ruby what happened? I saw..."

That was all Roy could say, she fell into his arms and cried against his chest. "It's Caleb, its Caleb." Roy tried consoling her with gentle pats while looking to the man who brought her in for an explanation. Collen Jr. introduced himself and guided them over to sit. For once the emergency area was practically empty but wouldn't be for long because Roy had called his male cousins who were on their way. He thought that would be best since he didn't know the seriousness of the accident. All he knew was Caleb had an accident, where or how was unknown. Collen began giving an account of what happened. He found it hard to believe, but listened attentively while trying to comfort Ruby. Caleb had been riding a horse since he was able to walk like the rest of them. They were all horsemen to their hearts. Uncle Pete had taught them all very well and he always said Caleb was the best. While the trio continued waiting for word Tiny and Doug came in with wild looks of fear._____

"Baby, quiet down now so I can hear what he's saying, continue Caleb." He explained the situation and told them their prognosis and the surgery that's recommended by the neurologist. He knew he had the authority to make whatever necessary decisions needed since he was next of kin present, with them in Denver. They were his parents and he wanted to show them the respect they deserved along with Ruby. No doubt about it surgery was crucial to relieve the pressure and internal bleeding from his brain; time was of the essence. "Caleb please do whatever you can for our son. I'm leaving everything in your hands. My nephews should be there by now for family support."

"Pray, Lawrence, please pray for our boy." Caleb Sr. was overcome with emotions for a second but had to be strong because he was going to be in the operating room observing. Yes, he was a remarkable neurological surgeon but this was too close. He would be there and ready to assist if needed.

"I will Caleb, get everybody in the conference room so we can get things underway." Charles Nason went to get Ruby and the nephews while Lauren went to get Mildred who was in his office with Linda and Collen Sr. who really preferred being with Ruby but he did it for his brother's sake.

Ruby and his cousins entered the conference room. Caleb Sr. hugged all three and told them he was glad they were there. He then took Ruby in his arms and softly explained to her they must be strong for Caleb's sake. He also needed her strength for him as well. She told him she would try as they held each other.

"Okay Lawrence, everyone is here."

"Ruby, Vera and I are giving you and Caleb Sr. the authority to make any and every decision concerning our son's well-being." Caleb Sr. signaled for the cousins and walked over to his wife who was asking why she was involved in making any decisions. Ruby's tears started flowing once again. Tiny held her in his arms with Roy and Doug on each side. Dr. Caleb along with the surgeons and neurologist explained in depth the situation and how pertinent it was for them to operate tonight. Ruby gave out a painful cry as she eased down in a chair.

"Be strong Daughter, be strong," begged Lawrence Nicholson who was now having a hard time controlling his emotions.

"Ruby do you have any questions," asked Dr. Caleb? "Tiny, Roy, Doug?" Everyone said no and the hospital representative brought the consent documents for their signatures while the doctors left to get ready for surgery. After the papers were signed Lawrence asked his nephew Roy to pray. His heartwarming prayer brought tears to every eye. Dr. VanLee and Dr. Nason assured the family they would be notified as soon as the surgery was over and excused themselves. Dr. Nason had the family moved to the nearest waiting area and called his house to request refreshments to be sent to the hospital. It was going to be a long stressful night and he wanted to make them as comfortable as possible._____

"Vera come on honey, they're waiting on us at the airport. Lawrence and Vera Nicholson's team minister and wife were there to help them pack and take them to the airport. They were flying in the company jet. His boss of thirty-five years, who was also a frat brother and longtime friend, insisted when he called to inform him about Caleb. Since Middleton was providing the transportation they were able to take the Stratton family as well. He called Tiny to give them the itinerary so they would have transportation waiting to take them straight to the hospital. Now if he could only get the women out of the house.

CHAPTER 26

Time was dragging unmercifully slow as the family and friends helplessly waited for the nightmare to be over. Ruby was now huddled between family. Lincoln and Heather stayed with the children. Her girls and Bro. Bruce and his wife had called to express their love and that they would be praying for them. Angela told her not to worry about a thing. She and Destiny would take care of all her business appointments and reschedule others for a later date. Ruby tearfully asked her to contact the wedding vendors and cancel all orders until further notice and offer her apologies and thanks for their time and efforts. She had to face reality a wedding would be the last thing to consider at the moment. The main concern right now was his health and him resuming a normal life again.

The Nicholsons and Strattons arrived at the hospital and were met by Tiny and Roy. They all embraced and told them there was still no word. Tiny and Roy were surprised that the Strattons still remembered them because it had been some years, but they did. The limo driver gathered the luggage with the help of the nephews and all went inside where the rest of the families were waiting. When they got off the elevator they met Dr. Caleb and Dr. Charles who were on their way to the waiting area.

"Caleb," called Vera Nicholson. "Please tell me my baby

is alright!" She could not hold on to her emotions any longer and had a total emotional outburst. Tiny picked her up and carried her to the waiting area. The Nason cousins and wives were sitting on one of the couches and quickly moved so they could lay her down. Vera being carried in alarmed the rest of the family. Ruby left her parents comfort and rushed to Dr. Caleb and Dr. Charles.

"Oh God tell me he's not..." the words would not come out. Everyone was now standing. Vera Nicholson kept mumbling *"my baby"* over and over as Lawrence tried to console her. Mildred gazed into her husband's weary face to try to get some kind of understanding with Linda and Lauren Nason by her side. Audrey Stratton walked over to Mildred and they embraced with tears streaming down their faces. They had lived this nightmare before when they lost their children thirty-six years ago. This time it was going to be different. Their grandson was going to be all right. He was going to have a long life and give them lots of great-grandbabies.

Dr. Nason held his hand up and asked everyone to remain calm. The surgery was over and had been a success. Caleb was now in recovery and would be moved to ICU sometime tomorrow until he regains consciousness. Basically his vital signs are good and he's stabilized. Ruby's lawyer instincts kicked in, she sensed there was something he was not saying and needed to know what it was. She looked at both doctors waiting for them to continue. She didn't want to alarm the family any more than they had been but she had to know.

"Caleb I feel there's something else, boys hold on to your aunt," said Mr. Lawrence as he walked over to embrace his longtime friend. He had a strong feeling he was contemplating whether to tell them now or wait. Caleb looked around the room at their extended family.

"Dr. C go ahead and tell us we can handle it," said Tiny. Caleb Sr. reached for Ruby's hand and held it in his. She knew then he was struggling with something powerful as tears formed in both of their eyes.

"Grandfather please tell us," she whispered. Those words broke his heart because what he needed to say would affect her more than anyone else in the room and he couldn't bring himself to hurt her again. That's why he had asked the doctors to explain the outcome of the surgery. As if summoned the doctors who performed the surgery walked in to explain what Dr. Caleb couldn't bring himself to say. One of the doctors asked if everyone there were immediate family members. Dr. Nason asked Lauren to take the Nason family and everyone else who was not family to the lobby for now except Ruby's parents, he knew she was going to need their support. Linda you stay with Mildred. Lauren Nason was not happy about her grandfather's request but she knew her grandmother would fill her in. Before leaving Ruby's new found friends gave her a hug and told her to be strong. Tori and Junior kissed her cheeks and said they would be right outside in the other waiting area with Q-Note.

The neurologist spoke for the group, "prior to surgery his MRI showed a hairline fracture on his left arm and a few cracked ribs. With a little bit of patience and support he will be good as new physically." Everyone was now waiting for *the but* and his demeanor said they were now coming to the real issue.

"Family before I continue there's one thing we all must agree and that is, it's all about Caleb and his recovery.

Every decision we make from here on out is strictly for his benefit and his benefit alone. Agreed?" The family consented immediately to the request. "Because of the delicateness of the surgery we deemed it necessary to keep him in a medically induced coma for a few days. Due to extensive swelling we cannot make any accurate prognosis of any permanent damage to the brain until he's conscious. Then we will administer another MRI and CT scan to determine the extent of the damages." He paused for a moment before going on to let what he said soak in.

Roy asked what everyone else was thinking, "Doctor are you suggesting there could possibly be some form of memory loss?"

Tears were now flowing down his father's and grandfather's faces for different reasons and for some of the same. Dr. Nason patted his shoulder while the nephews were doing the same thing to their uncle.

"Again we are unable to give a sound medical diagnosis until he's conscious. We only want to stress the actual facts for now and plead with the family for his sake; we must decide what's in Caleb's best interest for a healthy and trauma free recovery. We want it to be less stressful and painful as we can possibly make it. Therefore, Mr. and Mrs. Nicholson we suggest strongly that his grandfather be present when he regains consciousness. If there's any indication of memory loss and until we know the full extent, we think it would be in the best interest for Caleb's mental state to allow Dr. and Mrs. VanLee Sr. to assume guardianship only because of their relationship and him having his name. We feel this will give him an immediate sense of family ties and avoid a detailed explanation as to why he was adopted and raised by his parents' best friends.

Taking these preliminary precautions for now will prevent less confusion and stress."

"That's just too much to ask," moaned Mrs. Nicholson in her husband's chest.

"Caleb," spoke Mr. Nicholson through his own tears. "Do what you think is best just make our son well, that's all that's important right now. Just promise us that when he's strong enough you'll let him know about his family that's loved and cherished his very existence. He's been our life, our pride and joy. We've always tried to do right by the VanLees and Strattons in making all of you a part of his life." Like his wife said that was too much to ask. For once he felt helpless and cried like a baby. His nephews were now wiping tears as the other men surrounded the heartbroken family. Dr. Nason asked if the doctors would give the family a few minutes alone and they did.

Ruby sat numbly between her parents listening and watching the reactions of his family. The men that were trying to be strong for them were now falling apart as they let go of a barricade of emotions. The words, a *sense of family ties* played over and over in her mind. She couldn't believe this was happening. This time next week they were to be husband and wife. Now, it's a possibility he won't have a memory that she even exist, not to mention ever being a part of his life for fifteen years. Ruby recalls their meeting in the town square, the instant she looked into his baby blue eyes it was evident their love for each was stronger than ever. They both knew time was too precious to waste. Marriage was the best and most sensible step to take, especially since they couldn't stand being apart. He didn't hesitate asking her to be his wife and she has made plans to be just that, Mrs. Caleb Gerald VanLee and was looking forward to spending the rest of her life with him. It's just not fair she thought wiping away her tears.

Audrey Stratton, who looked like a movie star from the early sixties walked over and sat beside the Nicholsons. "Lawrence and Vera, I want you to listen to me and listen to me well," she reached for her husband's hand for support. If it had not been for the excellent job done by you two with our grandson…my snuggums…I don't know where I would be now. I was lost and in a dark place and caused my family to suffer as well."

"Oh Mother," said her oldest daughter. She looked at her daughter and told her she must.

"When my baby girl died I literally died too, never thinking of the beautiful grandchild she gave me and my own two wonderful children I had left. You and Vera went through all kinds of turmoil trying to keep us all a family and I know it wasn't easy." She looked over at Mildred who was one of her dearest friends. "Vera I know you'll remember this story and this is what changed my life. He came over to spend the weekend after spending two weeks in the country." Audrey smiled and continued, "He looked at me real serious like he had something on his mind when he sat his little backpack down to have milk and cookies. Chocolate milk that is and he did. He said, "*Grandmother Audrey you know you have such a long name. I already have a grandmother, a gram, and a nana; you need your own special name. That's what mama said, and she said me and you should give you one.*" Oh he was smart and a wise little fellow back then. To make a long story short we came up with honeybee and I still melt every time he calls me that. I'm his honeybee, well his and my other grands and great-grands now. That was such a special day for me Vera and you're responsible for that. I just want you and Lawrence to know how special you two are and you'll always hold a special place in all our hearts. Our snuggums is going to be just fine." Daniel Sr. patted their hands acknowledging he felt the same way. Caleb Sr. asked Charles Nason to send the doctors back into the room.

They returned to continue with the extent of his possible memory loss. It was agreed they could not promise or make any predictions as to how much if any was gone. They made it clear how important it was for the family to show extreme patience and not force anything on him for now. Less stress was best. The neurologist walked over and kneeled down in front of Ruby who had sat quietly during the consultation with very little emotions except for tears and soft sobs.

"Ruby, besides his parents you're going to have to be the strongest. I…"

"You don't' have to say the words Dr. Tmjarez, It's me and the love we share that's he's not going to remember. I already feel that," she whispered softly as she twisted her ring. There, she spoke the words aloud that had been plaguing her mind the moment Dr. Caleb spoke to them. She wiped her face and looked at Caleb's grandmother who was still sitting by his mother. "Mrs. Stratton I want you to have his mother's ring if it's alright with you Mrs. VanLee." Mildred was about to speak when Audrey Stratton caught her hand.

"Ruby the ring belongs to you. He gave it to you," said Dr. Caleb strongly.

"It's not fair for me to keep it Dr. VanLee. It's all over.

We can't get back what we had. He has a long ways to go and."

"And nothing, Ruby look at me, you can get back what you two had because it was genuine. Besides when he asked me for his mother's ring, his very words were; Honeybee no other woman is worthy enough to wear my mother's ring but Ruby Jewel McHarding. Honeybee I'm going to put this ring on her finger and I don't ever want it back and don't let her give it to you. She's that kind of woman very special and then he patted his chest. Is that what you all do frat?" She smiled.

"But this is his mother's ring, your daughter who's part of you and him."

"That's right Ruby," said Mr. Stratton, "she is a part of us and he's a part of her and you're a part of him and this ring will always connect us. He made that choice himself."

She was now overcome with emotions, "I don't' know if I can handle this," she cried. "I love him so much."

"Then Ruby show him," said Dr. Caleb. "Be there for him because he's going to need you and your strength. Like the doctors said we don't know anything yet, but it would be unfair if we were not completely honest with all the possibilities. We all need to remain prayerful for the best and not anticipate the worst. Regardless to what's going through our minds we must focus on Caleb because this is going to be a slow process and a long hard struggle for him more so. I need you to be strong for us all granddaughter, because it's you that has made the greatest change in him and made his life complete. You've given him that special love that only you and I mean only you, was able to give him, the woman he chose fifteen years ago." Ruby looked into the sad eyes of Dr. Caleb and told him she would. The doctors asked if there were any questions. Of course his mother asked if she could see him. Dr. Caleb pleaded with the rest of the family to go home and get a good night sleep and tomorrow they could all see him. He and Dr. Nason are staying the reminder of the night and will contact them if any changes occur. He looked at Vera and said her baby was going to be just fine; we need to be patient because we do have a ways to go. He gave her a big hug and told her she was going to need the kind of patience she had when she taught him how to tie his shoes. Although she didn't feel like smiling that treasure pulled a big one. She didn't think she would ever get him to learn how to tie his shoes but he did and at four years old. Mr. Lawrence told Caleb he felt confident with him and Dr. Nason looking after their son and trusted them whole heartily.

On his way out he walked over to Ruby and took her hand. "Come on and go with us Ruby, Henry Ray I'll take care of our daughter." Mr. McHarding patted him on the shoulder and said they would wait for them at the door.

God he looked so pale and helpless, like they all felt as they stood holding each other for support. The only way they knew he was alive was due to the machines and the frequent movement of his chest.

"You're going to be fine Baby," whispered Mrs. Nicholson to a sleeping Caleb. "Daddy and I are here with Ruby. You just rest and get well so you can go on with your life and give me some grandbabies." Mr. Nicholson patted her gently and suggested they give Ruby a few minutes with him alone.

"We'll be right outside the door Ruby."

She nodded her head and walked closer to his bed. Caressing his bruised cheek she told him how much she loved and needed him and to please remember her and their love. She leaned down and kissed the tattooed ruby on his chest that represented her and the love he'll always have for her. "I love you Caleb Gerald VanLee 3rd, please come back to me my ivory prince." Ruby felt a pair of strong arms holding her and looked into the face of Mr. Lawrence and his nephews. He whispered in her ear that everything was going to be fine. He knew she was frightened and feeling hopeless. But there was no need; their love was deep and embedded in his boy's heart and soul. He reminded her that Caleb did not have that ruby and the word jewel tattooed inside his brand for nothing. Mr. Lawrence told her he knew his son and sooner or later he was going to ask what does it all mean and he would make sure he knew the full significance. He hit his heart and said their love will always be and he meant every word. "Thank you Mr. Lawrence," she said softly. Together they walked out of his room to allow his grandparents to visit for a few minutes.

"You ready Baby," asked her father. She told them to give her a minute.

She walked over to his grandparents, aunt and uncle who were waiting for their turn. Ruby mouthed thank you again and gave each a tender hug and left abruptly without looking back. Her parent's rushed after her, but she was in her brother and sister's arms and together they walked to the elevator to take the hardest ride of her life. Ruby Jewel was leaving her first and only love and as far as she was concerned with her luck she anticipated the worst. It really was over and she had to accept that fact regardless if

249

anyone else did.

When they entered the lobby the Nason family was there to receive them. Words of gratitude would not leave her lips, her vocal cords had frozen. Collen Nason Sr. whispered for her to draw from that inner White-Cloud strength. She received hugs from her new friends Deb and Yolanda. Their husbands kissed her cheek and hit their hearts acknowledging their love for her and Caleb. Stumbling, her brother and father caught her and lead her out the door. She regained her voice and wept uncontrollably.

CHAPTER 27

Although it was only day four, Dr. Caleb had asked Dr. Tmjarez to stop the IV that dispenses the drug *Phenobarbital* which has kept him in a comatose state. He wanted him awake when Lawrence and Vera came for their daily morning visit. His vital signs were good and the surgery was healing fine. If things continue to go as expected he would be moved to a private room. Dr. Caleb also wanted him sitting up for a few minutes a day until he's stronger and then work toward being on his feet. His grandson was never one to sit around and get caught up in self-pity and they were not going to start now. He needed to get back to his life and Ruby. She had been to see him every day and according to Henry Ray then makes herself a prisoner in her room when she returns. She said it was depressing to see him lying there so helpless. He tried being encouraging and told her it wasn't as bad as it seems because he was constantly getting stronger every day, she just needed to stay prayerful....

Lauren Nason walked in, "Good morning Dr. Caleb, how's our patient today?"

"He's doing fine Lauren. Everything seems to be going well."

"Well good, I was just checking on him while on my way

to delivery. You have a good morning Sir."

"Thank you Lauren." He was told she was visiting him several times daily when no one was around. One of the nurses even caught her caressing and kissing his lips. He guessed he surprised her today because he was earlier than usual, but he had a goal and was very much aware of her intentions. But she could forget about his grandson because she's too superficial and the VanLee men did not like shallow women. His Mildred had her faults but she was sincere and a good hearted person except when it comes to her grandson. She thought it was her duty to find him a wife. Dr. Caleb smiled as he recalls Caleb putting her in her place when she first tried playing matchmaker. He didn't understand what she saw in Lauren Nason except she was Linda and Charles granddaughter. He was sorry that was not enough.

"What are you smiling about?" his voice was weak.

"Caleb, you're awake Son. How do you feel? Don't answer that!" Dr. Caleb pressed the button for his nurse.

"Yes, Dr. VanLee?"

"Page Dr. Tmjarez, please."

"Grandfather what happened?"

"You don't remember Son?"

"No, I just feel like I was stomped by a horse."

"That's pretty much what happened. You're in ICU and have suffered head injuries, broken ribs..."

"Where am I, this does not look like General."

"It's not son we're in Cypress right out of Houston."

"Texas," he moaned. Dr. Caleb gently patted his good side.

"It's alright son. You've experienced some serious injuries and need to be very careful and be still."

"Grandfather where is Mama and Dad?"

"They will be here shortly Son." Dr. Tmjarez walked in.

"How's my favorite patient?"

"Caleb this is one of your doctors. He's going to exam you."

"Grandfather I know the drill I've been a doctor for," he couldn't remember how long." Dr. Caleb patted him gently on his arm and told him that was okay. Lord he wished Vera and Lawrence was here now because he could tell he was getting agitated and needed the reassurance of his parents. He was a mama's boy and she could keep him calm. Dr. Tmjarez went about his job which was not easy dealing with a phenomenal young doctor who knew his profession. Dr. Caleb couldn't believe his eyes, Vera and Lawrence were peeping in the doorway. He stepped out to let them know he was asking for them. Relief covered their faces as they hugged each other. Dr. Caleb was relieved himself. He just prayed that whatever memory he's lost for the time being will resume.

Dr. Tmjarez stepped outside the door and they went to a small conference room to discuss his condition and him wanting to be a part of his medical team.

"Lawrence I don't know how we're going to keep him

from being involved since this is his specialty. And to be honest I'm just so thankful he remembers that he's a neurologist. But we do know he needs to take it slow and let his doctors do their job, and we promise that he will be kept informed."

"That sounds reasonable, let's talk to him. If you don't mind Dr. Tmjarez let us talk to him alone."

Vera and Lawrence rushed to his room and over to his bed side. They were so happy to see those baby blues looking at them, although he was extremely pale. They both kissed him gently on his cheek. Vera caressed his cheek while his father held his hand. Caleb was glad to see them because he needed some answers. Not that his grandfather could not tell him. He was like any other only child, spoiled and wanted his mama and daddy.

"Dad why are we in Texas? Is everybody in the family alright? Gram, Nana…"

"Caleb everybody is just fine. We're here because of your accident."

"Dad I can't believe I fell off of a horse." A frown spread across his face. He was trying to remember the accident.

"Son, don't worry about that right now, I want you to rest. Dr. Tmjarez told us of you wanting to be involved with your treatments. We want you to let your doctors do their job for now and you play the role of patient this time."

"But Dad, it's so much I don't understand." He was having a hard time staying awake but he knew it was a combination of the medicines, which he was going to wean himself off of right away.

"I know Son, we can talk about it later. You need your rest, besides Honeybee and Big D are here, plus your aunt and uncle. Rest now so you can visit with them later."

"Mama..."

"I'm here Baby."

"Where's Grandfather?"

"I'm here Grandson."

"Where's Grandmother?"

"She's here and will be by later today."

"Mama, don't leave until..." his eyes fluttered shut as he drifted off.

"I won't Baby." She held his hand to her face so he could feel her closeness and warmth. She knew he was spoiled but he was their only child and her spoiled baby as her husband has said so many times._____

Ruby pulled down the lace corset ruffle trim beige top she was wearing over her spandex-cotton denim skirt, with red lace appliqué flowers. Her mother had made her a French braid and wrapped a ponytail holder at the end to keep it together. She was ready to take that ride to the hospital to see Caleb, which she's done every day since his accident. She prayed that circumstances had improved some and she could smother him with love like her daddy said.

"I'm leaving Momma and Daddy, I'll call and give you an update on his progress," she said leaving out of the side door. She stepped onto the porch and admired the glorious morning, not a rain cloud in sight regardless of last night's light storm. It was clear with sunny skies and pleasant fresh scents, because of the light breezes. Ruby had a peaceful and restful night and felt everything was going to be just fine, besides it was just too pretty of a day to have any mishaps. She had her leather backpack with her toys so she could do a little work since she had planned to stay awhile._____

Lauren Nason just got off the phone with her mother who was fuming and fit to be tied. She only called to tell her the good news about Caleb. Leslie Nason chewed her out royally. Hosea told her about the warning he had given her concerning Weeboy. He told her no one should ride him, because he had not been himself lately and strongly suggested she choose another horse. Although she insisted, he felt terrible and blamed himself for the accident. She didn't mean for him to get hurt and end up in the hospital. He never should have fallen off his horse. He was supposed to have been a horseman, at least that's what he bragged about at the birthday celebration. She asked her mother whether or not she was going to tell her daddy and grandfather. Even though she had them wrapped around her finger they would be furious and not allow her to get by. She didn't mean him any harm, and hoped she convinced her mother just that. Lauren made a promise not to pursue him if she would just keep what she knew to herself. She actually had to beg her mother to remain silent. Leslie Nason said she would remain silent, with her promising to apologize to Hosea as soon as she got to the ranch. But under no circumstances was she going to let this golden opportunity to finally have the man of her dreams slip past her. No way and her mother will understand once he falls in love with her!_____

While Caleb was resting comfortably, Dr. Caleb encouraged his parents to go down to the cafeteria and have breakfast since they had arrived much earlier than usual today. He promised to stay by his side and requested the special for this morning. He looked at his grandson who was sleeping and thought he was going to need his rest because family had been notified that he was conscious and doing great, all except Ruby. Caleb Sr. wasn't able to reach her on the cell, so he called the house phone. Henry Ray said she was in route and should be there shortly.

"Dr. Caleb, we heard the good news," whispered Roy with Roderick by his side peeping into the room. "Is it alright if we see him?"

"Sure boys, he is asleep, but go ahead." He started to tell them not to pressure him about anything particular when Caleb asked who he was talking to.

"Say man why don't you open your eyes.

"Roy, it's been a minute cuz. How's everybody?" Roy hesitated for a second looking at his grandfather who was taking it all in.

"Everybody's doing great, little cuz. We're just worried about you. Mama and some of the family are on their way. The word is out that Frosty is back with the living. "

"Who's that you got with you?"

Q-Note jokingly caught his heart pretending to be hurt. "Auh man, you mean to tell me…"

"Q-Note, is that you?" Caleb held out his hand.

"Frosty man it's been too long my brother." He caught

the hint with his cousin. He gave him a big sloppy kiss and a pat on his good side.

"Please don't get mushy on me **Q**. What are you doing here?"

"I work here in the medical records department. But we have plenty time to talk about me. We promised Dr. C we wouldn't tire you out but I'll be back before I leave for the day, au ight?"

"Au ight, and thanks for coming by. When I flee this place we'll get together and hangout before I go back home…word."

"Word." He attempted to raise his hand, but it was difficult. So his frat brother patted his brand and then touched his. Roy told him he would be back when his parents come to visit. They said their goodbyes to Dr. Caleb and left the room. On their way to the elevator they ran into his parents and Ruby. They told them he was awake and recognized them. Ruby was so excited she hugged them both and rushed to his room. She didn't wait to hear the rest. His parents looked worried and asked Roy and Roderick not to leave. All they could think of was Ruby and what trauma her visit might cause the both of them. They approached his door, and heard Caleb begging him to calm down, everything had gone wrong. His monitors were beeping wildly signaling his vitals were elevating as his breathing became erratic. Vera rushed to his bedside with Lawrence and the guys behind her. Ruby was standing in the corner shaking like a leaf, tears streaming down her face.

"Mama why is she here?" He was shouting and actually trying to raise himself up when sharp pains rushed through his entire body. With all the pain he was experiencing he thought she had nerve coming to see him while he was flat on his back, pretending she was genuinely concerned about his welfare. How could she care about him? They haven't seen or talked to each other since he left PVU. She hurt him terribly and not one time did she ever say she was sorry. She refused his hand in marriage and has made his life a living hell.

"Baby stop before you hurt yourself." His breathing was becoming uneven. His doctor and nurse rushed in and asked everyone to leave.

"Mama, don't leave," was the last thing that slipped past his lips as he went into convulsions. Ruby didn't take her eyes off of him as she repeatedly whispered his name while being pulled out of his room. Out of the corner of her eye she saw Dr. Tmjarez give him an injection. She heard her name being called but she did not answer.

"What's happened," asked Dr. Nason with Mildred and the Strattons? Roy told them they were not sure, but he's having a seizure. His grandmothers and aunt became emotional. Dr. Caleb came out to tell them everything was under control. He was given a mild sedative and would be sleeping for a little while.

"Caleb, Roy said he went into convulsions, what brought that on? We were under the impression he was fine," asked Daniel Stratton 2nd while consoling his mother. Ruby whimpered it was all her fault. She was the reason for him having a seizure. Dr. Caleb walked over to her but she snatched out of Q-Note's arms and backed away from the entire group.

"Ruby, don't."

"No," she shouted as she pointed to Dr. Caleb. "You…you were there," she stuttered. "He…was beyond anger…he was outraged. His eyes were full of contempt and…and hatred for me." She hit her chest hard as she repeated herself as if she was making sure every word and twisted harsh look on his face was embedded in her heart. "He…he…hates…hates…me." This time Dr. Caleb and Dr. Nason called her name, but she held her hand up. "Please there's nothing to say. I will not cause him anymore pain. He does not deserve that." She took his ring off and walked over to his Honeybee and told her to keep it for him. "He does not remember giving me his mother's things and one day he'll ask for it."

"Ruby I thought we had been through this." Audrey took her hand, but she pulled away.

"I know, but we're not being fair to him now and it may upset him if he finds out I have his mother's ring."

"She's right Audrey," said Mrs. VanLee. "We don't need to upset and cause him any more pain than he's already experiencing and Ruby I don't think you…"

"Mildred," cried out Dr. Caleb.

"It's okay Dr. Caleb, I hadn't plan on coming back. I just need to get my things. Is it alright if I go back into his room?"

"Yes Ruby, he'll be sleep for a while." Ruby walked in and his mother was sitting by his bed holding his hand while his father was sitting by the window. She picked up her backpack and turned to look at her sleeping ivory prince. He looked so peaceful now. His parents walked out of the room to give her some privacy. She walked over caressed and kissed his cheek then his lips. She whispered she was sorry for causing him so much pain and she will always love only him. Ruby walked out of his room said good bye to his family and walked to the elevator.

CHAPTER 28

Ruby Jewel raised up to get her bearings, but her head started pounding. She was in her nightclothes and in her bed at her parents' home. She couldn't recall how long nor what day it was because she was surrounded by darkness and had been since that day. Her blinds and curtains were drawn to keep a dark gloomy room to match the melancholy mood she had. She never wanted to see daylight again, at least that's how she felt. She was content being behind closed doors. She had no idea the time nor did she care. What difference did it make? She had nothing to do or nowhere to go. She did not need to be around people spreading her misery. Her life was now empty and she felt completely alone. Her mother always said she would be by herself if she didn't change her ways, well she did and she's more alone than ever. She should have married him when he wanted her to, then maybe she would have some hope. It's her fault she's lost him all over again; Ruby turned over and cried herself to sleep...

"Henry Ray she's imprisoned herself in that dark room for three whole days now. She's had on the same night clothes, barely had anything to eat, and she won't take any phone calls. Dr. Caleb called to tell the good news about Caleb now in a private room and steadily improving. She wouldn't even talk to him; I had to deliver the message. Tori and Kami said she hardly said a word, they did all the talking and then she told them she needed to go. Go where? She won't even come out and eat. She's only had a bowl of cereal and half of a sandwich and those cocktails you've made her. It's not healthy for her to carry on this way. For once in my life I'm worried about my baby." Robbie Jean wiped the tears from her eyes. Henry Ray patted her hand and told her to stop worrying. He's sent for reinforcement that would arrive shortly. She couldn't imagine who but was glad. She thought Saturday night was bad when Ruby came home from the hospital; Wednesday morning she was a complete basket case. They were so thankful Roy drove her home. Dr. Caleb had already called and explained the situation and what to expect. He suggested they give her some time alone and he would keep in touch, but not to worry their children would get through this. He promised.

All they were able to do was help her change into a pair of pajamas and put her to bed. Her father fixed her a nice cocktail that helped her go right to sleep. Robbie Jean had never seen her fall apart like that since she's been in the world. Even as a child she was never easy to cry and always took what little punishment she was given well.

There was a knock on the front door. "There's the reinforcement I sent for. Come on let's let them in and get our baby back on the right track."

Robbie Jean was speechless when she peeped over her husband's shoulder. He was right he had brought in some real heavy reinforcements for sure.

"Oh give me this little angel." Kyla reached for Robbie Jean and gave her a big smack. Kellie told her she and her brothers were now into giving sugar especially to anyone with gray hair. "Where are the boys?"

"We left them with their daddy. This was a trip for girls only," announced Angela. "We've got work to do. Is she still in her room?" Mr. Henry told them yes and stepped aside to let them get started.

"I'll keep this little…"

"Oh no Ms McHarding, this is our secret weapon. Okay Kyla, Ruby…Ruby." Kellie and Angela walked to her door and opened it. The toddler ran to the bed chanting her name. Ruby thought she was dreaming and then the toddler began pulling her bedspread trying to use it to climb up. She couldn't believe her eyes as she set up to lift the little munchkin in the bed with her.

"Ru…by…Ru…by…kiss…kiss." Ruby's heart melted as she accepted a kiss from her special little angel.

"Okay Ruby Jewel McHarding, it's time for you to join the human race," said Angela. She hated to see her friend like this and couldn't believe she actually gave back her ring. Her father had already told them and asked them not to say anything.

"And when's the last time you had a bath or brushed your teeth? Don't you kiss my baby again," exclaimed Kellie. "Baby take Ruby for bath." Kellie opened the door so Kyla could see the tub. She was fascinated with bathrooms like all little people. She slid down on the floor holding on to the bedspread and pulled Ruby's hand trying to get her out.

"Look ya'll I appreciate…"

"Ruby Jewel you get your tainted smelling behind to this bathroom and we mean right now or we'll pull you by your hair girlfriend and we mean it." Angela and Kellie stood with their hands on their hips with a glare that emphasized they meant every word. Kyla looked at the two women and tried imitating them, but her little hands landed on her backside instead.

Ruby couldn't take it and burst into tears. After the sobs lightened up she told them how she felt. "Ya'll just don't understand. It's over...I've lost him. He'll never remember what we had. He actually hates me. You should have seen the way he glared at me when he asked me why was I there. It was just awful. I hurt him and that's all he remembers the pain and agony I caused fifteen years ago. He has no recollection that I love him. My heart is broken into so many pieces. I want to go back to the way things were. I want my daddy to walk me down the aisle Saturday. I want my life with him back," she cried. They patiently allowed her to get it all out as Kellie rocked her gently moving her curls from her face. Little Kyla climbed up in her lap and patted her wet face. Angela gave her a towel and told her to wipe Ruby's tears.

"Sweetie you know nothing can be done about what has happened, but you have to move forward. According to your parents, Dr. VanLee said the least little incident can spark his memory and cause him to remember the love you two have for each other. You just need to remain prayerful and give him some time; this is a must if you really want to spend the rest of your life with him. Now come on pull yourself together, let's get all cleaned up and have some lunch."_____

"Mr. Henry the lunch was delicious. It's always a pleasure to visit and sit on the back gallery."

"Angela please, porch.   This is Hempstead, Texas we don't have galleries."

"Alright Ms McHarding, porch it is." Her girls had a time getting her to cooperate earlier, but they had a secret welcome who did her job, thought Ruby as she peeled her peach. Babygirl had melted her all the way down. All things considered, they had a wonderful visit and lots of laughs with Kyla. She loved playing in the back yard and insisted on gathering every creepy crawler she could find...

"Well sistah girl we need to get down the highway. I want to get back to the city before it gets too late," announced Angela. Just be patient with his situation and give him some time. He is your soul mate and you need to give the both of you a chance to rekindle that love."

"She's right," said Kellie.   "This love affair has been going on for fifteen years and it's stronger than ever. Give Ruby sugar so we can go see daddy and brothers." The toddler did as she was told and also gave kisses to Ruby's parents. Then she chanted *da...de...bro...tha* all the way to the front door. "Me and my big mouth," taking the toddler's hand. The friends had a big laugh while walking to the car.

Ruby watched them drive off and decided to sit in her antique rocker for a spell. She waved at her parents neighbors who were coming from the grocery store. She was sure they were wondering why she was still home, that's never happened before unless there was an emergency. He was the emergency and reason why. She wanted to be there for him, but it wasn't a need now. She was no longer in Hempstead and may as well go home to resume what life she had before he returned. Besides, her parents had put their life on standstill to babysit her. They had not been to the center since she's been home. That wasn't fair, especially after her father had a hard time convincing her mother to sign up and participate. Ruby went inside the house to find her parents to tell them her decision…

"There's no reason for me to stay." Of course her mother was not happy, but her mind was made up as she packed her things while Robbie Jean watched.

"Baby can't you at least wait until the weekend since the wed… oh Baby I'm sorry."

Ruby stopped to give her mother a hug, "Mommy, an apology isn't necessary for the truth. You're right there will be no wedding."

"Only for now, everything will work out you'll see." She didn't comment one way or the other and put the last piece in her suitcase and zipped it up. "Ruby stay," pleaded her mother as she wiped a tear.

"Mommy please let me do this my way, remember I'll be back for Easter and then right back for Mother's Day. What's our color for this year? We haven't had a chance to pick a color since the…" she couldn't bring herself to say it. It had been a tradition for the McHarding women to wear a special color chosen by her mother for her birthday and this year it fell on Mother's Day. They had such a wonderful time two years ago at the Golden Regal Mansion and all agreed to make it their special outing every Mother's Day. So far it's worked out well, no cooking for the men and no cleaning up behind them for the women. She took her mother's hand and told her to think of the color she wants them to wear this year as they walked to the front of the house. Her father was waiting with a care package he had prepared. He took her luggage to the car with them following.

"You be careful Babygirl, we'll see you soon." He held open the door and kissed her cheek. They watched her drive off and then went into the house, but not before Robbie Jean told him he had been any help trying to talk her into staying. Henry Ray told her they needed to give her time alone. And she should get back to her routine instead of lying around there doing nothing. He didn't have the heart to tell them both he had visited the hospital yesterday, and saw Dr. Lauren Nason in Caleb's room. They looked pretty cozy to him, that's why he sent for the cavalry! _____

Ruby knew her father was right; work was what she needed at the moment. She needed to resume her life or at least attempt to work at it. Regardless of her feeling hopeless right now, she had to put forth every effort to maintain a positive attitude and be prayerful that all would pan out. Furthermore she had a business that needed her; but first she wanted to see Caleb one last time.

She was careful not to draw any attention to herself when she got off the elevator. She just wanted to get a quick glance and then leave; maybe she'll be lucky and catch him asleep. Then she would be able to go inside his room and caress his bruised skin with a tender kiss for the last time. What luck, his door was slightly opened; she heard voices and peeped in. Nothing could have prepared her for what she saw, Lauren Nason all over him with her chest grazing his face, fluffing his pillows. It didn't take all of that. She held her breath as her eyes clouded, she kissed her Caleb right on the lips and he didn't protest. As a matter of fact he looked like he enjoyed it. How long has this been going on? With her heart shattered, she walked away as quietly as she came in. The hope that she and everybody else wanted her to hold on to had just been destroyed for good...

Ruby Jewel drove straight to the business park minutes after Angela left according to the security guard. The cleaning crew was there now. She said her hellos and went straight to her office. Ruby didn't know how she made it to Houston; except by the grace of God. Opening her door; the first thing her teary eyes saw were the purple roses that she was sure had come today. Now letting her tears flow freely she flopped down in her chair and had herself a good strong cry. She knew it was over and she didn't have a chance getting him back, it was hopeless for sure. Looking at the purple roses she knew she needed to do something with them ASAP. No way was she accepting his roses; they didn't have the same mean. Wiping away her tears she had an idea and dialed the number on the card.

"Thank you Carrie, that's right send them to the hospital instead and reverse the charges to me. No, no messages and please I want this to remain confidential. Again thank you." She still couldn't help praying that one day he would get the true meaning of the purple rose. But she had to accept fate and continue her life without him._____

Cornelius Baines couldn't believe his luck when he saw her car parked in front. He heard about her fiancé's accident and memory loss; and hated it terribly. But he couldn't help thinking this was his chance, as he approached the door just as she was about to walk out.

"Mr. Baines, what can I do for you? The office is closed for the evening."

"It's what I can do for you and I won't take no for an

answer, and please call me Cornelius." The puzzled expression she had let him know he had better keep talking while she was still listening if he wanted things to go as he planned. "I'll bet you haven't had a thing to eat since lunch and I know this wonderful place that specializes in soul food with a nice view of downtown Houston's water gardens." Ruby smiled because she knew just the place, Soulsters. She heard about their fabulous second location but never had the opportunity to visit. Why not she thought and told him yes. *Thank you Lord*, he prayed silently to himself. "Okay, let's take your car over to the garage so they can keep an eye on it and we can ride in my truck."

"Alright Cornelius," looking down at her animal print sundress and black shrug.

"You look beautiful," and she did in spite of her being dressed casually.

"Thank you Cornelius." He loved the sound of his name coming from her lips. He told her she was welcome and could hardly contain himself; he was having dinner with Ruby...

Ruby what in the world are you doing? You know you're not being fair to him. Your heart belongs to Caleb. Humph, as far as she was concerned, he didn't deserve her heart or loyalty after what she witnessed today. And she didn't care if he had lost his memory. Her conscience would not let up as she sat across from Cornelius, enjoying a scrumptious mouthwatering meal that was cooked the way she liked; baby back ribs, potato salad, corn on the cob, Texas buttered toast, and lemon raspberry tea. The conversation was just as enjoyable. She learned some interesting things about him. He was a professional handyman which was good to know. He could fix most appliances and did simple plumbing jobs. The trades were mastered during his incarceration. That was the only subject he didn't care to talk about and she didn't press the issue. She couldn't help noticing his beautiful smile and his handsome face, and for just turning thirty he was quite mature. *And so what if he has a wonderful smile*. Ruby rubbed her temples trying to put a stop to her pestering conscience. She was just enjoying a friendly meal with a fine-looking gentleman.

"Cornelius, everything was delicious."

"I'm glad, how about dessert, their red velvet cheese cake is awesome." She told him she couldn't eat another bite."

"Fine, I'll get you a carry out and you can have it tomorrow." He signaled for their waitress. With their carryouts they had a pleasurable leisure walk to where he parked his truck. It was a typical spring night for Houston with favorable weather for a nice outing. Ruby was not ready to go home and face the memories, and was glad he suggested they stop at the big fountain located right in the middle of the theater district. Cornelius spotted an empty bench, caught her hand and they rushed over. They watched the waters change colors as it sprouted out. Downtown Houston had really changed he thought, or was it the beautiful company he had.

"It's a beautiful night isn't it," said Ruby looking up into the heavens. She noticed the formation of the stars and he came to mind, but she was determined not to let him spoil her wonderful evening. He was probably sharing his dimpled smile with that Lauren Nason.

"Ruby." She heard her name being called and gazed into his smiling face. "Where did you wander off to?"

"Oh I was just admiring the stars and their formation. Did you know that's…" He finished her sentence and enlightened her with an astrology lesson just like her….*He's not yours anymore.*

"Cornelius, I want to thank you for a lovely evening." She brushed her lips against his cheek and got in her car. He watched her drive off while feeling the very spot her soft lips touched.

CHAPTER 29

"Is the patient ready to have a little outing," asked Lauren, walking over to where chair he was sitting? He greeted her with his dimpled smile. She had been there faithfully keeping him company, making his stay at Cypress Memorial pleasant with her special treats. Yesterday she took him down to the hospital's cafeteria for dinner. "Yes, I'm ready to shake this place for a little while. I really want to thank you Lauren for making this easy. I couldn't have done it without you."

She blushed, "It's been my pleasure Caleb," she reached over and brushed her lips against his clean shaven face. The attendant came in with his wheelchair and helped him to his feet, then to the chair. "I have a surprise for you." He looked at her smiling because he couldn't imagine what the surprise could be. The attendant rolled him to the elevator. He was like a big kid; he loved surprises and insisted on her telling him. "I have a special picnic lunch prepared by Mrs. Perez and I thought we would eat out in the courtyard today and get a little sunshine. Would you like that?"

"Yes, that sounds great. I sure hope she fixed enough because I'm starving." As they entered the courtyard and found the ideal spot, Q-Note knocked on the window to get his attention. He was on his way up when he saw them going toward the courtyard. **Q** shook his head, he didn't like the picture he witnessed today nor the other times he's come down to visit. She was constantly around being extra helpful and sweet. At the rate things were going he and Ruby would never get back together. He was going to talk to his boy and find out where his head was for real. Looks like he was getting his chance, Caleb becked for him to come out and join them.

"Hey Frosty, how's my dog today?" He said that to vex Ms Lauren, she didn't like for them to talk frat.

"Yo dog is ready to steal away." The brothers hugged. "Lauren brought a picnic lunch, it's plenty. Mrs. Perez makes delicious roast beef sandwiches and pound cake that melts in your mouth dog."

"You know I can't pass up a deal like that." He pulled up a chair to join them. Lauren turned a nice shade of red like she was getting sunburn. "Boy it's a beautiful day and the sun is doing its thang. Lauren are you okay? It's not too hot for you?"

Caleb looked over at her, "You do look a little flushed. If you want you can go back inside **Q** can take me back to my jail cell when we're thru."

"Oh no Caleb, I'm fine."_____

"Caleb I'm sorry to tell you this but it seems we're in need of your bed." That was almost a week ago when Dr. Tmjarez dismissed him from the hospital. The two and a half weeks he spent in Cypress Memorial had seemed like two months. Now he was home and felt like a stranger and a prisoner. If it wasn't for his furnishing and personal belongings he would have thought he was in the wrong

place. It's amazing how the brain works and he knew better than anyone as a headache threatened. He knew he had to let it go for now. Caleb was bored to death and sick of being confined to the townhouse; except for the trips back to the hospital for therapy he had been grounded. He needed something to do besides read medical journals. Being physically active in what he loved was his prescription and cure. Whether his family approved or not he was planning to volunteer at the senior citizens center until he returns to the clinic. He walked out to his patio where the men were.

"Caleb, telephone," announced his mother. "It's Lauren," she whispered. His mother did not like the smile that surfaced, but what could she say. Ruby's name still brought tension and Mildred was having a field day singing Lauren praises.

"I'll ask them, hold on a minute. Mama, Lauren wants to know if we all want to come to the ranch for a causal dinner on the veranda. Mrs. Perez has fixed her famous beef enchiladas."

"Yes, Grandson that sounds like a great idea," said Mildred. Vera rolled her eyes because she really did not want to spend another evening watching Lauren Nason fuss over her baby. He looked at his mother to get her response. He was aware that she didn't care for Lauren but she has been very supportive and good company considering. It was at Dr. Nason's birthday celebration where he had the accident. According to newspaper clippings he's seen they were somewhat a couple. Right now he was just going with the flow, because of his memory lost. In all honesty he was having a difficult time believing they were actually a couple, but he knew time would tell.

"Mama, I'm waiting," he had his hand over the receiver.

"Son, I think I'm going to pass this time. I promised Lucille we would come over and visit with her and the new grandbaby."

"You're sure Mama." She walked over to him and kissed him on the cheek and said positive. He smiled because he knew her too well._____

 "Angela, I've gone out with him several times."

"Four times."

"Okay, four times and I've enjoyed his company. We've had some wonderful dates and I've even let him kiss me and I've kissed him, but..."

"But nothing! He's crazy about you according to Gregory." "Gregory, what does he know about him?"

"He's done some simple plumbing jobs at the business park."

"You need to keep dating and give him a chance."

"For what, I can't force myself to have feelings for him other than a friend. Trust me, I've tried and besides it's not fair to give him false hope."

"I still say you're not trying hard enough. Why don't you invite him to spend the weekend for Mr. Henry's birthday celebration and introduce him to your family? Then you won't have to entertain him alone, you'll have the entire family and lots of activities going on." Ruby sat quietly and Angela knew she was wearing her down. Ruby picked up her phone and shooed Angela out of her office. Angela

276

stepped out with a smile. She knew if she could get her home with her new beau Ms Robbie Jean could influence her to see, Cornelius Baines was a keeper.

It was all set; he was coming home with her for the weekend and meet her entire family. Her parents were happy she had found someone and was moving on with her life; Cornelius was thrilled; and her friend was ecstatic. Angela did have a point she wouldn't have to find something for them to do the whole time they were there. Her father's birthday was Saturday but they were starting the celebration Friday evening._____

Ruby and Cornelius arrived in Hempstead and was meeting her family at the farmhouse to start the celebration. Tonight was the weenie roast with all the trimmings. Her mother asked her to stop at Ms Dolly's for the desserts she ordered for tomorrow and Sunday on their way, of course she would also get her teacakes. She told Cornelius he hadn't tasted anything until he had one of Ms Dolly's teacakes. As usual the parking lot was full and she had to park around the corner. As Cornelius opened her door he observed his surroundings.

"This is a nice little town you have here Ruby."

"I like it; everybody knows everyone and the people are quite friendly. Tomorrow I'll show you around._____

"Pull up beside the SUV," ordered Caleb. He opened the door for his mother and Honeybee. "Come on family, you haven't tasted anything until you have Ms. Dolly's fried catfish, homemade fries, and peach cobbler for starters. Tell them Lauren, grandfather." Mildred looked at her husband. She didn't remember coming to this place.

"Yes, you're all in for a treat and will dine sufficiently ladies," he said opening the door. Lawrence noticed her car and walked over to his wife and pointed slyly to show her; they kept that to themselves. Caleb lead the group and for some unknown reason he felt a migraine coming on, why all of a sudden was a mystery. He hadn't had a headache for days, long as he does not stress himself out trying to recall past events, and of course the mentioning of her name. He had been looking forward to this all week. The Strattons just had a couple of days left and he wanted them to experience Ms Dolly's down home Texas hospitality. He had already called ahead to let her know he had a party of ten coming for her specialty tonight...

Ruby and Cornelius were sitting at the counter waiting on their orders. She ordered French fries and the house tea for them to share while they waited. As usual Ms Dolly was packed and a table for a large group had been set up. She was feeding Cornelius a fry and felt she was being watched, probably another classmate. She put another fry in his mouth while slightly turning her head. OMG...couldn't be but it was, Caleb with the look of dislike and animosity. Why was he still angry, he had gone on with his life? Lauren Nason was hanging all over him; the atmosphere was now thick with tension and hostility aimed at her.

"Ruby how are you Sweetheart." His mother and father embraced her with hugs and kisses, and then the Strattons with tender love squeezes while he stood tight lipped looking like he could kill. Dr. VanLee gave her a warm hug and whispered how sorry he was for everything. He said what everybody else wanted to say. She kissed his cheek and whispered it was just fate. She spoke to Mrs. VanLee, Lauren, and Caleb who barely parted his lips. Lord she wished she didn't care anymore, but she did. She introduced Cornelius as her friend. He played his part well by putting his arm around her as he shook hands with his family.

"Ruby your order is ready." Thank you, she thought and was about to tell them to have a nice evening, when she noticed his distorted face.

"Caleb are you all right?" He looked at her for a second and started massaging his temples. His breathing became rapid as if he was struggling. He was about to lose his balance, she reached out to him before she realized it. Thank God Cornelius was there, he caught him. It was total chaos and hysteria for a few seconds with everyone calling his name including Ruby. His father and uncle assisted Cornelius and they lifted him to a table that had been quickly cleared off.

"Son, can you hear me," asked his grandfather. "Vera, give me his medicine." Caleb blinked his eyes opened and looked over at his mother instead of Lauren and reached for her hand. He closed his eyes again and concentrated on slowing down his breathing while his grandfather took his vital signs. The sharp pain had actually snatched the strength from his body; just like he could snatch her and ask *Why?* "This was not bad at all son." He tried to sit up but his grandfather told him to lie still for a few more minutes. "He's fine, Daniel take the ladies over to our table."

"Lauren you stay with him," said Mildred.

"That won't be necessary, Vera will stay, Daniel."

Before leaving Mildred VanLee glared at Ruby. "This never would have happened if you…"

"Mildred that's enough!" barked her husband before she could finish her sentence. Ruby looked at Caleb lying there. She wanted to hold him and kiss away his hurt and pain; it was all in his face. But instead she said her goodbyes and left.

CHAPTER 30

"Angela please, just take my word for it, it was awful and a total disaster. The weekend had been ruined before it started, that's all I have to say. And poor Cornelius was such a dear; he had to drive us to my sister's with me balling like a baby. I tell you Angela I was never so embarrassed in all my life."

"Ruby, according to Gregory he had a wonderful time and he enjoyed being with you and your family, until you told him you didn't think ya'll should date anymore. I just don't understand you, what was so awful except running into Caleb and his wicked grandmother. That had nothing to do with you and Cornelius."

"Look Angela, I'm going to stop this charade before things get out of hand. I'm sorry, I just can't feel the way you want me to about him. And he's just too sweet of a guy to be used." She turned her back to her good friend, because seeing him again had nothing to do with their relationship except the obvious.

"Ruby."

She turned around to face her with teary eyes, "I still love him."_____

The Strattons were scheduled for an early morning flight

tomorrow. K & L Transportation Service would arrive at the townhouse at 8 AM and they would all ride to Houston to the airport and back to Hempstead. He hated to see them go but the holiday weekend was here and they did have families in Denver. Besides, they had been there ever since the accident. The grands had called to see if they were coming home for their big egg hunt and party which was always held at his grandparents' home. They couldn't disappoint them and he didn't want them to.

"You're still up nephew?" He knew he was not asleep. Because they were in the same area and he could hear him tossing about on his air mattress. They had removed the furniture in his kitchen nook which made a perfect bunking space for them.

"Yea, Unc, I'm too keyed up to sleep. More like restless and can't."

"Come on let's take a ride so I can enjoy this beautiful Texas night for the last time. I understand there's a truck stop that serves the best pastries and coffee this time of night according to Mr. C, you game?"

"Yeah, it beats tossing and turning." Yes sir, he had a sour disposition in addition to fighting a headache which has pretty much been his mood since Ms Dolly's. He and his uncle left through the patio door to keep from disturbing his aunt who was sleeping on the sofa....

Uncle Daniel pulled up and parked in front of the storefront and asked his nephew if it was anything special he wanted. Caleb looked at him with a blank expression. He was surprised his grandfather even knew of this place and couldn't imagine his grandmother sitting on a wooden bench even if it did have a cushion. He told his uncle he'll have whatever he's having and leaned his head back and closed his eyes. For some reason the closer they got to the truck stop the pounding became intense. He took some deep breaths to try and ease the tension that was creeping upon him....

Ruby Jewel couldn't believe her eyes. Caleb's uncle just walked inside the storefront and she had the nerve to duck behind the magazine rack. Once she was out of sight, she gazed out the big window for his truck. There he was reclined with his eyes closed massaging his temples. He opened his door to get out and she made a beeline to the ladies room. His uncle saw him coming inside with a frown and rushed over to make sure he was alright. He said he wanted a hot tea for his migraine. His Uncle paid for their purchases and they started toward the exit. For some strange reason Caleb stopped and turned around like he was expecting someone to appear. He waited a second and then walked out to the SUV, but not before gazing at the table in the middle of the courtyard. Something familiar was about that very spot and table; he just couldn't put his finger on it... that too must be a part of his past.

"What's wrong nephew?"

"Nothing I guess, except I had this strange feeling someone was watching me." He looked around the parking lot for a familiar car, but did not recognize anything. He leaned back to rest his head for a few minutes and then sat up to swallow his aspirins and sip his hot drink. His uncle even had a choice of pastries and a variety of sweet rolls. After they were situated they pulled out the parking lot but not before his uncle recognized Ruby Jewel McHarding in the rear view mirror. He wanted to say something but felt it was best he didn't, Caleb was already having a migraine all because he felt her presence....

They arrived at the townhouse and decided to sit on the patio to enjoy their treats and the serenity of a peaceful country night. Daniel Stratton pondered over whether or not he should mention that she was there, but again he thought he better leave well enough alone especially since he gets so upset with the mere mentioning of her name. So he decided the next best thing to do, keep his mouth closed and continue sipping his drink.

Gazing at the stars for a few minutes Caleb broke their silence, "You know Unc life is something. It's amazing how the decisions you've made in the past can still affect your future."

"Meaning nephew?" He knew where he was coming from but it was best to let him talk it out.

"Meaning, take me and Ruby for instance, we had our whole life planned to the letter. We would get married, hold off on having a family and attend medical school and law school in Houston. We were young and so in love and had our entire life ahead of us. Then the bottom fell out and she refused to give me a decent and acceptable reason why." He continued, "I have to admit it's hard to believe I actually moved to Texas after all these years." I guess with my family here it'll register sooner or later." He looked at his uncle.

"I understand nephew. I know we all have a special place in your heart but like you say, they are your family and you have been a part of their lives as well. And we all know you are well loved. The hospital was some crowded during your stay with the Nicholsons and Beasleys along with your frat brothers." They both laughed because the brothers did represent. He just hated he couldn't recall the fantastic reunion they had before his accident. His cousins and **Q** said it was in grand style, a ride around Houston in a chartered limousine with a spread fit for kings.

"Well nephew, I think we should turn in, we do need to be ready for eight."

Caleb was silent for a few minutes and then glanced over at his uncle and then looked away with his eyes filling up. Looking straight into the darkness he wiped his face on his shirt, afterwards he whispered, "I still love her Unc. All the love I have is only for Ruby Jewel McHarding and my life seems so empty right now. And now she's with someone else, who seems like a pretty good guy. I've lost her for good."

His uncle got up and sat beside him and held him as he cried in his arms like he did fifteen years ago. He had to do everything in his power not to say what he needed to hear, but he couldn't ignore the warnings and consequences given by his doctor and Dr. C. They made it clear bringing up her or the past was too risky, his reactions can be damaging. His migraines were not to be taken lightly; he saw that for himself at Ms Dolly's and tonight. The closer they got to their special place he developed an instant headache. It became more intense when they finally reached their destination more so because she was there.

"Son, that's because you've been tied down since the accident. Once you get out and back to work you'll begin to feel like your old self."

"I don't know about that Unc, but I sure hope you're

right." He sat up and cleaned his face. He had to admit he did feel much better and his headache had disappeared. Maybe that's what he needed a good man's cry.

"I am and you'll see." He was so happy to hear him admit he was still in love with her and knew things would work out for them._____

"Hey, how about going to the ranch for a little while, Charles said he had some new livestock. He bought two quarter horses and a couple of ponies and Mrs. Perez is making meatloaf sandwiches for lunch." Caleb looked at his grandfather with a big grin. That was a great idea. His parents were at the center and his grandparents stayed to keep him company. "Mildred we're going to take a ride to the ranch, you want to join us." He knew she did, but thought he would ask....

After a delicious lunch Caleb decided to go back out to the stable. He noticed whenever he was in Hosea's presence, he acted nervous and odd. They had always been pretty cool, but something was definitely bothering him. "Hey Hosea, your Mrs. did it up with her meatloaf. I know you're one happy man with a cook like that."

"You're right about that Dr. Caleb. So how have you been?"

"I'm good, just tired of hanging around the townhouse. I know it's only been a few weeks but it seems like months. Say what did ya'll do with Weeboy?" Hosea looked at him with guilt written all over his face. "Hosea what is it, get it off your chest man. I can tell whatever it is it's eating you up inside." It only took him a few minutes to spill his guts. What he had to say was shocking, knocking Caleb to his knees.

As if she had been summoned, Lauren waltzed right up to the stables. "Just the person I want to see," catching her arm, "excuse us Hosea." She had a smile on her face which vanished with in a hurry once she got a look at his scowled expression. She looked over to where Hosea was standing but had disappeared, her brain screamed he knows.

"Caleb let me explain."

"Explain what Lauren, how conniving and vicious you are. I've met some deceitful scheming selfish women in my time but you take the prize. Not only did you put my life in danger but innocent children." He wouldn't allow her to speak, so she did the next best thing in a woman's defense, she ran tears. "Don't you dare stand here and make up a cry; that won't work. As a matter of fact I want your deceitful malicious ass out of my face and stay the hell away from me, before I truly lose my temper and that you don't want to see. And another thing; if you say one word to Hosea or causes him any trouble in any way, I'll make sure everyone knows of your malicious scheme." Damn that felt good thought Caleb, as he walked off with her looking like the fool she really was.

CHAPTER 31

"I love you more than life itself and you've made me the happiest man in the world. I promise to be everything you think I am and more, my Ruby Jewel," he whispered as he trailed hot kisses down the middle of her bosom. Stopping to tease and suckle her taunt nipples, she caressed his powerful shoulders and nibbled his neck. She never thought she would get to hold him in her arms like this ever again. They had been so close to losing their precious love, but God made it possible. "Hold me tight baby. That's it baby I need to feel your…" bam…bam…bam…

"Ruby, come open this front door," screamed Angela. "NOW!" She had been knocking for almost five minutes. She could see her through the blinds sitting in her favorite chair, motionless except for the movement of her chest. If it wasn't so early in the morning she would have gotten her neighbor's key; she'll have her own after today.

Ruby looked around and saw that crazy won't take no for an answer Angela Lacey glaring in her window. The sun was barely out and she was already up interfering with her solitude. She went to the front of the house, disarmed the security system, and unlocked the door. Nothing was said as she walked back to her chair grabbing her pillow. She held it close to her chest and looked the other way. All she wanted was to be left alone, that was not too much to ask. It was nothing anyone could do; this was something she had to work out for herself.

"Ruby, you need to snap out of this funk, going only to work and worship is not enough."

"You sound like my mother Angela, and I left her at home."

"But she's right, and speaking of your mother she said you cancelled out on going home since you were just there for the Easter weekend. Now you know that's not being fair, you know Mother's Day is her special time with her entire family especially when her birthday comes on that day. She was looking forward to being with everyone that includes you, her first born. Ruby you can't do that to her, more so since you two have developed such a wonderful and loving relationship. Don't you be the one to spoil her weekend because of a man! I can't believe you're giving him that kind of control."

"I can't believe you actually talked to my mother?"

"Yes, I did talk to Ms Robbie Jean, you haven't been to work this week, wouldn't accept any of my calls, or answer my texts. What other options did I have?"

"Angela, I'm sorry, but I just wanted to be left alone."

"You've already been alone and what for; to sit around here in the dark feeling sorry for yourself? I'm telling you Ruby, you've had more than enough time to be alone it's time you get back to being the real RJ McHarding."

"You're right Angela but I can't seem to get past the last time I saw him with that Lauren Nason hanging all over him. I think I could handle it better if he wasn't with her. Every time I close my eyes I see him smiling at that witch instead of me. I keep thinking about the love we shared and how it's now over. Do you really understand what I'm going through? The man that I love despises me and all I am to him now is a constant reminder of heartaches and pain. Angela I can't even remember if I've ever told him I was sorry or not. I was so abrupt and harsh with him back then. It was like I was trying to punish him for the decision I made which has affected us all these years. And we both have been so unhappy." Ruby stopped to compose herself before she continued. She was on the verge of tears but refused to cry, she knew that was not the answer, plus it makes her feel worst.

"You know what I was doing when you were beating my door down?" She didn't give her a chance to guess. "I was dreaming it was our wedding night and we were making love. Can you believe that, Angela? I'm dreaming about a man that can't stand the sight of me." Shaking her head, "no, I wouldn't be good company for any one this weekend. And besides what if I run into him? I don't think I can face him again, not now."

"You saw Caleb the other weekend? What happened? What did he say?"

"Wait Angela, I saw him, he didn't see me and believe it or not I actually hid in the ladies bathroom for at least ten minutes. Then when I came out I stood behind the magazine rack like a stupid dim-wit to make sure he was really gone. Can you believe that me, Attorney Ruby Jewel Mc Harding, six figure career woman actually hiding in a stall. " She felt so sorry for her friend.

"Yes, I can believe it. And whether or not I want to accept it, you're still in love with him. You went to great lengths not to upset him, but that's not reason enough to stay closed up in this house with the blinds drawn. You yourself said it was over, and if you really feel it's truly over than move on with your life. Okay so it didn't work out with Cornelius, someone else may come along. I'm just asking you to keep the door to your heart opened, that's all. And furthermore, so what if you run into him again, ask him how he's feeling and keep walking. Because what you're doing now; I don't know how to describe what you're doing. It looks like you're just existing and it don't make sense. Your hair is a mess. You need a manicure and a pedicure and."

"I get the picture Angela."

"Okay, then let's do something about it right this minute. I've made an appointment for you at the beauty salon and Bronwyn is waiting for you. No one else will be in the shop except us and Kellie. Delana has already picked out two outfits in purple and accessories to match for the weekend. Now go take your shower and change while I get your traveling bag and shoes so you can spend the weekend with your family," she ordered.

"Now Angela, you've gone too far this time."

"No Ruby, you've taken this too far, you're acting like a grieving widow. You should be thankful he's alive and getting better each day. Once it's safe to probe his memory, maybe he'll remember the love he has for you. If he doesn't, than life must go on." With both their eyes filled with tears, Angela softened her tone. "We hate seeing you like this and we don't want you to push us away because we're here for you. We all love you Ruby and you've always been there for all of us, now it's our turn. What you're doing to yourself is not right nor is it healthy under any circumstances. Just for the record, I don't believe for one minute he's that serious about what's-a-face! Now go get cleaned up and put on something pretty so we can go." Ruby looked at her friend and knew she was right, she just wished her heart would accept the inevitable and free her from the anguish and emptiness she felt. The two friends hugged and walked to her bedroom._____

"Ruby, I can't believe you cut all your hair off! But girlfriend you really look like a sexy DIVA for sure. Look like you've lost a few pounds too and I mean that in a positive way, not like you needed to…to be glamorous." She and Kellie had schooled Cynthia well about a woman not being considered beautiful unless she wore a size less than a ten. "Talking about a new look is an understatement," she said. "You look absolutely fabulous and I'm sorry about Caleb. But remember, it's his loss and I do mean he's lost a good thing."

"I couldn't have said it any better," said Nisey. Ruby caught them both off guard when she embraced each one of them. They had made it a point to be there for her today and Angela was right she did need them.

"Thanks ya'll and being here today has really been good for me. Bronwyn thank you for the new make-over, I just hope I can keep this look."

"Just do what I told you Sweetie and you won't have a bit of trouble." Ruby looked in the mirror once more and had to admit Cynthia was right. She loved her new look and actually felt glamorous and sexy which was something she hadn't felt in weeks. "Okay girls, I'm on my way to the big city and I want everyone to have a wonderful Mother's Day. Tell Kellie and Angela I'll give them a call later." She pulled out her shades and waved goodbye._____

"Momma, I'm on my way right now."

"Oh Ruby, I'm so glad you decided to come home. Your sister and brother are here with the grands. It's going to be a wonderful weekend with all my children and grands at home. Baby we're going to Ms Dolly's for dinner so instead of coming home first meet us there. Your sister and sisters-in-laws are craving whatever is on her menu. And thank you Baby for making this weekend perfect."

"You're welcome Mommy. I should be pulling up in about thirty minutes. Love you." Robbie Jean just pulls the baby out of her and makes her feel so secure and that everything is going to be alright._____

"Mama, I'm tired of being cooped up in this house. I'm a doctor and I know what's best for me. I want some of Ms Dolly's fried tilapia and homemade fries and…"

"I get the picture Caleb, but you know what happened the last time. She didn't need to bring that incident up. He remembers perfectly well what happened, his Ruby was there with another man.

"Mother it's been days and I'm going to go crazy if we don't go out for a while." He walked over and eased down on the ottoman beside a unique sculptured cactus plant that was sent to him while he was in the hospital. The card was lost during transporting his things home and he didn't have a clue who sent it. All he knew it fit his décor. He was still puzzled about the two purple roses he received every day, they too came without a card.

"Maybe we can go to the ranch; you know Charles said

we were welcomed anytime. You enjoy sitting on the veranda."

"Grandmother I don't think so."

"Caleb what has happened between you and Lauren. I thought you two were becoming serious."

"Grandmother, let's just say she's not what she seems and I'm better off without her complicating my life any more than it already is. I would appreciate it if you don't bring her up ever." The look he gave her said he meant every word.

Dr. Caleb sat quietly and took it all in. He knew Lauren Nason's mess was not going to last long and was glad it was finally over. Daniel Jr. had told him about their trip to the truck stop that night and although he didn't see her he felt her presence. What was so amazing she was actually there! It was time they faced each other again since he's much stronger, because he knew he still loved her. He was also fed up with him moping around with his downhearted feeling lost attitude. Getting out will do him some good. Ms Dolly's sounds just about right. Naturally knowing the McHardings' were going to be there was a grave incentive, which meant so was she.

"As his father, I'm going to have to agree with Caleb, hell I got a taste for fried catfish myself." Father and son did a high five and told the women they had twenty minutes to get ready.

"I'll call Lauren and the Nasons to see if they're available to…"

"Grandmother, I'm warning you, invite the Nasons but leave that she devil where she is."

CHAPTER 32

Ruby drove around to find a parking spot but it was useless. It seems everyone had the same idea. She pulled up in the bank and parked like the other patrons and walked around the corner. The fresh country air would do her good because all of a sudden she became anxious and didn't know why; maybe she was anticipating her family's reaction to her new change. That has to be it....

As soon as Caleb and his family walked inside the dining area he saw the McHarding clan, all but her over to the other side of the diner. He gave everybody a hug and introduced his family to her sister and brother from out of town. The entire family was there for Mother's Day. They usually celebrate big and he was sure this year was more special with her mother's birthday falling on the holiday. Truly she wasn't going to be selfish and disappoint her. They even wear the same colors on all their outings, shades of purple must be it. Talk about a coincidence, he had on his favorite shade, a deep purple polo with black jeans.

Their table was set up on the left which was facing the Mc Hardings. The families exchanged niceties ending with enjoy your evening. He walked over to their table and took a seat where he would be facing her family which would make it possible for him to watch her when she comes in. His grandmother tried to get him to sit by her, but he wouldn't be able to see HER. He didn't know why he was thinking that way but he was. By the time they were all seated Ms Dolly came out to greet them.

He slowly stood to give her a hug. She told him she was glad to see him again and said someone would be with them momentarily and excused herself to greet her other guests. The house was full. Mildred asked his father to trade places so she could take in the atmosphere, she said. She too was waiting but not for Ruby. His father smiled and changed places because he knew what she was up too. He overheard her on the cell; she had gone behind his back and left a message for Lauren to join them for dinner. Thank God his mother was here to control him because he was not going to handle that well....

Ruby couldn't get inside the door good, before running into high school classmates that were also home for the holiday weekend. They exchanged hellos and engaged in chit chat.

"Aunt Ruby, its Aunt Ruby," sung her nieces. She walked over to her family's table.

It was her looking like she owns the whole world with short hair, probably cut it out of spite. She knew he loved her natural curls flowing around her beautiful face and down her back.   But even he had to admit her new look was absolutely gorgeous and becoming. She was stunning in an exotic kind of way, especially in her purple animal print tunic. He watched her give each family member a hug. Someone must have told her he was there. She turned to face him. Their eyes locked. He saw apprehension. For once she couldn't read his expression although it was much softer and calmer than the last time. She didn't see contempt or anger, but would be foolish to assume anything had changed. She told her family she would be right back.

He watched the sway of her hips with his eyes traveling up and down her luscious body to her ankle and purple sandals, while unconsciously fingering his diamond stud. All conversations had ceased or was it because he couldn't hear for the loud thumping sound of his heart pounding in his ears as she came closer. Lord he wanted to snatch her to his chest and ask her why, what was the real reason why they weren't together. It was good he was in an awkward position and couldn't just jump up. Yeah, it was best because he didn't trust himself where she was concerned. His emotions were unpredictable and on edge, right about now. If the truth be told, One minute he wanted to lash out at her and the next he wanted to kiss her senseless.

"Hello everyone," everybody spoke including him.

"Ruby I love your hair, you were brave to make that step. But I adore it and it's so becoming," said his mother, with everyone else agreeing except HIM.

She thanked them all and told Caleb how good it was to see him. She paused for a quick second while the table became still. She had something she wanted to say and then she would be done. "Caleb I have something to say that should have been said to you before we left PVU." Without hesitating she continued, "I am very sorry for the way I abruptly ended our relationship. I deeply regret my decision, and never meant to hurt or cause you any pain. I take full responsibility and ask your forgiveness for being insensitive and hope we can bury the past and be friends." She held her breath while waiting for his response.

"Of course Ruby, I forgive you and thank you for asking.

I would love to put the past behind us and be friends."

"Good, let's extend a hand of friendship."

"We can do better than that. Friends can embrace one another, just let me…"

"No don't try to move; besides your waitress is here to take your order, let's just owe each other a hug the next time. Okay friend?"

He gave her his enthralling smile that turned her heart to putty and said, "Okay friend." They settled for a lingering hand shake and she told them all to enjoy their meal. His mother's heart went out to her as she observed him watching her walk away.

She has certainly matured over the years, he thought as he absorbed her essence. He truly liked what he saw and knew that took courage for her to express her feelings in front of an audience, even if it was his family. But she did it with poise and dignity. He couldn't help analyzing every word spoken. Not one time did he expect her to admit her faults. She regrets not accepting his proposal, that's what she said as far as he was concerned. Can he assume she and Cornelius Baines are not in a relationship? He could only hope. One thing for sure, when he does get up he was collecting his hug. He wanted desperately to hold and feel her in his arms and he intended to do just that before the evening was over.

While taking a seat, her mother wanted to know if everything was alright. She told them yes and they would have to discuss it later because he was very good at lip reading, he was watching. So Robbie Jean changed the subject. "Ruby what made you cut off all your beautiful hair," her mother asked?

"I wanted a new look Momma. What do you think?" She waited anxiously for her reply with the rest of the family. They had already discussed there was something different about her besides her new hair style. She seemed to be more relaxed and poised, like her old self. It took nerves for her to go over to his table and apologize with his entire family listening and watching.

"I'm like the rest of the family, I love it. As Tierra put it you're jazzy!"

"Thank you Momma, I'm glad you like it. Believe it or not I was overwhelmed when I saw my hair in a big pile on the floor. But when I looked in the mirror, I was amazed and pleased with the transformation. What I'm really excited about are the different styles I can wear; curly like it is or spiked the next time, very versatile." Her father was taking in her new attitude and was delighted he had his Ruby Jewel back. He promised himself he was going to do something special for her friends.

The Nicholson and VanLee family enjoyed their meals and had a wonderful time. Between conversations with their families, Ruby and Caleb stole secret glances and displayed playfully flirty smiles at one another. She noticed his color was back and his hair had grown out. The light fuzz on his face was so sexy and inviting. She wanted to stroke his cheek and caress his lips, but knew that was not possible for now. Ruby prayed that someday he would love her again and she had made up her mind to wait, but that would be her secret.

The children and men were so excited and couldn't wait

to leave the diner. Tonight a big pajama party had been planned at her parents for the females, and the males were camping out at Lincoln and Tori's. As they prepared to leave Ms Dolly bought her a triple order of teacakes, and told her they had been paid for with compliments from her friend. She whispered for her ears only everything was going to work out while admiring her new look. In fact said she was glowing and to keep up whatever it was she's doing. Her father gave a nice tip to their waitress and put a little something in the busboy's pocket, his grands had a ball. The family gathered their carryouts and children and walked toward the front door.

"Dad, can you help me out here?" Although he was sitting on the end he was still blocked in because they were sitting pretty close together.

"Sure Son."

"Come this way Baby," said his mother. "I need to visit the ladies room anyway before we leave." She kissed his cheek and then patted it. Everyone was smiling and seemed pleased. Even Mildred who seemed to be on pins and needles showed relief once Ruby left. Vera Nicholson knew if the right questions were asked, she and Caleb Sr. were responsible for pressuring her into rejecting his marriage proposal. She hated she even told them his plans when came for his mother's jewelry. Ruby took all the blame, making it clear all was forgiven and he in turn forgave her. Audrey Lynn told her before she left her Snuggums was right about her. She was the only woman that deserved wearing her baby girl's ring, and that's why she left them with her to keep. She felt deep down in her heart Ruby would be asking for them soon.

"Ruby." She heard her name being called and knew it was him. He was now by her side. "I came to collect my friendship hug and thank you again Ruby. Let's put forth a conscious effort in being good friends." She agreed as they embraced taking pleasure in one another's' scent.

"Aunt Ruby, Aunt Ruby I need to go," announced her niece grabbing her hand. She smiled at him and said the joys of being an aunt as she was pulled in the direction of the ladies room. She bumped right into his mother.

"Oh excuse me Mrs. Nicholson; we weren't looking where we were going, huh girls?"

"I was Aunt Ruby but you were looking at that man you were hugging."

"Okay Dancy."

Mrs. Nicholson smiled, "What would we do without the honesty of the young?" The girls were just about to rush into separate stalls when the oldest stopped and announced they needed wipes. Mrs. Nicholson told them she had something better and pulled out her sanitizer spray along with something for Ruby, a velvet pouch. While the girls handled their business she opened the pouch and found her ring and keychain. She looked at his mother fighting back tears of joy.

"Thank you Mrs. Nicholson and please call Mrs. Stratton and thank her for me."

"No Daughter, I'm going to leave that up to you when you call and give her the news." She gave her a big hug and told her she was so happy for the both of them. Shortly afterwards the girls completed their hygiene and they walked out together. Their eyes locked once again both capturing each other's silent auras as they flaunted playful smiles...

Finally everyone was asleep including the little people, except Ruby who was wide awake and restless. She had been hugged, kissed, and pulled at all evening until the last little person fell off to sleep. Her family was so happy she had her ring, and the fact that they were back talking and grinning at each other. It was obvious to their families they were finally on the right track. Ruby checked the jobsite's email to do a little work, but her assistant had taken care of all. Another excellent decision hiring Danielle Callis, she thought walking out onto the back porch. Ruby sat on the swing to enjoy the fresh spring air while thinking how good it felt being in his arms even if it was as his friend. Her friends were right, they were soul mates and they would have the life they deserved together. This time she felt it in her heart and soul as she fingered her ring._____

His grandfather had noticed his cheerful mood the rest of the evening especially after she walked in. He couldn't take his eyes off of her the entire time during dinner. Her mere presence brightened his whole outlook. Without a doubt he still loved her in spite of losing a portion of his memory. He had a wonderful suspicion one way or the other, he was getting a granddaughter and a great-grandbaby very soon....

"Yes Eland, that sounds fine, I'll be ready. Thanks man." Caleb had a morning appointment tomorrow at Cypress Village Title Company to close the deal for his new home. Before his accident, Tiny's brother-in-law had been searching for him a permanent residence. He found the ideal place, a fantastic farmhouse which was move-in ready with wonderful antiques, a stable, coral and a modernized barn. Two small cottages were also located on the property which was included in the price. One was connected to the main house by a wraparound porch for his parents and another not far which the former caretakers had resided. His grandparents had also fallen in love with his townhouse and have already made plans to purchase it for themselves. He wanted his family close and for them to have their own private space. Things couldn't have worked out any better than if he had planned it himself....

"Here it is Aunt Ruby! Can we go in now? Huh, Aunt Ruby," pleaded her nieces. Lord how does she get in these fixes. She loves them to death but..."Aunt Ruby!"

"Yes, we can all go in and buy one item."

"Y e a h!" screamed the girls. They had driven to Cypress Village and walked the strand stopping in practically every shop. The girls were promised a video game, a piece of jewelry, and something for their hair. The girls were just about done once they stop at the jewelry store. Then they would have lunch and call it an evening. She was bushed and ready for a hot shower and relax in her rocker. Ruby passed the window to the jewelry store and stepped back to look at the wedding sets.

"They're beautiful aren't they?" Startled, she looked into the face of the man she was madly in love with. Although she didn't say anything last evening she liked the way he was wearing his hair; the wet look combed back gave him sex appeal along with his potent infectious smile. Her insides experienced little tremors; she never thought he would ever smile like that at her again. She longed to stroke his shadowy beard and kiss his adorable nose. Furthermore, to see the look of love and desire for only her touched her very spirit and soul.

She gazed at her hand and said softly, "Yes they are, but nothing compares to the one I have." He took her ring hand and kissed it gently and then took her in his arms.

"Marry me Ruby."

"When?" He captured her lips with a burning eagerness to taste the sweetness he's missed for fifteen years. Breathless she leaned against his broad chest, silently thanking the Lord for giving him back to her.

"Aunt Ruby," whispered her eldest niece, "Please, everybody is staring." He kissed her forehead while reaching into his pocket for a bill. Not one time did they take their eyes off of one another. Her niece took the money and went to the food court. They smiled and walked holding hands to the first empty table. Still holding her hand, he asked if she really meant what she said. She assured him she was serious and wanted to know when. He pulled out his cell to make some calls. She leaned over and kissed his cheek._____

"Granny, Aunt Ruby was kissing that white man from last night in public," said her oldest niece.

"That's right Granny, it was the same man we saw at Ms Dolly's," announced Dancy. Robbie Jean looked at her daughter. Ruby held her hand up and walked to the back porch where the men were. She needed a break.

"So you and Frosty were kissing on the strand." Ruby looked at her brother-in-law in disbelief because they just walked in the house and the girls were in the den.

"We got the text," replied Lincoln. Ruby's cell rang and she excused herself ignoring the stares.

"Girlfriend we are so happy for you," exclaimed whoever was speaking for the group because Kellie's name came up on her caller ID, but it wasn't her voice. Ruby shook her head because she knew this was going to be a long conversation. Her girls expected a detailed account and she thought it was best to move to the front porch. She didn't want to talk in front of the children. They were watching one of the movies she purchased and the oldest was playing her new game, but they still have big ears. She knew the women would listen which was fine that way she didn't have to repeat herself.

CHAPTER 33

It was a splendid morning, bright azure blue skies with white fluffy dancing clouds. He couldn't have picked a finer morning, thought Ruby rushing out to get in her car. She had been up at the crack of dawn getting ready as quietly as she could. Last night she had everything in the den's closet so she wouldn't disturb her family. She even used her father's bathroom to get ready since her room was occupied. Her siblings always used the bedrooms since they had small children. Lord next year it was going to be a mess, baby beds would have to be placed in each room for the new members. At least she wouldn't have to; she glanced at her diamond watch and couldn't believe the time. She had fifteen minutes to meet him. She checked herself in the mirror and was pleased. It was the suit she was going to wear that Sunday following their wedding that never took place. Ruby tiptoed to the front door disarmed the security system and was about to open the door when her mother appeared from nowhere. She had a large lace cream handkerchief and said it was her grandmother's. Robbie Jean kissed her daughter and whispered she looked absolutely gorgeous and shooed her out of the house. Ruby mouthed thank you Mommy and left....

Caleb was standing in front of his townhouse looking his savvy and handsome self, in his cream designer's suit, collarless silk shirt that was a shade darker, and matching shoes. His mother had pinned her diamond and gold broach at his neck before he left out of the house. She never said a word, just kissed his cheek and told him she loved him very much. Mothers he thought, as he took his coat off and threw it across his shoulder and waited impatiently for his ride. Just as he was about to check the time Q-Note pulled up with his wife Melissa.

"Hi Handsome, you ready to wear that dog collar," she asked with a bright smile. She got out letting him have the front seat. Roderick grinned at his frat brother as he waited for him to get in. They were to meet the judge in the court yard in ten minutes. When he called his frat brothers they were thrilled. Judge Marcus Ross was overjoyed and honored to perform the ceremony. *Q* and his wife had the same sentiments in being there witnesses. A beautiful bouquet of spring flowers wrapped in a wide cream satin ribbon laid on the backseat for Ruby along with a boutonnière for him and a corsage for after the ceremony.

"Hurry *Q*, I don't want to be late plus the judge has to get back to attend church with his mother."

"We all do," announced *Q* as he exited the complex and stepped on the gas. "Where are you and Ruby going to worship this morning? You certainly can't be in two places at one time and be with both mothers."

He hadn't thought about that, as they pulled into the parking lot facing the town square. A beautiful location for their outdoor ceremony had been chosen. He had everything under control except where they would worship. Today was very special for her mother because it was her birthday. And this was the first time he would be with all of his grandmothers and mother under the same roof except his Honeybee. Caleb smiled to himself because he knew he had made this day special for her already when he called this morning to give her the news. She told him he couldn't have given her a more precious gift and actually cried. Big D took the phone because she wasn't telling him fast enough what was wrong. One thing for sure he and Ruby will have to discuss this after they tie the knot, he thought, as they all got out of the vehicle. Melissa stopped him to pin his boutonnière and said how happy she was for the both of them.

The judge was sitting on the bench with his family. Caleb couldn't believe Yolanda and their kids were there which made it that much more special since they were not having family present. They decided to make it simple, avoid the drama and celebrate at the mansion with their families after worship. They were combining the Mother's Day celebration with their wedding reception. Caleb had previously reserved one of the large banquet rooms for both the Denver and Bellville bunch and ordered a special menu. He had them to add five more round tables to accommodate her family and if necessary, they could be moved to a larger room. He also ordered a wedding cake and ice cream for dessert along with the previously ordered cakes.

Ruby pulled right beside the Judge's Benz. She looked one last time in the mirror and opened her door. Caleb was about to go to her when **Q** stopped him and announced he would get the bride to be and told his wife to take Caleb to the Judge. Roderick got the bouquet and walked to her car. Marcus and his family met him and showered him with hugs and kisses. Yolanda wiped his face clean and took her seat on the bench next to two of her children. His name sake was the official photographer and was taking pictures of Ruby coming up the sidewalk. She was absolutely gorgeous thought Yolanda as she wiped a tear. She couldn't help being emotional, she knew the history. But that was all in the past and today they were starting a new life. Caleb and the Judge had chosen an ideal spot for their nuptials. They were surrounded by a variety of aged shade trees and assorted plants. One huge tree in particular was encircled with beautiful blooming flowers and small shrubberies was the setting for their private ceremony.

"Look at me I'm in love"...Caleb began singing an old love song while waiting for his bride who was a vision of pure loveliness. She was a portrait of elegant sophistication, in a satin and lace vanilla cream suit. The dramatic off the shoulder draped collar jacket with a crinkled scalloped trim bottom and skirt was stunning. Her eye-catching large fabric hat had a satin bow that looped through an oval pearl ring. Three strand pearl necklace set, stylish open toe cream pumps with pearl shoe jewelry, and matching purse put the finishing touches to her picture-perfect outfit. When she approached the bench she gave Yolanda her purse, but kept her lace hanky. Caleb reached for her hand and held it while he finished his song gazing into her glistening eyes. He kissed her hand and then enfolded her arm with his. Melissa reached for her flowers and then stood by her husband who caught her hand.

Marcus asked them to face him, "Caleb and Ruby I want you to know marriage is a joyous occasion when you have a loving and well deserving couple as you two wonderful individuals. You know you're very dear to my heart." He patted his chest as he spoke. "Caleb and Ruby face each other and hold hands. You have certainly had your trials, tribulations, sickness, and challenges; but with the grace of our Lord God and Savior along with your undenying love for each other you have prevailed over all. God has brought you to this point of your life where you desire to be one." Judge Ross smiled at the couple and told them to repeat after him....."Caleb and Ruby, I now pronounce you husband and wife. You may kiss your bride. "

"Good morning Mrs. VanLee."

"And what a beautiful morning it is Mr. VanLee." At last they were united as one, which will start the beginning of a new chapter in their lives. It was such a wonderful feeling to have all the obstacles they've encountered behind them. Caleb kissed his wife tenderly but with sheer passion while they lingered in each other's arms.

"Okay guys we would love to stay and watch this play of affection but we must get down the road or we're going to have some unhappy mothers," said Roderick. "Besides, I would like to congratulate and kiss the bride." Marcus and the ladies expressed the same sentiments including the groom. Caleb allowed them to embrace her while he received hugs and kisses from his sorors and friends. He thanked them for making this morning special. His name sake gave him the digital camera he used to take pictures to share with their family. They waved goodbye and walked to their car still in each other's arms. Q-Note backed up with Melissa calling their names. She jumped out to pin Ruby's corsage and kissed them both again and returned to her car.

Caleb looked at her, "Did I tell you what a beautiful bride you are?"

"Yes, but you can say it again," she said kissing his lips.

"Come on let's go get a quick breakfast sandwich and juice and decide where we're going to worship this morning." He looked at his watch and said they didn't have a lot of time...

Caleb and Ruby walked to where her family was sitting and took a seat beside her mother just as the service was about to begin. Bro. Allen was opening up and asked them to stand so the church could congratulate them. He understood they had a bright and early private ceremony. They were not surprised because they both said their mothers were up when they left and gave them their own special blessings. It was evident they were not going to be able to hold it in. Ruby was surprised that her mother had not uttered a word to the rest of the family including her father. He stood and looked at them in total amazement and gave her a kiss and hug and welcomed his new son-in-law to the family. Her shocked siblings did the same. They both kissed and hugged her mother as Ruby took her place beside her. After everyone quieted down Bro. Allen continued with the morning announcements. She was pleased he insisted they go to church with her family since this was her mother's birthday which made her day even more special. Robbie Jean was swollen with pride to have her first born and new son-in-law sitting beside her which made the beginning of this Mother's Day fabulous...

"They're here," announced Tiny, gazing out the window. The Nicholsons and Beasleys along with the Nasons who brought his grandparents were anxiously waiting for the McHarding clan. It had been a busy but fantastic morning as the wonderful news spread throughout the family. No one seemed to be upset with them having a private ceremony except Mildred VanLee, which was not a surprise. She was too upset to take the ride to Bellville and attended service with the Nason's instead, with Vera's encouragement. It was evident Caleb Sr. had warned her well because she had been pleasant and sociable along with the Nasons since they entered the banquet room. Everything was wonderfully done with fresh flowers centered on the tables and a Happy Mother's Day banner hanging on the wall. At the request of his mother a special table was placed in the corner of the room for the wedding cake that he ordered, with Aunt Ruth's modifications. She even had management to put a decorative arch as a background for the bride and groom's table which was centered in the room.

Charles Sr. was delighted to finally see his old comrades again and took seats right beside Uncle Pete and Arnold Sr. He introduced them to his family. They were having a marvelous visit talking about old times. Aunt Lucille did lay the law down; they could only talk shop until the newlyweds arrived who were walking in the door that very moment. The family stood and gave them a standing ovation. The happy couple embraced his family one by one starting with his mother who was in tears. All the grandparents were practically sitting together which made it easier. Her family took their seats after giving a general hello because it was his family's time now. Aaron was snapping pictures for their picture album that he and his wife were going to put together for them of their special day.

After everyone received their hugs and kisses the adorable attractive couple posed for pictures. No questions about it they made a stunning pair. His family came well prepared with their own cameras. The wedding cake was rolled in so they could get pictures of them cutting it. Caleb was surprised because it was actually decorated like a wedding cake with three ascending round layers, vanilla icing, gold trimming, and purple roses in the corners. A white groom and black bride had been placed on top. He knew nobody thought of that but his Aunt Lucille and thanked her with a kiss.

"Okay family, I know everyone is ready to eat including the bride and groom," announced his father. "But before we get started as always, we'd like to tell our women folk how special they are and how much we love them." All the men agreed with nods and applauds. He continued, "This year is very special because under one roof we have the groom's entire family plus a dear friend of Uncle Pete and Arnold Sr. and his family. We welcome them. But the main attraction is our new addition, my son's beautiful wife and her family. It was Caleb's vision to have his entire blended family as he puts it together and honor his mother, grandmothers, aunts, and cousins. Now I know he had no idea he would be honoring a beautiful wife, my new daughter." The entire room agreed by applauding. Caleb took her hand to his lips and kissed her fingertips; then her lips lingering just a bit too long. His mother and Aunt Ruth grunted and the room laughed. "Now, before we bless the food and have a delicious meal, I was asked by Caleb Sr. to allow him to say a few words."

Caleb Sr. stood and looked around the room of all the smiling faces and began. "I'm going to be as brief as I possibly can but I have something on my heart that I must say. I know you know my wife and me as grandmother and grandfather from Denver, but some of you have never seen us in the flesh. Well, for those of you who don't know we're Caleb's biological father's parents. This woman by my side gave me a wonderful son fifty-eight years ago. We raised him and married him off to a beautiful woman Bianca who just happens to be the daughter of Mildred and Linda Nason's best friend Audrey, Caleb's Honeybee." His male cousins started singing honeybee until their grandmothers gave them the evil eye. They apologized with Caleb 3rd giving them a smirk, but not a word was uttered.

"Continue Caleb," said Aunt Lucille eyeing her nephews.

"Thank you Lucille, in turn Caleb Jr. and Bianca gave us a beautiful and fine grandson Caleb 3rd. Lord we were so happy and as God would have it they were taken from us." Mildred wiped her eyes while he squeezed her hand. "As if that wasn't enough our only living flesh and blood was taken from us by the courts in spite of us putting up a strong fight. A document prepared by Caleb's parents stopped us from having custody. Now I know my wife may not agree wholeheartedly with me, but I must say this. We did a good job with our boy, but I'm convinced at our age Sweetheart we wouldn't have done his son justice. I'm coming to the climax of my revelation and I thank all of you for being patient with this old man. Lawrence, Vera and their families were God sent. We couldn't have picked a finer set of parents for our grandson in addition to this fantastic and loving family. They made sacrifices after sacrifices in raising this young man to become the man he is today. They refused financial support from both of his grandparents as well as refusing to use his trust fund that had been set up for him by his parents. They did it all, instead of you driving a Benz grandson, Lawrence said a Honda would do," everyone laughed. "We wanted him to attend an Ivy League university, PVU was his choice and there he found the love of his life. Thank God we didn't get our way." Caleb and Ruby embraced. "So I want to thank my wife for giving me a son and the matriarchs and patriarchs of this family for producing two wonderful people who accepted our grandson as their own flesh and blood and raised him to be a marvelous individual. Thank you for teaching him survival skills as he so often expressed and providing him with an abundance of love and the proper guidance. Because of this family he has a gentle, humble, and loving spirit which has enabled him to become an extraordinary doctor. I would like to thank Henry Ray and Robbie Jean for giving us a wonderful granddaughter who means the world to me and will always have a special place in my heart. Although she's never uttered a word, I was responsible for her turning you down grandson fifteen years ago. I'm so sorry for interfering but with that smile on your face and the one in my heart says you're going to have a fantastic life and I love you two very much." Caleb and Ruby walked over and embraced him and Grandmother Mildred with a kiss of forgiveness. "So my new family, you're stuck with us for life. We're moving to Texas along with Lawrence and Vera. Now let's stand and salute our women folk and then the bride and groom."

"Here! Here!" chanted the men with raised glasses.

"Caleb we all thank you and welcome you and your fine wife to our family." The family stood and welcomed them with applauds. The older gentleman was touched as he wiped tears from his eyes. "Now if we can get Uncle Pete to bless the food we'll get started and Uncle Pete don't forget it's Robbie Jean's birthday."

"Shouldn't we sing happy birthday first," he asked?

"Later Uncle, just bless the food now and be mindful of the little people." Aunt Lucille put her hand on her forehead along with some of the other family members as they bowed their heads waiting on him to get started because they knew it was going to be a long prayer.

"Okay. *Heavenly and gracious Father, who's the father of Abraham, Issac, and Jacob; we thank you for this wonderful occasion in more ways than one...Last but not least thank you for the meal we're about to enjoy, in Jesus name Amen."* The entire room said Amen as they looked at each other in disbelief, he didn't end with his famous words...

Caleb had truly outdone himself. Everyone had enjoyed a scrumptious meal of chicken breast and meatloaf both in a cream mushroom sauce; medley of vegetables; twice baked potatoes; lemonade and tea. Happy birthday was sung to Robbie Jean and delicious cakes were served. Next the grands gave her gifts, but her biggest surprise was her sister Rita and her family. They arrived right as they were serving dinner and was able to get in on the wonderful feast.

After dinner each mother was given a personalized basket of goodies; from cash to jewelry; gift certificates for beauty treatments to clothes; with everything in between. Robbie Jean was caught off guard again with her personalized basket of fine snacks from chocolates to fruit and twenty dollar bills rolled into flower blooms, compliments from all the families present. They even had extra baskets for additional guest and complimentary gift bags for the single ladies and girls. No female was left out except Ruby. She made it clear her gift could not fit in a bag and pointed to her husband. He was all the gift she needed for life. His male cousins told her to put it in writing, and were popped upside the head by their wives.

Her Aunt Rita had expressed the gift she wanted, the

outfit Ruby Jewel had on earlier. Her request was granted. While the baskets were being passed she made a quick change. She now had on a figure flattering cream and pink print sheath with a deep round neckline, butterfly sleeves, and a gathered side tie at the hip. She gave her aunt the complete outfit but kept the jewelry since it matched her dress perfectly, which had been the general idea.

One of Caleb's first cousins tapped his glass to get the room's attention. "Alright family and friends let's quiet down for the last presentation of the evening. Caleb, will you get your beautiful wife and come to the front." He found her at her parents' table. She had changed and once again she was a vision of pure loveliness. He kissed her lips, took her hand, and escorted to where Roy was standing. While pictures were being snapped, Tiny came in with a huge basket. "On behalf of your families, we're providing you with a honeymoon. You will spend two nights in Kemah in a luxurious suite at the Board Walk Inn for a late dinner and attend the blues concert. The next night you will enjoy a boat ride in the gulf aboard the party yacht. Afterwards, you will be driven to Galveston Island for the remainder of your honeymoon and stay at Hotel Galvez in another luxurious suite facing the beach. You also have tickets for the theatre, The Three Men Concert of Love, and Moody Gardens; in addition to a few extras to make this week special. Your limo is waiting this very moment and here is a little spending money." Roy then pointed to the window and sure enough a limo was out front. The couple looked at them in amazement and was about to speak.

"We know," said his mother. "You're not packed. Your grandmother and I packed your things."

"And Ruby yours are packed as well," said Tori.

"Well I guess, there's nothing for us to say, but thanks family," said Caleb.

"Man, I can't believe you're lost for words," exclaimed Tiny. "Please somebody take a picture of this moment." Ruby's brother told him he already had everything on camera.

"I do want to say on behalf of my beautiful wife and I; we're truly grateful and appreciative for this wonderful gift. And I do want everyone in this room to know how much you all mean to us and…"

"Okay man that's enough we don't want you to get sloppy on us and cause these women to turn on the water." Caleb shook his head in agreement because he was definitely becoming emotional. They had not planned a honeymoon of any kind. His bride had already touched his heart when she expressed she had all she ever wanted and that was him as her husband. Neither was looking for anything extra, including wedding gifts from each other. This display of affection was a total surprise.

"Alright, then I guess that's it and we'll see everybody next weekend." Tiny took the basket out to the limo as they embraced the family. Ruby was given more money from their fathers and grandfathers and both Nason men. They even hugged Lauren Nason who had been very low key during the entire gathering. As they left the banquet hall their parents were behind them chanting grandbaby…with the rest of the family joining in.

CHAPTER 34

The newlyweds' honeymoon was totally awesome, nevertheless it was over and they were back in the real world on their way to Hempstead. First, they were going to stop by her office so she could show him where she worked and introduce him to her friends and staff, *again*. Everyone had received the text and was aware the circumstances were still the same; Caleb had no recollection of his time there or of any previous introductions. His frat brothers Nathan and Aaron were also going to be on hand to help smooth over any slipups. It was very important for everyone to keep in mind Caleb and Ruby's lives did not begin until last week.

On a few occasions their honeymoon week had been taxing, but the ambience of their surroundings helped ease any tension that occurred. She was on pins and needles at times and had to be careful during their talks. It was imperative not to reveal previous activities they shared prior to his accident. His migraines were real, for that reason she was cautious not to trigger any distressful situations to the best of her ability. Ruby almost blew it when he told her he had purchased a farmhouse that was located on five acres of land and hoped she would love it as much as he does. She was thrilled, and almost slipped letting him know she fell in love with it the minute they walked the grounds the day of his accident, but she caught herself. As if that wasn't enough, she liked to have messed up again when she asked about the furniture that was left in the house. It was a blessing he was too excited painting her a vivid picture of their new home; her question hadn't registered. It was quite clear as he continued describing the place and the vintage furnishings that had been left behind, he was sure she would love. He thought what was there and between their two households the place could be furnished completely. It was ready for them to move in; their families and friends had taken care of that. She couldn't believe it, and then too she could. Angela and friends had packed her clothes and personals, all left were furniture and furnishings.

Regardless of the strain of keeping the past a secret, their honeymoon was absolutely fabulous. The evening strolls on the beach, the walk on the strand, visiting the antique shops in downtown Galveston, the train ride, the trip to the gardens, and most of all the candlelight dinners and concerts were fantastic. Their last night on the island had been heavenly, she thought looking over at her sleeping husband. They both were exhausted in a wonderful way. Last evening the love concert and the ambiance her friends had arranged granted them an unforgettable night of passionate love making. Their suite had been set up completely for a final romantic rendezvous after the concert with a delicious tray of goodies, chilled sparkling cider and a sensuous CD made for them. Needless to say every effort had been put forth in honoring the request of their parents. Of course that was another one of their plans before the accident to start a family soon as possible. Ruby just hoped it didn't happen before; now that would truly be something to explain. She kissed her husband and snuggled closer...

Angela checked her office once more to make sure

everything was like it was before he became a part of her life. She even placed the green plant at the front desk. Everyone was ready to meet Dr. Caleb Gerald VanLee 3rd *again*. She was nervous and couldn't wait until things were back to normal. When she talked to Ruby, she said they would just handle matters as they occurred.

"Are they here yet," asked Cynthia and Nisey out of breath?

"No, we're still waiting, and remember…"

"We know, we got the memo," exclaimed Nisey! "I'm going next door to see the triplets, text us!" Nisey walked out the front door and the happy couple was getting out of the limo. She rushed to them, gave Ruby a big hug, told her how wonderful she looked, and then waited to be introduced *again.* Man this was one fine white man, she thought as she noticed he too was wearing a new look that was very becoming. "It's really nice to finally meet the man that's captured my girl's heart."

"Thank you soror, and believe me she has mine on a chain as well," giving her a hug. They went inside and were received by the entire staff, including the new members. The introductions went well. Just as she was about to show him around, the Larson clan came in chanting her name. *Again* she made introductions and the boys began climbing his legs like they did the first time they met. Kellie tried to get them but he stopped her. Gregory walked in with lunch.

"Look *Da..dee* look," said the boys holding on to Caleb's legs.

"Say man look like you got your hands full or should I say legs." Everyone laughed as Kellie introduced the two men and they all followed them to the dining area. The boys giggled all the way which caused Kyla to whimper.

"Baby put her on my back."

"Kyla, hold on tight to Daddy." A fabulous lunch was ordered from Ms Janet's for everyone's pleasure. Nathan and Jazper came in with Aaron just in time. They were glad to see them together as a married couple and him looking like his old self. While the staff and children ate, Ruby and her girls walked to her office.

"Ruby Jewel, you are actually glowing girlfriend. Are we in the family way too," inquired Ann? "You know I can tell when a woman's pregnant. Remember I inherited the gift from my great-grandmother and her sisters. I told Kellie both times, and you my dear friend have joined the club."

"Ooooh...Ruby that would be wonderful if we're expecting together. We can whine to each other about our pregnancies." All eyes were on the two.

"Kellie, you're right, but I don't think this would work out for her at this time." Angela tilted her head toward Ruby who was not looking happy at all and her heart went out to her. She knew Ann had the gift if it was such a thing. She had been right with Kellie both times and everybody else at their church. But the pro was her Aunt Mattie. Ruby touched her stomach with mixed emotions. Her being pregnant was what their families wanted, but she needed at least a couple of weeks at least, into her marriage. She would definitely have to handle this with kid gloves to keep from causing him any anxieties about the past. OMG, she had a revelation. What if he thought she was pregnant for Cornelius, regardless of them never being intimate?

"I tell you what girls; let's just keep my condition to ourselves for a while. I'm too happy for drama right now."

"That's a great idea," exclaimed Angela and they headed in the direction of the dining room.

"Oh, this is going to be so much fun and guess who else is expecting?" Kellie paused to wait for their response when Ann blurted out, Grace and the preacher. They all stopped and looked back at Ann who threw up her hands and sashayed right past them.

"Here they are," announced Gregory, standing to seat his wife. "Ruby Jewel, I have to say there's something different about you," said Gregory. "Besides the new hair style and marriage, I can't put my finger on it."

"Baby can you get me a juice out of the fridge?"

"Sure, anything for the mother of my children."

"G-Man I'm with you," said Nathan. "It's something special about our girl."

"Nathan, maybe it's the pretty bright yellow sundress she's wearing causing her complexion to glow, will you put me some dirty rice on my plate honey." Nathan looked at his frat brother with a smile while putting dirty rice on his wife's plate.

"She's been frosted thru and thru," bragged Caleb flashing his dimpled smile. The men gave him a brother's cheer while they served the other ladies.

"Well Kellie looks like you will have another buddy," remarked Cynthia slyly and sipped her drink. The others gave her a mean look.

"Let's not jinx her cousin," said Nisey, "unless you're speaking of yourself."

"Girl please, this is one club I don't want to be a member of right now. Let me get married first. I tell you one thing; ya'll heifers better be able to wear your bridesmaid's dresses."

"Ruby I have all your mail and need to go over a few things before you leave," said Destiny. It was time to put a stop to this right now. She could tell Ruby was a bit uptight with all the attention. Destiny stood and expressed how nice it was to meet Caleb and she truly enjoyed hearing their love story. She thanked the Larsons for lunch and wished their visitors a good afternoon. The other staff members took the hint and gave their thanks and excused themselves. Lana told them she needed to get to class and her co-workers gave her that *yeah right* look. Sistah girl was courting hard and heavy now and everybody was expecting her to make an announcement very soon. Especially since her *Boo* was hired as the new minister for the congregation in Shadow Crest.

"Sweetie, I'm going to follow Destiny and chat with her for a few minutes while you visit with your frat brothers and Gregory."

"Baby you've hardly eaten." She told him she wasn't hungry and kissed his cheek before leaving...

"Girl thanks for getting me out of there, I needed a break, I was beginning to suffocate. I don't know how long I can keep this pretense up." Ruby took some deep breaths to settle her nerves. Angela walked in and flopped down in the empty chair next to her and let out a mumbled scream, then threatened to fix Cynthia once and for all. "That's my girl," exclaimed Ruby.

"She's not your trouble. Girl that husband of yours told us the most beautiful love story about you two that was so moving. He had us practically in tears, especially the part when you were looking in the window at the jewelry store admiring the rings." She recalled that very moment as Destiny continued. "Girl we were no good when he said you were still wearing his ring and he knew then you had never stopped loving him and he has always loved you."

"Destiny, that's such a touching story. He's so wonderful and I love him so much. I can't stand the fact that I'm keeping secrets and in reality, deceiving him," she starts to cry.

"Sweetie don't," pleaded Destiny.

Caleb walked in with a carryout and saw she was crying. "Baby what's wrong?" He had her in his arms and she literally fell apart. "Ruby, whatever it is we can work it out together." Her sobs became louder as he tried desperately to comfort her with his gentle caresses and kisses. Destiny and Angela stood against the wall with concerned looks. They had never seen her so upset in all the years of their friendship.

"Baby, you're going to have to calm down, it can't be that bad." Her weeping tore at his heart as he held her tighter rocking gently. It wasn't any need of questioning her. He just continued holding and rocking as she cried her heart out. Ann came in with a cup of warm tea. He held the cup coaxing her to take a few sips.

"Caleb, why don't ya'll spend the rest of the day here

and let her rest, I know you two are tired."

"Sweetie, would you prefer spending the night here?" She shook her head yes and continued hiding her face in the bend of his neck. Ruby knew she had made a spectacle of herself, but didn't care. All she had strength to do right now was crawl in her cozy bed and snuggle in her husband's arms. Ann left the room and took charge along with the Larson's. A car was driven in the back of the building for them to leave with her friends watching. Of all people, Cynthia wiped tears as she watched them leave. Never in a million years did she ever think she would witness the fearless RJ McHarding, Attorney at Law break because of love and that's exactly what has happened...

Gregory parked in Ruby's drive with Nathan right behind him. Caleb held on to her as they entered the house. He took full control as he put the keys in the designated tray and walked Ruby to the den sofa while pointing Greg and Nathan to the master suite. He instructed them to put the suitcases on the bench in front of the bed. He went to her pantry and got something for her headache and bottled water. Caleb knew she had to have one the way she cried, besides he could use a couple of aspirins himself, he too felt one coming. Ruby watched how he moved around her kitchen, like it was familiar territory. He even knew where she kept her medications. She prayed a silent prayer

"Here Baby take two of these and...and..." A knock from the patio startled them. Caleb stood still with a puzzled look at first and then walked to the patio door. "It's your neighbor, Baby. "Ms Johnnie, how good to see you again. Guys this is Ms John...Ms John...**Ruby, I've been here before, haven't I! I know your next door neighbor! Yes! You made me promise to be on my best behavior that night in order**

for us to sleep in the same bed…and I…excuse me Ms Johnnie, but it's true and now…"

They watched him pace the floor while he mentally recalled that day and the past events for the last few weeks. Everything came rushing back, his memory bank rewind like a video. After which seemed like forever but only a few minutes, her husband faced her with an stirring smile that slowly melted the tension and anxieties she's suppressed for weeks. It was all good. Ruby reached for him. Once again she needed to be in his arms. It was finally over and all she wanted to do now was snuggle with the love of her life. She shifted her body just a bit so they both would be comfortable. Caleb laid on top of her soft body and seized her lips with an eagerness to taste her sweet nectar that's been his daily feast for the past few days. He caressed her velvety skin as he nibbled the top of her exposed breasts. Greg and Nathan excused themselves and Ms Johnnie announced she would lock up.

"We ran our company out."

"That's okay, they understand," and he continued massaging her body that longed for his seductive touch.

"But don't you think you should call your parents and grandparents and let them know you got your memory back?"

"How about after I give you a thorough examination for symptoms, Mrs. VanLee?" Slowly getting up, he stood in front of her with a sensuous smile and evidence of her getting more than just a health check.

"Sounds good to me Dr. VanLee," she then got up and pulled him toward her bedroom which was now going to be theirs. "But on second thought text them so we won't be disturbed." The smile on his face said a wonderful idea …

"Mrs. VanLee let me help you undress and then we can start your examination." Facing her he pulled her dress over her head and then unhooked her cream lace bra watching her luscious breasts spill out excitedly. Stepping behind he scooped them up in his powerful hands kneading and fondling both. She leaned into him while he made circular movements around her tight buds. Enticing and exciting her more, he slid his hands down her body, removing her slip and undergarment all at one time while taunting her breasts. She turned around and attempted to unfasten his belt and pants. He shook his head and whispered, "I'm the doctor," and replaced a hand with his lips and hot steamy tongue. She held her breath, while her body was being saturated in hot moist kisses. Now easing down to his knees caressing and squeezing her voluptuousness, he stopped at one of her sensitive spots, her inner thighs. *Yessss* she moaned gasping and struggling to remain standing using his shoulders for support. Scorching her chocolate velvet skin with more hot kisses initiated deep shuddering breaths. He felt her trembles and had to make a quick decision the floor or the bed.

CHAPTER 35

The summer months had been very busy for Ruby and Caleb, starting with the excitement of her pregnancy. He was so sure she was *frosted* the first night at the townhouse. Her doctor stressed regardless of them thinking they know the exact date of conception, the delivery could come early late or right on schedule. According to Dr. Rosalyn's calculations she was due to deliver mid-December which would give them an early Christmas present. She wanted her delivery as close to the due date as possible.

Minor construction to the farmhouse had been completed. The front and back yards were landscaped with beautiful flower gardens and additional fruit trees were also planted. The Nicholsons and VanLees had made their transitions from Denver to Texas and were now happily settled in their new homes. Surprisingly enough his grandmother had mellowed down considerably and was enjoying country living. She loved visiting the farmhouse just to sit on the back portion of the wraparound porch and watch the hustle and bustle of the suburban and urban traffic. The ceiling fans, comfortable furniture, and the beautiful landscape made that area everyone's favorite spot.

Naturally they traveled back and forth to Houston until she was completely moved. Cynthia's wedding was a spectacular and memorable affair. Uncle Pete's Annual

Juneteenth Festival was bigger than ever this year with all the Nasons attending. They also enjoyed a week in Denver with the Stratton family and took family trips to Dallas and Atlanta to receive her awards. Grandmother Mildred was impressed with her granddaughter's accomplishments; and had both affairs put in the local paper._____

Hempstead was having some wonderful fall weather with just the right temperatures. On this beautiful late evening the mixture of fall foliage filled the air with fresh vibrant fragrances, thought Ruby as she caressed her protruding stomach. She and her in-laws were enjoying a pleasant evening on the front porch with her mother-in-law arranging pictures in the baby book for the umpteenth time. Her pregnancy was going well with her looking forward to motherhood. The nursery was completed due to over anxious grandparents and great-grandparents that were now eagerly awaiting the arrival of their little one. Because they still could not tell the sex of the baby the nursery was done in chocolate and sunshine yellow. So far baby VanLee has shown them their backside which seems to be the favorite position. Caleb tried so hard to coax the little bud to turn over, but it didn't happen. Next week she was scheduled for another ultra sound and the family was hoping the sex of the baby would be revealed. Everyone was baffled including her doctor, that each ultra sound showed the baby's bottom so clearly. Caleb was convinced they were having a girl because she had a cute little round tush that looked like hers. Of course they really didn't care although they referred to the baby in the female gender. Their main concern was a healthy baby.

"Oh Ruby, I still think this one of Caleb laying his head on your stomach should be the first picture," said Vera.

"What do you think Lawrence?"

"Yes Vera, I agree."

"Oh you two are no help. I'll just fix it like I want!" Lawrence winked at Ruby as he got up to go inside. It really didn't matter about the pictures. Surprisingly enough they all turned out very nice. She was hesitant at first to expose her stomach, but her husband insisted she was hot and sexy.

"Daughter can I get you anything?"

"A cup of tea would be just fine with some of that banana nut bread." Vera gave her that look, but she ignored it. She was eating for two and her baby wanted something sweet. Besides her doctor was very pleased with her weight, she had only gained a little over twenty pounds.

Phone "Hi Mommy, how's my baby."

"Hi yourself Daddy, your baby is having a sweet attack and grandfather is getting something to take care of it. Ooooh, now she's kicking, I guess she knows you're on the phone."

"Let me talk to her." Ruby put the phone on speaker and placed it on her stomach. He sang a lullaby which did the trick as the little one calmed down. "Ruby I'll be home as soon as the clinic closes, wait up for me Baby I love you." She teared up as she put the phone on the base. Lately, every time he utters those words she becomes overwhelmed with emotions and can't help thinking about how close she came to losing him.

"Here you go Daughter."

"Thanks Dad."_____

"Dr. Caleb I'm ready to lock up."

"Okay Andy, I'll be out in just a sec." Caleb was finishing up his reports because after tonight he would not be back at the clinic until Monday morning. He had been working late nights the entire week, so he could have Thursday and the weekend off for PV's homecoming activities. He and his frat brothers/cousins were truly excited and looking forward to them all being together for the first time in fifteen years. They had planned a big tailgate party with the works. It was going to be a grand occasion with the comforts of home thanks to the customized purple and gold RV and golf cart he purchased. It was already gassed and packed for tomorrow. He couldn't wait to roll up on the yard with the rest of the family. They were leaving in the morning. "Now Andy don't forget you and your family are invited to come by anytime and join our party." Caleb walked out the front door with Andy telling him he and his wife were looking forward to the visit. Everybody knew the Nicholsons and Beasleys knew how to have a tailgate party._____

Caleb parked in the garage and walked around the porch straight to their bedroom door. He could see candle light flickering on one of the accent tables near the window. When he touched the doorknob it opened. He heard soft music playing in the background. The love of his life was standing in the shadows of the night with a sexy lavender nightshirt that cascaded down the front. Her head was covered in a matching satin cap. The grin on her husband's face said he was pleased as he took her in his arms, he knew he was in for a treat. She whispered his water was running for his shower.

"Will you join me," he had to ask to be on the safe side? He knew she had a beauty appointment today and she was like any other sister when it came to her hair, especially since she was wearing it short. Ruby added a shower cap over the satin one which put a bigger smile on his face; the answer was yes. He untied her nightshirt, slipped it off of her shoulders, and let it slide down her body. She then took his hand and led him to their bathroom. With his assistance she stepped inside their custom-made shower and sat on the seat which had been built for two. She adjusted the water jets the way he likes while he discarded his clothes. He was by her side in seconds. He kissed the side of her neck and dragged more kisses to her cheek then her lips. Now kneeling and facing him, she took his favorite shower gel and sponged his body starting with his feet working her way up. Her gentle circling movements caused a slow seduction of his senses to be on edge as she teased and suckled his stiff nipples. She then covered every inch of him in a sensuous scented lather of cool mint blended with a splash of fresh mandarin and masculine musk. Now standing to rinse the soap he caught her around her wide waist and planted tender kisses down her bosom to the end of her birth line. Her soft moans told him they needed to take this to their room for safety reasons. Although they had intimate moments numerous times in the shower and jacuzzi, it just wasn't smart at this time. He knew he had been over protective with her, but he couldn't help it. After making sure he was soap free he turned the water off and grabbed two towels. He sat on her dressing bench and pulled her down on his lap. They toweled each other dry stopping for more intimate touches and kisses. He then led her to their bed. Positioning her body to receive her husband, stirring hints of enchanting ecstasy grew each second; both anticipating entering the passionate zone of intimacy. _____

The tailgate party was wonderful and everyone had

loads of fun, especially the grown kids. When they arrived, PVU's purple and gold flags along with the Greek sororities' and fraternities' decorative paraphernalia were visible throughout the campus. Rows of recreational vehicles, cars, and trucks were lined up in designated areas. It was truly a sight to behold. The weather had been perfect with clear pearly blue skies and welcomed cool breezes. Caleb and his family along with the brothers came equipped to have a fabulous time and did. Canopies, tents, and comfortable outdoor furniture were set up between and in front of the vehicles. One of the family's motor facility was stretched crossways the back for additional bathrooms. They also had motor bikes and three wheelers for the children as well as the men. Even Ruby's folks joined in with the fun. Lincoln and Henry Jr. had their camping gear to sleep on the side of the RV with Caleb. Naturally the females and babies were joining Ruby inside.

She couldn't believe the extent her husband went to with all of his new toys. He had new cooking gear; a deep fryer and a fancy medium size pit. Of course when it came to the canopy and the flat screen he had to have help from the pros as Q-Note put it to set it up. Everyone was still raving over the meals and who served the best besides the Saturday barbecue feast; that was a joint effort. The Nicholsons and Beasleys came in preparing chicken strips, fried fish, baked potatoes, salad and condiments for the group. The Collins and Hamiltons had the next night and prepared Cajun dishes, jambalaya and Boudain links, with all the trimmings. A variety of beverages, snacks, desserts were also provided. Between the families, they had enough food to feed anyone who was hungry. No one was turned away.

The concert was fantastic with artist for the old to the

young and of course PVU won their game and the band competition. Extensive plans were made for next year in making it a week instead of three days with everyone looking forward to another grand occasion._____

"Ruby," called Caleb. "It's time to go baby. I need to stop and pick up ice for the party and then do my couple of hours at the clinic." To give everyone a chance to attend the party the entire staff agreed to give a couple of hours toward the after hour care which worked out just fine. But Caleb was like an anxious child going to his first *Halloween Party;* he signed up first to do hours so he could join in with the festivities. He had already packed the car with the candy bags and pillows for her chair and was now just waiting.

"Okay, I'm coming as soon as I put my shoes on. Kiss the triplets and little Keyla Regène for me," whispered Ruby. She knew he would have a fit if he knew she was still on the phone talking to Kellie. She should have been off twenty minutes ago, but she wanted to hear her voice. The last time she called she was napping. Kellie told her she started to tell Gregory to just drop her off at the hospital when they left PV, she had a gut feeling she was going into labor that night and she was right. They had just settled down for the night when her water broke and the rest was history. Keyla Regène made her début a little after midnight and would be attending her first *Trick or Treat* bash at the business park. Kellie said they were going as some of the *Happy Feet* characters, in black jogging pants and white t-shirts with penguins on the front and back. She promised to take pictures and email them. This would be her first time missing the fun, but they were having a gathering at the center promising to be just as entertaining. The seniors and their families were having a combined funfest with all the trimmings.

Ruby made a loud sigh while getting into another position. It seems since they got the news she was having twins a boy and a girl doing simple things was a task. Now she was struggling to put on her black ballerina slippers. Looking up her husband standing in the doorway smiling with folding arms; it was no secret he was a proud poppa to be. He walked over to the chaise and took her shoes to do it for her. Once they were both on he pulled her up in his arms and whispered she was his beautiful pumpkin. He gave her a kiss on the tip of her nose and fondled her breasts and she gently pushed his hands away. She knew where this was headed and they didn't have time.

"Later Charlie," she said catching his hand to lead him out of their room. They were going as Charlie Brown and the Great Pumpkin. Her large round stomach was perfect in her orange bubble hem dress and black leggings. She had a green ribbon tied around her neck and a brown cap on her head with simple pumpkin jewelry for the occasion. He had on an orange t-shirt with a black stripe, black crop pants, tennis shoes, and shades. She thought he was absolutely adorable....

They entered the center and the party was in full effect with all kinds of costumes, from cartoon characters to famous celebrities. Everyone seemed to be enjoying themselves to the fullest. The orange and black streamers, posters, and decorations made the room real festive. Organized games, line dances, and refreshments had the party in full gear.

"Ruby Caleb, over here," called her parents who were sitting with Caleb's family and the Nasons. And they were all in costume which was surprising. She looked around for her siblings and their families; they were busy participating in the activities.

"Don't you two look cute," said Robbie Jean. "Come here Charlie Brown and give me some sugar. Look at our pumpkin Henry Ray, now she's too cute." They exchanged hugs and kisses with the family. He then fixed her chair and made sure she was comfortable before taking their contributions to the kitchen area. Ruby spotted her oldest niece and waved her over so she could give her the job of going around taking pictures. She had been given strict orders to stay put with her feet up until her husband returns from the clinic due to a little swelling. Of course she was going to do what she was told because he and her doctor had threatened her with complete bed rest if she did not start following orders.

"Baby I'll be back in a couple of hours, now do right please." She promised, he gave her a kiss, and told everyone at the table to make sure she did....

The big kid finally made it back and didn't know where to begin. He saw Ruby up doing the wobble with her sister and nieces and decided to join them. After two line dances and making sure she was off her feet, he was ready for some old fashion fun and games. After a couple of hours Dr. Caleb was all played out and ready to call it a night. Tomorrow was a regular day for the adults and children....

Entering the house and saying goodnight to his parents, Ruby was being pulled toward their master suite. With a wicked grin he reminded her it was later. He had them undressed in minutes, although he had a time getting rid of her black tights which caused her to giggle.

"Oh this is funny to you," he growled, nipping her chin while caressing and kissing her stomach, stopping at her navel. A quickie she thought as every nerve in her body was awakened and tingling. She loved his instantaneous lovemaking; he wasted no time hitting all the sensitive spots with his roaming hands and silky tongue. He traced the outline of her cute belly button then her tender breasts. She trembled at his touch. He rubbed his face in the middle of her bosoms planting wet kisses. Breathless urgent gasps escaped as she caressed and traced his brand. He grabbed her hands and pinned them above her head. She moaned as he continued using his torturous tongue, inflaming her velvety skin with fiery sparks. He captured her lips and seduced her tongue with his. Once again his captivating mouth trailed more wet kisses down her neck to her pregnant stomach. Her body moved on its own accord as his roving fingers from his free hand roamed all over her aching and throbbing body down to her jewels. "Oh Caleb," she moaned thrusting her hips.

"I know Baby, I know."

CHAPTER 36

Without any warning, the weather turned cold during Thanksgiving week, adding to the family's fun, putting them in the mood for *Christmas* which was knocking at the door. The city had been dressed in holiday array spreading the joy of the season right after Halloween. Holiday decorations in various festive colors were hung throughout the town. The airwaves were filled with *Christmas* music while several channels featured holiday movies and specials for all ages. Ruby and Caleb even had their decorations up along with an adorable table top tree for the young people who were receiving gift cards. It was a relief they didn't have to worry about being in the stores with all the hustle and bustle. Their families believed Christmas was only for children. The colors red, gold, and green were displayed throughout their home with their flower arrangements, poinsettias, and wreaths elegantly done by Grandmother Mildred with Ruby and Vera's help....

"Baby you look beautiful as always, come on now so we won't be late," Caleb pleaded. He walked over to slip her red jeweled ballerina slippers on while she put on a pair of silver dangling earrings and matching bracelets. Ruby had been moving around much slower these last few days and had become more emotional than ever, always second guessing her appearance. She was absolutely stunning with her protruding middle in a red umpire maxi length dress which had a jeweled neckline and long sleeves. He embraced his wife to reassure her she was his chocolate beauty more so than ever regardless of her added weight. Her heavy stomach had dropped and the babies were in position, and due anytime which has caused her to become overly anxious. All the preparations had been made, including the purchase of a new Mercedes Benz van which was already packed for the trip to the hospital. The only problem now was keeping her from being stressed and restless. Caleb gave her a kiss and helped her stand. He reached for her mink trimmed cashmere shawl and they walked to the front of the house.

Today was the last day of school and the children's holiday program which they had promised to attend. He would then report to work while she spends the rest of the morning with her sister unless he was needed. Caleb told their housekeeper they would be back the usual time unless he calls to inform her different, as they walked out the door. The luxury customized van was parked in the front of the house but at the ramp side. He nudged her lips again as he helped her in.

It was a beautiful airy morning with the sun adding just enough warmth to keep it from being dreadfully cold. Texas weather was truly something, he thought walking around to the driver's side. He looked over at Ruby who was holding her stomach and had a strong feeling she would not make it through the day, but he kept that to himself. He had already alerted Dr. Charlotte to express his feelings earlier. A few minutes later they arrived at the school. Junior was standing out front waiting with a parking spot he had saved for them which would put them in the door....

So far the morning was going according to schedule. They got through the jingle bells' rock, Rudolph the reindeers' step, Frosty the snowmen's wobble, and the winter wonderland twirlers. They were able to see all the

340

performances of their nieces and nephews. After quick hellos and I'm so proud of you, he kissed her in front of the children which caused giggles, and left for work. He knew he was leaving her in good hands, her mother and sister. Mrs. McHarding had decided to stay and help with the class party and keep an eye on her Ruby. She too felt this was the day and if so, it was going to be a very special one because this was Caleb's natural father's (Caleb Jr) birthday, *December 12*. If the twins come today, that would make this day precious for the VanLees.

"Thank you," sang Tori as she eased down in one of the children's chairs. She just said goodbye to her last child and it was still a few minutes before twelve, that's when the winter holidays were to begin. Ruby was reclined in her desk chair with her eyes closed. She had been pretty quiet once the children started leaving. Her mother had noticed her silence and sat beside her. Tori's little ones were busy coloring when they noticed their Uncle Caleb standing in the door way with his arms folded across his chest. He had decided to stop by after a morning visit to check on her before returning back to the clinic.

"Uncle Caleb, Uncle Caleb did you see us on the program," shouted Lincoln and Torrin.

"Of course I did munchkins," lifting them both in the air. Ruby opened her eyes and was so happy to see him. She was not feeling the best and the babies were so active in an unusual way. The look on her face revealed it all as he walked over and kissed her gently. He caressed her stomach which calmed them down some. With a smile he carefully pulled her up and held her as close to his heart as he could and whispered they would be at the hospital in twenty minutes.

"Aunt Ruby is it time," screamed the children along with their mother. Mrs. McHarding remained calm and called her husband to tell him she was riding to the hospital with Ruby and Caleb. Tori told her she would be there as soon as she takes the children over to her sister-in-law. Her mother instructed her to ride with her father so they would not have a lot of cars to drive back. Caleb called his parents and grandparents to let them know he was taking Ruby to the hospital as he put her shawl around her. It was now a little cooler than earlier, regardless of the sun shining. They were in the vehicle, buckled up, and on their way. Lord he loved this woman so much. She was his life and now was about to bring into the world two more lives that they made together with the help of the *Master*. Caleb kissed her hand and then drove quickly but cautiously to Cypress Memorial....

6:00 pm

The twins Lawrence Nicholson, *6 lbs. 5 ozs* made his appearance at 4:40 and Bianca Denise, *6 lbs. 4 ozs* followed at 5:15. Ruby was now resting while the babies were on display. Caleb had been her strength as she delivered their children. She hoped next time she would only have one, twins were a job. Their proud father along with the rest of the family was in the nursery window *ahhhhing* and *ooooohing*. Lawrence and Vera shed tears of joy when Caleb announced the babies' names. It was an extremely special day for the VanLees because this was their son's birthday and the Strattons because Bianca Denise was named after their beloved daughter. *(Bianca birth mother's name, Denise adoptive mother's middle name)*.

"Oh Ruby the babies are absolutely beautiful," exclaimed her mother as she fingered her short hair into a style. Robbi Jean had slipped away from the others to spend some time alone with her daughter even though she was going home with her for a few days. "They're both completely bald," she whispered as if someone else was in the room. They both smiled because it was definitely a black thing and a strong indication she would be combing hair for days. A few minutes later the rest of the family came in with flowers and balloons.

"Aunt Ruby the babies are here and we saw them," announced Hayward. "But Aunt Ruby they don't have any hair." Everyone laughed because he called himself whispering. Ruby caught her stomach and as she let out giggles.

"The innocence of the young," said Grandfather Caleb as he walked over to her bed to kiss her forehead and give her a gift in a worn velvet box. She knew it was something special and old because of the worn faded fabric. Ruby opened the box and gasped. It was a mother of pearl ring surrounded by diamonds that she had seen on Caleb's grandmother's finger. He told her it belongs to his mother who passed it to the mother of their grandson and now they wanted to pass it on to her. Ruby couldn't get past the word *they* as she looked at Grandmother Mildred. She kissed her cheek and confirmed it was a gift for their granddaughter who has blessed them with their first great-grand. Caleb stood bursting with pride because he knew how sacred the ring was. His grandmother had worn it next to her wedding ring and never took it off except to have it cleaned. To give it to Ruby was truly saying she was very special. Caleb's cell vibrated it was his family in Denver. Honeybee and Big D were still emotional about the birth of their great-grands and the entire family had made plans to spend the *Christmas* holidays with them._____

Christmas Day

"Ru...by," shouted Uncle Pete standing in the doorway of the family room. "Is the food ready, I'm ready to say the blessing so we can eat?" Everyone knew what was coming up. Caleb shook his head as he pushed the stroller which held the sleeping twins beside his Aunt Bea and Gram who was now sitting at the table. He then took his Uncle by the arm and escorted him to his chair at the head of the table where Ruby was standing. Caleb invited the rest of his blended family to take their seats. He kissed his beautiful wife as they watched their kin. They were such a handsome couple in their black slacks and red tops, he had a red polo and she a shimmering print swing with holiday jewelry.

"Do you think we need to say something to Uncle Pete before he blesses the food," whispered Ruby?

Caleb looked at his wife and whispered, "Nope, let them get christened, that's my uncle being himself in his own way. Besides, he looks forward to doing that every time he prays at a family gathering. They may as well get use to him if they're planning on visiting me because I truly love that old man." Everyone was now seated. Caleb and Ruby welcomed and thanked their families for making their first *Christmas Holiday* special. Then Caleb asked his favorite uncle to bless the food. And yep, after his Amen he ended with his famous words: *Lord ha'm mercy upon us, every time we git somthum good to eat sumbody here to eat it up from us.* Caleb had the biggest smile on his face as he said Amen again._____

New Year's Eve, 11:45 pm

Ruby stood at the nursery door watching her husband

who was standing over the cribs smiling down at their sleeping babies, who had a full day. He gently stroked their bald heads and chuckled quietly. She couldn't contain her own laughter because she knew what was going through his mind. Little Hayward was so amazed that Bianca Denise was still bald with a lace headband instead of bows. His little sister came with a head full of curly hair, and now has little ponytails. He didn't understand why his cousin was still without hair. Caleb looked her way and held his hand out for her to join him. He kissed her hand and pulled the love of his life into his arms. He reached into his pocket and pulled out an exquisite gold angel charm bracelet which belonged to his birth mother. He had added another angel with diamond wings to match the original one since they had twins. Their eyes locked as he put it on. Words were not needed between them. Ruby was honored and proud once again to inherit another piece of his mother's jewelry.

"Come on Sweetie it's almost time for the fireworks and the family is waiting." Ruby kissed her husband's cheek and pulled him away from the cribs.

"Here they are," announced his dad. "Come on you two, we thought we were going to have to welcome the New Year in without you." His parents and grandparents were sitting on the screen-in porch where they had spent the remainder of the evening. Caleb had the area nice and cozy with a portable fireplace and flat screen. They had been watching a holiday special and the preliminary fireworks, while enjoying a light snack. Everyone was now ready to toast in the New Year and watch the special fireworks to welcome another year. His mother gave them all a glass of sparkling cider and then Grandfather Caleb cleared his throat to begin his toast.

"Within the last year our lives have undergone some phenomenal changes thanks to the grace of God and the humble spirit of my lovely granddaughter. We're thankful for the determination of my grandson in being his own man and obtaining the desires of his heart and soul. Because of these two wonderful people we have been blessed with new additions to our family...grand /great-grandchildren. So, I would like to thank God for blessing us with a New Year, good health, prosperity, and most of all the love of family." Just as they completed their toast and shared hugs and kisses, the sky lit up with vivid sparkling displays of fireworks in assorted designs and colors.

"It's a beautiful sight, isn't it," asked Ruby staring up into the sky?

Dr. Caleb Gerald VanLee 3rd gazed into the face of his chocolate beauty with so much love, devotion and admiration, the mother of his children, his best friend and soul mate, his life line, his world. "Yes she is," he replied.

She looked at her husband and smiled as she ran her hand through her short hair style, "I'm talking about the fireworks silly."

"Nothing compares to the fireworks I have in my heart for you, nibbling her cheek. Attorney Ruby Jewel McHarding-VanLee still finds it hard to believe she was now married to her first and only love, plus a mother in less than a year. She silently thanked God for making it all possible. Cuddling in his arms, she kissed his lips and they continued watching the awesome displays.

Dear Readers,

I hope you've enjoyed reading Ruby Jewel and Caleb's love story as much as I did writing it. Wasn't it a pleasure to visit old friends from *Senseless Misconceptions* and *Destined to Be?* Thanks so much for the kind praises for *PROMISES*. The next set of stories will take place in a small town called Allanville, Texas. Jetta Faye and Tyson's *Valentine* love story, *YOU WERE MEANT FOR ME* will be the first. Be sure to keep an eye out for it in February. I look forward to your feedback as always and wish you lots of love and romance.

Email address wparksbrigham@writeme.com

W Parks Brigham

 PO Box 330353

Houston, Texas 77233

ABOUT THE AUTHOR

W Parks Brigham lives in Houston, Texas and has two adult daughters. She holds two degrees; a BS in Social Work with a Child Development / Psychology minor and M.Ed. in Education. She has spent her adult life teaching small children and loved every minute of it. She is now a retired (*Halleluiah*) teacher of thirty plus years. Her main interest and hobbies includes active participation in her church, listening to her own radio station designed especially for her, playing spider solitaire, working bent and wiggly word search and Sudoku puzzles. W Parks is an avid reader of Black Romance which prompted her to write and self-publish her own.

www.ingramcontent.com/pod-product-compliance
Lightning Source LLC
Chambersburg PA
CBHW050543260626
47157CB00002B/416